**IN THE GRIPPING SAGA OF THE APACHE
NATION LIVE THE MEN AND WOMEN OF
HISTORY AND LEGEND**

GERONIMO—The fearless leader whose awesome
powers defied explanation.

TOM HORN—The salty Indian scout whose hatred
for authority was equaled only by his admiration
for Geronimo.

COCHISE—The tragic, aging warrior still craving
revenge against the white men who murdered his
kin.

CHOKOLE—The brilliant woman guerrilla warrior.

Together they struggled against the relentless tide of
history and wove the rich tapestry that was an Indian
nation and the great American West.

"VIVID, RICHLY COLORED . . . FIERCELY EF-
FECTIVE."—*Kirkus Reviews*

"A STIRRING NOVEL!"—*The Nashville Banner*

"PROBABLY THE TRUEST HISTORY WE HAVE
HAD OR MAY EVER HAVE OF THE APACHE
INDIAN NATION."—*Chattanooga Times*

CRY GERONIMO!

(Formerly titled
Watch for Me on the Mountain)

Forrest Carter

A DELL/ELEANOR FRIEDE BOOK

Published by
Dell Publishing Co., Inc.
1 Dag Hammarskjold Plaza
New York, New York 10017

This work was first published under the title
Watch for Me on the Mountain.

For information address Delacorte Press/Eleanor Friede,
New York, New York.

Dell ® TM 681510, Dell Publishing Co., Inc.

ISBN: 0-440-11039-4

Reprinted by arrangement with Delacorte Press/Eleanor
Friede

Printed in the United States of America

First Dell printing—March 1980

*To Geronimo's Children
and Chokole*

Were half the power, that fills the word with terror,
Were half the wealth, bestowed on camps and courts,
Given to redeem the human mind from error,
There were no need of arsenals or forts:

"The Arsenal at Springfield,"
HENRY WADSWORTH LONGFELLOW

CRY
GERONIMO!

1

SAN CARLOS RESERVATION:
CAMP OF APACHE CONCENTRATION

Sun mottled through the brittle brush, camouflage fashion, over the Apache sitting beside it. The bush had no leaves. Naiche, the Apache, smiled inwardly, knowing this. There was no need for concealment. When they decided to kill him, they would. It was Apache habit to sit thus.

Sand flies darted through clouds of gnats, biting his face and hands. He did not brush them away. He was watching a spot of horizon sky to the southwest, lining it with his eye above a dark grouping of horsemen that came. In this way, he judged their progress. They were moving slowly.

He looked behind him, surveying wickiups that scattered away to the north. They were set in uneven lines, wavering on the bare banks of a creek. Stunted cottonwoods among them were without leaves, fired by sun and swept by wind.

Constructed by nature for torrents of water, the creek banks were wide apart, but held only a stagnant stream no bigger than a man's finger. Alkaline and bitter water. No one moved.

They are in the wickiups, Naiche thought, *enduring away the heat of midday, waiting.* His eyes fastened on his own hovel. He fancied he could hear his wife crooning tones to their baby; rocking, seated on the ground and brushing away flies. Making her mind empty.

He felt a surge of emotion toward the half-decision he had made. He knew he would have to decide. The prisoner the soldiers were bringing would force the decision.

He knew he, himself, was not wise. He had never regarded life soberly enough to be a decision maker. When his father died, he had asked his sons to keep peace. His older brother, Taza, had done so; but then Taza had been trained by his father to chieftainship. Naiche had not. His father had wanted no rivalry between his sons, and so Naiche was trained only in loyalty, to support his brother, the chief. But Taza had died. Naiche became Chief of the Chiricahua Apaches. Neither his father's nor Taza's spirit had returned to counsel him. Naiche had prayed for their counseling. It did not come. He was alone.

He turned back to watch the progress of the horsemen, distorted and dancing in the heat haze. Now he could make out the colors of the horses and of the coats of the horsemen. The coats were blue.

They came from the direction of Fort Thomas and the agency, where each month all Apaches must walk to receive their ration. Naiche led them on ration day, walking across the desert. If an Apache did not go, there was no ration. Some of the old people hobbled twenty miles across the desert to receive their ration. Those who were sick had to be helped by others. Some were carried. There could be no excuse, for this was when they were counted.

Every Apache wore the metal tag around his neck with markings. Even the babies. When they received their ration, the bluecoats counted the markings on the tag. The rations were always the same: a handful of meal, live with weevils; sometimes a slice of beef, stringy and half-rotted. Naiche felt the burden of their starving and sickness. He had sought counsel with the bluecoats.

His father had always said, "The time for counseling with others is in the waxing of the moon, toward the full." Naiche knew this was true. People felt and thought less narrow. They were more giving. It was time the coyote was more successful in hunting; and the cougar.

Faithfully he had marked each day before the moon waxed full. He had risen early and trotted across the plains, past the agency building to Fort Thomas. He always walked through the gate of Fort Thomas in the heat of midday when no one was outside. He stood on the parade ground until he was seen by the bluecoats, and he came forward to always say the same words: "Old people dying. Babies dying. We are of the mountains, not the desert. Let us go to our valleys of the mountains to raise our own food. Guard us there." He never understood their answers. He knew few words of the white eyes. Each time they cursed him and waved him away. Sometimes the bluecoats shot their guns at his feet and pointed to the pole. He had left each time, hoping his words would be heard.

The pole stood at the parade grounds. On top of the pole was the skull of Delshay, Chief of the Tonto Apaches. Naiche remembered when they had mounted it, sodden and bloody. The blowflies had laid eggs in the head and worms ate out the eyes. Birds had fought over the rotting flesh. Now there was only the skull of Delshay, grinning.

Naiche thought of Delshay. He was always afraid. How many times had he surrendered his people? Always surrendering. Each time, he became frightened. Soldiers, even the officers, would shoot at him for "sport" as he walked near the fort. He would run back to the mountains. From there, he would send them word: He would surrender; but he was afraid. So they cut off his head. *He is not afraid anymore*, Naiche thought.

Naiche looked again to where the soldiers were

coming. They were closer. When he gazed slightly to the side of them, the heat haze was diminished and he could see on the rim of his sight. Their horses were plodding in the sand. The decision would have to be made soon. Anxiously he searched his mind for words of his father.

But now he could remember only the ending of the old free ways. The ending of his father, when he was old and weary of fighting and his people ragged and starved from running. How his father had met the bluecoat star chief. The star chief had wanted very much to accept his father's surrender. It would have meant much glory to him, for Naiche's father was a great man. He was Cochise.

The star chief had said he wanted peace. Cochise had answered that he too wanted peace, and had said, "Then it is decided. We will live in Cañada Alamosa, our old home; here in this valley of our mountains. We will farm corn in this valley. We will be at peace. It is my word."

The star chief had shaken his head. "Three hundred Mexicans," he had said, "have become citizens of the United States and now own property in the Cañada Alamosa."

Cochise had argued with the star chief: "There is room for all. Let us live farther down the valley. We will also become citizens of the United States and own property and take your ways."

The star chief had looked at Cochise a long time, and answered, "You cannot become citizens of the United States. You cannot own property."

"Why?" Cochise had asked.

The star chief had shrugged his shoulders. "Indians are not people. It is the law."

Cochise had ridden away, angry. For a year they had run; but too many were dying. Cochise had surrendered and said, "There is no place for the Apache. There is a place for all others. But there is no place for the Apache." And he had asked, "Has God forsaken the Apache?" And when the soldiers came in a short time, to break their final promise and remove the Apaches from the valley reservation onto the desert camp of concentration, Cochise could not go, for he was dying. At the end, he had spoken to God, his voice far away and his eyes fading, dimming the mountains: "The Apache carries his life on his fingernails. The Apache wishes now that the mountains would fall upon him. The Apache wishes to die."

Naiche stood and looked back to the wickiups. *Is that what they are waiting for—to die?*

The soldiers were close now. He moved behind the bush and watched. A dozen bluecoats. They angled their horses toward a wickiup that sat apart. As they passed, not talking, their horses snorted and blew their nostrils, smelling Naiche, but the soldiers did not notice. Now he could see the man they were leading.

The man was short and powerfully built. He stepped and jogged jerkily, lifting the chains that shortened his stride. He was barefooted, and leg irons hit the protruding anklebones as he walked. Blood was on his feet. He was filthy. Excrement had caked and dried on his pants. Naiche knew he had been in the hole. His hands were bound with chains, and the soldiers led him by a rope looped about his neck.

They passed close to the bush and Naiche stood stoically, not looking at the soldiers, only at the man. Bushy hair fell down about the prisoner's bowed head, but as he passed he turned his face slightly. His eyes fastened full on Naiche's. The eyes gave no evidence of his humbled and chained condition; they flashed black and fanatical. He said nothing. He was Geronimo.

The soldiers stepped before an old wickiup with leaning mesquite branches for sides. One bluecoat dismounted. He took the chains from the prisoner's hands and, lifting the rope from around his neck, slapped him with it across the buttocks. The bluecoat said something, and the soldiers laughed.

Geronimo stood, head bowed, with his hands still crossed before him, as though the chains were still there. *He pretends submission,* Naiche thought, *but must hide his eyes from the soldiers.* The soldiers whirled their horses and cantered away, wanting to be free of the desert. Naiche watched them growing smaller to the southwest. They had not taken the chains from Geronimo's legs. The irons were banded above his ankles.

He walked in a jerky half-shuffle and dropped heavily on the ground, his back against the wall of the wickiup. Sprawling his legs before him, he picked up sand, tossing it at his feet. Clouds of flies rose in the air. The sand stuck and coated the blood, covering it from flies. He did not look up.

Wind, lifting whirls of sand, rattled brittle brush and sage, strumming a thin whine through the cotton-woods' naked branches. No Apache appeared. They knew why he was here. No army could capture Geronimo; this they knew. No fear of death, no weariness of war could induce his surrender. He never wearied of war. His surrenders were shams of cunning, designed to bring him amongst them; to call them to keep the Faith. He was a War Shaman. Even the great chiefs—Cochise, Juh, Mangas Coloradas (before the white eyes cut off his head and placed his skull in a trophy case)—had often chosen Geronimo to lead on the trails of war.

War was sacred. So far back that the great-grandfathers could not remember the long line of great-grandfathers who had warred. It was said, once in a dim time, their people had planted corn in the valleys and harvested their food. The Spaniards had come. They had greeted the Spaniards as friends but were taken to be made slaves, and so broke away. They could plant and harvest no more. The Spaniards waited to kill them when the corn ripened in their valleys.

War kept them free; kept them from the deep mines where peon Indios of the south labored for the Spaniards. War kept them from the lash of black-robed Church priests. War made them free from the soldiers who spread blight among the peon Indios and killed them and defiled their women, causing them to die.

If it had been that a god kept them free of this, then the god would be sacred. It had been War. The arrow, the lance, the bow, the knife—even the food on the trail of War—was known by a sacred name.

Now, caught between the Mexicans and the Americans, running and dying on the trails and in the camps of concentration, the Apache was lost. There had come an uncertainty, even evidence that War would no longer keep them free. The Faith was dying.

In making treaties, the Apaches found they were not people, by the Law. They could not be citizens. They could not own property. And as animals, they could not entreat that their concentration camps be located in the valleys of the mountains they loved. They were placed on the desert. They could raise no corn, gather no mescal bulbs or piñon nuts; make no flour from the yucca. Rations were cut to the borderline of starvation, leaving them weak, sickly; dying.

The desert camp was the oven of extermination. "Extermination," General Sherman said, "is the only answer. The more we kill this year, the less we will have to kill next year." Sherman's faithful apostle, Sheridan, echoed his leader with a vengeance: "The only good Indian is a dead Indian."

Only the desperate Faithful now followed Geronimo. There were some among the Apaches whose minds sought the Reality superior to the physical world, as one awaiting execution despairs and seeks life in the spiritual. Most clung to the despairing material world, hoping to keep alive their physical bodies. Many hated Geronimo for continuing a hope-

17

less war, and they blamed him for the disasters that had come to them.

The magnificent Cochise had warred, but even he saw the inevitable, and surrendered. Mangas Coloradas, respected and revered throughout Apacheria, had decided upon and sought peace. When the soldiers, beneath a truce flag, cut off his head and held it, dripping and unreal, it was the Lesson: The soldier government expected gratitude from the Apache for prolonging their lives. There could be no equal meeting to agree on peace. A people do not meet with a god to exchange agreements. Even the youthful and impulsive Victorio had seen. Three times he sought to live in peace, and three times betrayed, bitterly announced his fight to the death; and died.

Thus, dozens of the great chiefs. All were gone. But always in the shadows of the campfires, appearing briefly at the rancherias to harangue and recruit warriors, there was Geronimo, thirsting for War; raiding, striking Mexicans and bluecoats, and bringing disastrous retribution down upon the Apache. No entreaties tempted him. No argument appealed to his reason. And so there was hatred for him. Fear and fascination too; surviving warriors told stories of how Geronimo had called up the wind with blowing sand to hide them from pursuing soldiers. Of how he could "see," telling them of events that would come; and it was so.

Some had spied on him, dancing alone in the mountains with strange chants that brought the Gans, the mountain spirits, to dance with him; and had seen him purifying himself of the soul-destroyers.

He was a Shaman of War, they said, and there is always a fascination of the Unknown; and fear.

Naiche stepped from behind the bush and walked across the open ground to where Geronimo sat. When his shadow fell across the bloody feet, Geronimo looked up. The dark hole, where they had held him prisoner, had lined his face and made it haggard.

18

"Naiche." His greeting was flat and toneless.

"Yes," Naiche said, and seated himself beside Geronimo as he continued tossing sand at his feet. Naiche studied the cottonwoods along the creek. Politeness required a period of silence. The wind made flute sounds through openings in the mesquite wall.

"Before I surrendered," Geronimo announced softly, "I took cattle and horses from the Mexicans." He stopped flicking sand and looked away toward the eastern sky. "I sold the cattle and horses to Texans and bought good guns and bullets. I have them hidden to the south."

It was the decision. Naiche hesitated. "The chains?" he asked.

Geronimo shrugged. "Bring me a piece of iron. The chains will come off."

The silence came back between them. It was Geronimo who waited. A baby cried, far off, weak on the wind, whimpering. Naiche listened to the cries, dying in snuffling sobs.

"We will go," Naiche said. Geronimo looked hard at him. Far back behind the blackness of his eyes, Naiche saw a light that moved and danced. A Spirit, some Apaches said. Others called it the flames of War and Death. Briefly Geronimo clasped the arm of Naiche. "It is good, brother."

"Yes," Naiche answered, "it is good."

The baby was crying again. The decision had been made.

2

Westward, a low horizon swallowed the sun, belching red skyward and turning the desert purple. Fires flared before wickiups. Geronimo picked up the heavy iron and worked at the clasp lock on the leg irons. Naiche had brought him the iron and a water bag. He had refused the maize cake, knowing it was a full day's ration for Naiche. He had observed Naiche's appearance; though he was young, his muscles were stringy, standing bare in flabby flesh. Naiche was being consumed by starvation. *He is giving his rations to his wife and baby*, Geronimo thought.

He paused to look at his own body, naked where he had stripped away the filthy clothing and washed. Despite his time in the hole, he was hard. The months in the Sierra Madre had given this to him; venison and yucca meal, shudock berries, mescal and Mexican beef. Clean water.

He grunted, twisting the iron, and the clasp lock sprang loose. He was free.

The footsteps were light. He heard them and sat without moving. She was small, even for an Apache; a calico skirt ballooned around her in the wind. Her hair was pulled back severely from an oval face, knotted and tied behind her head. She knelt without speaking and placed a long knife by Geronimo's hand and set boot moccasins by his side. Over them she laid a long breechclout, and silently she began ministering to his deep-cut ankles. Using powdered root of ocotillo on the wounds, she bound them with cloth.

"Thank you," Geronimo said politely. She was tying the cloth and did not look up. "I am Zalah," she said and, finishing with the bandages, moved to lay wood for a fire before the wickiup. The twilight deepened as she worked, and Geronimo watched her impassively, but with suspicion. The bluecoats had many spies among the Apaches; those who would ferret out information in return for extra rations for their families.

Rising from her work, she whistled, and a small boy ran out of the dark, carrying a glowing stick that she placed within the wood. A flame flickered, and the boy stepped back shyly behind her, into the darkness.

"You have a family?" Geronimo asked. He slipped the long knife from its sheath and slowly honed it on the leather, slapping and sliding the blade.

"I . . . have my son . . . Sanza," she said, hesitating, watching the blade moving up and down the sheath. "My husband was killed by the Tucson white-eye raiders where we farmed. My baby girl died . . . here."

He did not look at her, but pausing from his blade sharpening, he carefully selected a hair from his head. Jerking the hair loose, he held it dangling in the air before him and swept the knife in a vicious quick swing. The blade did not cut the dangling hair. He resumed the monotonous honing.

Zalah spoke loudly now, as if to call his attention away from the slapping blade. "My son is almost nine years. He is almost a warrior. Once," she said, as though delivering a prepared speech, "he defied the soldiers. When my baby was dying, he ran beyond the boundaries and dug mescal and brought it back, hiding from the soldiers all day as he came . . . trying to save my baby. The soldiers would have killed him. He . . . is very brave." She reached hastily behind her and pulled the boy forward to stand with her. The fire played on spindly legs and arms. A small stomach paunched beneath the rib cage over his breechclout, bloating. The boy studied his feet, staring at them as though he had not seen them before.

Geronimo gave no indication he had observed the boy. The knife slapped back and forth on the leather. The fire crackled higher.

Her voice was hollow now, brave and prepared like a schoolgirl's: "I know how to fire a gun. I am strong and can fight like a warrior . . . I . . ." Her voice trailed away.

Geronimo stopped the knife and looked at her across the fire. "The boy is no warrior," he said flatly.

Sanza shuffled back, away from the hard eyes, and secreted himself behind his mother. But Zalah did not retreat. Instead her eyes met Geronimo's boldly. She patted her hair into place, smoothed her face with her hands, and where her nervous fingers found a torn place in her skirt, she folded it away from notice. "I am still young," she said. "You have . . . no one. I will . . . do as you want." She tried to smile coyly, but her chin trembled.

Geronimo stared at her. "I will not marry you," he said harshly.

Zalah bowed her head, and in a moment the whispered words of Apache disgrace came across the fire: "I will not ask you to marry me." Geronimo held the knife suspended in the air, watching. Slowly she raised her head, and her face was wet. "I know you are going," she said weakly. "I . . . know . . . all say that you have surrendered only to come and take others away. I . . . must go. I must save my son. I want him to live."

"He can live here," Geronimo sneered. "He will be fed enough to live."

"No," Zalah whispered, "I want him to live where he is not told where he must walk and what he must do . . . where there is no power over him . . ."

"You want him to be free?" Geronimo asked, and for the first time his vóice carried a hint of reason.

"Yes," she answered, "to be free . . . in the mountains."

Geronimo resumed the slapping of the knife blade. "You may go," he said casually. Sanza, the boy, peered from behind his mother and looked at the hard face lighting and shadowing in the firelight; the terrible Legend of Blood and Death who casually ordained their freedom while he sharpened a knife.

Zalah moved toward Geronimo, but he held up the knife, halting her. "No, you owe me nothing, and so I will accept nothing. You will pay enough for freedom . . . maybe you will die." He paused and looked hard at her. "There is something you may do."

"Yes?" Zalah asked.

"You may go to every wickiup this night and tell them Geronimo knows that they know. Tell them Geronimo has already placed warriors in the bush, and any man, woman, or child who walks toward the fort will be killed."

"I will," Zalah said.

Carefully he selected a hair from his head, holding it dangling in the air. The knife swept, snakelike, sparkling in the firelight. This time a short piece of hair was left hanging. Geronimo grunted. He rose and walked away into the darkness. Shyly Zalah called after him, "When . . . will we go?"

"I do not know" came floating back. Geronimo was gone.

He found Naiche outside his own wickiup, sitting, waiting. Squatting beside him, he asked, "Are there some you can trust?"

"A few," Naiche answered dryly.

"Then send them into the brush with bows and arrows. No one must take the word to Fort Thomas." Naiche slipped away. And through the night Geronimo visited the wickiups.

He squatted by the dying embers of Chato's fire and said nothing. Chato knew why he was there, and after a long time, spoke. "No," he said.

Geronimo rose, looking into the glow of embers, not at Chato. "We are going south, into the Sierra Madre. Do you wish to live in this way?"

"No," Chato said, "I do not wish to live in this way, but I am not a fool. Now, there is no other way," and stared stonily before him as Geronimo walked into the shadows.

Loco poked at his fire. Geronimo had not spoken; he had appeared and squatted across from him. Loco spoke into the fire: "The old way of freedom is gone, Geronimo. It is hopeless." And as Geronimo rose, Loco stood. "Still," he said wistfully, "it would be good to see the mountains again; to be free for a little while." Then suddenly, "I will go."

And so through the night Geronimo appeared at the wickiups. He listened and spoke little. He did not answer the questions: How can you hope to outrun the soldiers' horses so far . . . to the Sierra Madre? The Sierra Madre is far away; how can you survive to reach her?

But by morning excited talk ran through the wickiups of those who were going. They talked of plants still bearing fruit in the mountains: the yucca; there would be piñon nuts in cool groves; the berries would be gone, but they would make flour from the palo-verde seeds and shinoak acorns, rich flour, full of life. Some recited places they knew where cold water ran from rocks in shaded canyons.

They began to pack meager rations of meal and to fix *tsochs*, the slings, to carry babies so they might run faster. Men were fashioning crude, short bows from cholla sticks, twisting the fiber of 'guilla to string them. Using reeds, they split the ends and precariously secured pointed stones for arrows.

Dawn came glaring and hot over the eastern rim of desert. The rumors were spreading. Old stories of

Geronimo were recounted. He was untrustworthy. His trail of war was littered with the dead of his own people. He was often drunk on tiswin.

Naiche sought him out and found him in the creek bed. He was studying the tips of bare cottonwood branches. Naiche knew he was looking for omens. Perhaps even Geronimo needed reassurance.

For a while Naiche followed him, pulling down the branches Geronimo had been holding. At their tips there were the scars of fallen leaves. On each scar was a face. Some of the faces were smiling, some were frowning, some were fierce. Other faces looked weird and monstrous. Geronimo sat down on the creek bank, holding his head.

"Tomorrow," Naiche said quietly, "is counting day."

"Yes," Geronimo acknowledged. He would say nothing more, but rose and walked away, crossing the creek bed and disappearing in the brush.

By midday wind began to blow. After a monotonous moan it lifted, whimpering in bursts. In early afternoon sand clouds appeared in the north, rising a thousand feet into the sky. By mid-afternoon the wind was screaming. The sun dimmed yellow and changed to a pale green lemon, easily watched with the eye. The horizon and the sky were gone.

Geronimo appeared before the wickiup of Naiche. "Tell them to gather here at darkness. We will leave." He disappeared in the whirling sand.

Naiche would always remember that day. How the air had grown sullen and heavy in the morning. How the tongue tasted of metal. How, in the beginning, bushes had moved without wind.

They gathered in dusk's half light and came close to one another, peering through sand to recognize a friend. Many who had said they would go did not come. Sand, driven in rasping bursts by the wind, struck the sides of the wickiups and kept them inside.

Geronimo moved among those who had gathered,

separating women from men. He lined the women in a long column of twos. The young woman by the side of the old; the woman without a baby beside the woman who carried a baby in her breast sling. The women had covered their faces with cloth and placed wet clothes over the heads of the babies.

Behind the women, in the same column of twos, he placed the children. The older by the younger; the boy by the girl. After the children, he spread the warriors in a column three abreast, slightly wider than the women and children's. The warriors must pick up the child who fell; help the baby-laden woman who faltered; seize and carry with them the old woman who lagged behind.

Apache fashion, they carried nothing except the barest necessities for survival: small food sacks and water bags, knives, and the warriors, their crude bows and arrows.

Twilight deepened. Those who could watch from their wickiups barely saw the figures now—a long line bending their backs against wind and sand from the north, the children standing uncertainly between the women and warriors and seeking assurance, holding one another's hands.

Geronimo was bitterly disappointed: eighteen warriors, fifty-three women and children. Most of the women were widows, desperate to save their seed— babies, children; bits and pieces of families destroyed by the soldiers. They stood like sheep, dumb and apologetic that they endangered all the lives with their cumbersome flocks.

He began at the head of the column. Grasping Zalah and the woman beside her by the shoulders, he shouted in their faces, "We will *live* at the *mountains!* Say it!" His face was fierce, eyes hypnotic. The women shouted back, "We will *live* at the *mountains!*" Down the column he moved. An old woman, standing silently in the column, was seized by the throat and slapped brutally, again and again, as Geronimo shouted at her. Several warriors moved toward him, but backed away as the old woman began to shout. He shoved his face close to the children's, and when they mumbled, he shook them and made them shout at the top of their lungs. By the time he reached the warriors, the entire column was chanting, screaming, "We will *live* at the *mountains!*" Standing before the warriors, he pumped his arm like a choirmaster, leaping and jumping, churning the air with his arms.

Imperceptibly the screaming changed tone; the forced desperation gave way to a rhythmic harmony, and in the harmony there rose a note of exuberance. There in the whipping sand and roaring wind, an exulting Spirit, as if an anthem, invaded the minds of a group that only shortly before had been seized with doubt and fear, and cringing before the storm. Warriors, feeling the exuberance, began to dance, in the grip of the Power; children stomped their feet in unison, and cloths fell from the faces of women. They no longer felt the sand.

Abruptly Geronimo whirled, trotted to the head of the column, and waving his arm, led them in a quick shuffling gait toward the southwest.

Naiche, at the head of the warriors, noted the direction Geronimo led; it was almost directly toward Fort Thomas and the soldiers. Only dimly did the thought flicker in his mind to protest. He was too caught up in the chant . . . the blind faith in the Something Geronimo had created.

The Dragoon Mountains lay behind Fort Thomas, and the Dragoons ran south toward the Sierra Madre. Any other course would have been a loop around the fort, costing time they could not afford and effort they could not survive. Geronimo knew the sandstorm would hide them from the soldiers, and no one questioned the faith that the sandstorm would last to carry them past the fort.

As they ran, the chant ceased. Breath was needed for running. But Naiche remembered the sensation.

The words rang over and over in his mind: "We will *live* at the *mountains!*"

"*Live . . . mountains!*" The two words boomed in the conscious mind. Later no one remembered that night run across the plains. They remembered beginning; the short times they were allowed to rest with Geronimo moving among them chanting, "We will *live* at the *mountains!*" They remembered the ending.

With the chant the Shaman Geronimo had placed their conscious minds at the mountains where there was life—their prize. Their conscious minds, which would have picked and worried over the stumbling step, the distance, the soldiers, the storm—all were suspended. The fumbling, failing human body is controlled by the conscious mind, and having forced them to set it aside, Geronimo induced them to allow their spirit mind to control them. And so they became of the Spirit, and performed the unexplainable "supernatural" effort.

Geronimo had suspended the material space between them and the mountains. He had suspended the time to reach them. There was no space, there was no time—the illusions of the conscious mind.

United States Army officers would later record that the remaining Apaches at San Carlos lied; that it was impossible for humans to have left at the time given by the Apaches and reached the Dragoons when they did. But the army officers were using a scale of measurement that was material. They lived and worked and fought in time and space, and did not know the world of Geronimo.

When they forded the Gila River, they could have easily seen Fort Thomas, or been seen, had the sandstorm not covered them. Between the river's banks, it was calm, with wind whipping overhead. Dust dropped, choking. Briefly they rested. The women wet cloths from the stream and wiped the faces of children and babies.

Geronimo, turning slightly south, led them over the

farther bank and back into the storm. The wind was squarely at their backs now, pushing them away from Fort Thomas. No one knew when the wind died. They became aware that it had, leaving a smothering dust cloud through which they ran. Suddenly they ran out of the cloud, gasping clean air and seeing stars, millions of light dots above them.

After a time the lights dimmed, and pink shafts shot skyward from the east. They saw the mountains. The Dragoons were rocked against the sky. Geronimo increased their speed.

The sun was well into the cloudless sky when they reached the canyon. They rested, touching one another, shocked, as if just awakening to this thing they had done together. The warriors brought an old woman to the canyon shade. They had been supporting her, running. The women shared meal cakes and passed the water bags among them.

Geronimo stood apart, looking back toward Fort Thomas. Naiche walked to him, and they studied the horizon through Naiche's Spanish binoculars.

"Now they know," Geronimo grunted. "From where the wind died, they will follow our tracks."

The canyon sliced into the side of the mountain, narrow and sand floored. Perpendicular, smooth-rocked sides stood three hundred feet above them. Along the floor Geronimo ran, turning to wave them on. They felt weariness now and each time he stopped were quick to sit, resting against the scant shade of the eastern wall.

At noon the canyon turned west. There was no shade. The air was thick and suffocating. Babies cried and sweat stuck the women's dresses to their bodies. Geronimo stopped. Motioning to Naiche, he began to search out hidden hand holds, carefully climbing the canyon wall. Fifty feet above the canyon floor he found the small opening, and reaching inside, he pulled out rifles and cartridge belts, tossing them down to Naiche.

Twenty rifles. Most of the warriors knew only the blackpowder musket. Geronimo dropped to the canyon floor and showed them how to work the rifles. These were breechloaders, United States Army issue, Spencer rifles. The eyes of the warriors gloated over the quickness of loading. They sighted along the barrels, ran their hands over the smooth stocks. These were the guns of the bluecoats!

An old warrior felt the power of the gun. He raised his rifle, waving it high over his head, and screamed the Apache war cry, echoing down the canyon. All the warriors joined in, echoing a confusion of screams and chants; except Geronimo. He stood head down until, seeing him standing silently, they became quietened. The last sound died. The silence was heavy on the air. Geronimo looked down the canyon, the way they had come. "Brothers," his voice echoed, "the horses and soldiers are moving toward us." He spoke slowly so that echoes would not confuse what he said. "These mountains are no wider than a snake lying in the desert. These mountains end to the south . . . end; and where they end there is a full day's running across the desert before we reach the Madre. This canyon"— he pointed ahead down the narrow sand floor—"runs west. In a little while there is a place we must leave it and go south. The soldiers will come down this canyon. When they see our tracks turn south into the mountains, they will ride back to the plains; back to the canyon mouth. They will ride fast, south, beside the mountains. They will be waiting at the end and kill us on the desert we must run to reach Sierra Madre." He paused and paced before them, head down. A gloom spread over the band. Women held their babies tighter and children came close to their mothers. The warriors stared at their feet, fingering the rifles and feeling foolish for their outburst of a moment before.

Geronimo stopped and stretched out his arms, as if to touch the canyon walls. "Here," he said, "the walls can be climbed. There must be a warrior who climbs to the top of each wall. When the soldiers come, only one of the warriors fires his gun. He fires it many times from the top of his wall. The soldiers will stop. They must send men back to the canyon mouth; send them along the top of the wall." He swept his arm in a wide arc. "When the soldiers reach this warrior, he must fight them until . . . he is gone. The soldiers will go back and come again down the canyon. This time"—Geronimo pointed to the opposite canyon wall—"the second warrior will fire, many times, and stop them. They must go back again to the canyon mouth and come along the top of this warrior's wall. He must fight them until . . . he is gone. The soldiers must be made to wait, here, a long time before they find our tracks turning south. Brothers . . ." He stopped, turning his face to the sky, as though praying, before he looked at them again. "Brothers . . . there must be two among you who have no wife; no children." Silence. A breeze, whispering through the canyon, moved the bushy hair of the warriors beneath their head bands. A baby cried and was hushed by its mother.

There was a rustle among the men as a slender brave rose in their middle. He held his rifle before him, across his chest. "My wife and children were killed by the soldiers," he said. "I am called Boto. I will stay."

No one spoke. An old warrior stood. His buckskin war band held in place bushy white hair that framed a wrinkled face. "I am called Tana." His voice was thin with an old quavering that broke. "My wife is old. If she could be . . ."

"She will be cared for," Geronimo said.

The old man walked toward him. He limped. Slapping his crooked leg, he laughed. "See! Now I will not have to run like the rest of you! I will rest on the canyon wall." He laughed hollowly, feeling foolish that no one joined in the mirth of his joke. Geronimo embraced him, and they stood for a moment, arms about each other. Boto followed him, and he too was embraced by Geronimo. No one talked. There was nothing to say.

Geronimo walked a little way down the canyon to the west. He waved his arm forward and turned away in the shuffling trot. The women tiredly fell in behind him, followed by the children and the warriors. As they ran, an old woman stepped from the line and stood, waiting for them to pass. Her white hair was long, almost to the waist of her dress, faded and torn, covering a tiny frame. She began walking slowly back.

As the Apaches shuffled toward the west they heard the chant rising and echoing in the canyon: "Only the mountains live forever . . . only the rocks live forever . . ." The Death Chant. Geronimo looked back. Boto and Tana were standing in the middle of the canyon, singing. The old woman was holding Tana's hand.

3

The sun tilted, changing its light rays, filtering through the earth haze and playing with the colors of the canyon walls. Rock streaks of green melted subtly into blues; pink pastels darkened into reds, and sandstone yellows spread liquidly, like paint, mixing and changing with the delicate brush of light.

Tana and his wife, Watashe, sat cross-legged on the canyon floor, their backs to the southern wall of narrow shade. Boto returned from his scouting to the east, the way the soldiers would come. He sat down by the side of Watashe, resting his rifle across his knees. From his loose blouse he took three husks. Placing one between his lips, he politely passed the others to Watashe and Tana, and striking a sulphur match on his cartridge belt, he lit their cigarillos.

They breathed and held the smoke for long intervals before releasing it, luxuriating in its soothing assurance. Watashe and Tana had closed their eyes, and Boto watched the colors changing on the opposite canyon wall. He was a man in his prime; beneath the war band his face was firm, strong, and his legs, above the boot moccasins, showed sinewy muscles.

"Tana?" He addressed the old man without looking.

"Yes." Tana did not open his eyes.

"You know the soldiers better. You were with Nana and Victorio. When . . . do you think . . . they will come?"

"I have thought on it," Tana said. "At the counting this morning, Chato would tell them first . . . before they discovered. But they will be confused in the beginning. They will think, perhaps, that Geronimo has gone to Ojo Caliente." Tana drew smoke from his cigarillo. Boto considered the old man's answer.

"But," Boto argued, "Naiche has said that Geronimo told Chato we were going to the Sierra Madre."

Tana laughed. "Yes. Geronimo is cunning. He thinks twice . . . maybe three times. He knows Chato. When Chato tells the soldiers, first they will think it is true. Then they will argue among themselves and say Geronimo is treacherous. They will say Geronimo knew Chato would tell, and so he is going to Ojo Caliente instead of the Sierra Madre. Then they will argue some more. They will, in the end, ride in circles, around and around . . . until they find our tracks. I think"—Tana paused and glanced quickly at the sun—"they will be here when the sun begins to turn red. It will be a little while." He thought on what he had said and laughed low. "Geronimo makes them work like a burro instead of thinking like the eagle."

A breeze touched the sand floor and was gone. "I walked the length our guns will carry," Boto said, patting the rifle. "There is no place, no boulder behind which they can hide. They must go back a long way when we shoot."

"Yes," Tana answered, "Geronimo did well to pick this place."

Now there were light shadows flickering in the colors of the canyon wall, as though a shadowy hand, etching faintly with gray, feverishly erased its etchings, only to draw again. A cliff hawk sailed smoothly down the canyon. Feeling a slight cooling caused by the slanting of the sun's rays, he came from the plains to search out snakes and rodents, soon to be moving among the rock crevices. Swooping before

34

them, he screamed at their presence and sailed to the canyon rim to perch and consider them.

Tana said, "He has left the desert early; too soon. Perhaps something there has caused him to leave."

Boto stood erect. "Yes. The hawk has come to call us."

Watashe struggled, slow in rising, to stand with Boto and Tana.

Boto motioned to the wall opposite them. "I will take this side if . . ." He looked questioningly at Tana. ". . . you think it better that I . . . go first, Grandfather?" He used the old term of respect.

"Yes, Grandson," Tana answered, "your testing will come while it is still light. You have the strength of the wolf and can move quickly." He laughed, slapping at his crooked leg. "Watashe and me, we cannot move as fast. But in the night, after you are . . . gone, we have the hearing. Our years will help us in the dark, like the coyote."

Watashe touched the arm of Boto, sliding her hand down to hold his strong hand in her old one. "Grandson," she said softly, "when we were born, we chose to put our spirit bodies into these bodies, and to test our spirits and make them stronger—if we win the tests. Now we will be born again, back into our spirit bodies. It is good, and we will be together."

Impulsively Boto squeezed her hand and looked into the old, watering eyes. "Yes," he said shyly, "I believe this. When Geronimo hugged me, he said he had seen the other side and it is good for the strong spirits, for they are in the light. We will be together."

He left them, walking across the canyon's floor. The hawk flapped upward and sailed farther down the canyon. He placed his hand, searching for the first hold on the wall, and turned to face the old couple standing, watching him. He remembered the centuries-old good-bye of the Apache sure of death. "It is a good day for dying!" he called softly. They smiled at his remembering and answered him, "It is a good day for dying!" And the canyon's echo of the words was soft, sighing with a peaceful reassurance, a comforting authority that this was so.

Tana tore a strip from his blouse and tied the rifle around his neck. He pushed Watashe ahead of him, up the wall. She was light, and if he had gone first, and his old leg failed, she could not have held him.

She was slow in her movements, but sure, not slipping. Halfway up she found a sandstone ridge that angled toward the top and toed her moccasins deftly in the crevice. Tana followed, pulling himself over the top of the wall, directly behind her.

They lay for a moment, panting. Tana looked down the way they had come. The canyon floor was far below them, a white strip of narrow sand between the walls. He was pleased with the rocks and boulders here. A good place. But their perch was only a narrow ledge, for almost immediately the mountains rose upward, steep and bouldered.

When the soldiers came to kill them, that was where they would hide, up there, and shoot down on their ledge. It could not be helped. They must lie close to the canyon's edge.

Across the canyon they could see Boto's head. He had settled himself in the place he had chosen, behind two boulders. Tana and Watashe waved and saw the hand of Boto lift in answer.

Behind Boto's narrow ledge, the mountains rose too, with heavy boulders. The boulders made shadows now, lengthening. Where the sun touched them, they were red.

Tana rose and walked among the rocks, searching for the place they must have. He found it a little farther up the canyon, but close to the edge. A big rock sheltered them from sight across the canyon; before them two boulders formed a V through which they could see the way the soldiers would come. Tana lay down and Watashe lay beside him.

The rocks still held their heat, but the air cooled with the sun's rays' lessening slant. Tana lay on his stomach, his rifle before him. Watashe studied the old face, dark and lined, sagging cheeks wrinkling downward. They had been together since they were very young. A snake rustled in the rocks, moving away from their presence.

"Tana," Watashe whispered. She knew a voice tone would carry far.

"Yes," Tana said, not moving his eyes from the canyon.

"You remember Ojo Caliente, with the water spring and the piñon grove?"

"Yes."

"Where our children are buried?"

"I remember," Tana said.

Watashe smoothed the faded calico of her sleeve. "When we . . . go, you may go first. I will follow. We will meet Boto. If . . . we are separated, can we meet there . . . by the children?"

Tana took his eyes from the canyon, looking into her own. A smile creased the lines of his face. "Yes, Watashe. We will meet there. I will remember and put it in my spirit mind. We will meet there." He reassured her, placing his hand over her tiny one.

"I will do this too," she said simply; and satisfied, lay beside him, watching the way the soldiers would come, down the canyon.

The shadows lengthened and narrowed the lighted sand strip of canyon floor. They sensed the coming. It was before their ears heard it. A slow pulsating of air. A rhythm that was slow. Watashe saw Tana stiffen, and she, too, felt the air rhythm on her senses.

The sun was a red ball behind them. Its light, sifting through dust particles, spread a red haziness over them and into the canyon. The redness deepened.

Now a sound touched their ears. Muffled and shuffling in sand, but ominous in its depth. There were many horses. Far ahead, where the canyon bent, Watashe saw them. Even with her age-watered eyes, she could make out walking horses. They came around the bend. More and more of them came. There was no ending to the line. Now she could see figures on the horses.

Riders were coming directly toward them, and the lead horses were strung out, not ridden abreast, like soldiers' mounts. They were Indians.

"Scouts," Tana whispered. "Papago . . . and some . . . are Apache." Watashe could see them now. The Papagos wore their hair short and had hats on their heads. The Apaches wore war bands holding their bush hair in place. Cartridge belts crossed their breasts. They rode slowly, studying the sand.

Behind them came the soldiers, riding three abreast. Watashe could see the sun make red sparkles on their metaled guns. The soldiers rode two hundred yards behind the Indian scouts, cautious of an ambush. The dark line of soldiers lengthened toward them, passing through shadows by the walls. Still they came around the bend; more soldiers than Watashe had ever seen.

The scouts were close now. One of them looked up, scanning the canyon rim. Watashe looked away from him. He would know if she watched him closely. The lead scout was Papago. He was watching the ground, hat shadowing his face.

A rifle startled the quietness, booming. The Papago instantly threw his hands wide, hat tumbling. His horse broke into a run and he tumbled backward, dead. An Apache riding behind him whirled his horse about. Before the echoes died, the rifle boomed again, hitting the Apache between his shoulders, knocking him over the horse's neck. The horse, startled by the sound, reared and bucked the Apache into the sand. Boto had begun his ordeal.

Shouting came from the soldiers. Above their confusion an officer's command rang out. They turned their mounts, retreating back down the canyon. The Indian scouts were scrambling their horses, following the soldiers.

One had jumped from his horse. Holding the reins, he backed against the canyon wall, almost directly below Tana and Watashe. The soldiers had halted, disciplined, halfway down the canyon. They faced about, watching the dismounted scout. He was looking, scanning the canyon top from where the shots came. Now he shouted, "*Yeh. . . . ooooooooo-oooooooh!*" and pointed to Boto's hiding place.

As he pointed, Boto rose in the rocks, aiming his rifle. The shoot boomed and the scout was flung against the wall. He died slumping to the sand. His horse, released, drummed down the canyon westward. The thunder of the shot made rolling echoes that followed the horse farther and farther away. There was heavy silence.

Watashe and Tana saw Boto now. He was climbing a huge boulder on the canyon's edge. He reached the top, in sight of the soldiers. For a moment he stood motionless, skylined before the red ball of setting sun. His hair was whipped by the wind. Slowly he raised the rifle with one hand above his head. As he shook the rifle for all to see, a sound began deep in his throat and, rising from far away, scaled to a high-pitched scream: "*Eeeeeeeeeeeeeeeiiiiiiiihaaaaaaah!*" The war cry of the Apache. The scream bounced, echoing fiercely between the walls. The blue line of soldiers rippled in movement.

Boto lowered the rifle and turned his face to the sky like a wolf, savage and mournful. "*Haaaaaaaaaa-aaaaaaaaoooooooooooooooooooh!*" The Death Call. The Apache scouts would know and so would tell the blue-coat chief. To go this way, they must kill the Apache. There was no other way to pass him. He would fight and die.

Watashe thrilled at the cry and saw Tana's figure shiver on the ground. The soldiers dismounted and stood against the wall with rifles. Shouted commands floated up the canyon to them. A group of soldiers and Indian scouts mounted horses and drummed back toward the east, searching for a place to climb the wall.

Wastashe saw Boto descend from the boulder, but he did not leave the ledge. He did, however, change his position, moving closer to the soldiers. He rose above the rocks; aiming his rifle, he fired toward the soldiers, sending them scrambling farther back along the canyon. The reverberating sounds had not died when he fired again, and again.

Tana turned to Watashe. "Boto does well. He has added many steps to the women and children following Geronimo."

"Yes," Watashe said, "I can hear them running. They are running far away. Boto is giving them many steps. The soldiers must wait."

The sun slipped behind mountain crags, flaming the sky and bringing shadow in the rocks. Slowly the sky flame died, taking away its light. The first star appeared, blinking wakefulness in the east.

Tana gripped Watashe's hand. "See," he whispered, "they are coming." Watashe strained, watching the darkening rocks across the canyon. Then she saw, first one figure, quickly outlined before melting behind a boulder, then another, and another. They were moving toward Boto's place on the ledge.

Circling, they were coming down the mountainside. Suddenly a rifle cracked, and another. A volley of rifles opened up. Tana chuckled. "They are searching for Boto, but he will not answer and tell them where he is. They must come closer and pay for their knowledge."

As Tana spoke a Papago scout leaped atop a boulder and shot down at the ledge. He was answered immediately by Boto's rifle. Slumping, his gun clattering loud in the stillness, the scout rolled from the boulder.

Before his body came to rest, the rifles set up a deafening roar, firing repeatedly at the place of Boto's muzzle flash.

Watashe and Tana saw the figure rise from the ledge rocks. It was Boto. He staggered, stumbling, and fell just as the rifle volley spoke again. From where he had fallen, his rifle answered back. Again he stood. This time he fired before the rifles hit him, turning him as he fell.

Now there was a quietness. Cautiously the figures moved, bending behind rocks as they came toward Boto. Then boldly standing over him. From where he lay, Boto's rifle cracked, striking upward at the figures over him. One of them toppled, sliding in the rocks.

This time the soldiers' rifles fired long and continuously where he lay. After a time they melted back into shadows and drifted along the ledge toward the east.

"Boto is gone," Watashe whispered.

"Yes." Tana raised his rifle, placing it between the two rocks; pointing it toward the soldiers.

Dusk slipped away, retreating toward the west. A tide of stars advanced out of the east bringing silver light to the canyon. The sand floor beneath Watashe and Tana shone white.

Far off a coyote yelped high, tenor voiced. The mountains echoed, hollow. There was stillness.

Tana pulled cartridges from the belt and laid them by his hand. He said, "They are coming." The canyon whispered with a stirring of air that many bodies make in their moving; a creak of leather; a muffled sound of horses' hoofs striking sand.

The scouts were separated this time, riding closer to the canyon's walls, keeping to the shadows. Tana picked the lead scout across the white floor. He fired. The scout fell backward with the rifle crack. Hastily Tana worked the breech and pushed in another cartridge. The scouts had turned their horses.

Tana shot and a horse fell, screaming. Again the shouting of commands.

Tana began a steady firing toward the soldiers, filling the canyon with echoes following echoes until it seemed a dozen rifles were shooting.

The sounds of horses and men moved farther away. The silence came again. Tana sat up, watching for signs of life. There were none. Starlight deepened the seams in his face. His eyes glittered beneath the war band. "Boto gave us good night cover. Now we will use it." Watashe nodded. She knew Tana was a great warrior. His old and wrinkled body was scarred in many places. Guns of the soldiers had crippled his leg. He had been a warrior with Nana, and with Victorio. He had fought the star chief Carleton and Gray Wolf Crook of the bluecoats; the soldier chiefs of Mexico, Terrazas, and Trevino. He would use the darkness.

He stood, pulling Watashe up beside him. "Look," he said, and opened the rifle breech, placing a cartridge in it. He cocked the rifle. Easing the hammer into place, he handed her the rifle.

"Now, you must do this. Take out the bullet. Put it back in the rifle." Watashe fumbled with the gun. She managed to do as he had instructed. He took the rifle from her, slipped the cartridge belt over his shoulder. "I will go to meet them along the ledge. You will hear me shooting. Then"—he pointed up to the mountainside crowding above them—"I will run, up there. I will shoot at them from the mountainside. While they are shooting at the mountainside I will come back, here. I will leave the rifle for you and go back to the mountain. I will let them see me . . . up there . . . but it will take awhile before they can find me. In this way"—he turned his face toward the stars, speculating—"we will make them use more time." Watashe nodded. He embraced her briefly and she laid her head on his chest, long hair silvering in the moonlight. Releasing her, he was gone, limping across the rocks.

Watashe sat down, smoothing the billowing calico dress that fell to her ankles. She had always loved him; fully, finding even the little things to love, the weaknesses and the faults. They had become one, growing together over a long time, and now they were to share this short time; she and Tana, giving steps to the women and the children.

She would have to move quickly in the rocks when she had the gun. She stood and pulled the calico dress over her head, dropping it to the ground. Except for the boot moccasins she was naked.

Far down the ledge a rifle cracked. It was Tana. Again. Now answered by a staccato of rifle fire. Again the single rifle shot. This time closer. When the soldiers' guns answered, she could see the spouts of flame. Tana was moving up the mountain above her. A long silence. A coyote yelped. He was answered by another and another. Watashe thought, *Stupid Papagos. Tana knows they are not coyotes. Why don't they shout at each other? They are yelping so each will know where the other is. So they will not shoot each other.* She nodded knowingly in the moonlight. One of the yelps would be Tana's. He would join their game, and they would be confused, not shoot at his place.

A pebble fell, rattling on the rocks. It was near her and she pressed close against the boulder. In front of her a shadow fell on the ground. It grew larger. The owner of the shadow was crawling up the boulder directly above her.

From far up the mountain a lone shot spouted flame. The shadow rose, stiffening. Watashe looked up as the Papago screamed, losing his balance and falling, straight-bodied, over the canyon edge.

Tana has been watching over me, Watashe thought, *but now they will know where he is.*

Rifles chattered along the mountain, making tiny flames that sputtered in the shadows. They were moving toward Tana's place. She strained to listen when the guns quieted, but could not hear him.

He slipped through the rocks and was before her, pulling the cartridge belt from his shoulder and laying the rifle on the ground. Neither spoke as their eyes met, and he was gone. He moved low, crouching, dragging the crippled leg heavily, and when Watashe picked up the rifle, it was wet with blood.

He would show himself now. She watched the mountain, dappled in the shadows of boulders. Somewhere a heavy rock crashed, and guns volleyed at the sound. Tana had tossed the rock.

Then she saw him, far away from where the rock had fallen. He had raised himself in full view, standing on the boulder in the light. Suddenly he collapsed, throwing his body from the boulder as rifles opened on him.

They did not shoot him, Watashe thought. *Tana is wilier than a coyote.* When the rifle had fired this time, they were closer together in a half ring, moving in. When the last rifle shot died, the coyote yelping began again. They were moving up the mountain.

Then, "*Haaaaaaaaaaaaaaaaaoooooooooooooooo!*" Mournful and long, the cry carried hauntingly into the stillness. It was Tana, and it was the death cry.

This time the rifles did not stop firing as the flame torches moved closer together and joined into a ring. For a long time they boomed and cracked, and echoed. There was a silence. Then the shouts. Tana was gone.

Watashe slipped cartridges from the belt and placed them in her mouth. The cartridge belt was heavy; she would not need many bullets. She crouched waiting. She could hear them now, coming down the mountain. They were talking. Rocks fell and rattled as they approached the ledge, coming directly toward the small clearing where she crouched.

Now she could see them, a dark bunching of men. They wore hats, shadowing their faces in the star-

44

light. Bold and confident, they talked loudly. One of them laughed. Something was scuffing over the ground, loosing pebbles; they were dragging Tana's body. From the shadow of her boulder, Watashe saw clearly now as they came onto the ledge. Two of them held Tana's feet, pulling him on his back, and the lifeless head bobbled and bounced over the stones. Now they were on the ledge in full sight.

The tallest of them stepped to the rim of the ledge and, looking up the canyon, wigwagged his arms in the starlight—a sign to the bluecoats that all was clear. As he swung his arms he shouted the signal to them: *"Hey-oooooooooh!"* Watashe raised the rifle on her knee and sighted between the shoulders of the shouting man. She fired. The rifle explosion boomed in her ears, deafening her, but she heard the man's shout instantly become a scream. He pitched headlong into the canyon. That would tell the bluecoats, Watashe thought. The canyon was not clear. They could not pass.

With the booming of the rifle the dark knot of men instantly melted into the boulders' deeper shadows. They left Tana's body lying on the ledge. Watashe could see the face, turned up toward the stars. There was a deep stillness. She reloaded the rifle, sliding in the cartridge, careful to muffle the click of the breech. She felt a great calm. Her hands were sure and deft.

Here on the ledge the air was still, but far below her in the canyon she could hear wind. At first she was alarmed, for the wind rippled and pattered, and she thought it might be the bluecoats trying to pass, but it was not the sound of horses, or of men running in the sand. Then she knew. It was the wind bringing back to her the sound of the women and the children running. They were still running, following Geronimo. She smiled slowly in the darkness of the boulders and a deep comfort came over her.

Faintly, to her right, she heard a stone turn, and with the born instinct of an Apache warrior she moved backward, rapidly and silently, to escape being surrounded; but she would not move away from the ledge. She could not give up the ledge.

She paused, listening, trusting her ears. Cloth slithered faintly on rock. The sound was in front of her. She had beaten their circle. Now the contest would be their eyes against her ears. She half-raised in the shadow of a huge boulder and bent her body forward in an unnatural, grotesque position. In the illusion of light and shadow, the eye searches for the symmetrical lines of the human body; not the grotesque outlines of rock outcropping. She waited.

Far away down the canyon a bluecoat officer shouted. She could not understand his words—words that echoed hollow and angry. Watashe smiled again. The white-eye chief was impatient. In answer to the shout, a shadow grew quickly atop a boulder, anxious to please the officer and have done with the ambush. The shadow grew, lumpy and moving. The scout was crawling.

Watashe laid her cheek on the rifle and waited patiently for her swaying sights to cross the figure. The sights wavered, moving back and forth. In the center of the shadow now, she squeezed the trigger. Flame reached for the scout not ten yards from her, and with the echoing boom of the rifle the figure half-rose, clear in the starlight. The head flopped against the rock, knocking a hat cartwheeling across the ledge and into the canyon.

The figure jerked and twisted, and gurgled, rolling from the boulder. Striking loose shale from the ledge rock, the body of the scout slid noisily across the ledge and dropped from sight over the edge. Watashe listened but could not hear the body striking the canyon floor. A small avalanche of shale rattled hollowly, following the body into the canyon.

She knew she had caught them moving. If they had seen her muzzle fire, they would have shot. But they knew their encirclement had missed. They would widen now, coming in behind her.

Carefully she opened the breech and inserted another cartridge. She knew Tana was hovering near her, watching. She could see his body lying fifty yards ahead of her on the ledge.

"See Tana . . . Boto . . ." she whispered to herself. "I am helping too. All the great bluecoats still cannot move . . ." The stillness was so heavy that her own whisper startled her. Faintly, far away in the canyon, so dim that it seemed a memory, she could hear the light patter of wind carrying the sound of the footsteps; the women and children running behind Geronimo. For a moment she listened dreamily to the sound. The patter made a rhythm; the wind carried a melody. It was a song.

The song was beautiful, reassuring. Quietly a wisdom thought came into her mind: *This time, I will not be afraid when I am born into the spirit body, as I was when I was born into the earth body. I fought then . . . thinking that to be born here was death. It was not; only a visit. I will not be afraid.*

She shook her head, flopping the long white hair around her shoulders. She must move, but where? Slowly, painfully on the shale, she began crawling toward Tana. Carefully lifting the rifle and placing it down before her, she inched forward, making no sound. Close to her right in the boulders a whisper sound came, very near. It was a moccasin sliding over rock. She paused, turning her head toward the rocks. Too late. The man stood above her in full view, his rifle already pointed. He fired and the flame leaped down at her. She felt the shock, but there was no pain. The blow tumbled her across the ledge, losing the rifle. Frantically she grabbed at the loose shale, at first searching for the rifle, and then, seeing the edge of the canyon's lip sliding perilously close, to hold herself from falling over into the canyon.

The man leaped toward her. A long knife blinked

in the starlight. On her back, looking up, she could see the man clearly in the air, leaping. His face was shadowed by a hat, but she could see his teeth, bared by lips drawn back in the effort. He came down on her, spread-eagled, and plunged the knife. She did not feel it, only a faint tap as if someone had nudged her with a stick.

He rose to his knees astraddle her body. Now she could see the knife handle sticking up from her chest. Instinctively her foot came up between his legs, searching, and found the crotch. She was lying with her head close to the lip of the ledge. With an easy, almost effortless motion, she lifted the man on her foot, using his own momentum as he sought to rise. Needing more power, she deliberately pushed backward, turning her body over into the empty air above the canyon. The scout grunted in surprise, then screamed as he and Watashe shot out over the canyon's edge, falling through the air.

The sound came rushing to her ears as she fell—the sound of the women running; distinctly she could hear the patter of the little feet, the children. She smiled, floating in the wind.

Major Morrow looked down from his horse. Two broken figures lay near each other on the canyon's floor. One was his scout. The other, a tiny bloodied old woman with shrunken breasts. Her hair spread silvered on the sand, incongruously beautifying the scene of blood and death.

Morrow sighed. "After all these years, I shouldn't be surprised at them."

Captain Beyer, beside him, agreed. "Disgusting. Naked like an animal, by God!"

Morrow motioned to the dark clump of riders behind him. "Better roll the body aside. The horses will shy at the blood."

A lean figure dismounted. "I'll take care of it, Major." The figure was buckskinned. A sloppy cowboy hat shadowed his face. While Morrow and Beyer watched he laid a blanket over the body of Watashe with an awkward, courtly gesture. Kneeling beside her, he meticulously tucked the blanket beneath her before lifting her in his arms. Without a word he passed Morrow and Beyer, walking back down the canyon, carrying the tiny body with a tender attentiveness.

Captain Beyer spat, "A hell of a man for chief of scouts, Major. Tom Horn is more Apache than the goddamned Apaches."

Morrow grunted. "I came to that conclusion a long time ago, Captain."

The story was brought to Fort Thomas and San Carlos. All Apaches know it: How the running steps were given to the women and the children. They do not name them. Apaches do not name dead bodies, for those bodies are no longer the identity of the spirit that was in them. But they remember there were three warriors who fought. They have not forgotten Watashe. The place is called the Canyon of the Three.

4

The Three had added more steps to the women and children than was at first apparent. In a matter of four hours Major Morrow had lost ten scouts. Needing his scouts for the final search and kill, he determined to lose no more.

And so he dismounted his soldiers, resting them and their horses against the canyon walls. Lighting no fires and with guards placed on the canyon rims, he waited for daylight.

At dawn he proceeded, this time with scouts afoot on the ledges of the canyon's rim, far in advance of his column. There would be no more surprises; but the pace was slower.

Thus it was noon before his scouts reported; ahead the tracks had left the westbound canyon, turning south. They had followed the tracks for an hour before reporting back. There could be no doubt—Geronimo was racing south, leading his band through the length of the Dragoons. The only possible destination was the Sierra Madre.

Morrow turned his column about and pushed them hard for the canyon's mouth. From that point they would have the smooth valley floor to ride, fast, with the Dragoons beside them and excellent prospects of intercepting Geronimo at the Dragoons' southern tip. Perhaps catching them helpless on the stretch of plains between the Dragoons and the northern point of the Sierra Madre.

Major Morrow was a veteran Indian fighter. He

knew Apache warriors on foot could cover a hundred miles in a day; but with women, babies, and children, running through mountain terrain—that was another matter.

In the late afternoon they emerged from the canyon's mouth onto the valley floor. He ordered the horses, whose saddles were ringed with lather, to be sack-wiped and rested. For half an hour the soldiers tended their mounts and tightened gear on the pack animals carrying three weeks' ration; preparing for a faster pace.

Commanding parts of the Ninth and Tenth cavalries, Morrow had under his command Captains Beyer and Dawson, both veterans. In addition he had left Fort Thomas with nearly forty Indian scouts, Papagos, Pimas, and Apache policemen of the reservation. It was a large and highly competent force.

As the men began to loiter, completing their tasks, he called for mounting. With scouts flanking, he headed the column south, keeping the Dragoons on his right. The pace he set was a fast canter, raising dust. Four times faster than an Apache on foot could sustain. Even a warrior.

An hour later they crossed the Butterfield Stage Line route that wandered west through the Dragoons toward Tucson. Here he paused briefly to send a messenger east along the route through Sulphur Springs and on to Apache Pass and Fort Bowie to apprise General Crook of the "Geronimo development," and his own subsequent maneuvers.

By the time sunset flamed red over the ragged peaks of the Dragoons Morrow's detachment was far south of the stage line. He brought his command to a halt beside a brackish pond on the salt flats and ordered a timed rest while they ate and tended their horses.

After unsaddling and graining their horses, the soldiers sat on the ground, rising to walk and stamp their legs and feet, as they ate cold rations. Dismounting, Morrow handed his reins to an orderly and walked with his peculiar dragging limp away from the camp. He had never admitted to anyone his love of the morning and evening panoramas on the plains. His men were encamped in the purple dusk shadow of the Dragoons, and far to the east he could see the Chiricahua peaks across the valley, flaming red like torches where the sun still touched them.

Except for the limp, Morrow's bearing was West Point. The army was, had been, his life. His hair showed white beneath the brim of his cavalry hat; he was nearing the end of his career. He was given now to long periods of silent retrospect, as is perhaps every man of thought approaching the end of a career . . . or a life.

He had acquired the shattered hip, and the limp, at First Bull Run. His first day in the first battle of the War, as a lieutenant in McDowell's command, had fulfilled all his glorious expectations of war. They had turned the Rebels' flank and, before sundown of that first day, were confident of victory, except for a small hill of stubborn resisters commanded by a Rebel leader named Jackson.

On the following morning they had fully expected to sweep the hill, but Jackson held, stubbornly, fanatically. Then a sound, first far away, growing in volume and intensity, rolled toward them. It was the sound of guns, but mixed with a low ground rumbling of thousands of men, running. The rumbling of the feet came closer, and men were yelling and screaming wildly. Suddenly the sound burst on them . . . and the sight: their own men, running toward them. They had thrown away their guns and scrambled like a mob into his troops. Behind them gray horsemen burst from the trees waving sabers, riding with reckless abandon, and from them came screams so chilling that Morrow had felt his first flash of fear. He had watched, fascinated, horrified, unbelieving as the gray horsemen came on, led by a red-bearded giant he was later to learn was Jeb Stuart.

In that instant the rifle ball had struck his hip, knocking him from the saddle. By some tenacious will he had clung to a stirrup while the horse plunged with the mob, dragging him back. When the horse had become entangled in the brush, he had with superhuman effort, pulled himself into the saddle, and the horse had joined the stampeding men.

Dimly he remembered the wild hysteria of the rout, wagons with mules tangled in harness, horses falling, men tromping men as they rushed, like a tide of unreasoning storm, down on the fringed carriages of the ladies in pretty frocks and men in top hats who had journeyed down from Washington to watch the "victory." It had been a nightmare of unreal horror, carried along by the mob that crushed over screaming women and wrecked carriages.

Through the long months of hospital beds he had felt disgraced. The haunting flash of fear never left him. With his unreasoning military temperament he could not resolve the feeling.

When he was released from the hospital, he asked, then begged, to be returned to the Southern Front. But all his requests were denied. There was even doubt that he might remain in the army. He was sent west.

First to Fort Ridgely, where the white tide had enveloped Minnesota, and the Santee Sioux. He had seen action in dealing with the Santee and Little Crow. But half-starved Indians with bows and arrows, running to protect their women and children, were not Jeb Stuarts. He could not resolve the haunting doubt.

He was at Denver when the War ended, engaged in operations against the Arapaho and the Cheyenne. On July 4, 1865, he stood on a street corner watching a victory parade in which he had declined to ride. Colonel Chivington's troops had paraded, riding horses behind the military band while thousands lined the streets and cheered.

Standing next to him had been an old bearded man, buck-skinned and moccasined, who stank of whisky and filth. As the band had proceeded past them the old man drank from a bottle, and muttering unintelligibly at first, then shouting, began pointing at the passing soldiers and their horses. "Look!" he yelled, pointing. "See the women scalps!" Cupping his hands, he had shouted at the soldiers, "Women killers! Baby killers!"

Around him the crowd had begun to grumble, but the old man didn't notice, or didn't care. Staggering halfway into the street, the old man had pointed to a soldier. "Look at his *hat*! He's got women's private parts all dried out and looped on his *hat*! Look at all their hats! Cut out'n from 'twixt women's laigs, by God! Look at 'em! All of 'em!" A soldier, infuriated, had leaped from his horse onto the old man, knocking him to the ground. Before the crowd could come close, the old man had risen with a triumphant scream of defiance. The soldier lay with a knife sticking upward from his chest.

Morrow had testified for the prosecution at the trial of Daniel—the only name the old man would give the court. There was no presentation of defense. No attorney would take Daniel's case. When the judge had asked the defense to present its case, the old man had risen alone from his table in the squared section set aside for the prisoner and said, "Judge, I ain't got no deefense. I was too drunked up to recollect stabbing that . . . soldier." He had paused and looked coolly around him at the packed, quiet courtroom before he laughed. "Onliest regrets I got, Judge, is not recollecting the satisfaction of it, but I'm prouder'n hell the sonofabitch is dead." The crowd had roared, animal loud, threatening, and it was a long time before the judge could gavel quiet in the courtroom. The jury never left the box. After a short whispered consultation their foreman rose and pronounced the guilty verdict and recommendation of death by hanging.

Daniel rose at the judge's command and with a surprising smooth grace walked to stand before the judge.

"Do you have anything to say before I pronounce sentence?"

"Well, yeah, Judge." Daniel grinned and, turning, swept the courtroom with his gaze. His eyes locked on Morrow's for an instant, and Morrow had felt the shock of clear blue—and somewhere behind the eyes, a twinkle of grim, sardonic humor. Morrow had felt like a child, looking into the eyes, before Daniel swept them away, over the courtroom that had fallen silent, waiting with a fascination to hear words from the dead.

"Well"—his voice was soft, almost musical—"reckon I can ramble some, see'n as it's my neck." He paused, breathing deep. "First, I ain't skeered of dying; 'bout time for me to go anyhow. I'm old, but I seen some things and I know fer sure there's a balancin' out . . . always, there's a balancin' out. Takes awhile . . . but there is. Hell"—he swept his buckskin arm around the court—"we're all criminals here. Me, I ain't the only one, but I'll claim my part. When I come west there was beaver everywhere. The beaver is gone. The buffalo is going. I've helped to kill 'em both off. The Indian is going. What's left of 'em will live on reservations like maggots." His voice changed and dropped almost to a whisper. "I had a 'rapaho woman and a young'un at Sand Creek. They wa'ant any warriors at Sand Creek . . . jest women and children butchered by the soldier boys."

A low rumble rolled through the crowd, and Daniel grinned wide and snaggle-toothed. His eyes crinkled with grim humor. "Yep, that's the truth and you know it. The antelope is going . . . the trees . . . even the air, by God! I've mule-packed, three hundred pound to a long ear, into the mining camps, where there ain't nothing but grubbing night and day fer money and whores and whisky. Where everybody is ganging up doing nothing but grabbin' and shittin' all over each other."

The old man stopped, looking reflectively above the heads of the crowd, and narrowed his gaze to a point above them. "When the last tree's been cut . . . when the last buffalo's gone . . . when the last gold nugget's been grubbed out and the last Indian's been killed . . . whatche goin' to do then? Watche goin' to do with all the big-power greed ye got built up in ye? That ye've passed down to yer young'uns? Whatche goin' to do then? I asks. There won't be nothin' left fer to vent it on . . . 'ceptin' yerselves."

Serenely calm, he stopped and looked over the courtroom. "I ain't no Bible toter, but sum'eres I heerd it said that when ye set out to unbalance the laws of God, then ye got the seeds of yer own destruction set in ye. That's why"—he slapped his chest and spread his arms wide, grinning broadly—"I don't feel a thing agin' ye, fellow criminals . . . not a thing. Shore as God hung the moon, all of ye, and yer children's children, is in the boat with me." His voice dropped and he looked dreamily out a window. "Naw, I ain't sorry to go. Come to think of it, everything I cared about has already left anyhow." Abruptly, he sat down.

Morrow had risen and left the courtroom. He had not waited for the judge's sentence. The old man's words were obviously insane; everything his career stood for, the progress of the country, his country, the old man had blasphemed. As he stepped into the street his foot struck a whisky bottle lying by the door. He kicked it viciously toward the curb, where it struck and crashed against more bottles.

From Denver he was sent north to help bring order to Virginia City, Montana. Red Cloud had closed the Bozeman Trail, and the Murphy wagons no longer brought supplies to the mining camps. There were bread riots of hungry, desperate men. Coal oil was selling for twenty dollars a gallon in greenbacks, nine dollars in gold. In fact, greenbacks were selling, one dollar for forty-five cents' worth of gold.

A week after, he arrived with his troops (he was a captain now); bread riots tore the town apart, flour was six dollars a pound. As he and his troops faced an angry mob of shouting, cursing miners the face of old Daniel in the courtroom floated before him, grinning. *What the hell are you doing here anyway?* The question flitted at his thoughts. He shrugged it off: *Well, they're here trying to get money; me, I'm here because I'm a soldier, and a damn fool for asking.*

He was at Fort Cobb, standing in the officer ranks behind Generals Sherman and Sheridan, when the huge Kiowa chief Satanta addressed them: "You cut down our trees. You slaughter the antelope and the buffalo, and yet you do not eat, but leave them to rot. You dig in the ground and toss your waste in our streams that one time were clear. You burn everything. What do you want? Are you crazy?" Sherman had ignored the rhetoric and the questions. The general, who never smiled, had simply issued a curt series of threats to Satanta: The chief must bring his people in and stay on land guarded by the United States Army. Sheridan had spat on the chief's feet.

Promoted to major, Morrow was assigned, from Fort Robinson, to assist in carrying out Sherman's "burn" order. Coming out on the high plains, he and his detachment were forced to ride through thousands of rotting buffalo carcasses. Only the skin had been taken from the beasts, and the stench was unbearable. Blowflies, working at the maggoty flesh, darkened the air and even attacked the soldiers' horses.

When they had come up on the buffalo hunters, grizzled, whisky-soaked men, Morrow had ordered them to move away from the large herd grazing beyond a brow of hill.

"What in hell fer?" the bearded leader asked belligerently.

"We're setting the grass fires," Morrow had answered coldly. "Get out."

"Fire! Fire! What the hell you settin' the grass on fire for, man . . . you'll burn everything! Are ye crazy?" The buffalo shooters were incredulous. Old Daniel's face floated back; now he was laughing uproariously. Morrow had gazed over the miles and thousands of putrid flesh humps left by the buffalo men. "Yes," he had snapped at them, "I'm crazy . . . Sherman's crazy . . . you're crazy! The whole goddamn world is crazy!"

They had set the fires, lighting wagonloads of coal oil in twenty-mile lines; and as the flames whooshed thirty feet high the wind caught the wall and raced it toward the west, moving, moving over the horizon, intent, it seemed, on burning the world. Where a moment before there had been lush grass, flowers, birds, animals . . . now the earth was black, parched, barren.

Even the soldiers under his command had questioned the far-reaching orders. "It's simple," Morrow had explained sardonically. "Sherman says, 'No grass means no buffalo. No buffalo means no Indian.' Very simple."

It was. And now, as the Dragoons' purple shadow lengthened across the valley, he shrugged and shook his head to clear the thoughts that came more frequently these days. He reflected rather bitterly that he seemed destined to ride out Old Daniel's prediction. The Apaches were the last. Maybe Geronimo was the last of them . . . the Last Indian. He, Major Jack Morrow, seemed destined to taste the bottom of the cup, whatever that might hold for the tongue; and with the final Indian War Leader, who didn't even hold the rank of chief.

In the deepening dusk he consulted the big watch he carried in his coat. Fifteen more minutes of rest. The troopers were sprawled on their backs, making the most of their time off the horses. A hundred yards away he saw his chief of scouts sitting alone, as he always did. He was watching the same red of the Chiricahua peaks, dimming now, like embers dying in a fire. Cutting chunks of jerky beef with a bowie knife, he plopped the dry meat into his mouth, chewing methodically.

Morrow began walking slowly toward him. Horn's cool and flippant disregard for command irritated Morrow. On this ride Morrow had wanted Sieber, but Sieber was passed out drunk, and he had been forced to use Tom Horn.

Horn was in his early twenties and at one time had lived with the Apaches and spoke their language fluently. Morrow considered this to be his only claim to qualification as a chief scout. He had been a friend of Geronimo's, and some claimed he still was. At any rate, Horn had several times refused to betray his "word," defying command requests that he arrange conferences with Geronimo. His refusals were accompanied by dry, laconic statements that he did not trust the army's "word." Apparently he had no such distrust of Geronimo.

Horn was never without his low-slung .44 Colts, and well-founded rumors claimed several shoot-out killings to his credit. To his discredit, as far as Morrow was concerned. He had no use for gunslingers. But there were other, more solid reasons, in Morrow's mind, for his distrust of Horn.

First, Horn was a Missourian of that peculiar wild-breed border fraternity who were somehow lacking in civilized standards and seemed hell-bent on pursuing some reckless objective for the sheer joy of recklessness. He had no respect for any institution of a civilized nature, so far as Morrow knew.

Second, his father had been a Confederate cavalryman, of which Horn frequently and loudly boasted. Although Horn had twice been recommended for valor, officers with cooler heads, including Morrow, had seen that the recommendations were buried.

As Morrow approached him Horn pretended not to notice. He continued his methodical chewing and gazing toward the Chiricahuas. Deliberately, Morrow thought, and felt a fresh flood of irritation with the man. Suppressing the feeling, he spoke calmly, within two feet of him. "Horn?"

Horn watched the far mountains for a full two-second count before turning his head. "Major." He always uttered titles with a tinge of flippancy, as though officers were jokes dressed in play uniforms.

Morrow caught himself, cleared his throat to keep down the outrage that the man inspired in him. "What do you think of our situation?"

Horn looked up from beneath his wide-brimmed hat and his eyes twinkled humorously. He plopped a chunk of beef into his mouth before answering. "The situation we're settin' in, I reckon?"

"Obviously," Morrow replied dryly.

"Well," Horn said lazily, pointing the bowie knife back toward Apache Pass and Fort Bowie, "it's shore the end of ol' Crook. No doubt about it. The ol' bastard's tried to change a lifetime of criminal ways in the last year or two. Got in pistol range of being decent, askin' for real food for the concentration Apaches, hollerin' to stop the Tucson ring of army contractors from stirring up the war . . . sich as that. Yep"— Horn stretched his arms and grunted—"he has reformed toooo damn decent to be a general. The politicians and profiteers won't put up with it." He waved the bowie, pointing it at Morrow. "You can put it in the tally book, Major. Ol' Shit-Don't-Stink will use this excuse to git Crook's scalp. You take when Crook said that peace would kill the goose that lays the gold egg for the Tucson army contractors . . . well, they got powerful friends in Washington and Shit-Don't-Stink is one of 'em."

"I suppose so," Morrow said stiffly. No need to question who Shit-Don't-Stink was. Morrow knew. Horn delighted in using his own versions of descriptive names in the manner of the Indian. He had a total irreverence for Custer's memory and insisted on referring to him as Hard Backsides, the original name given to Custer by the Indians.

Shit-Don't-Stink was Sheridan. Horn had gone into elaborate detail in explaining this name in the saloons of Tombstone and Tucson. His story always brought gales of laughter from the drinking fraternity. Shit-Don't-Stink, said Horn, knew very well that his shit did stink, but he wanted *you* to think that *he* was mighty sure it didn't. Reason for this, Horn explained, was Shit-Don't-Stink hid out the first three years of the War, excepting when he was caught by Southern cavalry and got his butt tanned. Then in '64, when the Confederates didn't have mount replacements for their cavalry, no powder, and not much of nothing else, out comes ol' Shit-Don't-Stink and Strike-a-Match Sherman and start in to settin' fires. According to Horn, if Strike-a-Match spent the night in town, you'd damn shore better shake him down and hide the matches. "That sonofabitch *loves* to watch fires . . ." always brought roars of laughter.

"While," Morrow said somewhat sourly, "you're giving me your refined opinion on Washington, would you care to throw in an opinion on what we may expect in the case at hand—namely Geronimo? Since that is what you draw your pay for doing."

"Why, yes," Horn said pleasantly. "First off, like I told you before, ain't but one thing happens when you follow Geronimo into a mountain . . . or a canyon. You get chewed up. Maybe a little at a time . . . but you still get chewed up. Ol' Geronimo is heading straight as a ruttin' buck for the Madre. That is, if he don't decide to stop off at Tombstone and burn it to the ground on the way. Who in hell knows what Geronimo is goin' to do? Ain't nobody ever handled him, Major, and that includes Crook. Nobody. Never captured, and never will be. You can tally that down too. It's fact," he announced with finality. "But," he added humorously, "we can get a little ridin' in. And since we don't care how many Indian scouts gits chewed up, that being the general idear—killing Indians—anyhow, if we're lucky, we might skim off a few of Geronimo's crowd. Best we can hope for," he added cheerfully.

Morrow consulted his watch, frowning against the darkness. He made a mental note; his eyes seemed to be failing him lately. But he was pleased that the feeling of irritation had left him. It was always that way with Horn, once you got past the abrasive irreverence of the man. Like bitter beer.

Still holding his watch, Morrow was tempted to extract more of the twisted thinking from the voluble scout. "Tell me, Horn," he asked conversationally, "since you're such an admirer of this bloody renegade Geronimo, why don't you join him?"

Horn felt the edge of hostility in the tone. He looked keenly at Morrow. A chuckle deepened in his throat and broadened into a laugh. Smiling good-humoredly, he drawled, "Well, Major, first off, there you go . . . pure army . . . gittin' the harness tangled before the buggy gits started. Geronimo's bloody, that's fer shore; but a renegade? A renegade, Major"—his tone mimicked a schoolmaster's—"is someone that deserts a faith or a cause; now, you shore can't accuse ol' Geronimo of that, no matter what the newspapers say. You fellers holler 'renegade,' because Geronimo won't let you sucker him into being a pet Indian fer *your* cause. And what is your cause . . . and my cause . . . and these miners' cause that's digging up all this silver and copper hereabouts? Why our cause is thievery, plain and simple. Only difference is, I know what I am. You and the U.S. Army, by God, call it glory. Now"—Horn rose, sheathing the bowie and stretching his arms—"reason you won't find me joining Geronimo is simple 'rithmetic. The pay ain't much good, and Geronimo is a hero. Yep"—he pulled his hat from his head and inspected the brim philosophically—"a bloody hero. He ain't fightin' fer no money, er glory, er promotions, not even fer land. That makes him a hero, Major, and you show me a hero where everybody thinks he's jest the opposite, and I'll show you a tragedy. And"—he clapped the hat on his head—"Mama learnt her boy Tom not to git mixed up with no tragedies and get hanged; leastwise while so young. Hell, I ain't seen the elephant yet, ner heard the owl."

Morrow sighed and turned, walking away. Stopping, he called back at the young man, who was chewing the last of the jerky and gazing at the stars, "Horn, do you think we can catch him on the flats?"

Tom Horn didn't take his eyes from the stars. "Only thing I can promise, Major, is we'll make the flats come morning. If Geronimo don't fly, we'll cut it damn close to rounding 'em up. You understand, I said *if* he don't fly."

Morrow shouted mounting orders, and as he swung into the saddle he could hear Horn speaking rapidly in Apache, Papago, and Pima to his scouts. *His* only *damn qualification for chief scout*, Morrow thought. He suspected Horn's flippant bitterness covered his feelings about losing the scouts in the canyon. Morrow made a mental note to check the length of Horn's contract with the army. It ought to be terminated.

5

Geronimo had been chased many times by soldiers. As a young warrior with Mangas Coloradas, and after the old chief's death, with Juh and Cochise, he came to know how doggedly the blue soldiers would hang on a trail. But while a quick ambush did not stop them, it did make their officers cautious of losing men. Knowing this, he counted heavily on the ambush of Boto, Tana, and Watashe to delay the soldiers for a night in the canyon.

When he led his band south, turning from the westbound canyon, they passed through a piñon grove, over a range, and into an arroyo running south. The arroyo continued for several miles through a hogback and dropped dramatically into a deep canyon. The last hundred yards of the arroyo's entrance into the canyon was a sloping bank of shale. Women and children fell and slid down the banks, holding on to one another.

The canyon had come from the east, but twisted southward. Deep, with limestone formations and sharp outcroppings overhanging its rims, the canyon floor was lined with live oak and piñon. Through its center fresh spring water ran clear over rocks.

Geronimo rested them here while the women emptied brackish water from bags and refilled them with cold water from the spring.

These mountains had been the principal lair of Cochise. From their peaks his warriors could see the wide sweep of plains on either side; all the way to

Apache Pass, where the freight wagons came through, moving across the salt flats toward the Dragoons and through them to the mining camps and Tucson.

Geronimo had stood on these peaks with Cochise; knew where water rushed from rocks and where raceways interlaced, running south. It was down this canyon, later to be named Cochise Canyon, that he led his band, running and resting through the night while Major Morrow waited for dawn, halted by the Three.

After midnight of the following day, while the major led his troops, running on the salt flats, Geronimo brought his people down the last slope of the Dragoons and onto the plain.

To the south his band could see their destination: the peaks of the Sierra Madre, looming high. The Mother Mountain, hereditary refuge of the Apache, sprawled her skirts a hundred miles wide. She plunged over a thousand miles into Mexico with endless trails and hidden sanctuaries in her bosom.

Using Naiche's binoculars, Geronimo studied the valley to the north, down which the soldiers would come in pursuit. He saw no dust cloud in the starlight and so set the pace, walking, across the plain. For over fifty hours, with only short rests, they had been running. There was a limit, even for Apaches.

Now they rested more frequently, walked slower. More than half the warriors carried children who could no longer walk. But night is the best time to cross the dangerous open ground of the plains, and Geronimo wanted most of the openness behind them when light came.

In the gray light before dawn they looked back and saw the wisdom of Geronimo's urging through the night. There were dust clouds behind them, coming fast. The cavalry of the bluecoats.

No urging was needed now. They began to run. Every man and woman carried a child. Straining the last of their reserves, they fixed their eyes on the Mother Mountain looming close, and ran.

Geronimo led them straight to a shinoak grove at the foot of the first mountains. As they passed under leafy, sheltering branches he halted them. Frantic women, knowing soldiers on the chase killed children as indiscriminately as men and women, sought to run past, holding their children on hips or leading them.

Geronimo seized one woman carrying a baby and, flinging her to the ground, grabbed another. Zalah blocked the path of the women, fighting them. Gradually their hysteria was calmed.

"Loco!" Geronimo waved to the old warrior chief. "Lead them. They must follow you single, one after the other, so your tracks are small and we may cover them when we come." He pointed Loco toward a dim trail that skirted the mountain, running south. "Follow the trail. When the sun is overhead, you will see a tall mountain. Turn away into that mountain. Behind it, you will find water. Wait for us there."

Loco shouted to the women and children. He led them in single file down the trail.

"There is no hurry," Geronimo called reassuringly to them, but they anxiously crowded on one another's heels. Geronimo sent three warriors behind them.

With a dozen warriors now, he came back to the edge of the shinoaks. The column was plainly in sight, two abreast. The horses were walking. Major Morrow had pushed hard to overtake the band on the plain; failing that, he knew the campaign would lengthen in the mountains. The moment had passed for a quick death blow. Now the test was stamina; they must keep pressure on the band and allow them no rest.

Geronimo placed the warriors in a long line. Each stood beside a tree, facing the plain. From this shelter they had a clear view of the column approaching across flat ground. Geronimo turned to Naiche. "It is for you and me, brother, to go out and meet them.

When we shoot, shoot the scouts. They will be more dangerous in the mountains."

"I am ready," Naiche said.

Before them on the plain old and withered purple blossoms dipped in the wind from chest-high pea-bushes. Crouching, with Naiche on his heels, Geronimo ran among them, directly toward the approaching horsemen. Their heads never rose above the blossoms. They ran erratically, dropping to their knees, stooping to run again through drying sunflowers, yucca, and walkingstick cactus. The swaying, dipping pea-bushes kept movement before the eyes of the soldiers and so confused the movement of Geronimo and Naiche.

So close; now they could hear saddles creaking, horses blowing. Still Geronimo ran toward them; seventy-five yards . . . fifty. Naiche could see sweat standing on the face of the nearest scout. Geronimo stopped, kneeling. "Now," he whispered and raised his rifle. They shot together. A scout slipped sideways from his horse; another flipped backward.

Even before the rifles' reports had settled in the air, Geronimo had whirled, running toward the shin-oak grove with Naiche on his heels, dodging left and right. His action, cat-quick, was only a half-second faster than Major Morrow's. Morrow shot his hand in the air, waving the troopers in a full charge after them.

Morrow shouted, harsh in the wind, "Charge! Charge!" To his left a voice yelled, *"No! No! Stay back!"* It was Tom Horn, but the yelling troopers drowned his shouts in the wind.

Geronimo and Naiche had nearly a hundred yards to run for the shelter of the shinoaks. Scouts to the right and left of them fanned out in an effort to squeeze their route of running into a straight line. The horses, gaining stride, thundered the ground with pounding hoofs. They gained rapidly on the pair. Soldiers began shouting triumphantly, shooting at the dodging, ducking bushwhackers. Spouts of sand hit left, right, behind . . . now in front of them. The gap was closing. The two would not make the shinoaks.

The horses were charging headlong, necks outstretched, when the withering rifle fire opened from the trees. It was rapid, practiced, disciplined fire that had no pause. Half the warriors in the trees were firing while their other half were reloading. It was deadly. Three scouts were knocked instantaneously from their horses; Captain Beyer's horse stumbled and flipped, throwing Beyer forward. A soldier screamed, falling backward from his mount. Two horses fell, coughing, carrying scouts with them.

The bugler sounded retreat, and Morrow moved his men, cursing and shouting, back beyond rifle range. The troopers were fighting lathering horses, heated and excited from the charge. Morrow slid his own mount to a dust-choking stop beside Tom Horn. "Where the hell were you?" he shouted angrily.

Horn did not look up. He had dismounted and was kneeling over a scout. Morrow climbed from his horse, and Captain Dawson joined him. They watched while Horn painfully pulled the blue coat from the scout, lying on his back; life was bubbling from a huge ugly hole in his chest. The scout was Apache. Horn finished stripping away the blue coat and stepped to his horse, where he rummaged in saddlebags and returned with a small can. He spat in the can and, poking his finger inside, knelt by the scout. The Apache was conscious and watched him with calm eyes as Horn withdrew the finger and rubbed it across the Apache's cheekbones, leaving long streaks of yellow. The streaks were the markings of Geronimo's warriors.

Blood burbled through the lips of the Apache. He opened and closed them, but he could not speak. Horn wiped away the blood. He pulled the long knife from the sheath of the scout and tried to place it in his hand, but the hand couldn't hold the handle, and so he placed it on the skinny chest, heaving erratically. The Apache's eyes had followed every movement, and now a serenity came into their blackness as he looked at Horn. He raised a hand halfway. Horn clutched it, holding it briefly, and laid it on the knife. "*In-gew*," Horn said softly. "All right." He picked up the blue coat and, standing, held it before the eyes of the Apache; drawing his own knife, he slowly, ceremoniously cut the coat to rags, throwing it at the feet of the man. The eyes blinked a silent gratitude and rolled back. He was dead without a word.

Morrow, Dawson, and a half dozen men who had gathered watched Horn lower his eyelids and rise. Dawson spoke for all of them, his voice harsh and loud: "What was that silly paganism about?"

Horn grinned. "Nothing silly, Captain. I give my word to all my scouts; if I found 'em hit and dying. Same as you'd like to have one of yer priests er preachers. You see"—Horn was addressing no one in particular now, for he had lifted his hat and was thoughtfully scratching his head as he gazed south at the mountains—"yer army and yer government can blackmail these scouts into knuckling under. They draw the extry rations and they do loyal work fer you; Talo there on the ground had a wife and three young'uns and they was starving in yer camp. But they're different from white people . . . you didn't buy his soul. Nope, that knife there"—Horn replaced his hat and looked down at the sprawled figure— "that represents what has kept him free . . . all his people for hundreds of years . . . free from shitty politicians and governments and armies. Ye might say I laid a Bible on his chest, where he could see it. He'd of held it if he could." Horn looked up steadily at the lean faces around him. "Yeah," he said thoughtfully, "you bought his mind and his knowledge, but not his soul. His soul is with Geronimo."

A trooper cursed and spat on the Indian. Morrow

shouted to the medics tending Captain Beyer in the distance before he turned back to Horn.

"I asked you a question, Horn," he said stiffly.

"Oh, yeah." Horn looked insolently at him. "So you did, Major. Well, I was right about here, where I am now." He tapped his temple with a forefinger. "I'm paid fer brainpower . . . which I tried. I yelled not to charge, but you went and done it anyhow."

Morrow came close to the scout. "Don't tell *me* how to fight Indians. I was fighting Indians when you were sucking a tit, by God!"

"Why shore you was, Major," Horn said soothingly, "no argument there. But when you're fighting Geronimo, you don't go by Indian-fightin' rules. You go by Geronimo-fightin' rules. One of which, by the way, you jest broke; which is," he added easily, "don't *never* charge Geronimo when he's trying to git you to charge him. Come to think of it," he said meditatively, "don't charge him when he *ain't* trying to git you to; that's a pretty good'un too."

Morrow whirled from the chief scout and strode away. Beyer's arm had been broken, and medics, splitting his tunic, set casts. Somewhere ahead of them a wounded man moaned as medics worked over him in the brush. The sun had moved, hotter, past noon.

Now on foot, with Horn close beside him, Morrow ordered the men forward cautiously. Scouts were out in wide flanks. After fifty paces Morrow ordered a raking fire laid down on the shinoak grove. There was no answering fire.

The sun had tilted well into the afternoon by the time Morrow and his soldiers had infiltrated the grove. They found no Apaches; only a single file of moccasin tracks leading south along the edge of the Sierra Madre.

6

His powerful legs swung easily, running through afternoon shadows lengthening on this apron of mountains. Behind him, single file, a dozen warriors matched him through creosote and burro bush and under the dark of ironwood trees.

There was no sound of their running. Only wind from the east, whining off the dreary Chihuahua plain, where heat devils curled and danced away the vision so there was no horizon.

They ran steadily to the south beneath the shadows of the Mother Mountain, looming high and broken, tucking the sun behind her and sheltering them in her cover.

Geronimo slowed and walked, and stopped in a thicket of mesquite. The warriors, gathering around him, followed his look eastward across the prairie. The wind rushed from the flat plains heat into the coolness of mountain shade, bending sparse bunchings of galleta grass and shaking the bushes of sage. The prairie was alive, dancing in the wind and heat.

Geronimo pointed. "Gosoda." Naiche raised the binoculars to verify what he could not see. Through the glasses the Mexican village was clear: adobe buildings squatting on the plain with a cathedral tower rising from its middle. A low white wall circled the town, broken by a gateway that was the only entrance. Naiche could even see a guard walking on the wall. The guard seemed to dance, but Naiche knew it was a trick of the glasses and heat breath and so did not trust his eyes.

Tiny adobe huts with thatched roofs hugged close against the outside wall of the village, and near them a high-railed corral held mules and horses. Naiche grunted when he saw the corral. He passed the binoculars to the warriors near him.

Geronimo walked alone down the back trail from where they had come. He disappeared in the shadows, pausing to listen, walking again.

The confinement of the hole and his days at San Carlos had deadened his trail senses. When running through the live oaks and piñon of the Dragoons, he had begun to feel them again faintly; the return of their life thoughts . . . their rhythms. Entering the shinoak grove, he had felt the return stronger, more intense.

Now, seating himself beneath a desert hackberry in full foliage, he watched a deer bird picking the yellow berries and dreamily relaxed the thinking of his conscious mind. Eyes closed, he shut out the senses of sight and sound.

Here, there were a community of plants, traveling together. A million years ago they had set out from the south, conditioning themselves as they came north, lengthening their roots to gather more drink; sparsing their foliage to release less of their moisture and their breath; heightening their perceptions for survival.

They had kept precariously between the Mother Mountain and the hot, dry plain to balance their needs. Their life rhythms were harmonious; they required order to survive. Their perception of danger was finely honed, not sluggish. They were alert.

Softly Geronimo chanted. Not words, but tones that matched the rhythm of their harmony. The tones were soothing and beautiful, rising and falling without break or abruptness. The rhythm became stronger. A haunting odor came to his nostrils from the leaves of creosote bushes. The burro bushes moved their branches in unison to the chant. Slowly Geronimo felt the rhythm tightening. Were the danger moving from them, the rhythm would have lengthened, growing more languid. Now, faintly, breaks of excitement came, staccato; and he knew the soldiers had not stopped. They were coming.

He rose, touching the trees and bushes lightly, and trotted back the way he had come. His warriors waited.

"They will be here soon," he said, and turning from the prairie, he swung into the mountain, toward the west. The line of warriors followed.

Dull brass from cartridge belts picked light from the shadows. Here and there along the line an arrow quiver slapped the thigh of a brave still carrying a short Apache bow on his shoulder.

The shadows deepened as they ran into the foot-hills of the mountain. Twilight came and the wind died. Then darkness. Still they ran, into the deeper darkness between shoulders of mountain.

Brilliant stars brought a faint glow of light as they emerged from the shoulders and climbed upward along the sides of a majestic peak. Thickets of piñon scattered the starlight, making silver slashes on the ground. A night hawk whistled alarm, and far off the scream of a cougar echoed hollow and alone.

Their breath came heavier as they climbed. Stars trekking westward with them marked an hour, then two as Geronimo unerringly found a narrow canyon and led them through the mountain. He slowed, walking still farther downward into a ravine.

The floor of the ravine gave off the warm smell of sweet grass in a clearing between the mountains. Water splashed from rocks. Only Naiche and Geronimo went to the stream to drink. The warriors stretched on the grass. Muscle response in their legs was gone. Stamina, even wakefulness, was sapped by over seventy hours on the trail.

A sliver of old moon edged over the mountain pass to the east. It shafted light down on the meadow and darkened the mountains, but none of them sought the safety of the shadows. Geronimo walked into the water. He splashed it over his body. "Look, brothers," he called softly, "the water will help us if we help ourselves. The soldiers will come here soon." He came out of the water and walked among them. "The soldiers will be tired, as we are. They will like this water; this place. They will stay here."

No warrior raised his head.

"Listen, brothers." Geronimo spoke loud and harsh. "We are few. We are Apache. We must last beyond what the soldiers do. This is their way, to run us until we fall. Wet your feet in the water. We must each leave here alone. Each in a separate way, so the scout dogs will believe we are frightened and scattered. When you have run a long way, you must begin to move up to the rocks and hide your track. When you have done this, turn back to the east. We will meet at that place where we saw Gosoda. Then we will rest."

Naiche walked from the stream to stand by Geronimo. "Get up!" Naiche shouted. "Remember the women and the children."

Ahkochne, a father of two, was the first to rise. He pulled another warrior, staggering, to his feet. One by one, they lunged toward the stream. Some of them sat in the water, but soon they were splashing and throwing water at each other. Geronimo was among them.

He sent Ahkochne to the south, shuffling away into the shadows; another warrior to the southwest, another to the west. As the last warrior disappeared in the shadows he touched Naiche's arm. "Come," he said and walked to the steepest slope of mountain.

They pulled themselves up, grabbing brush and cedar, outcropping from rock. Two hundred feet above the meadow Geronimo pushed his rifle onto a ledge of rock that overhung the clearing. Swinging up, he pulled Naiche after him.

They sat cross-legged on the ledge, shadowed by the mountain behind them. Far below the grassed clearing showed bright in the moonlight. The spring flashed a thin necklace, glittering, but they could not hear it. On the ledge there was wind.

Naiche dozed, snapping awake once when an owl called close by. For a moment he watched Geronimo, sitting straight-backed, watching the clearing below. He awoke again when Geronimo touched his leg and knew he had been sleeping for a long time. The moon had tilted toward the west. It was colder.

"They are here," Geronimo whispered. Naiche looked below. The meadow was empty. He watched the shadows. A deeper shadow moved; then another. The mountains' shadow ring, surrounding the moonlit clearing, was alive with darker, flitting ghosts.

"Scout dogs," Geronimo hissed. A coyote barked sharp and sudden directly below them. Naiche laughed low. "He sounds like a dog puppy." The bark was a signal to others.

There was a clatter of iron-shod hoofs on rocks. Men leading horses walked into the clear moonlight of the meadow. Soldiers. The line, single file, came on and on out of the pass. Naiche whistled beneath his breath, "There are many!" It was a full troop of United States cavalry, eighty men. Pack mules followed them.

Leather creaked and slapped as horses were unsaddled and led to water. A murmur of men talking came faintly to the ledge. Cooking fires flared, and sentries with shouldered rifles came from the fires and paced into the mountain shadows.

"See the weakness of men," Geronimo commented soberly as they watched. "We make them tired, but we give them a good place with water. They forget why they have come. They want to sleep and eat and drink the cool water. Like the white-eyed soldiers train the camp Apache to do," he mused softly, "un-

75

til he forgets he must be free, and is grateful for the soldier guard camp where he thinks only of enough to eat and water to drink. How easily people forget the food their spirit body needs and are made slaves to the powers that will feed their earth bodies."

"Yes," Naiche answered; it was a surprising thought. His eyes picked out movement, a darkness that wiggled up the side of the mountain. He touched Geronimo's arm and hissed in his ear, "See, the scout dogs are moving, up here, on the mountains to find our tracks."

Geronimo watched the dark movement Naiche had indicated and near it another, and another. Small, imperceptible; like black worms moving upward on the blacker wall of the mountain. The movement was everywhere. He stood, pointing below them. "They are coming here too." White teeth flashed in a wicked smile at Naiche. "Come, we will leave them a gift, so that when they find it in the morning, they will believe we are still here on the mountain. It will make them timid."

They climbed the perpendicular bank behind the ledge, finding foothold in the rock, and squatted beside a cedar, bushy and stunted. The cedar, restless in the wind, moved, alternating shadows and slashes of light over them, so that their shapes beside it were continually changing. A searching eye could not determine a man's form in the fluid drawings of light and shadow that made a thousand forms.

Somewhere on the mountain below them a hawk was disturbed and rose screaming in the moonlight. Naiche felt Geronimo tense. A small pebble rattled and fell below them near the ledge. Geronimo rose beside the tree. He had drawn his long knife. There was no following sound. The wind whined where it cornered the ledge of rock.

A shadow rose at the ledge's end. It grew imperceptibly and stopped, becoming a part of the ledge shadow. A long moment passed. The shadow grew taller. It became a man standing on the ledge. Wind whipped the bush hair beneath his war band. He wore a blue soldier coat and knelt, studying the disturbed gravel of the rock. Geronimo leaped.

He struck the kneeling man in the back, flattening him and knocking the wind from him with a grunt. He had not used the knife. Naiche jumped to the ledge beside him, and as Geronimo rose, Naiche seized the man and pulled him erect. He was Apache.

The blue coat hung loose over his small frame. Long sleeves were rolled back from his hands. He was young. Naiche easily pinioned his arms behind him, facing Geronimo. He did not struggle.

"Marteen," Geronimo whispered.

"Yes." The scout looked at his feet.

"Why?" Geronimo asked.

Marteen studied his feet and did not raise his face. "To eat," he said. "My woman . . . children." There was no pleading in his voice. It was a statement, flat, without emotion. "The Apache are all going to die."

Geronimo turned the knife's handle, bringing the sharp edge up, and held it slightly away from his body. Marteen raised his head and looked into the eyes of Geronimo.

"Is it . . . could I . . . take off the blue coat?" he whispered above the wind. Geronimo nodded. Naiche released his arms. Slowly Marteen unbuttoned the coat, letting it fall to the ground. He was bare above his breechclout, frail and skinny. His eyes did not move from Geronimo's.

"Forgive me, Usen," he said, and his voice changed into a low chant. "Only the mountains live forever . . . only the rocks live forever . . ." Geronimo moved smoothly toward him; his arm shot bullet-fast with the knife, burying it below the breastbone. Marteen flung his arms upward and clasped them about the neck of Geronimo, hugging him; cradling his head like a child on Geronimo's shoulder.

They stood, swaying, holding each other in the

moonlight and the wind; the stocky figure, head bowed over the frail, boyish-looking scout who clung to his neck.

Naiche's vision blurred, watching them. An over-powering, aching hurt came over him. He wondered whether it was for Marteen, the traitor. Or was it for Geronimo? Or was it for them both?

They left him there, on the ledge, taking his rifle and cartridge belt. In the morning the soldiers would find him. Beside him they would find the blue coat, slashed to rags. He would be staring at the morning star; beneath his head would be a smooth rock, and in his hand, clutched tightly, they would find a stick, representing the Apache arrow. As clear as the bene-diction of any priest who sought to save and restore the prodigal son to his faith.

When they left him, they scrambled upward, Geronimo and Naiche, hurrying against time. Up, past the tree line to the rocks before they turned east along the ridge, leaving no track.

The swaying tops of trees hid their running. If a man could have watched from the meadow, which he could not, he would have seen the squat figure in the moonlight, leading the tall, jumping from rock to rock. The powerful shoulders sagged unnaturally, and the head was bowed. But the strong legs drummed hard. Running toward Gosoda.

7

Come, warriors, like the eagle, free.
Come to battle like the eagle.
  —A Chiricahua Apache chant

Day dies easily, gracefully slipping its life beneath softening shrouds of twilight, bringing the first stars of promise before sleeping in the night-death. But then day, being light and therefore life, has strength and faith in rebirth. Man and animal, tree and bush, repose confidently in twilight; as they do in approaching death, once they resolve to put the light-life behind them. They are imbued quietly with the knowledge of eternity, confident death is a passing door to dawn-birth. Life is eternal.

It is not so when night dies. Night withdraws quickly and without grace. Hating life and the dawn-birth, it departs without waiting. There is a brief time before the faintest gray of light permeates the black when the sun, far away in the universe, blots out the stars. But its own light has not reached the earth. It is at this time, when night leaves and dawn has not arrived, that the darkness is deepest. The night feel is gone. The day feel has not arrived.

It is a time when no coyote yelps nor wolf howls. No tree stirs nor bird ruffles. It is a time when the sickest die. For in the Law there can be no revolutions of the Life Wheel without the door of Death. One without the other cannot exist, and so the night-death feel is, itself, a part of Life. When it is gone, there is no life-death feel. It is the limbo where man, plant, and animal ebb lowest.

And so it is the time when the Apache, trailed by enemies on all sides, must choose to gather. The enemy does not have the spirit will of the Apache. Enemies lie in the limbo.

They came singly, melting out of blackness to where Geronimo and Naiche waited. Each warrior had guided himself back to this place where, the day before, they had seen Gosoda across the Chihuahua plain. Each had waited in the shadows of the mountain for this time.

Sound is alien and harsh to that time between life and death, and so the whisper of Geronimo floated light and ethereal to the warriors: "We will scatter" —he waved his arm toward the mountainside—"and sleep. We will meet here when the sun dies."

And so they left, each seeking his own bush or tree, away from the others. Now they would rest while the sun rose and passed, and died. Naiche, the chief, took the highest point on the mountain as a rallying place in alarm. Geronimo, the War Leader, at the foot of the mountain, closest to danger, would give that alarm; and so he walked not far from the faint trail at the foot of the mountain where the plains came perilously close. Gingerly stepping through a desolate patch of prickly pear, he knelt and crawled beneath the low branches of a single mesquite bush standing nakedly among the cactus. In this exposed area, with no surrounding cover and where no man would seek to hide, Geronimo curled his body around the bush's small trunk. Laying his rifle under his hand, he slept before first light touched the east.

His years of age were now well into the fifties, and the restless dreams that forever haunted his sleep were becoming more real, like visits into another time.

A thousand times he had dreamed it. He was in a cart, standing, with bright ornaments around him. Horses pulled the cart through a great city. Men alongside the road raised instruments of metal to their mouths and blew through them, making a loud noise.

He left the light and was enclosed by moving, shapeless muscle that gave him feelings of comfort and security. He did not want to leave the comfort for he considered it Life; to leave would be to die; but instead he was born. He recognized the eyes looking at him. He knew the soul in the eyes from another place. Now as she crooned to him and talked in the strange language he came to know her, this time as mother. So it was with the man who he came to know as father.

He swung in the *tshoch*, the sling, strung between cottonwood branches. The wind pushed him and pulled, playing. The sun was warm with life.

By the time he learned the language and could talk he had mostly forgotten the other Time; only briefly and in snatches did he speak of it. His father and mother laughed and called his talk child's fancy. And so he had put it aside.

When he became five, he knew where he was on earth: in the beautiful mountains near the headwaters of the Gila. His mother and father had taken him to the exact spot of his birth and turned him, lying on the ground, in the four directions; center of the Wheel that was everywhere and had no circumference.

He stood before his father, still almost a baby with the play beads in his hand. His father said, "See, these are your hands. Look at them. They are your friends. You must depend on them. Your arms, your legs; they are your friends. Breathe deep and know this is your friend. There will be a time when these will be your only friends; these and your eyes. Your life is to be running . . . running, and fighting the Enemy, so that your soul will not be a slave to them." His father had pointed at a far-distant mountain. "Run to it. Run back. Run. So that you will learn not to tire, nor fall. To tire or fall when the Enemy is chasing you is death."

He had run. When he first felt the wind, exuberance rose in him and he moved in its life-wildness. In the beginning the wildness was undisciplined, but his sense sharpened with running. He began to feel throbbing moods, changing from softness of play, sometimes to fretfulness, depression, anxiety, alarm, or wild anger. He gave himself to it and became a part of all life feelings that talked on the wind. He did not question it, as a baby does not question sight, but naturally accepts what is brought to the senses.

And as with the baby seeing, at first the senses were blurred, but he soon discovered the objects of his feelings. The stunted cedar living precariously from the rocks, the cactus on the desert; these were sharp and alert in their feelings for survival. He felt them and used the rhythms of their perceptions. Their rhythms of alarm were quick and harsh.

When he wanted rest, he sought the mesquite growing close to the stream, secure in its life, cared for by water and silt. It was lazy, languid in its rhythms. He would lie beneath it relaxing, yawning and luxuriating in the low beats of feeling that surrounded him.

In the soft mountain twilight of evening his parents, sitting before their tipi, watched him beneath the mesquite. Before he was six, they named him Gokhlayeh: One-Who-Yawns.

By the time he was seven, he was the most adept at Apache child games. The children stood in long rows, facing one another and throwing rocks. They learned quickness and agility in dodging missiles of the Enemy. Shooting simple wooden arrows at one another, they dodged, sometimes grabbing the arrow in the air with their hands. Always they ran.

He helped his father and mother in the valley fields below the mountains, planting corn, beans, squash, and pumpkins. Many times they could not harvest what they had planted. The Enemy came and they were fighting, running . . . always running, to hide among the mountains. Men and women, placed high on the mountain peaks, watched for the Enemy: the Mexicans. The Mexicans meant death. His father sat beside him in the evenings and talked: "Be watchful for the Enemy. If we do not fight them, they will make us slaves to work below the ground digging their metal. If we do not fight them, they will make us beasts without spirit life—beasts that come to think only of food to feed the earth body; shelter for the earth body; medicine for the earth body. Food for the spirit body will be forgotten. The spirit body will die; it must have freedom to live. To War is to live."

Gokhlayeh listened solemnly, nodding his child head, and knew this was so. His round, chubby child face grew solemn as he thought on these things. His father explained, "Maco was my father, your grandfather. He was a great warrior and Chief of the Nedni Apaches. I married your mother, who is Bedonkohe Apache, and so I gave up my right to chieftainship of the Nednis to follow her here. We are Bedonkohe Apache now, but not chiefs. The man must follow, to be with the woman. The man is the planter, like seed in Mother Earth, but he sometimes dies quickly in War. It is the woman who is There, and brings life to the Apache. This is important, for the Apache are not many." His father spread forth his hands. "See, we are like the fingers, separate: the Bedonkohe, the Nedni, the Chihenne, the Chiahen, and many more. We are also Chiricahua Apache. There are Tonto, Jicarilla, Mescalero, Mimbres, and others, but we are all Apache. We must live, so, in small bands. If one band is destroyed by the Enemy, all others may live. But"—and he closed his hand into a fist—"we come together to make War." And so Gokhlayeh came to know who he was, a part of the people. He was to be a part of the War. A great yearning came upon him for the day he would go south with the warriors to beat back the Enemy.

Riding recklessly, he hunted buffalo with the lance; and with the ponies he and other youths drove turkeys from mountain ravines onto the plains. Chasing the turkeys until they tired, the boys swooped among them, snatching them from the ground. He became a magnificent horseman, using the quick ponies to chase even rabbits, killing them by throwing a club from the back of the ponies in full flight.

Before he was twelve, he was assigned to stalk the deer. Moving a small bush before him, he crawled, pausing for long intervals as he watched the deer for signs of alarm. Lying flat, waiting to crawl again across miles of prairie. He learned the excruciating patience necessary to kill the deer; or the Enemy.

Entering his teen years, he was allowed to track the bear. Rounding a point of rock high in the mountains, he came face to face with his first grizzly. The bear rose towering above him. In that infinitesimal moment of the bear's indecision that only the eagle recognizes in the snake, Gokhlayeh shot forward between the massive arms and plunged his lance into the bear's heart. He dodged the crushing sweeps of paws, running, inches from death, until the grizzly fell.

Gokhlayeh came to know that he was born with an instinct that few could ever learn—to sense that flash of indecision in the bear, or the Enemy, and to instantaneously strike boldly with killing ferocity.

Gokhlayeh's father died of a sickness. They dressed him in his most colorful clothing and streaked yellow beneath his eyes so that he would not lose sight of the sun on his journey. Chanting his deeds as a warrior, the band had led him on his best horse far up a canyon. There they placed him in a cave with his bow and arrows, his lance and war knife. They slew the horse and laid it beside him and closed the cave. He would lie, waiting for the journey, while the pines sang low around him.

Gokhlayeh was summoned before the council and given his duties and the Law. A person who will not support aged forebears, or who neglects the sick or abuses them, or is guilty of cowardice or laziness or infidelity is banished from the band; messengers are sent to all bands of the Apaches so that none will receive him. Gokhlayeh was not yet a warrior, and so could not marry, nor receive the full charge of responsibility from the council.

After his father died, they burned the tipi home in which they had lived and gave away all his father's possessions; for no Apache could benefit from the death of a family member lest desiring that death for material riches might enter and weaken his spirit body.

He was a dutiful son and supported his widowed mother. He helped his mother build a tipi and furnished it with skins and fur of mountain lion, bear, and deer.

He fretted to go on the trail of War. Already he had seen the Enemy many times and the bodies of men, women, and children in a band who had been killed by the Enemy.

At sixteen years of age Gokhlayeh was five feet nine inches tall, tough, wiry, thick of shoulder and arm. He could run seventy miles in a day and hold water in his mouth for half a day, running, before swallowing.

The Apache spiritual will to discipline and overcome the physical needs and wants was strong in Gokhlayeh. With lips cracking, tongue swelling from thirst, to pass the water hole without giving thought to drink if drinking brought danger; to lie in the blazing oven heat of the desert and not seek the shade of tree or bush if doing so endangered the raid, and not feel the heat; to run past the point of endurance when men succumb to the belief that the aching legs will carry them no farther, and to know that the legs will: This was the "inhuman" will of the Apache, strong in Gokhlayeh.

He possessed something more than this will. His mind was a naked nerve, sensing the emotions around him. As a people of solitude may sense the feelings of others without their speaking, so Gokhlayeh sensed his world, equaling the deer who snatches its head from the grass at no sound or smell or sight, but at the feeling that comes, clean and sharp as a thunderclap.

At seventeen, he was ready for War.

Mexican troops, probing north, forced the Bedonkohe band to flee their rancheria, leaving behind most of their provisions for the winter. Mangas Coloradas, known among all Apaches and Mexicans for his skills and wisdom in the ways of War, was Chief of the Bedonkohe band. He commanded power and respect from many bands. His three daughters had married chiefs; one was the wife of Cochise, Chief of the Chokonens.

But he called on none of these for help. Instead, he led his people south, into the San Antunez mountain range, deep into the bosom of the Enemy and close to the Mexican settlements of Sonora. His objective was food.

They traveled by night so that no scout should see them, and walked through the mountains in long horizontal lines, like infantry advancing, so that they left no single trail to be followed. No woman snagged clothing on a bush; no child dropped an object to be found. There was no talk, no laughter. Farther and farther south they walked, where the Enemy was strongest and therefore confident; off guard and lazy.

In a small deep canyon they set their rancheria of tipis and ate sparsely of piñon nuts.

On the trail of raid and War the council fire is lean, tiny—giving its light of sanctity to the council, but hiding from the Enemy's eyes. Flickering, the fire played light and shadows over the face of Mangas. He stood, six feet four inches above the fire, and placed the buckskin war band about his huge head.

Sitting cross-legged before him, the warriors watched, and each, as he was selected by Mangas's pointing finger, stood and placed the war band about his head. Twenty warriors were standing when Mangas saw the squat figure hovering hungrily on the fringe of firelight.

"And you, Gokhlayeh, may go," Mangas said. No warrior exercised his right to object, and so Gokhlayeh was apprenticed to the trail of War.

They left in the night, running south in single file with Mangas leading. As an apprentice, Gokhlayeh ran behind. He was not allowed to speak unless spoken to, nor to assume any position to which he had not been ordered. Carrying bows and arrows, lances and war knives, they wore only breechclouts and moccasins.

Two days and nights they ran. Stopping at intervals to sleep in brief naps, they pulled the breechclouts from their waists, using them as covering to break the chill of the mountains.

The sun was lowering, red over the Sonoran plains, when they came down out of the mountains on their second day. Distant on the plain, white adobe buildings marked the village of Crassaves. Evening cook fires sent smoke rising above the houses.

Mangas halted his warriors on the edge of the plain as a cathedral bell tolled, murmuring small and monotonous in the emptiness. The sun's red ball touched the far horizon, striking the faces of the Apaches kneeling in the brush. They watched a herd of cattle and horses being driven from grazing land to the south, toward the night corrals of Crassaves. The cattle were bawling, anticipating water.

Carefully Mangas counted the herdsmen. There were three. Sombreroed, they slouched in their saddles, moving languidly behind the herd. Mangas verified his observation by raising three fingers in question, and warriors answered him, raising their fingers in the air. They had all seen only three.

Now he made a final inspection of the horizon. Nothing moved. The village showed no saddled horses or soldiers. Holding up an open palm to his warriors to signal that all was clear, he received their open palms in answer. None saw danger. Mangas was about to motion the line forward toward the cattle when a low whistle came from the line's end. It was Gokhlayeh and he had raised a fist. Quickly Mangas and the warriors sank down behind the brush. At first he saw nothing, but no Apache advances in movement when a warning has been given. Then, far on the horizon, his eye caught a red flash. Sun had touched metal.

Slowly they came. Mounted soldiers riding two abreast. They were riding out of the sun, a large body, moving toward the village. Reaching the village, they did not stop but came on, directly toward Mangas's band. He motioned his warriors back to the mountainside and waited.

On they came, directly toward the mountain. Now Mangas could see the beards on their faces. Before them a single soldier rode carrying a bright-colored flag, holding it aloft. Sabers flashed in the sun and iron-tipped lances, socketed in the stirrup of each soldier, pointed skyward, making a grim double fence that rode above the horsemen. They halted at the mountain's edge, directly below Mangas and his men. Dismounting, they set camp fires. This was to be their night camp.

Silently Mangas motioned his men back, farther up the mountain, and signaling toward the ground, indicated that here they would stay. Mangas was bitterly disappointed. He could afford no battle with the soldiers. His band desperately needed food. But how long would the soldiers stay? He knew they might remain for days. His people could not afford a long time; they must have food. He decided to wait out the night.

Twilight deepened. Night dropped black before the moon's rising. Torches of fire came from Crassaves, bobbing across the prairie toward the soldiers. The sounds of Spanish guitars floated soft and melancholy to the silent, watching Apaches. Women were laughing. It was they who had brought the torches from the village.

From his place alone on the mountain Gokhlayeh watched the distant fire flickers and listened to the sounds. He had seen the Enemy many times, but only while running from them. He moved down the mountain, unseen by Mangas or the warriors. At the mountain base he could see the fires plainly, a long necklace of light wavering.

The nearest campfire was a hundred yards from him on the prairie, and he crouched, stalking as he had stalked the deer, moving toward it. As he came closer he dropped to his belly and pulled himself, snakelike, along the sand floor, keeping close to bush and mesquite.

Within ten yards of the campfire he lay watching. The guitars were strumming fast, a heavy and sensuous beat, and women in colorful skirts were dancing around the fire. Gokhlayeh had not seen this kind of dancing. The women stomped their feet, lifting curving hands that stroked their breasts, moving their hands upward over their heads. The women flicked their skirts, tantalizing the soldiers with bare thighs and buttocks.

A bottle thrown from the fire landed close to Gokhlayeh's face. It lay, glittering, tossing back the light of the fire. A soldier and a woman broke from the circle, coming almost directly toward him where he lay in the sand. The soldier half-pulled, half-dragged the woman, her hair falling around her face. She was protesting shrilly, and the soldier was laughing. Gokhlayeh pushed backward quickly, barely escaping their path, and they passed within a yard of his head.

With his cheek pressed close to the ground, Gokhlayeh had been listening to the drunken talk of the campfire. Spanish was spoken fluently by his people, and he understood much of what was said. Now he was caught between the campfire and the struggling couple, who had stopped near him and were wrestling, the soldier tearing at the clothes of the woman. A few yards from him they fell to the ground, the soldier struggling to a position on top of the woman. The rising, boisterous shouts and drumming music around the campfire drowned out the woman's screams of protest. Now Gokhlayeh was forced to turn his attention from the campfire to the couple on the ground. From his sheath he slid the war knife and placed it between his teeth.

The soldier had pushed his pants down and was between the legs of the woman. Gokhlayeh saw the white of his buttocks rise and fall and heard the woman scream; but behind him there was no break in the campfire's carousing sound. The soldier's face was pressed down on the woman's, turned away from Gokhlayeh; but the woman's face, beneath the soldier's, was turned directly toward him. He could see her eyes, looking at him, but she did not see. Her feet rose from the ground, jerking in the air, kicking, dancing grotesquely; and her bare legs slowly entwined around the soldier's back. Her feet moved together, locking and holding the soldier. Her eyes were glazed, far off in the feeling. He waited for the moment to move.

Furiously the soldier was pumping, but the woman could not turn her face from Gokhlayeh. Her mouth was open, gasping and exploding breath in tiny screams and yelps. Her hair had fallen over her face and her eyes. Gokhlayeh began to move, when suddenly the soldier stopped. He rolled from the woman and stood, pulling at his pants and fastening them. The woman lay looking up at the soldier. Her mouth was open and her legs still twitched spasmodically. She said something. The soldier laughed and kicked her naked stomach. Turning, he staggered drunkenly back to the campfire.

Gokhlayeh held his position, frozen, prone on the ground, but now his toes were dug deep into the sand, ready for quick movement. The woman sat up. With incongruous modesty she combed and patted her long black curls into place while her large rounded breasts danced nakedly above the torn blouse. Her dress was above her hips. She raised her head from the combing, and Gokhlayeh, watching with a cat intensity, saw her eyes travel downward. First, she ran her hands over her large breasts, smoothing at the bruises left by the soldier, fingering the stiff, protruding nipples. Her eyes moved downward to her dress. Gokhlayeh hoped they would stop there, that she would rise like the soldier and go back to the campfire. But the eyes hesitated on her legs, remembering something she had seen . . . and yet, not seen, when the soldier was upon her. The eyes lingered on her feet, then began languidly traveling across the short space toward Gokhlayeh.

His muscles coiled, and by the time the woman's gaze had lifted, he was already moving. The force of legs trained to run seventy miles in a day, to leap an arroyo, to run backward for thirty miles shot him forward like a catapult—in the same, almost prone position, without his knees touching the ground—across the short space to the woman.

She never understood. Looking up, she saw magically and terribly the hard face striped with paint and the glittering eyes framed by black bush hair. Her mouth fell open before the hand seized her throat, whipping her head backward and breaking her neck. Only her legs twitched. Gokhlayeh lay beside the woman for a moment, watching the campfire. The music and shouts were still loud and uninterrupted.

He reached across the woman; grabbing her arm, he rolled her onto his back like a sheepskin over the the back of a wolf. Slowly, painfully, he pulled himself across the desert, tuning his ears to the campfire sounds, for he could not watch the soldiers now.

For an hour he moved thus, the woman grotesquely dangling her head beside his, with legs astraddle his hips, flopping and dragging on the desert floor. In the shadow of the mountain, he rose and, lifting the woman to his shoulders, trotted into the trees.

Mangas was dozing and did not hear Gokhlayeh approach. He sat up quickly at the touch and saw the young apprentice still carrying his burden slung over a shoulder. Gokhlayeh flung the woman on the ground.

"The soldiers will leave in the morning," Gokhlayeh said softly. "They will go north for four days. There are no soldiers in the village and few horses."

Mangas looked at the dead woman sprawled in the brush. "How do you know?" he asked.

"I have been to their fires," Gokhlayeh said flatly, without boast. "This"—he pointed to the woman—"is a loose woman of the soldiers. She saw me, but she will not be missed." Turning silently, he faded away into the shadow of the trees.

Watching his retreating form, Mangas felt a great conflict of emotion. The information was very valuable to know; not only that the soldiers were leaving, but their length of travel, the village's resources of horsemen and soldiers. But he felt an outrage at an apprentice warrior's daring an exploit that not even a seasoned warrior would attempt without proper consultation. Slowly a suspicion of knowledge invaded his thoughts.

There was no arrogance in Gokhlayeh's manner, no boastfulness, yet he assumed authority as though it was due him. His sighting of the troops when he, Mangas, and warriors seasoned by a hundred raids had not seen—Mangas thought on this. He tried to reject the suspicion, but it remained; only a Shaman of War returned from the past would act so surely. There had been none in his lifetime, nor his father's, but there had been stories told of Shamans born to lead and born to War. The growing certainty of this in the mind of the powerful and influential Mangas was to have a great effect on the destiny of Gokhlayeh.

At dawn the soldiers broke camp, mounting and trailing north. The camp women shouted after them, waving. And as the soldiers grew small and dim to the north the women straggled back to Crassaves. Before the night was over, they would know how close they had lain under the eyes of Apaches.

The sun rose and herdsmen brought cattle and horses from the village, driving them toward the mountain. Reaching its base, they turned the herd south and settled them grazing galleta grass that grew along a sluggish stream.

Still, Mangas did not move his warriors. Patient, perching like eagles over prey, they waited. The soldiers must travel farther north before they moved. The plains blew white-hot under a sun tilting past noon. Nothing moved except the cattle and horses grazing in the distance, and it was not until the sun reddened, lowering to the horizon, that Mangas gathered his men. They moved, crawling onto the prairie. Scattering in a long line, each warrior crouched beside a bush, directly in the path the herd would take on its course toward the village.

A dog barked far off in Crassaves, and the cathedral bell began tolling the sunset. The herd moved. Coming toward the familiar night corrals of the village, the herd needed no point riders, and the vaqueros rode drag, behind them. These were Spanish cattle, long-horned and of a suspicious nature, but now, bellies full on grass and a long day of sapping sun behind them, they plodded, senses dulled and secure.

Every warrior squatted like stone beside his bush. The cattle came on directly toward them, and now were all around the Apaches, passing among them. A cough, a scrape of the foot or movement of the head would have sent the cattle running.

Gokhlayeh was at the end of the line near the edge of the herd. He stared stonily at the cattle's legs brushing past him. A longhorn ripped through the sage covering Gokhlayeh as a steer, fighting flies, shook his head through the covering. The sharp horn tip whipped inches from his throat, slicing a narrow gash on his shoulder, but he did not move. Stifling, the dust rose around the crouching warriors, and through the dust cloud Gokhlayeh saw the end of the herd.

"Vamos!" The shout of the irritated vaquero startled Gokhlayeh; the man was almost upon him, hidden in the dust and cattle. He had a bearded face and wide sombrero. He rode lazily, a rifle across the saddle. His horse came on, a shaggy pony, plodding as listlessly as the cattle. Now the pony was passing close beside Gokhlayeh.

With his knife held flat between his teeth, he slipped easily beside the pony, almost under it. Leaping, he slid behind the rider, and before he had settled or the pony had crowhopped in astonishment, the long knife whipped viciously across the throat of the vaquero with a swishing whisper through the flesh.

Reining the pony only slightly, Gokhlayeh pushed the rider to the ground, snatching the sombrero and placing it on his own head. The entire act was fluid, swift, silent. Scarcely a ripple was made in the easy motion of herd and pony, but every warrior watching saw Gokhlayeh's actions. The warriors rose and pulled the two remaining riders from their horses.

Looping rawhide jaw bridles on the herd horses, all the warriors mounted and slowly turned the herd away from the village toward the mountain. They did not run, and within an hour Crassaves had dropped peacefully from sight behind them.

In the morning the villagers would find the bodies of the vaqueros. They would send riders north after the soldiers; others would follow the tracks of the herd until the tracks turned into the mountains. There they would turn back. Only an army followed Apaches into mountains.

8

Low throbbing beats of *esadadnes,* the hoop drums, greeted the raiders as they drove the cattle into the shadowed canyon of the rancheria. Dancing began, celebrating the gift of food and offering thankfulness to Usen.

Gokhlayeh and the warrior Kahtala were sent back on the trail. If they came, the soldiers must be watched. From a solitary perch high on a protruding butte, Gokhlayeh could hear the tone chants of the celebration and the dancing. They spoke his name and told how he'd seen the soldiers and kept the raiders from death. But he did not hear the words. He felt uneasy in the moonlight, looking far along the broken peaks of mountains. He felt the soldiers were coming. He knew this, but he could not yet see or hear them.

All night the dancing continued, and in the morning the people began slaughtering the cattle, drying meat to be placed in hides for easy carrying. Gokhlayeh was not sent for and so he stayed on the butte. Careful not to silhouette himself against the sky, he lay full length atop a boulder, facing north. He watched the sun chase away fog from hiding places below the peaks.

The sun rose higher, heating the rock butte where he lay, but he did not move. He could hear the bawling of the cattle and, faintly, murmurs of talk. Noon passed and the sun tilted west. Lazily buzzards assembled, cycling higher and higher above the rancheria, anticipating remains from the cattle slaughter. The buzzards were dangerous. They marked the place of the rancheria for faraway eyes.

West the sun moved to meet the earth rim, and the first touch of cool wind diminished the heat waves. Far away on the mountains a cloud of specks rose in the air. They did not circle but straightaway flew westward toward the plains. Crows. Gokhlayeh placed a stone before him and marked the length of its shadow on the boulder. Now he watched intently. The stone's shadow lengthened.

Suddenly, closer than the crows, a single speck shot skyward, up, up, and turned, arrowlike in flight, toward the west. A badly frightened hawk. Gokhlayeh marked the shadow's length at the sighting of the hawk and so knew the time progress of the troops.

Carefully he leapfrogged his sight, first to a position directly before him that represented the distance from the crows to the hawk, then farther away to a like position, until he reached the point from which the hawk had flown. He calculated the distance, the time. The soldiers, easily following the beaten trail of cattle, would be at the rancheria before midnight.

Looking across the wooded ravine, he searched the high naked rock where he knew Kahtala lay. There was no sign of him. He had not seen the soldiers coming. Rising to silhouette himself against the sun, Gokhlayeh sent a piercing hawk whistle echoing among the rocks. Kahtala's head slowly rose above his perch, watching him.

Raising his left hand high above his head, Gokhlayeh clenched his fist and crooked his arm toward the rancheria: The Enemy is coming. With an exaggerated movement he swept the open palm of his right hand across his eyes: They will arrive after dark. Lifting his open hand straight above him toward the sky, he slowly changed its position, slanting the hand toward the east: They will arrive here on the east side of midnight . . . before midnight.

Kahtala stood and swept his arms wide. He had understood. It was for Kahtala to report this to Mangas. Gokhlayeh stretched his powerful body, glad of the movement, and before he lay again on the rock took a disciplined mouth of water from the skin bag. He knew when Kahtala reached the camp, for a sudden silence stopped the voice murmurs; then the voices became louder and there were sounds of great activity.

He heard Kahtala coming up the butte behind him and sat upright. Kahtala's head appeared over the butte's edge, and he pulled himself, grunting, beside Gokhlayeh. He was not young. Beneath the buckskin war band his face was lined. Downward from his naked chest a purple scar ran, smooth, marking the symmetrical sweep of a Mexican soldier's saber in a long-ago contest for life. The Mexican had lost. Kahtala sat down. "How did you tell?"

"Crows. Not circling. The same as, later, the hawk," Gokhlayeh answered.

Kahtala grunted approvingly. "Our people will scatter so there will be no trail. They will meet across the mountains, east, at the Chihuahua plains."

"And then?" Gokhlayeh asked.

"Mangas says they will turn north. We . . ." Kahtala paused. "We will follow, after we have helped the soldiers find what they want."

Pulling two pieces of fire-blackened beef from a pouch, he handed one to Gokhlayeh. They sat, chewing meditatively on the tough meat. Gokhlayeh was hungry, and the meat juices were good in the dryness of his mouth. They ate silently. The earth rim touched the sun. Where there had been noises from the rancheria, now there were no voices. Kahtala rose. "Come," he said and slid down the rocks.

Gokhlayeh followed him into the canyon. Where the rancheria had been, now there was nothing. Even the campfires had been buried and covered in brush.

Cattle grazed along the banks of the small stream. Two horses were tied to a piñon.

"We must ride the horses," Kahtala said, "and take the cattle back along the trail we came, to meet the soldiers." Dusk had settled by the time they had rounded up the cattle, heading them through the narrow arroyo along the back trail. Stars came well before the old moon.

The band had slaughtered half the captured herd, and nearly a hundred head of cattle began lowing protests, echoing far through the mountains. Kahtala pushed his horse close to Gokhlayeh's. "We must make them go faster. The soldiers will hear them soon."

But the trail led upward along a ridge, and no amount of charging the ponies at their rear took the leaders past a plodding gait. For an hour they herded the cattle along the ridge, over a small rising back of mountain, and downward into a canyon, keeping them on the well-marked back trail. In the canyon there was grass and the cattle began grazing.

"We must set camp here," Kahtala said. "Soldiers are coming." Gokhlayeh and Kahtala gathered wood and made separate piles along the canyon floor. While Kahtala set fire to the piles of wood, Gokhlayeh cut tipi poles, scattering them near the fires. The fires shot high in the air, etching shadows on the canyon walls. They stood for a moment, watching and listening.

"The scouts," Gokhlayeh said, "will come before the soldiers. We will not hear them."

"Yes," Kahtala said. "Come." They swung on the ponies, riding them up and down the canyon among the cattle, making many tracks, and then turned westward, leaving the canyon. Behind them the glow of campfires reflected in the sky.

For two hours they rode west until, sighting the Sonora plains, they turned south. As day broke they rode the ponies onto rocky ground and, pulling their bridles from them, left the ponies to wander. On foot they ran east across the mountains toward Chihuahua.

Before midnight scouts reported to the Mexican *comandante*. They had discovered the Apaches' rancheria. He approached his troops cautiously, keeping them clear of the camp until his scouts had examined the flight tracks of the Apaches.

Only two ponies had left the camp, running west, their tracks easily found on soft ground. No more. The *comandante* shook his head in frustration, but it was an old and familiar frustration. Once in the mountains, the Apaches were known to fly from their rancherias like birds, leaving no trail to follow.

The *comandante* never questioned what he had found. The rancheria was the object he had set his mind on discovering, and having found it, he searched no further. This the Apaches knew of men and their body minds; and so they gave him the illusion of what he sought. While the Apache was skilled in many things—survival, the ways of the plains and mountains, war and the raid—he was first a master of illusion.

For two days Kahtala and Gokhlayeh ran across the mountains. Sighting the Chihuahua plains, they turned north and struck the trail of their people. Another day of running brought them into camp. Mangas was leading them home.

Crossing the desert north of the Sierra Madre at night, the band saw a campfire to the east of their path. Scouts reported it to be the camp of a mule train, heading south. At the sight of the Apaches coming close, the drovers fled, leaving their mules. Thirty mules carrying loaf sugar and bacon.

The band threw away the bacon. No Apache eats peccary or fish, for both are known to eat reptiles. What loaf sugar they could not use they would trade to the Navajos for blankets. Adding the thirty mules to their already large remuda of horses, they continued north into the Dragoons. They were rich now;

loaf sugar for use and trading, beef and mules for winter meat; horses. Deep in the Dragoons they encamped their rancheria.

On this first night of encampment and celebration Gokhlayeh was called before the council. Mangas Coloradas sat in the center of the warriors. He looked across the council fire at the youth standing impassively before him.

Wearing breechclout and moccasins, the young man's body rippled with power of leg and shoulder. His square-jawed face was framed by black bush hair; his lips were so thin they appeared to be a slashing scar. The eyes held Mangas; black, burning, perhaps old eyes, Mangas thought, perhaps eyes that saw something in the past, or future. Haunted. Mangas shook his head, clearing his thoughts, but the suggestion would not go away, and he remembered Gokhlayeh's prowess on the raid. Was he a War Shaman—born, not learned? Born again from the Great Wheel?

First, the responsibilities of a warrior were explained to Gokhlayeh: to protect the safety of his people; to see that all his people were fed and the sick and aged cared for; to show courage, honor, and dedication in the exercise of these duties even in the face of death by the Enemy. The responsibilities were many and varied, but all were rooted in the strength and practice of the simple spiritual values. The rights were few and followed on the performance of these responsibilities.

Apache practice allowed for no politician to alter this equation by relieving the responsibilities of those who would give him power. To do so would bring chaos and death to the society. And so the logic and practice was firm. Ignore responsibility, lose rights. The resulting judgment, harsh or benevolent, followed the Law, and was therefore Justice. The Apache society remained strong.

Gokhlayeh was awarded six horses. He was also rewarded the right to marry. He was a Warrior.

Walking away from the counsel with the beat of *esadadnes* and chants throbbing behind him, he followed the water spring, sparkling in the moonlight. Sounds of the rancheria faded. Ahead through the shadows of the trees he saw her. She sat on a rock, trailing her feet in the water. Alope.

She did not look up as he walked to her, but watched moon reflections in the spring. Long black hair fell over the white deerskin dress, her best. She was slender, even dainty—tiny-breasted and slim-hipped. Some women called her frail, but she was a hard worker and a dutiful daughter to her widowed father. Her love of creating beautiful things showed in the decoration of her slippered moccasins and dress. Gokhlayeh sat beside her on the rock.

They sat for a while without speaking. They had loved each other for a long time, and speaking was often an intrusion on their thoughts and feelings. How many times had they slipped away to watch the sunrises and the sunsets—the birthing and dying of light —experiencing together these two great events of all Life? There was no need for each to tell the other "I love you." Words too often lie. And so the Apache brought action to expression. How can action lie? Loyalty, consideration, faithfulness, duty, hate, anger, love—actions are the truth of these feelings and therefore do not lie.

And so Gokhlayeh and Alope enjoyed the richness of knowing. No clutter of misused words or superficial wit or sly mastery of tongue brought doubt to their feelings.

Gokhlayeh spoke first.

"It is done."

"Yes." She did not look up from the water.

"May I ask your father?"

Her tiny hand moved to hold his and she looked at him, the smile flashing shyly. "Yes." She always

101

thrilled him with her touch and her smile, more so because she did not contrive to do this.

Gokhlayeh appeared early in the morning before the tipi of Noposo. He knew there was no question. The father could not deny the daughter who had consented to marriage unless he could find flaw of character in the young man.

Old Noposo sat before his tipi to receive Gokhlayeh. He was torn between pleasure and reluctance. He was pleased that this new warrior, already talked of by the people for his prowess, would marry his daughter. After all, Gokhlayeh was really the son of a chief. At the same time, he was reluctant to give up this dutiful daughter, who had added beauty and comfort to his life.

Noposo sighed and looked resignedly at the young man standing stoically before him. "Yes?"

"I have asked Alope," Gokhlayeh said politely. "She has agreed. We want to be together. Our lives to go the same way."

No arrogant speeches of warrior power or boasting of his hunts. Noposo was pleased with the young man's simple modesty. Still, he wanted to test the depth of feeling for his daughter. Was he sincere? Did he place high value on his feeling? Noposo knew the council had awarded Gokhlayeh six horses, and so deliberately he raised his hand, spreading the fingers wide: five. "Horses," he said quietly, "not mules." It was a staggering recompense for losing his daughter.

Gokhlayeh neither hesitated nor argued. "I have six horses. You may choose your five from them." Gokhlayeh's feeling was full and true.

This was their marriage. No other ceremony was needed. Gokhlayeh built a tipi near his mother's. Alope brought her robes and deerskins and added paintings to the walls of the tipi, decorations to moccasins and clothing.

But first, they went away. Taking buffalo robes,

they climbed the canyon wall. On a mesa high above the rancheria they spread the robes beneath piñon trees. Here, away from the noise of people, in the sweet smell of piñons, they consecrated their beginning of one life from the wedding of two, suspended in a spiritual ecstasy which overpowered their physical union. From the start, they were one.

Moonlight silvered the canyon below them, sprinkling sparkles on mountain rocks far away. Lying on the buffalo robes in the shadow of the trees, Alope moved her small hand to touch Gokhlayeh's.

"Perhaps," she whispered, "when you find something, you are afraid you will lose it. I am afraid, Gokhlayeh. Will our time be short?"

Gokhlayeh tightened his hand around hers. "Once," he said slowly, "my father told me to run to a mountain. I ran for three days across the desert. My mouth was dry and cracking and my tongue swelled from thirst. I came upon a fresh spring of water falling over rocks in the mountain. I wanted to rush into the spring and gulp the water so that my mouth would quickly lose its thirst. But I did not. I lay down beside it. I touched my lips to the water and felt its coolness. I took a little sip of water and felt it roll in my mouth and my mind, and my spirit felt the sweetness. I did not measure the time. How long did I lie there? I do not know; maybe a season, maybe a moment; maybe ten seasons. But I did not measure it. It will be with my spirit always. And," Gokhlayeh said, "I thought, a man might be born beside this spring and live his life here beside this spring and his spirit never know what mine now knows. Perhaps he would never let his spirit feel this, though he lived beside the spring a hundred years."

Alope slipped her arm around him. "May we do this then, Gokhlayeh? And there will be no time?"

"There will be no time," Gokhlayeh answered. Alope's instinct was right. The time would not be long as measured by men. But these were to be the richest years of Gokhlayeh's life and Alope's and of the short time that was left to Alope.

A son was born the first year, and within four years, two daughters. But the years were not tranquil. Mexican soldiers were coming farther north. Four times in a year the band was surprised by them and forced to flee, losing warriors, women, and children. On every occasion Gokhlayeh distinguished himself, fighting off the soldiers while women and children escaped. He killed more of the Enemy.

It was during this time that the Apaches first saw Anglo white men. They were driving sticks in the ground and sighting along them. The Bedonkohes went down on the plains to meet the white men and gave them venison and meal. The white men gave the Apaches shirts and money. They shook hands and promised to be brothers; soon the white men left, and the Bedonkohes were sorry to see them go.

There was nothing for which the money could be used, but on a trip north to trade, the Navajos told them the money was very valuable. Gokhlayeh traded his money to a Navajo for a small trinket. It was a tiny doe, head raised in sensitive alertness. Exquisitely worked in silver, it reminded him of Alope.

From her hair Alope cut strands, weaving them into a delicate braid. In the center, she fastened the silver doe and hung it about her neck. She never took it off. At first some of the women laughed at Gokhlayeh's trading money for a trinket; the money could have brought several blankets. Seeing the secret smile of Alope and her love for the silver doe stopped their laughter. It was the last present Alope would receive.

White men came again. This time they rode horses and wore blue coats. They carried guns. When Mangas and his band sought to visit the white men, they shot the guns at them, killing a woman, and the Bedonkohes fled back into the mountains. Mangas determined to lead his people south. This would give time for the white men to go away. Traveling at night, they crossed the desert into the foothills of the Sierra Madre and made peace with a Mexican village the Apaches called Kaskiyeh. The treaty was for ever.

9

The sun was still bright on this late afternoon of spring. The shallow arroyo of the rancheria was filled with sound. Women prepared supper. Children ran, splashing and shouting in the narrow stream. They had been encamped here almost a week near Kaskiyeh while the men traded venison and bear robes for cloth, iron utensils, and knives. Soon the men would return for supper.

Spring rains had set frogs to singing farther along the water spring, and bees hummed around early opening blossoms. Alope paused beside the cook pot. Her eyes followed Tala, her son. He was leaping into the shallow stream. Spraddling his chubby legs, he splashed the water high with his fat bottom. Leta, her four-year-old daughter, was trying to imitate her older brother and was tumbling after him. Water, showering high, silvered over them. Alope's mother-in-law, standing beside her, followed Alope's look and smiled.

"They are strong."

"Yes." Alope laughed. "Almost too strong for me." The baby daughter, swung in a *tshoch* between two live oaks, was playing with a bead string hung above her.

It was a good time. Looking at her children, Alope felt an exultation. Springtime did not account for all the feeling. She felt whole, satisfied with this union encompassing all her family. Gokhlayeh loved the children as she did, without reservation. When he was away, they watched for his return, shouting with delight as he snatched them all into his arms and tumbled with them on the ground. Even the baby had come to anticipate her father's step, squealing as he tossed her high in the air, catching her in his arms while Tala and Leta tugged at his legs to pull him back to the ground. Life was good.

They were at peace and soon would return home, when the bluecoats had gone. No guards were even necessary for the rancheria. Her father, Noposo, was the only man left behind, and he stayed because he did not want to walk to the village. He sat dozing against a tree. Alope smiled. She would take him food at suppertime. The old man still depended upon her.

She bent to her cook pot. Something was wrong. Quickly she looked toward the children; they were still laughing, splashing water. Her mother-in-law had walked to the *tshoch* and was crooning low to the baby. She looked down the arroyo: The women were cooking, calling out to each other, laughing. Children ran, playing games. The feeling would not go away. Anxious, she felt a knot rise in her throat. The frogs had stopped singing.

She took a hesitant step toward Tala and Leta, playing in the stream. Stopping, she looked around her again. She saw them. They stood in a long line on top of the arroyo. Soldiers. In their hands were naked sabers. Some carried long lances tipped with sharp iron. They were bearded, and grinning as if at a joke they were about to play. The line extended past the women farther below her. Slowly sound died in the arroyo. Talking stopped, but some of the children, still unmindful, laughed and shouted in the stillness.

Old Noposo, wakened by the silence, sprang to his feet. A soldier leaped, plunging a lance through the old man's body, bending him, doubling over the lance, to the ground. The action triggered wild screaming that filled the air. A great roar came from the line of soldiers. They lunged downward into the arroyo among the screaming women and children.

Alope ran toward the stream. A blow knocked her to the ground. A soldier fell on her, ripping at her dress. She twisted, kicking, beating at him. She surprised the soldier with her strength; bucking beneath him, she tossed him rolling on the ground, and scrambled on hands and knees, trying to locate her children through the dust cloud. The soldier, cursing, scrambled after her; grabbing her by an ankle, he jerked her naked beneath him and, turning her body up to him, struck brutally at her face. The blow stunned her hysteria. Through a haze she looked wildly for her children. No longer defending herself she sought only to move her head, her eyes, in all directions, looking.

A woman struggled past her, borne to the ground by a shouting soldier who rode her back, weighting her down. A young girl flopped naked near her. Her eyes were wild, unseeing, as her long hair swept the ground where her head jerked convulsively. Her mouth was open and she was screaming. A huge man was on her, between her childlike legs that kicked and beat the air. Women and children were milling in confusion, running one way to escape and darting back, pursued by individual soldiers.

She saw her mother-in-law holding the baby in her arms, running past her. A hand reached into her line of vision, snatching the old woman by her long hair; another hand swung a saber across her back. Grotesquely, unnaturally, the old body folded backward, the trunk almost severed. The baby fell to the ground, crying. Alope tried to reach for the baby, a few feet from her, but she could not free her arm.

Through the dust she saw Tala running toward her from the stream, his chubby legs rising and falling. Behind him Leta ran, tumbling down, getting up. Leta was crying, rubbing her small fists at her eyes. On Tala came. He was not crying. His small round face held a stubborn determination; like Gokhlayeh, Alope thought crazily. Another soldier came into Alope's vision. He was moving toward Tala.

Alope screamed, "Run away, Tala! Run away!" The soldier swept a saber in a practiced, powerful arc. Tala's head tumbled from his body. Blood fountained high in the air from the neck stump. Still, the chubby body took another step, headless, toward the mother. Another; fat arms pumping, swinging; and fell near her.

Alope didn't feel the soldier on her, or within her, nor the teeth biting her breasts and face. Dust enveloped Leta and she could no longer see her, but she could tell her screaming from the others'. Again she tried to reach for the baby, jerking an arm loose, stretching across the short space between them where the baby wailed on the ground. A soldier stooped, picking up the baby. She saw him fondle her, almost tenderly. She watched her baby's wailing soften; saw her small button eyes open in wonderment as she sniffled, holding back baby sobs that shook the small fat body.

The soldier shouted to another, and back and forth between them they shouted a wager. The baby was thrown high in the air. The second soldier raised his lance. Alope could see the long, sharp point, glinting in the sun. Beneath the point, a piece of red cloth fluttered. Her eyes glazed, watching the short, fat arms flailing in the air, higher and higher. Now she was falling, and alarm opened the little black button eyes wide. The baby's mouth was open, the wind and the high toss taking her breath. The lance point shot up, snake quick, meeting the falling body, spearing through the stomach, projecting stark and bloody from the back. Her baby's face was frozen in astonishment and shock.

Alope's mind faded. She did not see the baby thrashing on the lance; nor Leta, disemboweled by a saber, crawling over the ground, intestines snagging at the rocks as she tried to reach Alope. She didn't feel the other soldier on her; not even the knife that slashed away her small breasts, poking them obscenely into her mouth. She had died with the baby, on the lance.

A movement on the prairie caught the eyes of the Bedonkohe Apaches returning from Kaskiyeh. It was a woman waving her arms, and she was dying. Dropping the goods of trade day at the town, the men ran into the silence of the arroyo. Here and there a weak cry came from the wounded and dying, but mostly the bodies, bloodied and tangled, were silent. From surrounding trees emerged the women and children who had escaped. Slowly their crying and moaning rose, filling the twilight of the arroyo with an eerie sound.

Gokhlayeh first saw his mother, broken; old eyes glazed at the sky. Near her, the bloody round flesh ball that was his baby. His eyes followed the dark trail of Leta over the rocks where she reached to touch the foot of her mother. Alope; by her side the headless body of Tala curled, seeking and finding the mother comfort. One hand of Alope's was outstretched, reaching for the baby. She was gone. Alope was gone. They were all gone.

He stumbled among the bodies, going again and again to each, looking down at them, stumbling away in an aimless circle; only to return again. He did not touch them. Now he became obsessed with destroying, wiping away all that he could find. Setting fire to his own tipi and his mother's, he threw everything into the fire; feeding the flames to keep them alive. He found the little bow of Tala's, the buckskinned stuffed doll of Leta's. Throwing these in the crackling flames, he crawled on his hands and knees around the bodies, searching. He found the bead string extending from the baby and lifted it, jerking. It had been clutched, frozen in the tiny fist.

Most of the bodies in the camp had been gathered,

fires had been set. Men and women passing watched Gokhlayeh crawling among his family's bodies. Stopping, he sat down and snatched from his feet the moccasins that Alope had made and threw them in the fire. He ripped away the blouse he was wearing, tearing at the decorations Alope had sewn on the front, and fed the flames. He stood naked except for his breechclout. Looking emptily at the people near him, he turned and walked away. He did not look back at his family, nor make any attempt to bury them.

Walking far down the arroyo, he stood by the stream, looking into the water. The water was empty. Darkness had come, and behind him the fires were dying. The crying and wailing had settled into a monotonous moan that chorded the air with a hopeless dirgelike sound.

Gokhlayeh could not bear the anguish. His physical mind retreated, leaving a vacuum filled by something more overwhelming. His Power spoke to him.* "Gokhlayeh! Gokhlayeh!" His Power called the name four times. "Gokhlayeh! Gokhlayeh!" So clear was the call that he answered verbally, "Yes, I am here." His Power spoke, clean and sharp to his mind. There could be no misunderstanding: "You love deeply, Gokhlayeh. This is good. This is good for your spirit body, Gokhlayeh. Here in this shadow world, peopled by shadow bodies with shadow minds, used by the recurring spirit bodies as they try to strengthen themselves, it is necessary that you love deeply and strengthen. But, Gokhlayeh, legs are made strong by climbing mountains, not by retreating from them and resting in the shade of self-pity. Your spirit body may retreat and grow weaker, or you may climb the mountains of your anguish and your obstacles. Keep the Faith with your spirit body, Gokhlayeh, and no

---

*Apaches knew that a Power spoke to those with special purpose. This was not regarded as a supernatural phenomenon.

weapon shall destroy the shadow body you have chosen. But you will lose much and you will sorrow in many losses before you grow old and shed the body of the shadow world." And so there, in the arroyo filled with the smell of blood and the sound of dying, Gokhlayeh knew with certainty there was a Purpose. He was not yet sure of what that Purpose was, or how it should be brought about; but he knew it existed. He did not know he stood by the water for hours, for it seemed only briefly before Mangas touched his arm, and then gently took him by the shoulders to face him. The great chief had, himself, lost a child.

"Gokhlayeh," he said softly.

"Yes."

Mangas looked into the eyes that met his and the eyes were red, deep within the blackness. "We can do nothing more here, Gokhlayeh. We have no weapons. We must go back north." He looked hard into the eyes. "Do you understand, Gokhlayeh?"

"I understand."

And so the Bedonkohes left in the night, walking north. Behind them, distant, a figure stumbled and weaved uncertainly, leaving a trail of blood from bare feet torn on the rocks and brush of the trail. It was Gokhlayeh.

Some of the warriors killed game, but he would not eat. He slept apart, away from the camp, and walked so far behind that Mangas often sent runners back to confirm that he still followed.

Gokhlayeh had died with his family at the arroyo, and out of the ashes of that death would rise a spirit with flames of violence so terrible that Kaskiyeh would mourn its rising; as, indeed, would all of northern Mexico and the southwest of the United States. The flame would rage against the final darkness of the Apaches and, for their salvation, light a secret passage.

10

Summer was dying. The red fruit of strawberry cactus still dimpled the desert floor, but the deep pink flowers of devil's head had shriveled. Women of the Bedonkohes had long since picked the blossoms of the guajacum, rich with honey, and the yucca and varnished acacia had yielded their seed to be pounded into flour.

It had not been an easy summer. Even for a people whose gene memory of centuries carried the knowledge that War and Death were the life of their Way. The Bedonkohes had lost almost a fourth of their women and children at Kaskiyeh. Many families had been touched in the slaughter. Gokhlayeh alone had lost all.

The Nedni and Chokonen bands had sent food and clothing. Coverings for tipis and weapons had come also from the Mimbres. And as with all things of this world, the wounds were gradually healed; the routine of life was resumed—except for Gokhlayeh's.

He set his tipi apart, high on the canyon's rim above the rancheria. He hunted, but ate little, giving away most of his kills to the old and the sick. Those rising in the early gray of morning saw Gokhlayeh first, kneeling in prayer before his monkish, sparsely furnished tipi. In the evenings of shadow twilight they saw him again, praying.

Mangas often visited him, sitting beside him, cross-legged, before the tipi. And though Gokhlayeh was polite and soft-spoken as he had always been, now he answered only when asked a direct question by Mangas. He was constantly at work before his tipi on pieces of iron, shaping and sharpening the pieces into lances and arrow tips.

Deep in the blackness of many nights the rancheria heard chants, far away and high in the mountain; chants that rose thin, unearthly, and caused the mother to rise and pull coverings tighter over her children and the man to roll a buffalo robe heavier about himself and his mate. The chants were not a harmonizing with the earth, the plants, the wind; nothing of this earth. They were tones that invaded the spirit and sought harmony with the Gans. Sometimes they were deep, savagely growling on the wind; sometimes the chants rose high, screaming, breaking from the screams into a whimpering moan, as a soul, tortured, might cry in hopelessness.

A runner from the Tonto Apaches visited the rancheria with a message: The bluecoat soldiers and white eyes were taking metal from the ground and, seeking to repay the Apaches in a spirit of friendship, had invited them all to a feast. Council fires were lighted and the Bedonkohes gathered to give their opinions of the invitation and to discuss its meaning. Most spoke in favor of going. There would be food and presents. And going would assure the bluecoats that the Apaches were a peaceful people when treated fairly. The bluecoats had not gone away; they were increasing in numbers. It would be good to make treaty with them.

Gokhlayeh had stopped before the council fire, and people were silent. "The ones who go are fools!" he said harshly. "There will be no guns seen at the feast, but the bluecoats do not come with peace; they come with death! I see the Apache lying on the ground and dying. There is no peace!" The Bedonkohes had not gone, and the people of the Tonto, the Coyotero, and the Mescalero who had feasted with the bluecoats had died, writhing in agony on the ground. The food had been laced with strychnine. Had Gokhlayeh seen? Was he a Shaman? The whispered questions ran through the Bedonkohes and added weight to the growing conviction in the thoughts of Mangas.

The closing days of September were hot, the mountain nights cool and crisp. In a canyon removed from the rancheria a great fire provided warmth and threw its flickering light high against the darkness. Three hundred warriors sat on the sloping sides of the canyon, on ledges and rocks. They smoked cigarillos, silent, while the firelight played over impassive faces that masked the excitement inside them. They were watching and listening. This was a meeting of three bands—the Bedonkohes, the Nednis, and the Chokonens—all of whom would be known in history as the Chiricahua Apaches.

They were here in joint council to consider the growing boldness of the Mexican Enemy raiding farther into their mountains and the rapid multiplying of the bluecoats. In the center, seated near the fire, were the three chiefs of these bands. Mangas Coloradas, Chief of the Bedonkohes, in the middle; on his left, a heavily muscled giant rivaling Mangas in stature. He was Whoa, pronounced *Who Huh*, but called Juh. On Mangas's right, the lithe, tall Chief of the Chokonen, with high forehead and calm eyes. He was Cochise. The chiefs listened as warriors advanced, singly, to stand before the fire and the chiefs and give their thoughts on the matter of decision.

Bluecoat soldiers were everywhere about them. Miners were flooding into the hills and canyons, taking metal from the ground. Settlements of white eyes were rising magically in every direction, to help supply Mexican troops moving in raids against the Apache.

For two hours every warrior choosing to do so exercised his right and expressed himself before the council and the chiefs. As the last speaker walked away Mangas stood, looking around him.

"Is there one among you who has not spoken and chooses to do so? Remember, speak now, so that all know, whatever we decide, we are bound to honor that decision."

From out of the canyon's shadow the short powerful form of Gokhlayeh walked into the center of the firelight. He faced Mangas and the chiefs. "There was a time when we were like the panther, moving to strike the Mexican slavemasters and returning to our den. Now we are like the wolf who is wounded without a home. Our Enemies are all about us and every hand is turned against the Apache. Already the bluecoats have slave camps for us and many of our brother Mescaleros, Mimbres, and Tontos are dying there. They made treaty to live, but they die in slavery. Some here tonight have said they want to make treaty. If this is what the chiefs and council decide must be done, then kill me *now*, here, tonight in this canyon, for I will honor no treaty! I will make no peace! Would you save your bodies by killing your Spirit and your Life? Kill my body now, for I will not surrender my Spirit to death. I am a Warrior! I say leave the bluecoats to wonder and doubt what we will do. I say strike the Mexicans at our front while the bluecoats cannot decide our intentions at our back. I say"—and Gokhlayeh raised his fist, shaking it toward the south—"I say the time is for *War*! All summer we have mourned and the time for mourning is over. Drive the Mexicans back as our grandfathers before us have done. I will mourn no man who falls and I want none mourning me. I say kill Kaskiyeh! Kaskiyeh, where lies the blood of our women and babies. *I say War!*" He stood for a moment, glaring across the fire and sweeping his eyes around the canyon's wall of warriors while "*War!*" rumbled, echoing away, repeating and dying in the distance of darkness. A deep stirring of sound was rippling through them. Then he turned and walked away, into the darkness of the canyon.

Slowly the sound of rumbling voices subsided into whispers and then into silence. The crackling and popping of the wood fire echoed hollow and loud. A warrior had defied any decision for treaty or peace, and in the shock of silence that followed, Mangas sat down between Juh and Cochise. He looked in the flames and saw Gokhlayeh speaking, and felt the savage thrill of his voice.

Cochise leaned close to Mangas. "Is this the man who saw the Apaches dying at the feast? The one of whom you spoke, who has lost all his family?"

"Yes," Mangas answered, "this is the man."

Juh smiled broadly, breaking the tension, and firelight played on the teeth of a meaningful smile. "I . . . am ffffor . . . thththth . . . this man." He heaved the words out in a loud voice, overcoming his speech impediment. Juh knew Gokhlayeh well; they were cousins, and Juh was for war, any war, against any enemy.

Cochise spoke low in Mangas's ear. He favored the views of Gokhlayeh. He appreciated the cunning that delayed action against the bluecoats, who were close to them. War against the Mexicans was traditional. Cochise honored tradition.

It was Cochise who nominated Gokhlayeh; Mangas and Juh agreed. Perhaps Cochise felt something in Gokhlayeh that Mangas felt. Perhaps he only appreciated the craft of the man's thinking. Mangas stood to announce the decision. His great voice boomed in the silence: "We say this: Let us all go as one. Let us follow a single Leader to guide us. Let him lead us on the trail of War! Let him lead us to Kaskiyeh! *Gokhlayeh—War Leader of the Chiricahuas!*"

Screams tore the air, chilling with their tone of unreasoning abandonment. Instantly the low throbbing beat of *esadadnes* filled the canyon, beginning the Dance of War; harmonizing the Spirit in the body to meet the contest of Life and Death with a fanatical courage of conviction—to kill or be killed.

Above the great mass of warriors, dancing now and chanting, Gokhlayeh sat cross-legged on a ledge. He watched them with a stoic brooding of face, and in him was no exuberance; only the surety that had begun his Purpose.

It is obvious and known why the Indian family walks single file, the man in front. Ahead is the unknown and therefore a possible danger to the family, and the man must meet it first. But why the Indian warriors run single file is not understood, except by genuine frontiersmen and scouts. Obviously, in meeting danger ahead, the warriors present the target of only a single man; but there is another reason. All trackers know that a man's normal stride is three feet. A warrior running behind the man before him need not place his foot directly in the print of his predecessor. His foot may fall anywhere in that three-foot stride, as may that of the man behind him. A tracker crossing this trail can count with certainty up to three warriors and guess as high as six or seven. Beyond that, he is helpless to estimate with any accuracy the number of warriors who have passed.

And so, two days following the naming of Gokhlayeh as War Leader, they ran, single file, into the twilight of late September. They took no horses. A horse must be cared for on a long journey, watered and fed. An Apache can run a hundred miles on a mouthful of water, a handful of piñon nuts. A horse cannot.

Lean and hard of body, they wore breechclouts, boot moccasins, and war bands holding bushed black hair in place. They were armed with lances, bows and arrows, and war knives slapping sinewed thighs in their sheaths. Twenty paces ahead the short powerful figure of their Leader swung easily in a slow run, and behind him ran the three most feared Apache chiefs in the Southwest: Mangas Coloradas, Juh, and Cochise. The long line of warriors following stretched a quarter mile.

The orders of their Leader were simple: Kill the owner of any eyes that saw them. Even two Apache warriors on the warpath struck terror into the populace of entire settlements. And three hundred! To be seen and reported would send frantic messages of alarm in all directions for two hundred miles.

First to the southeast they ran, with the lights of Tucson twinkling far off to their right. Touching the edge of the Dragoons they waited in her tree fringes for day to pass before running past the lights of Tombstone. Onto the empty prairie, running in the darkness that winked with the fires of mule trains on their way to the mining camps. The drovers of the mule trains were blessed that night, for the Leader swung wide with his warriors, and so their eyes did not see and the drovers lived.

Entering the Sierra Madre, they did not take the familiar paths along her edge of the plains, but used the war trails, more difficult and less traveled, in the interior. Now they traveled by day, resting at night, and on the evening of their fourth day after entering the Madre, Gokhlayeh led them down from the mountains. Far away on the prairie, perhaps a dozen miles, night torches blinked and flickered in the prairie wind. Unerringly Gokhlayeh had brought them to Kaskiyeh.

Some slept beneath the trees. Most of them sat alone, watching the distant lights. Every warrior knew what the morning meant. It was not a raid for food and provisions. This would be a battle called forth by the Apaches. Only the winners would leave the field. The losers would stay.

In the deadness before dawn Gokhlayeh called them about him. They prayed to Usen, not for help, but that each man would not abandon his courage,

119

living or dying. Some knelt in their praying, some stood, looking to the sky and the mountains.

Gokhlayeh explained how they must place themselves. He talked slowly and quietly as if he were explaining the way to hunt turkeys or rabbits. Lifting his arms, he formed a U. The mouth of the U, he explained, would face the gate entrance to Kaskiyeh. Mangas would command one prong of the U; Cochise the other. At the bottom of the U, stretching back toward the mountains, Juh would command. The warrior line making up the U would connect the chiefs.

Cochise stepped forward. "Do you say the Mexican soldiers will come into the U, down the middle between our lines?"

"Yes," Gokhlayeh answered.

"How?"

"I will lead them," Gokhlayeh said quietly. Cochise looked thoughtfully at Mangas and Juh, and then away toward Kaskiyeh. He said nothing more. Gokhlayeh's mystery of how he could lead the soldiers belonged to Gokhlayeh. Let him do it.

While the gray before dawn still ghosted the prairie, distorting shapes of cactus and bush, the Apaches moved into position. Silent, crouching in their running no higher than brush tops, they moved toward Kaskiyeh. Coming close, they began disappearing one by one, taking their places in the lines. Before the sun rose, before the first village cock crowed thin and strangling against the wind, they had disappeared, leaving the prairie as they first saw it, empty and waving in the wind.

Cathedral bells broke the sun's rising over a clear rim, red and cloudless. As the sun lifted itself from the earth dust and changed its redness to a pitiless white, Kaskiyeh awakened to its last day of life.

11

An hour before dawn broke over Kaskiyeh, the town had begun to stir. This was a feast day, a holy day. Cathedral bells broke the prairie's emptiness, clanging hollow with that peculiar futile sound given to all things of disturbance in that vastness where no obstacle rises to echo a knowledge that the sound exists. By the time high Mass was over, tradesmen were setting up their stands in the uncobbled plaza, ankle deep in dust.

Father Dominque, walking among them, noted the monotony of their wares—baskets and bags woven from basket-grass, gourd bowls and wooden trays lacquered with the oil gum of insects, pottery with designs of flowers. As he walked he nodded continually to the mestizos; the men snatching their sombreros from their heads at his passing, their women performing clumsy curtsies. Already he could feel the heat through his robe and sweat trickling down his legs. He passed workmen finishing the wooden podium where he would sit, presiding over the pageant, and turned down a narrow street enclosed by adobe houses. His destination was the *cárcel*, the jail, squatting one-storied at the end.

The sergeant was awaiting him, anxious to be relieved of his prisoners so he might join the celebration. On this day Father Dominque had the power of dispensation. The sergeant, a huge bearded man, swaggered to meet the father.

"*Buenos días*, Padre." He smiled expansively.

"*Buenos días,* Sargento," Father Dominique responded, and stepped with him into the coolness of shade. He was a little man, though growing heavy around his middle, and he puffed slightly from the walking and the heat.

"How many?" he asked the sergeant.

"Thirty-five." The sergeant looked uneasily at Father Dominque and added, "Thirty of whom, Padre, are your prisoners."

Father Dominque nodded irritably; he knew how many he had charged. They were all Indios charged with the same offense—failure to work their prescribed days of tribute for the Church on its lands and in the silver mine, situated a dozen miles from Kaskiyeh at the foothills of the mountains.

"I dispense with their punishment," he mumbled, a formal rote that he delivered in a singsong voice. "And the five?"

"Military, Padre." The sergeant added hastily, "But all minor offenses, drunkenness and property destruction . . . maybe a little too much *rapiña* in the quarters of the Indio women . . . small things of no consequence."

"Then tell Capitán Felipe I have no objection to their release if he and the *alcalde* can agree upon it." He shrugged his thin shoulders, walking away from the relieved sergeant; turning, he called back, "And tell El Capitán that I wish for *all* Indios to be permitted . . . ah . . . brought into the plaza to view the pageant. It is necessary for their learning."

"*Sí,* Padre," the sergeant called after him.

Father Dominque retired to the coolness of his chambers. He always felt irritation at the conflict of powers between the Church and the military. In truth, he had the right to dispense all punishments for crimes, whether civil, military, or Church charged. But in the last few years the gradual incursions of the military into the powers of the Church had opened the way for jealous donkeys like Capitán

Felipe to insinuate themselves into positions of power. He resented the incessant quibbling and discussion that occurred as a consequence between himself and the captain, with the whining fat *alcalde* always presenting himself, as mayor, to represent what he liked to call "civil authority."

From the window of his chambers he could see streamers of bright colors fluttering across the square, and a faint hint of perfume came from flowers decorating his podium. The crowd was growing large and noisy as the peons with colorful serapes and the women in fringed *rebozos* mingled with soldiers. Here and there, people of higher stature and wealth wore costumes of Old Spain.

A band of musicians strolled through the crowds, and the high whine of a flute lifted above the drums and guitars. The musicians attempted *flamencos*, exciting the children, who chased one another around the plaza. Now the tempo of the music quieted, and the flute began a haunting strain of forgotten Moors.

He sighed, turning from the window. None of the extravaganza excited him. Twenty years ago he had received his holy orders in Mexico City and come north with great enthusiasm. The enthusiasm had long since disappeared. True, he had, with moderate success, managed the Church properties and dutifully enriched the coffers, but he felt that the Church had little challenge spiritually. Since the Indios were not people of "reason," he could not administer the Holy Eucharist to them, nor confirmation. He had baptized some, to wash away sin, but they were still lost, kept barely within the bounds of civilized action by the whipping post and the stocks standing close by the cathedral. There was even doubt and animated debate within the Church hierarchy as to whether the Indios in fact possessed souls. Father Dominque was sure they did not.

Clapping his hands briskly as he sat down at his table, he reached for the wine glass extended to him by the servant girl who had instantly appeared. Her hands shook as she handed him the wine, spilling a few drops on the table. Quickly she withdrew—an Indian girl, small, with long black hair and lithe movements. Father Dominque noted her shaking hands without comment. He knew the reason for her nervousness; and the loose-fitting white dress she had taken to wearing. She was carrying a child. She would have to be sent back to the Indio quarters. No child of a priest could be born in a priest's dwelling. To do so would bring disgrace. He always hated the scenes, though they never protested; mutely looking at the floor or crying, hanging their heads like dumb animals and dreading to leave the security of the Church to go back to the brutality of the soldiers who administered the lives of the Indio quarters. She would have to be replaced. Today, while he sat on the podium, he would look for one among the Indio families; young, as yet undefiled by the bestial soldiers.

Outside his window the crowd noise increased; black powder, cupped in tiny containers, was being exploded. There were shouts and singing, laughter. A girl screamed. Father Dominque knew he would be forced to enter the plaza soon, to begin the pageant; the soldiers, despite his request to Capitán Felipe, were growing drunk on pulque and tequila. Soon the plaza would be a spectacle of drunken, celebrant soldiers and girls too afraid to resist them.

Kaskiyeh was now filled to overflowing, as pilgrims had come from villages fifty miles away to help celebrate Kaskiyeh's saint day. All the towns and villages of Mexico had a patron saint, and today was the holy day of Kaskiyeh's. The patron saint of Kaskiyeh was Saint Jerome—in Spanish, Santo Geronimo.

He rose, walking through the cool corridor. Adjusting his robes, he stepped into the hot plaza. He passed the tables set beneath a live oak, loaded with dishes of turkey cooked in sauces of chile, chocolate, sesame, and spices. There were huge bowls of *atole*, wrapped around pork and chicken and boiled in corn husks to make tamale dumpling; cinnamon chocolate whipped into foam. It was an extravagant feast for the peons.

As he walked, somewhat majestically, toward the podium, the crowd quieted and parted before him. Ahead he saw Capitán Felipe weaving unsteadily in his polished buttons and shining boots. He was drunk. The captain bowed as he passed, doffing his cap and smiling. As he ascended the podium to his thronelike chair the fat *alcalde* followed halfway up the steps, making small murmuring, whining sounds of abeyance. He was stopped from ascending the podium only by Father Dominque's quick look backward of disapproval. The *alcalde* refused, however, to give up the progress he had made; he halted midway on the steps and held his ground, bowing and smiling at the crowd. Silence descended on the plaza. The wind, rustling leaves of the live oak, rattled a sound of dried castanets. The day was September 30.

The gates of Kaskiyeh were open wide. Here, in this important center of mines, ranches, and farms, on a direct route of the mule trains traveling north and south, there was little to fear from the Apache. Stationed here under the command of Capitán Felipe were two companies of cavalry and two companies of infantry. A large enough force to deter any ragtag group of savages.

Father Dominque sat quietly on his throne, surveying the bared heads of the men and the shawled women and girls. For all his hardships, he was due these brief moments of undivided attention when the captain and the *alcalde* could not intrude. For weeks he had coached the pageant players. They were to reenact the life of Santo Geronimo; how the Santo had appeared, a hermit out of the desert of Chalcis, in Antioch, to be ordained a servant of God. His podium faced the wide gates where the first player would appear, coming from the desert as Santo Geronimo had done.

Now he lifted his hand and waved it, beginning the drum roll that heralded the entrance. The drums were muffled in the beginning, rolling softly, growing louder, reaching a climactic burst. At that instant a short stout figure appeared in the gate. The figure was dusty and unkempt; around his head, holding bushy hair, there was a buckskin band, across his cheekbones, a yellow streak that emphasized the hard, vicious lines of his face. He wore boot moccasins, breechclout, and a loose blouse of polka-dot red. He was an Apache!

The crowd instinctively shrank away from the gate, and a rumble of alarm swept over the plaza. But the Apache seemed unmoved by the crowd's reaction. Father Dominque could see his eyes, pinpoints of concentrated hatred; like the eyes of a tiger he had once seen chained in Madrid. However, the Apache was unarmed and alone.

Capitán Felipe, seeing the moment as fated for his appearance before the crowd, weaved into the center of the plaza. He held a tequila bottle in one fist and, waving it toward the Apache, shouted, "*Hola*! Behold! Santo *Geronimo*!"

Relieved, the crowd burst into laughter. The captain sought to extend his comical farce. He bowed toward the Apache, grinning, white teeth beneath his trim mustache. "Enter, Geronimo!" And turning to the laughing people, he shouted, "Let us welcome Santo Geronimo!" The crowd, laughing and shouting at the joke, began a chant: "*Geronimo! Geronimo! Geronimo! Geronimo!*" The chant grew in rhythm and volume, thundering louder as the wind rose, sweeping the chant across the desert . . . to the ears of Apache warriors, lying tense, waiting, with their Leader among the Enemy.

Inwardly Father Dominque raged. Capitán Felipe was cunningly making a joke of his, Father Dominque's, efforts for the pageant, and at the same time acquiring the center stage before the crowd; but he smiled benevolently. There was nothing else to do in the face of the crowd's hilarity. Curiously he watched the Apache. Now he saw him reach upward under his blouse. When he withdrew his hand, he held a short bow and feathered arrow. Slowly, methodically, he raised the bow, fitting the arrow. As he drew the string back, back, toward his ear, the crowd silenced, watching an unreal performance, fascinated. The arrow zinged in the air and buried itself in Father Dominque's chest, feathers fluttering before his eyes, in the wind.

Father Dominque did not lose his smile. He tumbled, still smiling, from the throne, down, bouncing on the podium and puffing dust where his body fell at the feet of the *alcalde*. The seconds of silence ticked over the stunned plaza.

And into the silence the Apache spoke. He smiled, a thin slash of teeth across his face, and bowing mockingly in imitation of Capitán Felipe, he said amiably, "*Adios!*" as though he had politely opened a door. Turning his back on them he trotted easily, arrogantly, into the desert.

Behind him the plaza erupted in an animal roar of outrage. A priest had been murdered before their eyes! Soldiers tramped over people, rushing for guns and horses. Some of them, not seeking to arm themselves with guns, snatched sabers from their scabbards and fought the milling crowd of women, men, and children, trying to run after the Apache.

Capitán Felipe was the first to gain a horse and, roweling his mount recklessly, drew his saber, waving it warningly at the crowd. He finally managed to speed through the gate. Ahead of him a few soldiers on foot were running, sabers drawn. They stood no chance of catching the Apache, who was fleeing ahead of them, gaining as his powerful legs ate the ground. Capitán Felipe slapped his horse with the saber. The murderer stood no chance of making the mountains, fully a dozen miles away. The captain would be the one to reach him first and bring back his head to the people of Kaskiyeh.

Behind the captain more horses were drumming, and men attempting to cheat him of his prize were pausing to aim their guns and fire, but the Apache was zigzagging in a crazy pattern that defied marksmanship.

The squat figure was an impossible target, bobbing over the rolling prairie, running left, then right, but always in a line for the mountains. He was two hundred yards ahead of Capitán Felipe in the beginning, but as the horse stretched out into a hoof-drumming run the distance shortened rapidly. Now it was a hundred yards . . . fifty . . . and behind Capitán Felipe the last of the soldiers poured through Kaskiyeh's gates, joining the chase. Twenty-five yards, fifteen, and the captain leaned from the saddle, holding his saber wide, ready for the cut.

Suddenly the Apache whirled in a tight half circle, and faced him! He was grinning wickedly at the captain. Beside him a huge giant of an Apache rose from the desert. Reality exploded in Capitán Felipe's brain, but it was too late. The squat Apache screamed, leaping at him, and a long knife glittered brilliantly in the sun. It was the last sight Capitán José Ernesto Felipe was to see. An Apache war scream was the last sound. The Leader had reached the bottom of the U, and it was Juh, the giant, who rose beside him.

As the last soldiers ran through the gates into the desert two tall Apaches appeared from bush on either side and closed behind them; as magically as they appeared, other Apaches materialized, running from each side of the U. The soldiers were caught between them. Mangas and Cochise had closed the top of the U to make a circle.

The entire populace of Kaskiyeh rushed to the walls, first to watch the chase of the Apache, then, upon seeing warriors rise from the desert, to watch their soldiers destroy them. In the beginning there were shots fired, but gradually the shots diminished. Plunging horses and fighting men created a huge dust cloud that enveloped the scene. The villagers could make little of what was occurring. They could hear shouting, screaming, knives striking sabers, and the heavy parrying of lances.

Here and there a horse ran, riderless, out of the dust cloud with reins trailing. The sounds began to change. The yells and screaming stopped; the clang of iron striking iron diminished into a slow, methodical sound of thuds—iron striking into unyielding flesh and bone.

Slowly as a coming sunrise, the dust cloud began settling. As the cloud fell, first revealing shadowy shapes of men, then clearing, the villagers were stunned. With the clearing of the dust absolute silence had settled over the battlefield. Everywhere, Apaches stood, as if at attention. Among them, on the ground, were mangled, bloody, and headless soldiers. Horses lay, lances standing stark from their bodies. The Apaches were looking toward the center of the field.

As the villagers watched, the squat, powerful Apache who had appeared at their gate and killed their priest walked slowly to the field's center. His blouse had been torn from his body. In his hand he carried a saber, and slowly he raised the saber, pointing it toward the sky.

Blood was over his face, splattering across his chest, even his legs. The saber, pointing upward, ran rivulets of blood down the blade onto his hand and arm. He turned toward Kaskiyeh, still holding the saber high, and tilting his head backward toward the sky, he screamed—a fanatical wild scream of unreasoning terror.

A lower sound began, muffled beneath the scream, and rose higher in volume and intensity. Gradually the sound became intelligible. The Apaches, raising bloody knives and lances, jabbing them at the sky, were chanting, "Geronimo! Geronimo! Geronimo! Geronimo! *Geronimo! Geronimo! Geronimo! Geronimo! Geronimo!*"

12

The War Leader Geronimo was born where Kaskiyeh died. Some of the villagers escaped from this
greatest disaster suffered by the Mexicans in a long
history of war with the Apaches. Others, huddling in
their cathedral, died in the flames as Geronimo led his
chiefs and warriors running with torches through the
town.

The two unmistakable signs of trouble on the
prairie—black, billowing smoke and hundreds of
spiraling buzzards—brought soldiers riding from all
directions. They found Kaskiyeh embering in the
adobe skeletons of buildings and walls, and before
the gates a field of bloating bodies that had been
soldiers. From the battlefield they found the thin,
single-file trail of moccasins that aimed like an arrow into the looming Sierra Madre.

Some Apaches say that Geronimo had no way of
knowing, nor cared, that Saint Jerome was the patron saint of Kaskiyeh, or that September 30 was
his feast day. Others, noting his astuteness and fantastic ability to grasp and analyze situations alien to his
culture, say he knew; that as he lay on the desert
studying the plaza of Kaskiyeh he planned his the-
atrical entrance with a knowledge of what was trans-
piring in the town.

By accident or by plan, the results were explosive
and instantaneous over all of northern Mexico. His
appearance out of the desert at the precise moment
of Saint Jerome's entrance, to replace Saint Jerome;

his calm, deliberate killing of the priest, and his mocking bow and "*Adios!*" smacked of the supernatural. Within forty-eight hours of Kaskiyeh's death, soldiers, mule drovers, and refugees of the town had carried the story into Sonora, through Chihuahua, and even south into Durango. Geronimo, killer of Kaskiyeh, was proven beyond all doubt an evil saint, risen from the lower regions.

The bounty for an Apache male's scalp was a hundred pesos (soon to rise to three hundred), for an Apache woman's, fifty pesos, and for an Apache child or baby's, twenty-five pesos; but instantly the bounty for Geronimo's head was posted at two thousand pesos, twenty horses, and fifty cattle. But only for the head; no scalp or thin claim would do. The reward would increase. The Guerra con los Diablos, the War with the Devils (Apaches) became the Guerra con Geronimo, the War with Geronimo. Many years before the United States Army learned the name "Geronimo," his fame, or infamy was widely established in Mexico.

From the battlefield Geronimo and his men carried fifteen slain brothers, and deep in the recesses of the Sierra Madre they buried them in hidden caves where no Mexican could find and defile their bodies. Then, pausing briefly, faces to the stars, as Geronimo asked Usen to consider their courage and cause in admitting them back to the Great Wheel, they raced north through the broken peaks and ridges toward the sanctuary of their people's rancheria. They were running ahead of an alarm that swept behind them, fast as the wind. Resting in short stops, they did not sleep, and reaching the northern tip of the Madre on a late afternoon, Geronimo headed them, running boldly, across the plains in the red glow of a dying day. Through the night they ran with the Dragoons just to the east of them before angling northwest across welcome, broken ground that offered day cover. On the following day they entered the Santa Catalina range, and Geronimo slowed their pace, to bring them trotting into the large hidden settlement of their combined people.

The victory celebration was tempered by mourning for the lost warriors. Despite a life way of War and Death, the Apaches regarded the death of a single person as an event of great concern and deep sorrow. The bonds of affection within families and throughout a band were strong, and it was not unusual for for the death of an individual to be mourned for many months. The fires of victory were solemnized as fires of remembrance for the dead.

Geronimo sat with the combined councils and the chiefs. He talked persuasively for a permanent coalition of the bands, a forming of a single nation from the three. He urged immediate and total war against the Mexicans. But he was not a chief. Perhaps his arguments were regarded as would be those of any man proficient in a special field who seeks to promote that field's activity and, in so doing, enhance his own position.

Geronimo's abilities as a War Leader were secure, even regarded with awe by many. But his arguments were not successful. The chiefs and councils maintained they must regard other matters than war—the safety of families and the securing of the best life possible for the people to whom they were responsible. When Geronimo responded that he could "see," that there would be no life at all for the Apache unless the commitment was made now to total war, his arguments were dismissed.

And so, with typical Apache independence, the bands went their separate ways. Cochise took his people into the mountains of Dos Cabezos and the Chiricahuas. Mangas Coloradas, longing to visit Warm Springs Mimbres relatives, led his band, drifting, across the Mogollons into the Black Mountain range. Juh, with his Nedni nation, traveled south with the boldness that marked his nature, back into a Mexico stirring like a hornet's nest. But once in the Sierra Madre, he took them deep into their native stronghold at the headwaters of the Yaqui River.

Before Juh left, he married Ishton, a favorite "sister" of Geronimo, and the bonds between Geronimo and his cousin Juh were strengthened. Geronimo followed Mangas Coloradas, but he made a mental note of Juh's location; the headquarters of the Nednis intrigued him, in the heart of the Enemy.

Oral history of the Apaches recalls little of the second wife of Geronimo. Her name was Nana-tha, a quiet and sturdy girl of the Bedonkohes who was cheerfully oblivious to the brooding air of the War Shaman. A baby son was born, but while the boy was still an infant Mexican troops, striking north, overran the Bedonkohes and killed the infant and mother. The predictions of his Power were to come to pass in the life of Geronimo. He was almost fatally wounded in the battle, lying close to death for weeks. He recovered, and struck back. Receiving no commitment from the band, he recruited individual warriors to follow him. With twenty warriors he was identified at Fronteras. Out of the burning town he carefully gathered supplies—food, weapons, clothing, utensils, to carry back as an enticement to the warriors. If they would not be spurred to further action by his prophecies of enslavement and death, perhaps they would follow him for war prizes.

But he had lost four men at Fronteras, and fewer warriors listened. With a dozen running at his heels he hit Nacozari, and when the Indian slaves fled across the plains into the mountains, he followed them. They cringed on the ground beneath the trees as he spoke earnestly to them of their need to join his fight against the Mexicans. But they had been too long in slavery and sat helpless in freedom, like chickens still caged. He had walked away.

Needing warriors, he recruited from the band of Cochise and attacked Janos, then Arispe; but the flood

134

of Mexicans continued north, attracted by the settlements of the white eyes. The attraction was wealth, supplying needs for mining camps, forts, and towns. Mule trains carrying these supplies grew longer and more numerous, heavily escorted by Mexican troops.

The Apaches were at peace with the United States Army despite new mineral discoveries and settlements that miraculously flourished in the Big Burro Mountains and the Santa Rita range. The California Road had been opened through the heart of Apacheria, and wagon trains, stagecoaches, and troops were seen daily on the road. They were not molested. Cochise, Mangas, and other chiefs had given their word of peace. It was kept. Apaches had begun participating in the new civilization that was approaching and surrounding them. They cut wood for the stage stations and even raised feed for mules and horses in exchange for money and supplies.

The United States Army had established a strong system of forts in West Texas: Forts McIntosh and Duncan and Camp Hudson on the Rio Grande, with Fort Inge and Camp Clark to the north; northwest of the Pecos, Fort Lancaster, with Fort Stockton just to the southwest. Fort Davis was established in the heart of the Davis Mountains of the Big Bend, the eastern range of the Mescaleros. West of Fort Davis was Fort Quitman, and still farther west, at El Paso, the biggest fort of them all, aimed like an arrow at the homeland of the Apaches, the propelling force which launched the rolling tide of bluecoats: Fort Bliss.

Out of Fort Bliss and El Paso, the California Road wandered north along the Rio Grande, turning west at Doña Aña to dip south of the Santa Rita and Big Burro Mountain ranges, crossing the vast flats north of a new settlement called Lordsburg and through Doubtful Canyon of the Guadalupe Mountains. Plunging west out of the canyon, the road crossed the San Simon Valley and through Apache Pass of the Chiricahua Mountains to emerge onto the salt flats of Sulphur Springs. From this valley the road proceeded through the Dragoon Mountains and, emerging, ran north of Tombstone, westward through Tucson.

Two years following the word of peace given by the Apache chiefs, Geronimo rode alone along this road. No white man saw him, for he did not travel the wagoned tracks of the road, but kept to brush and hill, riding always at a distance and lying still, often in the light of day, while the white men passed on the road. He was alarmed at the growing numbers that came, day after day. There was no end to their coming.

From the foothills of the Santa Catalinas he watched a new fort just north of Tucson: Fort Breckinridge. Following the Santa Cruz River south, he was forced to hide in an arroyo from bluecoat patrols out of Camp Calabasas on the Mexican border. Turning east, he was surprised by soldiers riding out of Fort Buchanan and escaped, riding fast before a fusillade of bullets (the peace was to be kept by Apaches only; lone Indians were considered "fair game"). Running north of Lordsburg, he sought refuge in the Big Burros and found more forts, more bluecoat patrols riding from them, crisscrossing the Apache homeland. Fort McLane, north of the California Road, was in easy riding distance of Silver City, where a metal strike had been made and white miners rousted for rich ore. Riding south to north on the Rio Grande, there were Forts Fillmore and Thorn, Craig and Conrad; east of the Grande a huge fort dominated the flats: Fort Stanton.

His ride had taken him a month, and as he turned his horse west, to cross the Black Mountain range, he was shocked to find bluecoats there. They had a home and base called Camp Ojo Caliente in the heart of the Warm Springs Apaches. From a high peak he studied them through the day, using his Spanish binoculars. Mexicans, peon Indians, and here and

136

there an Apache were cutting dried adobe bricks and laying them in walls that formed buildings. All around them soldiers carried guns and guarded the perimeter. Their manners were not those of men at peace but of men at war. Twice in the afternoon he watched patrols riding into the compound and reporting.

With darkness, he slipped away and rode north along the Alamosa River. As he rode he paused frequently at the mouths of canyons that opened onto the sluggish stream. Each time, he drew in long breaths of air through his nostrils, as a man might taste soup with his tongue. Near midnight, at the entrance to a deep-cleft canyon, he sniffed the sign—a light, barely perceptible warmth that floated on the dry coolness of mountain air. He turned into the canyon and rode cautiously between the high walls. Two hundred yards into the canyon the heat of human bodies funneled toward him, intensified by the spice of cooking food threading the air. He stopped, and tilting back his head, he yelped coyote style, five times— once more than the coyote's limit of four barks—and was instantly answered in the same manner.

The tipis were set well back in the shadows of the cliffs, ringing a small spring and grass meadow. It was a large rancheria. Geronimo rein-trailed his horse on the meadow grass and walked toward the fire burning low before a large tipi. He sat down cross-legged in front of the fire. In a moment an old Apache emerged from the tipi. His face was wrinkled and his hair was white. He held a blanket around his shoulders and sat before the fire without aid of his hands, opposite Geronimo.

The old man was Cuchillo, Chief of the Warm Springs band of Mimbres Apaches. Another figure, a younger man, materialized out of the shadows and sat down beside him. The younger man had earned his name on the battlefield against Mexican troops. Once, in a desperate fight, he had dashed onto the field, running crazily among a hail of bullets to lift a wounded brother on his shoulders and carry him to safety. The Mexicans had called him Loco (Crazy). The name had stuck. Behind Cuchillo and Loco warriors silently assembled, standing in the shadow to see the man of whom they had all heard: Geronimo. There could be no mistaking his identity—the strong muscled body that rippled above his breechclout, always the war band, and above the thin slash of lips, across the cheekbones, the streaks of yellow paint. He gave no indication that he saw the warriors facing him; instead he stared, eyes glittering, into the fire.

Cuchillo broke the silence that politeness had required.

"We are pleased to have you here, Geronimo."

"Thank you," Geronimo answered politely, looking up into the old chief's eyes. "I have traveled through the patrols of many bluecoats to reach here."

Cuchillo smiled. "Yes, there are a good many of them, but I think maybe there are no more than these. There is room for all."

Geronimo looked hard at the chief's face. "There is no end to them, Cuchillo. They will not stop coming."

Cuchillo laughed. "There is an end to everything, Geronimo. Anyway, they are our friends. They have said so. They are not like the Mexicans. They have not attacked us. They do not wish to make us slaves."

Geronimo sighed. For the first time he looked beyond the chief, to the circle of warriors. He spoke as though directly to them: "The bluecoats are not our friends. They will kill us and make us slaves, as the Mexicans do, when there are enough of them so that they feel strong."

Cuchillo's face hardened. It was ill-mannered of a welcomed guest to argue with a host, but Apache independence dictated his right to do so. Cuchillo's tone harshened: "The Word has been given, Geronimo—by me, by the Chiefs of the Coyoteros and the Mescaleros, by Delshay of the Tontos, by Mangas and

Cochise. The Word will be kept. That is the Law."

Geronimo rose from the fire, rudely and quickly. He turned away toward his horse.

"You are leaving?" Cuchillo asked, more to emphasize Geronimo's rudeness than to determine his actions.

"Yes," Geronimo said.

Loco rose and, holding his palm in the air, called after Geronimo, "Peace, Geronimo!"

Geronimo paused, turning back to face them. "War," he said dryly. "War, Loco. Any people can have body peace if they will sell their souls for it. Peace is a condition, Loco, not an end. It is a condition our souls can live with only if our souls and minds are free. Unless"—and his eyes burned red toward the fire—"you will buy peace for your body with the most violent of war: murder of your soul." He whirled and, leaping on his horse, was about to turn its head when a young warrior stepped forward, holding the horse's head. Geronimo jerked at the rein, but the young man held on, looking up at him. "Do you believe the bluecoats are so many as you say?"

Geronimo looked down at the young man and saw a strong face with square jaws and high forehead. "How are you called?" he asked.

"I am called Victorio," the young man answered.

"Yes, Victorio, they are more than the rocks you see in the mountains and," he added bitterly, whipping the horse away from the young man, "you will live to see and count them as a slave . . . or before you die." He rode hard out of the canyon.

Within a year Cuchillo would be killed, "by mistake," when he waved a friendly greeting to a United States Army patrol. His successor, Delgadito, would last hardly another year. While walking away from Camp Ojo Caliente after a visit with his bluecoat "friends," he would be shot in the back by an army trooper for "sport." A young War Chief would ascend to Delgadito's position, and many people would die. His name was Victorio.

Geronimo reported the findings of his long scout to Mangas and Cochise, but his arguments were met with the same unyielding beliefs with which Cuchillo had faced him. Geronimo disappeared. On the morning of his disappearance the Bedonkohes found a row of stones laid before his sparse tipi in the form of an arrow. The arrow pointed south.

He was Mexico's most wanted man. Every mule train attacked, every village, town, or rancho raided for cattle and horses identified the leader as Geronimo. His "head" had been offered for reward in a dozen towns, but the reward had never been paid. Conflicting reports of his appearance at two places at the same time served to strengthen the argument of his supernatural evil. Despite this, Geronimo rode alone into Mexico—across the barren flats south of the Chiricahuas, hiding by day, riding by night, and into the safety of the Sierra Madre. His destination was the stronghold of Juh on the Yaqui.

The Yaqui River moves slowly across the rolling plains of Sonora. Burdened with silt, it approaches the Gulf of California with a wide-banked quietness of its waters, relieving its burdens into the gulf. If a traveler traced the Yaqui backward, to where it emerged roaring from the western side of the Sierra Madre, he would enter a canyon deepened by a million years of the river's activity. As he traveled up the canyon the river would grow smaller with each tributary passed, and the water would become sparkling clear, tumbling over rocks, downward from the elevations of the river's birth. The canyon would narrow, but always in its depths would be lush grass, greened by the river's moisture, piñon trees, mesquite, live oaks, and wild bursts of flowers carrying a warmth to the cooling air of high elevations. Fifty miles into the interior of the Madre the traveler would arrive at the headwaters of the Yaqui—its birthplace, with crystal springs high in elevation but deep-cradled in the canyon. This was the home of the Nedni Apaches.

Geronimo did not trace the Nednis' home by traversing the Yaqui's length. He rode the spine of the Sierra Madre, sure of the place, and found them. He was welcomed heartily by Juh. In reality this was the home of his heritage. His grandfather had been chief of this band and was remembered as a leader of honor and great integrity.

The tipis of the Nednis were scattered among trees of the canyon for a half mile bordering the clearwater stream. The high altitude lent a crisp coolness that was invigorating but not uncomfortable. It was an idyllic setting for life and living. But Juh was troubled. In his stumbling speech he poured out his anxieties to Geronimo. Ishton was dying. The birth of her child was due, and she had been in pain and labor for a long time. Although she made no complaint, Juh knew she was suffering greatly.

The huge man had never left her side, tenderly stroking her forehead with wet cloths, holding her hands in his rough futile attempts to comfort her. Juh loved the calm, intelligent Ishton with all his heart. He knew Geronimo felt deeply for his "sister."

Before the fire of late evening he paced back and forth as Geronimo watched the flames. All reserve was gone. Tears tumbled down his cheeks and his great chest heaved in sobs. He stopped, looking down at his cousin, sitting cross-legged by the fire.

"I," he said loudly, preparing himself to force the words past his stuttering, "I . . . am a simple mmmmmman, Gee . . . Gee . . . *Gero*nimo. I ddddo *not* dee . . . dee . . . de*serve* Ishton. No *ppppower* has ever spoken to *mmmmmmme*. If it was *thththat* I had a *ppppower*, I wwwwwould make a *trade . . . anything* ffffffor Ishton." He paused in his labored speech before heaving his chest again. "I have *ppprayed*, but I have no *pppppower*." He stood helplessly before the fire and Geronimo, looking pathetically like a great bear humbled and begging without hope of reward.

Geronimo stood, facing him. "I will go up there," he said, pointing to a peak looming high above the tree line. "When Ishton is well and the baby is born, send for me." He walked away toward the mountain.

Juh followed him for a ways, trying to speak, stumbling, then, too overcome by his emotions to attempt further speech, watched silently as Geronimo disappeared. Then he turned and ran, lumbering into the tipi where Ishton lay. He had full faith in Geronimo's Power, and holding her in his arms, he told her the good news.

Geronimo walked upward, through the tree line, onto the barren ground, whipped by wind that exposed the teething of rocks and boulders. The air was sharp and cold. At the top of the peak, on a small plateau, Geronimo began his prayers to Usen and the talks with his Power.

He took no food or water with him, nor did he have shelter from the biting wind. For four days he prayed, asking for assurance that Ishton would live. Below him a great calm settled over the rancheria of the Nednis, and Juh did not move from his place beside Ishton. On the morning of the fourth day Geronimo's Power answered him, calling his name four times: "*Geronimo! Geronimo! Geronimo! Geronimo!*" And from his knees, looking to the sky, Geronimo answered, "I am here. I have been calling. I wish to ask that Ishton might live. That she might not be taken as one I love. Let her live and I will ask nothing more." And his Power answered, "You chose to come back to the earth world and place your spirit body in conflict with the forces of the lower planes. You chose, Geronimo, to strengthen your spirit body. You may keep the Faith with your spirit or you may weaken and surrender your soul to the lower planes. You may have the child to comfort you at the time your earth body is old. You may have Ishton for a short time with Juh. Ask nothing more, Geronimo. No weapon will kill your earth body. Ask nothing more. Only you may kill your spirit body." Geronimo answered, "I will ask nothing more."

When the messenger climbed the peak, touched red by the setting sun of that fourth day, he found Geronimo seated. He was at peace, calmly watching the sun slipping away behind the mountains. The messenger told him a son had been born to Ishton; that the mother and child were well. Geronimo answered, "I know."

Geronimo's unshakable faith in the prophecies of his Power stayed with him throughout his life. One might wonder at his thoughts as he descended the mountain. Certainly he was happy for Ishton and for Juh; but also within him he knew for a certainty that he could expect nothing more of his Power to soften the straitness and punishments of his destiny in the physical world.

Juh was jubilant. He met Geronimo, almost dancing in his relief and exuberance. Lifting his solemn cousin high in the air, he bear-hugged him with his great arms and called for a celebration.

The hardy Ishton was carried from the tipi and placed on a bed of boughs and skins so she might see the fires and celebrations. She was pale, but smiling. When Geronimo knelt beside her she raised her arms, pulling him close, fully confident that it was he who had saved her child. As he rose from his knees she held up the baby to him, and Geronimo took the boy in his arms. Ishton watched his tender holding of the child. She knew Geronimo's affection for children, and she watched the hard face soften, the fierceness recede from the burning eyes. Geronimo had lost most of those he loved.

That night there was feasting, dancing, songs, and chants. The Nednis named the boy Daklugie—a description of his birth which means "One who fights his way through."

The celebration lasted a week, a momentous occasion in the history of the Nednis. After Ishton had regained her strength, the band moved leisurely down the canyon of the Yaqui. They had two purposes in their movement. One was to bring their base camp closer to the Sonoran plains, where their warriors might strike the mule trains moving north through Nuri, Ures, and Arispe to supply the white-eye settlement of Tucson, far north. This was at Geronimo's urging. He was haunted by the flourishing activity of the bluecoats in the north. The peace word given by the chiefs there prevented his attacking the bluecoats directly, and so he sought to weaken them in this manner. Juh agreed.

Their second purpose was to come closer to the mountain slopes where mescal might be gathered and cooked. As they moved toward the plains, parties of women and children scouted the slopes in search of the plants. This was the month of June and during this month the mescal, a large agave plant with thick, fleshy leaves that spike murderously outward, opens massive red flower stalks that make it easy to spot. The women looked for large patches of the plant and were gone, often, for days. When they found a suitably large patch, they placed four-foot piñon sticks, flattened at one end, against the base of the leaves. Using hatchets or stones, they hammered the ends of the sticks until the leaves were cut away; only then could they dig out the huge white bulbs, sometimes three feet in circumference.

When they had accumulated enough bulbs for a band the size of the Nednis, probably a ton, they dug a ditch four feet deep and about twelve feet long. Placing stones in the bottom of the ditch, they built fires to heat the stones, and when these were sufficiently hot, they piled the bulbs into the ditch, covering them with grass, followed by a thick layer of soil. For twenty-four hours the mescal cooked in this efficient pressure cooker. While the mescal cooked, a member of the party ran to summon the band. All gathered for the uncovering of the pit. While still warm the mescal is a flavorful syrup and called for a festive occasion. What was not eaten was spread into thin sheets and dried on flat rocks. These sheets were cut into small squares that could be carried for food and would keep indefinitely. They retained a nutritious food value of great use to the Apaches.

In a leisurely month of travel and camping the Nednis enjoyed two great mescal cookings. As women of the band searched for a third likely patch they were moving dangerously close to the eyes of the plains.

13

Clouds, lowering and heavy, settled on the western slopes of the Sierra Madre. They had come, washed on the winds of Sonora, from the great waters beyond. Now the clouds dropped thick fog, glistening on rocks and trees. In the deep of the Yaqui's canyon the Nednis lit small fires before tipis, chasing the moist chill from their doors; few ventured outside. They expected rain and had, the night before, carefully moved their tipis farther from the river to higher ground.

It was early morning, too early yet to know the sun's decision—whether the clouds were thin enough to be chased away or whether they would bring rain. In the grayness of fog and early morning two girls of the Nedni band walked away from the rancheria. Climbing a path in the canyon wall, they moved leisurely across the mountain slopes.

One was named Lucia, and a week before she had reached the age of sixteen years. At the full of the moon she had been given her womanhood ceremony. Her companion was Mathla, a girl of eighteen who had acted as her attendant. Their announced purpose was to find a new mescal patch, but this was only an excuse. Their real purpose was to exercise the new independence of Lucia; to gossip and relive the thrill of the ceremony and discuss likely prospects of marriage. They were accompanied by an unwelcome follower. Lucia's nephew Noshe, five years of age, tagged resolutely at a distance.

Twice Lucia had stopped to scold him, waving him back from his position twenty paces to the rear. His only concession to her scoldings and entreaties was to place his thumb uncertainly in his mouth, sucking speculatively through her tirade while his shoe-button eyes regarded her in calm stubbornness. Womanhood ceremonies meant little to Noshe. He regarded Lucia from the wisdom plateau of his five years as quite simply a girl; furthermore, a girl he had known all his life and who exercised no authority whatsoever that he could determine. And so, on his stubby legs he followed, climbing determinedly over rocks the pair of leaders easily stepped over. But he was strong and able to stay near enough to keep them in sight.

Once he paused to observe a red racer scooting across the ground; again he stopped to investigate a fringe-toed lizard whose tail was protruding from a rock. He contemplated catching the lizard by the tail, but he had caught them before and there was nothing new to be explored about lizards. Contrary to the girls' suspicions, he was totally uninterested in what they were discussing. They were discussing boys as they walked farther into the fog haze. Boys and the recent ceremony: How it had begun, with Juh directing the singing of all the band. How the War Shaman Geronimo, himself, had directed the dancing as all the people joined hands and danced in a circle. For hours the celebration continued, until the moon passed its zenith and began its descent. Then the older people retired; the young single men gathered in a tight circle, surrounded by a larger circle of the girls. The throb of the *esadadnes* stopped, and as Lucia stepped forward first, to select the young man with whom she would dance, the lonely, thin wail of the flageolet carried through the moonlight. She was beautiful in her costume of white deer-skin and flashing beads, and she had chosen the shy young man with whom she had exchanged long looks

147

over a period of time. Then all the other young women selected their partners and the lovers' dance went on and on, until the moon was paled by the sun's rising. At the closing of the dance each young man presented his partner with a present.

Mathla was already engaged to be married, and so with some difficulty she assumed an air of superiority to Lucia's girlish excitement; but not for long. Gradually she succumbed as the two sat down on a boulder, chattering. Lucia's young man had given her a valued gift, a Navajo blanket, and she was sure their ways would soon be together, to go as one.

Noshe, keeping a guarded distance, sat down on a stone, reflecting with bored second thoughts on this trip that had yielded nothing new or exciting. Something scurried under the stone, and he knelt beside it. Placing his cheek to the ground, he poked a stick experimentally under the stone and was rewarded when a grasshopper mouse made a terrified dash into the open. He was about to run after the mouse, looking up to where the girls were giggling and talking, when he saw the gray shapes in the fog.

The gray shapes were in a circle, all about the girls, who had not noticed them. They were moving slowly, cautiously, toward the two girls. Noshe would have called out, but the shapes were too close to the girls now. His five-year-old Apache mind told him that silence was best. As he watched, loops from lariats shot out from the gray shapes, falling over the heads of the girls, around their necks, and they were dragged, choking and fighting, from the rocks. The gray shapes, Noshe knew, were the Enemy.

Quickly he looked about him. He had not been seen. Survival came first. He crawled, round belly on the ground, to a large boulder and, holding its edge, slid himself tightly under a cleft. Now he watched.

The gray shapes had large hats on their heads, and beards. Noshe could see them as they seized the girls, tying their hands behind their backs, jerking them brutally with the ropes about their necks. Some of the Enemy laughed, and disappeared with the girls down the slope of the mountain, half-dragging them with the lariats. Others began walking about in a widening circle. Two of them came directly toward Noshe, and he squeezed tightly under the boulder. The two were talking, but Noshe could not understand their words. They stopped beside his boulder, and the toe of a boot stuck under the edge, not two inches from Noshe's nose. The boot was black. Noshe had a short knife hanging from his breechclout. Slowly he pulled the knife and placed it between his baby teeth. If the boot kicked him, he would stick the knife in it. He waited, regarding the boot with stoic attention. It moved, away from him, and the voices faded as the men walked with heavy tread down the mountain.

Now there was silence. A light rain pattered faintly on the boulder and across the ground. Still, Noshe did not move. He knew there might be others, and so he waited. The fog lifted as morning passed. The rain stopped. Cautiously Noshe slipped his head from beneath the boulder. Across the clearing he could see a red-tailed hawk, preening feathers industriously on a piñon limb. Somewhere he heard grunting and, turning his head to locate the sound, saw a mother peccary with two of her young. They were rooting at the base of a bush. Confidently he pulled himself from the boulder and stood up. The hawk flew, and the peccary, with her pigs, trotted away. He was alone.

His first instinct was to follow the trail of the Enemy. Perhaps he could kill them. He considered this for a while, seating himself comfortably against the boulder, but thought better of that plan. The Enemy were many, even for an Apache. He would need help. And so he began retracing his tortuous route across the rocks and boulders to the canyon. It was late in the afternoon by the time he arrived at the bottom of the canyon, having carefully negotiated the descent. He knew precisely where to go.

He presented himself before the tipi of Juh, and told his story. He told it again when Juh shouted and the War Shaman Geronimo came and warriors began to gather. Snatching guns from tipis, they ran, with Juh carrying Noshe in his arms, to the exact spot at the base of the canyon wall, where he pointed upward to the path he had followed. He would have liked to tell it a third time, but he was left suddenly and unceremoniously alone at the base of the wall, and his mother captured him again into babyhood.

It was after midnight when Juh, Geronimo, and the warriors returned. Noshe was awake and crawled, without being seen, to the shadows nearest the fire. They were gathering guns and ammunition. They had followed the tracks, and the tracks led to the town of Nuri. Noshe saw Ishton laying out articles for the warriors from a storehouse of captured supplies. He watched the hard face of Geronimo in the flickering shadows that worked across the circled, listening figures. Ishton was talking. She had a plan. Lucia was Juh's younger sister.

Nuri was situated on a plains plateau of two thousand feet. Close to the Sierra Madre foothills and astride the freight trail running north and south, Nuri was more than a town. It was a fort.

Colonel Luis Gomez, commanding three hundred troops, had many responsibilities and therefore much authority. There was a constant shuttle of patrols through his garrison, with troops moving south to meet the freight trains coming north and escort them into the enclosure of Nuri's ten-foot walls for safety before leading them north to Ures, to Arispe, from there to the new border town of Nogales, and thence to Tucson.

For years the mule and ox trains had carried a variety of supplies to the Anglos of the north: loaf sugar from deep in Mexico, bacon, cloth, mining tools, and flour. An ox could easily carry fifty pounds of flour on its head while saddled with three hundred pounds of goods on its back. Mules, properly fed and handled, could carry up to three hundred pounds through the rugged terrain that crossed mountains, plains, and deserts.

There was now less demand for these goods. Colonel Gomez had heard of the Anglos' opening of the California Road with its huge wagons freighting from Texas all the way from San Antonio to supply the growing mining industry of the Arizona territory. Of late the long freight trains of mule and oxen out of Mexico had become specialized. From shallow three- to five-hundred-foot shaft mines to the south, cinnabar ore was extracted and heated to drive off the sulphur. From this, mercury was obtained. The mercury was transported by mules carrying hundred-pound iron flasks hung on each side of their backs, in trains often extending to a hundred head, in single file. Mercury was in great demand by the miners to the north. Crushing their gold or silver ore into a powder, the miners mixed the powder with water and poured the mixture over thin copper plates which they had painted with mercury. The gold or silver combined with the mercury to form an amalgam, from which the earth and rocks were washed away. When intense heat was applied to the copper plates, the mercury boiled and became gas, leaving pure gold or silver. Mercury, therefore, could not be reused. Because of this, and the fantastic increase in mineral strikes, it was in tremendous demand.

The Anglos were not alone in the need for mercury. New silver mines being shafted along the foothills of Mexico's Sierra Madre had first call on the mercury supply. This led to another of Colonel Gomez's responsibilities and irritations. Mercury brought higher prices from the Anglos, and it was his duty to stop and divert those freight haulers who sought to bypass the

Mexican silver mines in favor of the greater Anglo riches.

With four captains and eight lieutenants under his command, he had his men divided into small patrols that constantly shifted east and west to apprehend those who sought to slip around Nuri with their mercury freight; as well as his regular escort patrols plying their routes north and south. Recently a new use had been found for mercury. Mixed with alcohol and nitric acid, it is highly explosive, and its use in the new percussion caps of cartridges had further increased the demand. The responsibilities were heavy on Colonel Gomez. In addition he was constantly harried by his superiors to furnish another expendable product for the mines of Mexico: Indio slaves. The demand was of major importance, affecting, among other things, Colonel Gomez's career.

Pressing demands from the south came from powerful figures in the national government who could, with a flick of their fingers, reduce Colonel Gomez to a peon. And the local demands made by the two silver mines in the immediate area required unerring diplomacy and complex manipulations. One of these, Church owned, was administered by the priest of Nuri. The other was owned by a coalition of powerful dons.

The quiet godly air of the priest did not in the least allay Colonel Gomez's fear of his power. Given the intricate political workings of the Church, only a word was necessary in Mexico City to end his career . . . even his life. The same with the politically potent dons. And they gave him no respite. The dons, with blustering demands, and the priest, with quiet insistence, constantly pushed him for more Indio slaves.

The mortality rate of the mine-working Indians was appalling; like mercury, they were used quickly and gone. But unlike mercury, the supply was diminishing. Four years was the average life span of an Indian working the mines. Carrying bags of ore weighing up to four hundred pounds up long ladder poles from varying depth levels for fourteen to sixteen hours a day, some never saw the sun. The Indians' alarming rate of death was overreaching the births.

The Church, struggling to keep its mines operational, had launched a long-range plan that was apparently failing. Ordering that no female Indios be used in mine labor, the Church had urged a breeding program with an announced birth goal of four children per Indio male, in four years' time. But the Indios failed in this propagational program; births were few. Perhaps, Colonel Gomez had suggested to the priest, the hours were a little too long; perhaps if the workday was shortened to, say, twelve hours . . . after all, a man . . .

The priest had shrugged, turning up his hands in a hopeless gesture, but assured the colonel he would forward his suggestions to higher authorities. The ominous tone of the priest's "forward your suggestions" made Colonel Gomez apprehensive.

Consequently, nervous about his career, and his life, Colonel Gomez had for the past six months instituted a two-pronged program designed to meet the demands for Indio slaves and relieve his anxieties. He had begun enlisting what were politely referred to in military circles as *guerrilleros*, irregulars. Cloaking them in a similegality, Colonel Gomez had sworn in hundreds of the *bestia* bandidos. They operated without regular pay and were clothed in bits and pieces of uniforms such as the colonel could supply. Ostensibly they were under his authority; but they reported to him only when they pleased, and this was when they brought in the source of their pay: captured Indios.

He had begun the bounty at two hundred pesos per male or female Indio, delivered to him at Nuri. But the price of Indians was determined by the price paid for Apache scalps, and the price of Apache male scalps had lately risen to three hundred pesos. Consequently the irregulars had begun selling scalps, fashioning all hair in the manner of an Apache, so that it was difficult to determine the nationality of the scalp's original owner. Colonel Gomez had been forced to raise the price to three hundred and twenty-five pesos per Indian. To restrain the beastliness of his irregulars, he had laid down rules: The Indio male must be in good health, able to work. The female must be unraped or if raped, the female organs must be undamaged. This last rule was crucial to the second prong of Colonel Gomez's program.

Directly behind his quarters at the western end of Nuri's long cobbled street was the garrison for his soldiers. In the middle of the soldiers' compound squatted a long adobe building sectioned into two parts. In one section were kept the male Indios during their short stay; in the other, the female Indios, who stayed longer. The female Indios were impregnated by his soldiers.

The growing evidence of the success of his program had led to a quiet exultance in the cautious colonel. The male Indios, costing him three hundred and twenty-five pesos, were selling for six hundred locally, to the priest and dons. Those he shipped south brought as high as a thousand pesos per head. He was able, therefore, to satisfy the local powers and yet make a profit for his army superiors, himself, and his captains.

He kept records on his program and laid down careful rules. All Indios were medically inspected, washed, and redressed in sacking. No female Indio might be brutalized any more than was necessary to force her to submit to sexual relations—and that only in the beginning, for after the first or second time, the women became pliable. Assigned to cleaning detail in the barracks and his own quarters, they were held until showing pregnancy and then brought as high a price as males, with the purchaser anticipating a birth that would add to his wealth. It was a brilliant, productive program that satisfied both current and long-range labor objectives. It was a program that was spreading over Mexico, resulting in a large population of mestizos—mixed bloods. Except for Apaches.

The day after Lucia and Mathla's capture Colonel Gomez sat at his desk, facing the open window, from which he could see the long street and front gates of Nuri. He was examining his duty officer's report of the night before. Neatly dressed with epaulets shining, as befitted his nature, he alternated between sipping wine from a long-stemmed glass set on his desk by his Indian concubine and puffing a black cigarillo. Frowning at an entry, he went over it carefully, tracing it with his finger. The entry was noted by the duty officer as paying out six hundred and fifty pesos to irregulars in exchange for two female Indios. It was the notation following the entry that caused his frown. The notation was: Apache.

Closing the record and placing it carefully in his desk, he stared out the window and breathed, "*Excremento!*" The curse was used frequently in Mexico in dealing with the Apache. The Apache refused to be dealt with in any civilized manner. Whereas history proved to the Spaniard that all Indios could be reasonably subdued, and eventually civilized, the Apache was a frustrating enigma. When the Spaniards took Apache as slaves, they retaliated by taking Spaniards as slaves! Unthinkable! When the Mexican soldiers used lances upon them, the Apaches adopted lances, using them with more imaginative cruelty than the soldiers.

Military campaigns against them resulted in long marches of frustration that yielded nothing except retaliatory attacks on villages and towns equaling the horrors of an Attila. Whereas most conquered Indios came to recognize Christianity as their salvation, respecting the Church and its authority, the Apaches blasphemed the Church, burning cathedrals, desecrating altars and the cross, murdering priests and other

155

men of the cloth with indiscriminate abandon. Their murderous practices had led to their name: *los Diablos*—the Devils. As slaves they were intractable, escaping at the slightest opportunity, and even when kept under tight security, becoming homicidal monomaniacs when they obtained alcoholic spirits, murdering anyone within reach.

Colonel Gomez squinted against the sun's heat, rising higher and beating off the cobbled street through his window. He repeated, *"Diablos! Excremento!"* Sighing resignedly, he pushed back his chair, rose, and placing his ornamented cap carefully in place, strode briskly down the cool corridor that led to his troops' compound. Outside he returned the salute of a bearded sergeant who followed him into the compound at a respectful two-step distance.

In the middle of the compound short, sturdy tables were placed against the wall of the Indios' building. There were six of the tables and on them were cages. Built of thick cedar, the cages were small, four feet high, four feet long, four feet wide. These were the "Apache cages," reserved for the infrequent captives of the Apache nation. They were designed so that no freedom of movement was allowed the caged. The inmate could neither stand up nor lie down, but must remain crouched in a folded position.

Colonel Gomez looked through the bars at Lucia, her hands still lashed behind her back. Her head was down between her knees. She did not attempt to look up. He stepped to the adjoining cage and inspected Mathla, in the same position.

"Young!" he said, without looking at the sergeant.

"Sí," the sergeant answered. Colonel Gomez mentally toted up the figures and arranged his arguments to the trader, plying south, to whom he must sell the Apaches. No purchaser in the north of Mexico would buy Apaches. To do so was to court disaster from their bands; besides, being so close to their homeland, invariably they planned escapes. Apaches must go

156

a thousand miles to the south, hauled in cages on the *carros*—the carts. Every Apache thus sold must be clearly branded with an A on the shoulder, so that any purchaser might be forewarned of the possible trouble he was buying. It was a good law that prevented unscrupulous traders from foisting off an Apache as a common, passive Indio.

Colonel Gomez indicated the cages. "Pull them, Sargento. Let us have a closer look." And as the sergeant moved forward, Gomez cautioned, "Remember, they are Apaches . . . watch it!"

The sergeant grinned. Unlashing the cage door, he reached inside, grasping a big fistful of Lucia's hair. In one practiced, powerful motion he jerked her through the door and onto the ground. The sergeant knew that he had great latitude so far as the brutal treatment of Apaches was concerned. Lucia lay on her back, looking up at the colonel and sergeant. Her calico blouse and skirt had been torn, ripped down the front. Now it fell open showing copper skin and small rounding breasts with delicate nipples. An ugly blue knot had formed over her left cheek where an irregular had struck her. Her eyes revealed nothing to the men standing over her. A glaze of stoicism had dropped a curtain over the black pupils. Colonel Gomez stepped close, almost directly over Lucia. He was about to stoop, his hand reaching to fondle at her breasts, when the sergeant shouted, "Colonel!" and jumped, kicking Lucia in the side, rolling her over. Colonel Gomez leaped back as Lucia's feet grazed his pants leg, narrowly missing his groin with a viciously aimed kick. Gomez looked ruefully down at her. "A shame that such a body belongs to an Apache! That we must ship such a *querida* south . . . a shame!"

'Sí," the sergeant agreed. He unlashed the door to Mathla's cage and, grabbing her hair in the same manner, yanked her sprawling onto the ground. He did not loose his hold, but dragged her until she lay alongside Lucia. Her mouth was swollen, caked with blood; the mud smeared on her face might have been the result of tears, but the colonel knew Apaches had no feelings and therefore did not cry. He turned to the sergeant. "Sargento, if you wish, you may summon help. I want it done as quickly as possible. They must be ready to go south *mañana.*"

"No, Colonel," the sergeant replied hastily. "If you please, Colonel, I can handle this. We have only our relief patrol and they are sleeping . . . ah, the wall *guardia* . . . no need to call them from duty."

"All right," Colonel Gomez responded crisply, "get them ready."

The sergeant was a big man. He knelt between the girls and, using the hair of each in turn, lifted their heads, hooking his arms around their necks. He rose with each in a headlock, half-dragging them into the adobe shed.

Colonel Gomez stepped into the doorway to watch the procedure. The room was small with only a high window that gave a twilight to the interior. The floor was stone, and in one corner a blacksmith's pit was flued by a stone chimney. Across the low ceiling a long pole was suspended by a chain at each end, looped around the pole and fastened to the ceiling. The only furnishing was a large wooden tub filled with water.

On entering the room the sergeant flung the two girls, like grain sacks, forward onto the floor. He walked to the blacksmith's pit, where he pumped energetically at a bellows until red glowed through the charcoal. Turning, he picked several iron bars from a corner and nestled their heads in the red coals. Then with a brief look of inquiry at the colonel, and at Gomez's nod of approval, he leaped violently on Lucia's upturned back, striking her with both knees and knocking the wind from her body. Quickly he drew the knife from his belt, slashing the hand ties. Before she could recover, he rolled her to her back.

Whipping the ties expertly, he bound her hands in front. Rising, he repeated the violent operation on Mathla. Now he rose, puffing from his exertion, his cap askew on his head. He was sweating, the moisture rolling from his face downward into his beard. Again Colonel Gomez nodded. The sergeant was a veteran who knew Apaches.

Recovering himself, the sergeant seized Lucia by her knotted hands, jerked her upward, and grabbed her around the waist in a bear-hug. In a quick rush he slammed her against the stone wall, at the same time bringing up a knee to her stomach. She doubled from the pain and loss of breath. While she was in this condition he used one hand to lift the horizontal pole out of its chain loop, the other to raise Lucia's bound hands, then slipped the pole between her arms and raised the pole's end back into the looped chain. She was suspended without a struggle, hands around the pole, her feet barely touching the floor.

He paused, glancing at the colonel. Colonel Gomez nodded. Seizing Mathla from the floor, he repeated the procedure. As he slammed her against the wall a short cry burst from her, then a slight whimper as he strung her hands around the pole's opposite end. Colonel Gomez smiled knowingly. "This one"—he stepped forward to run a hand over Mathla's full breasts—"could possibly be broken in . . . to . . . ah, serve." But as he and the sergeant studied Mathla she relapsed into the blank stoic stare of the Apache.

A shadow fell on the ground at the corner of Colonel Gomez's eye. He turned, irritated at the interruption. "Sí?" he half-shouted at the corporal, who was standing stiffly at salute.

"Colonel?" The corporal was taken aback by the colonel's fury. After all, he had good news.

"Sí! Sí!" Colonel Gomez shouted.

"The wall corporal reports *guerrilleros* coming from the north, Colonel. They have many captured Indios, sir."

159

"Ah! Well . . ." Gomez was mollified by the news. "Many? You say many? How many?"

"The wall corporal says maybe forty . . . maybe fifty, Colonel."

Gomez thought for a moment and snapped his orders at the corporal: "Notify the *alcalde*. For that many, he will want to be present. Tell the wall corporal to break out a squad. Escort the *guerrilleros* down the street and halt them before my quarters. I will be there to settle their claims and receive their Indios."

"Sí, Colonel." The corporal trotted away across the compound. Colonel Gomez started to follow, then, remembering, turned back to the door. "You may stay here, sergeant, and proceed."

"Sí, Colonel," the sergeant answered. He waited while the colonel's back retreated from the door, then watched him disappearing through the rear of his quarters. When the sergeant turned from the door, his expression was changed. He did not wear the mask of subservience on his face. Grinning, white teeth flashing in his beard, he drew the knife from his belt. The girls were watching him now, heads raised, facing each other across a space of six feet. Their eyes were glazed blank, appearing almost uninterested in his actions. But they watched.

With an exaggerated slowness he slid the knife under the clothing of Mathla, slitting the dress, front and back, until she hung naked. His breath was quicker as he finished cutting away Lucia's clothes. He stood back surveying his work.

The girls were slender, supple, Mathla more full-hipped. Their feet supported none of their body weight, and their bronze bodies stretched upward toward their bound hands, the tension emphasizing the curving of hips into slim waists and flat bellies. The strain rounded their thighs subtly, and their taut arms pulled their shoulders back, tightening muscles that pointed the small bud breasts of Lucia upward and thrust the firm, full breasts of Mathla outward.

The sergeant dipped a bucket of water from the tub and, pouring it over Lucia's head and body, began slowly lathering her with soap. Setting the bucket down, he used both his hands. The sergeant intended to enjoy his work.

Colonel Gomez stood attentively before his window, looking down Nuri's lone cobbled street, lined with the adobes that housed stores, cantinas, and cafés. He was watching the open gate at the street's far end. Having ordered the irregulars to be escorted down the street to meet him, he knew it would be improper for him to appear outside, waiting. They must wait on him. He was by nature disciplined, restrained, but even so, it was difficult to contain his exultation. This was the greatest single haul of captive Indios since he had begun his campaign! Forty! He began a mental computation: forty, even at local prices—and this would please the priest and the dons—perhaps a profit of eleven thousand pesos; selling them to the south, as high as twenty-seven thousand. Perhaps he could split them up, selling half to the priest and dons, half to the south. He grew impatient, even with himself. Leaning out the window, he shouted toward a small squad of soldiers standing stiffly at attention beneath him. "Corporal! *Reporte!*"

The corporal detached himself from the squad, running, and inside the building, trotted, panting, to attention before Gomez.

"Colonel?" He saluted.

"How long? Where are they?"

"They are near, Colonel, they . . ." The corporal could see the street through the window; he pointed. "See, Colonel! Now they come!"

Colonel Gomez whirled to the window. The first horses were rounding through the wide gate, entering Nuri's street. Two riders fronted the procession. Behind them a column of riders rode on either side of the prisoners, who walked between them. The irregulars were typical *guerrilleros;* large sombreros shadowed hard and brutal faces. Their uniforms were bits and pieces of cast-offs, here an army coat, there a fancy pantaloon, but all wore crossed *bandoleros* of cartridges on their chests and all carried rifles across their saddles. The rifles, *bandoleros*, and sombreros seemed to be their only common accouterments. This was an unusually large force with perhaps twenty riders flanking single file on either side of the prisoners.

The sound of the horses and the shuffling, dragging feet of the prisoners mounted a low echo in the street. People began gathering on either side to watch. A few soldiers straggled from barracks to stand in the crowd. Merchants came from their stores, and women and children lined the route. As the procession came on, silently, an excitement rose in the voices of those watching. Colonel Gomez strained to see the cause. The two riders leading blocked much of his view, but as the lines stretched out, coming toward him, he could see the prisoners more clearly. They were women! Apache women! There could be no mistake. Their long dresses of calico, torn and muddied, the fashion of their hair identified them beyond a doubt. Gomez saw blood on their faces—the result of having to subdue them. They advanced sullenly, straining back against the ropes about their necks that led to the saddles of the riders. Their hands were tied behind their backs. As Gomez watched, one of the *guerrilleros* sidled his horse toward a prisoner; swinging his rifle in a vicious short circle, he knocked the woman headlong into the street. A cheer rose from the crowd.

"Por Dios!" Gomez exclaimed softly. "They have captured an entire band of the murderers! An entire band!" Colonel Gomez was leaning forward, attempting to estimate the size. Counting the prisoners was difficult, as the *guerrillero* riders, irritated at the prisoners' holding back on their neck ropes, had

begun dashing their horses into them, striking them with rifles and loose ropes.

The corporal was saying something, but Gomez interrupted: "They must have killed the males. I see none of the males as prisoners. The *bestia* have scalped them for bounty. I . . ." The corporal was speaking again, low, but insistent and anxious.

"Eh?" Gomez whirled on him. "What is it?"

"I said, Colonel . . ." The corporal hestated. ". . . that . . . well . . . the horses they ride . . . they make no sound on the cobbles . . . they are not shod."

Gomez looked blankly at the corporal. Somewhere, far back in his consciousness, a warning signal was buzzing at the corporal's remark, but it did not fully register. He moved close to the window, leaning out. The crowds had swelled, lined four deep along the street. More soldiers had come to watch. Someone raised a long cheering shout, and the crowd took up the cheer, chanting, "*Bravo! Bravo soldados! Vivan los soldados de Mexico!* Long live the soldiers of Mexico! *Muerte a los Diablos!* Death to the Devils!" The crowd was stamping time to their chant, tossing hats in the air. This was the greatest delivery ever seen of the Devils, who had caused the dread of sleepless nights, the anxiety of breathless days. The citizens' relief was an avalanche of sound. Colonel Gomez felt a surge of exultation, and suddenly he saw his plan in a new light: Begun as a program to supply slaves, suppose it developed into a campaign to rid northern Mexico of the Devil Apache! Nearly three hundred years had met with failure by generals, presidents . . . even kings! The name "Gomez" would be acclaimed throughout the parliaments of the civilized world!

The *guerrilleros* had halted. Behind the two lead riders Gomez saw some activity among the prisoners. They appeared to be pushing, obviously still unsubdued! As he watched, the prisoners fumbled with their

163

clothes, and their skirts fell to the ground! Gomez's first reaction was disgust at their immodesty; standing half-naked openly before the citizens! But—his thoughts became jumbled, jigsaw-puzzled; their hands were tied! How could they. . . . ? He watched, detached as in a dream cast in the bright, scalding sunlight. There were rifles dangling beside the legs of the prisoners! The prisoners had all carried rifles under their skirts! Colonel Gomez looked dazed, questioning, at the two mounted leaders sitting facing him, not twenty feet away. One was a huge man, the biggest Gomez had ever seen. The other was a blocky soldier who rode slumped in his saddle, his sombrero tilted forward and down. As Gomez watched, the blocky soldier slowly raised his head. He was looking directly at Gomez. He flashed a smile, showing white teeth between thin, slashed lips. Across his cheekbones were two bright stripes of paint. The paint was yellow.

Colonel Gomez's brain would tell him nothing. He was frozen. His lips fumbled with the name of the yellow-painted soldier . . . he knew it from description, but his mind would not yet let him recognize the reality of an impossibility. The crowd's chant was still loud but dying in volume as those closer to the prisoners saw something as unreal as had Colonel Gomez. The chanting was coming from the rear of the crowd, from those who could not see.

Calmly the women prisoners raised their rifles as they turned, backs to one another, to face the crowd on either side. They began firing! The first discharge of rifles clapped thunder between the buildings. The firing was point-blank into lounging soldiers, women, children. For an instant the crowd stood like sheep, waiting to be slaughtered. In that moment the mounted irregulars kicked their horses into action, dashing in quick maneuvers that blocked the open gate of Nuri. Others drummed their horses down the side streets. Hysteria took control of Nuri. People screamed, wild and unreasoning, running squarely into the sides of buildings in blind flight. The "prisoners" were upon them, shooting rapid fire and killing indiscriminately.

The two leaders had raised their rifles and fired point-blank through the window at Gomez and the corporal. The corporal fell, dragging at Gomez with his hands, trying to hold a fading balance. Colonel Gomez felt the blow strike his chest. He staggered, kicking at the corporal. The floor tilted under him. He struggled with his mind, confused still; *all* of them were Apaches! The *guerrilleros* were Apaches! He struggled with the name of the face with yellow stripes. Geronimo! Trying to say the name, coughing great gushes of blood from his mouth, he fell against the wall. It was a trick! He felt hurt at the unfairness of it all.

Blood was pumping from his chest, running down his coat. He stared at the blood; messy. He would need a clean uniform before he went outside to meet the *guerrilleros* and pay them for the Indios. Dimly the screams came to him through the window—horrible, hysterical screams of terror. Some of them choked off quickly. Some trailed away hopelessly like lost souls crying. Rifle shots were exploding, scattered over a wider and wider area. The Devils were in the buildings. They were all through the town, all around him. A soft thud entered the room. Colonel Gomez, his head nodding and wavering, looked up. The blocky soldier was standing before him. But now, he was not a soldier. He had shed his hat, and a war band held his hair in place. Above the waist he was bare, muscles glistening and cording through sheets of sweat and blood. Beneath the stripes of yellow across his cheekbones the figure smiled wickedly. Gomez could not focus his eyes, but the figure helped him; padding softly across the room, he knelt and, extending a hand, held Gomez's head erect. In his other hand he held a long, slender knife. The blade was already bloodied, dripping onto the colonel's uniform. Gomez looked waveringly into the fierce black eyes not six inches from his own. Finally he could say the word, softly.

"Geronimo."

"*Sí*," Geronimo answered as softly. He held the knife blade before the eyes of Gomez. "For your sins, Colonel." And with a quick motion shot the knife into Gomez's throat. Colonel Gomez died without a sound.

Both Lucia and Mathla heard the shots and turned their heads toward the door, but the sergeant smiled. "*Celebración!*" He had washed the girls, fondling their breasts, squeezing and poking, even biting the large breasts of Mathla. After the washings he had taken ropes from the wall and, looping the left ankle of each girl, had drawn the left leg of each outward and upward, tying the end of the rope to the pole.

Now taking an iron from the coals with tongs held in one hand, he advanced to Lucia. The iron bar was a branding iron and the A was glowing red. He hesitated briefly as the shots continued in the distance, growing more numerous, accompanied by wild screams. He shrugged. Lucia watched him, calculating. He moved with apparent carelessness toward her, unbuttoning his pants as he came closer.

Quick as an eyelash she lifted and kicked with her free right foot. As quickly his left hand shot out, grabbing her kicking leg at the calf and pulling it close to his hip. He laughed. "Apache panther, eh? I will give you something you need." Inching his way along her leg, he moved his hand to her knee, now her thigh. Her left leg was helpless, suspended in the air. He was close between her thighs now, and he reached around her left thigh with the hot iron, holding it six inches from her buttocks. He was sweating profusely, panting. "When the iron hits your butt, *querida*, you will bring your treasure to me . . . quick!" He drew back the iron, but could not see as well; the light from the door had suddenly been shut out. He stopped, looking to the door, and blinked his eyes, more at the man standing there than to adjust his sight. He was the biggest man the sergeant had ever seen, completely filling the doorway and bending his huge head and neck to peer inside. The man wore a sombrero, and his chest was crossed with *bandoleros*; a *guerrillero*.

"*Vamos!* Get out!" the sergeant shouted, infuriated at the giant; but the giant did not move. He did not even look at the sergeant. He spoke to the girl! The words were unintelligible to the sergeant. The giant's chest heaved to get out the words: "Lucia, hhhhhave you aaaaaand Mmmmmmmmmath*la* bbbbbbeen hurt?" He spoke Apache! The sergeant dropped the iron clattering on the floor. Foolishly he began buttoning his pants. It was easy, there was no hardness to prevent his action. He backed away from the girl. Lucia smiled. "No, Juh, we have not been hurt," she said calmly. In the sudden quiet, Mathla giggled. The giggling turned to laughter, a little hysterical. Lucia joined her. The scene was insanely ludicrous. The girls, tied naked, suspended from the ceiling, laughing hilariously now. The sergeant stood dumbfounded, not able to take his eyes from the giant.

Juh still had not looked at the sergeant. He was looking at the laughing girls. His craggy face broke into a grin, and he stood for a moment like an embarrassed overgrown boy. Then, as though suddenly remembering, he fastened his gaze on the sergeant. The grin disappeared, and the girls' laughter died. Lifting a gigantic paw to his hat, he pulled it from his head, dropping it to the floor. His hair fell from beneath the hat, framing his face below the war band. The horror struck the sergeant. "Apache!" He screamed the word, unbelieving, and repeated it: "Apache!" He looked around him wildly. It was unreal. No warrior Apache could enter Nuri! There was a mistake—a joke! But he knew it was no joke. His rifle was stacked outside the barracks. He pulled his knife. Holding it before him, pointed at the giant, he backed, taking quick glances behind him. If he stumbled, he knew he would die.

Juh moved after him, padding with the soft, fluid motion of a lightweight. Backing, the sergeant moved left to give Mathla a wide berth. Juh followed, crouching with his arms held wide, like a wrestler seeking a grip. At his waist he carried a holstered pistol and a knife, but he made no move toward either weapon. In the distance rifle shots were cracking, exploding in rolling echoes with yells and screams; but in the room there was only the sound of the sergeant's heavy boots scraping stone, and the breathing of both men. Juh did not move in close; instead he allowed the sergeant to back slowly away. He followed, keeping a short distance between them.

Rifle shots were closer now, in the compound outside the room and in the soldiers' barracks. There was a sudden explosion of rapid fire, yells, screams, and the flurry of firing subsided to lone, spaced shots.

Neither of the two men paid any attention to the sound of rifles. They were watching each other's eyes. The sergeant's back touched the corner of the walls. Quickly he looked. There was no more room. Carefully Juh took another gliding step toward him. The movement brought desperation to the sergeant. He lunged, knife pointed forward like a fencer, straight at the giant chest. The chest didn't move, but from the side a huge hamlike hand moved faster than the sergeant's, swooping and grabbing the wrist of the knife hand. The grip tightened. The sergeant swung his left fist at the hard face and felt his left wrist seized in the same manner. The knife fell ringing on the floor.

Now they stood, bodies almost together. The sergeant was a big and powerful man, but his head reached only to the chest of Juh. Slowly Juh forced his hands upward, still gripping the wrists. Below his beard, great cords of effort stood ridgelike on the sergeant's neck; sweat popped in great balls from his face. Every ounce of strength in the sergeant's powerful shoulders could not stop, or even bring pause to, the inexorable movement of his arms, up and back. His mouth flopped open. He screamed at the same moment his arms cracked like dried sticks. Juh released him and glided back a step. Then, sweeping his big hands together, Juh seized the sergeant's head from either side, viselike. He placed his thumbs in the sergeant's eyes and pushed. The eyeballs popped, spewing miniature shots of blood and jelly onto Juh's chest. The sergeant's screams were inhuman as Juh threw him to the floor and stood over him, watching almost meditatively while the helpless arms flopped without control, attempting to claw at the bloody sockets where eyes had been.

"Juh." A quiet voice spoke from the door. Juh whirled. It was Ishton. She was carrying a rifle, and around her waist, a cartridge belt. Instead of a skirt she was wearing a warrior's breechclout. Juh's eyes softened. The wild light died and reasoning returned to them.

"Kill him, Juh," Ishton said. "Kill him now." Stooping and wrapping a hand in the sergeant's hair, lifting his head, Juh swung his right hand in a swift ax motion and chopped the sergeant's neck, breaking it. Without a word he padded through the door, outside into the compound, leaving the care of the girls to Ishton.

Dead soldiers lay in uniformed wheat rows. They had rushed confused from the barracks and had dashed into withering rifle from the building tops. Milling about, running first in one direction, then another, they had fallen in almost neat files across the compound. A few citizens and soldiers had escaped Nuri, running through the back gate, leaping from rooftops over the wall. It was they who later identified Ishton as the leader of the women warriors, and Juh, whom the Mexicans called Capitán Juh. This

Apache guerrilla-leader team of husband and wife was already infamous in Mexico. Their successes in planning and executing unorthodox warfare would inspire books studying their tactics. Identified also at Nuri was Geronimo.

Silhouetted atop a building above the compound, he was even now directing quick operations below him. A long string of mules and the best horses Nuri had to offer stood in the compound, brought from the corrals. The Apaches were working swiftly and silently, loading the mules. First to go on the packs were the war weapons of the Enemy: rifles, pistols, cartridge belts, boxes of ammunition. Next, cheese, sugar, flour, dried beef, and fruits, and last, bolts of cloth, iron tools and utensils, soldiers' uniforms and women's clothing.

Geronimo alternated his attention between directing the activities in the streets and sweeping the horizon with binoculars. The sun was tilting toward the edge of the plains in the west. As the last mule was loaded he leaped from the building and mounted his horse. This was the signal, and every Apache, man and woman, mounted behind him on files of horses flanking the long line of mules. With a silent arm wave he led them out of the compound, past the rows of dead soldiers, horses shying and snorting at the smell of blood and death. Enormous black clouds of blowflies had already begun their work. Their instinct told them they must be quick, to eat and lay the fast-hatching eggs that would bring maggots to feed, and so propagate their kind.

Down the long cobbled street of Nuri the procession moved, slow and shuffling. The clouds, earlier chased away by the sun, returned in the coolness and drew a shadow over them. The horses picked their way over and around the crumpled bodies. The pack mules were not so well mannered. They were watched by many sightless eyes. A woman sat, legs sprawling, in a doorway. Her head rested comfortably against the doorjamb. Long black hair tumbled over her shoulders, and she seemed to be leisurely watching a parade, except her eyes were dead. Many lay or sat in calm repose, while others hung from windows they had tried to crawl through. Where buildings came together to make sheltered corners, small piles of bodies lay as though swept there to be gathered later. Where they had cowered, huddling together in horror, they had been shot. The cooling of twilight brought wind sighing softly down the street, lifting and picking at the clothing of the dead as if urging them to stand, to come to life. Around the building corners the wind whined and whistled through crevices and windows. The scene would shock Mexico and bring rage to the state of Sonora.

Through the gate, the procession swung wide and turned into a half circle to stop, facing Geronimo. Here, he called for volunteers, and when half the riders stepped their horses forward, he rode among them, selecting only three, placing his hand on their shoulders. These three aligned their horses beside Geronimo, and they watched as the Nedni band, in practiced precision, split their force into small groups. Each group consisted of four to six Apache men and women. Leading mules, these teams moved away toward the Sierra Madre. They proceeded fanwise from Nuri, each on a separate course. They would leave twenty thin and difficult trails to follow, keeping their initial direction for three days and nights over mountain backs, through canyons, and along rocky slopes before they began converging on the east side of the Madre at a rendezvous of all their people. The team including Ishton and Juh was the last to leave. As they walked their horses and mules across the plateau both turned, and Ishton called, "We will wait at the place for you. We will wait." Juh swung his arm high in farewell and was answered by Geronimo and the three, waving. Then, they were gone.

With their leaving, Geronimo and the three dismounted. They donned soldiers' coats, crossing *bandoleros* of cartridge belts across their chests and buckling pistols around their waists. Pushing their hair up into the sombreros, they laughed shortly, with a grim humor, at one another's appearance. Mounting, the three trailed closely behind Geronimo. The trail led north.

The twilight had deepened. Behind them a dog barked, then howled, frantic and alone in the death of Nuri. The wind, blustering sand bursts, swung the hanging body of Colonel Gomez back and forth from the crossbeam of the town gate. Driven into the ground at his feet was an iron with its brand pointing upward toward the colonel. The brand was an A, the iron a symbol the Apaches hated even more than the Spanish lance.

14

Generals of field armies plan maneuvers and logistics of attack. The more successful study the characters of the opposing generals, and spend much time theorizing about their opponent's reaction to their own actions, and from there the countering action they will initiate. Buffs call this "Death Chess," a deadly game that has fascinated "civilized" men for centuries. On occasion, the generals must plan holding actions, even retreats, but they are relieved of the dual planning that weighs heavy on the guerrilla leader. The generals have no need to plan escapes.

Apache guerrilla leaders depended upon surprise for the initial success of their attack. Surprise, often heightened by the Apaches' ability to create illusions, brought a momentary immobility, stunned their opponents. Instant action and merciless execution developed that immobility into terror. Terror developed chaos and unreasoning action, which did not allow the mental recovery necessary for a counterattack by superior numbers which could have overwhelmed the Apache.

Illusion, surprise, terror—all mental reactions which were the weapons of the Apache guerrillas. Always, they were numerically inferior, usually more poorly armed, and were forced to strike the enemy deep within his own territory, away from their beloved sanctuary of the Madre. Thus, the plan of escape was of equal importance with the plan of attack.

When the Nedni band discovered Lucia and

Mathla's capture, they knew they must strike quickly to save them. Apache male captives were usually killed by the Mexicans, but Apache females were shipped far south to slavery without delay. Few escaped to make the long trek back.

While Ishton was the author of the attack plan on Nuri and much of the tactics belonged to Juh, the overall direction of attack and escape belonged to Geronimo. Immediately upon learning the whereabouts of Lucia and Mathla, Geronimo had put his preparations in motion. He sent two scouts with binoculars to a prominence overlooking Nuri. Those men, women, and children not in the attacking force broke camp and scattered to the southeast across the spine of the Sierra Madre, toward the rendezvous on the eastern slope of the mountains where the attackers would meet them after Nuri.

By the time the attacking force left Yaqui Canyon, the two warrior scouts gave Geronimo detailed descriptions of the soldier patrols—the direction they took, their size, the number of pack mules accompanying them, telltale evidence of distance they planned to cover from the town.

The attack was successful, no Apache was killed. But even as the fighting continued, Geronimo was atop a building, studying through binoculars the route of those who were escaping on horses. He paid no attention to those running on foot. Those on foot run in terror *from* something, and so their direction means nothing. Those on horseback, more secure, run *to* something: the nearest known concentration of soldiers. The riders had fled north.

This was the direction in which Geronimo now led the three riders behind him. They were to meet, halt, and divert several hundred soldiers riding head-on toward them. The Nedni band was in need of time to escape across the Madre. Geronimo and the three others were to give them that time. Typical of the Apache mind, they did not envision failure in meeting a force of overwhelming numerical superiority. If their people had done so, they would never have fought slavery against just such odds for nearly three hundred years.

The binoculars hanging about his neck were useless to Geronimo now. Darkness was lowering. The wind quieted and died. Behind him the three rode in single file. Although he had picked them with a seeming casualness, this was not so. He knew their particular characters.

Immediately behind him rode a slight warrior called Fun. He had acquired the name from bluecoats of the north where he was a victim of the white man's peculiar sadistic pleasure in making the Indian appear ridiculous in the ways of white society. Fun, believing all actions were honest expressions, endeavored to be friends with the white eyes. He drank with the soldiers and accepted their lavish offers of more drinks, in the eternal Indian naïveté that sees no ulterior motives. When the soldiers induced him to dance, he danced. It made them happy, for they laughed. Fun laughed too. When they began shooting at his feet, he had run drunkenly, trying to escape the shots, alarmed at the soldiers' sudden enmity. They had called him "Funny"; the name had been shortened. Many soldiers would die at the hands of Fun. His name would figure prominently in United States Army records. He was lighthearted, a daredevil, but he was also a sensitive, skilled, and deadly warrior.

Chokole rode behind Fun. She was a handsome woman, strong-faced, lithe of body. Over fifty years of age, she was a benevolent grandmother to the two children of her daughter. Twenty-five years before, Mexicans had captured her husband. When the Apaches found him in a ditch near Honas, he was still breathing. His eyes had been poked out; strips of skin had been peeled from his body and his genitals cut off and stuffed in his mouth. Since then, Chokole had

175

refused all offers of marriage. Nuri had not been her first battle engagement nor was this her first action of rear-guard diversion. She was quick and sure with weapons, suicidally fearless. She would not be known to United States Army records, but in Mexico she was well marked for death, second only to Ishton among the women warriors.

At the rear old Nana rode. He was crippled, and wrinkled with age. Deeply loved by all Apache children, he was a kindly grandfather who told them stories without end and laughed at jokes they played on him. He was a whittler of toys and maker of dolls. For well over fifty years, before any of the other three had been born, he had been fighting and killing Spaniards and Mexicans. Although a close friend of the young Victorio, like Geronimo he had come south because there was the word of peace in the north. Nana was a man of war. Thirty years later, United States Army authorities would piece together an incredible (to them) story; how this old man, whom they had ignored as senile and crippled, had led bands of Apache warriors that devastated thousands of square miles in Arizona and New Mexico. The Mexicans knew him well, having for many years placed a high bounty on his head. They would never have to pay.

Minuscule in size, this force of Geronimo's had combat capabilities that included absolute coolness under fire, the boldness required for guerrilla skills, and high kill-power. Military miscalculations were continually made by United States and Mexican generals, who looked upon individuals as ciphers in a numerical mass. To the Apache, few in number, the individual was viewed as a unit of one with strengths and weaknesses thoroughly analyzed by war leaders such as Geronimo.

Thus Geronimo knew the strengths of his force, its greatest being that there were few, if any, weaknesses. The plan he had outlined briefly at the gates of Nuri had met with no objections from the three. Now, as they rode farther north in the darkness, ears alert for sounds of horsemen ahead of them, there was but one weakness in the plan—none of them knew the identity and thus the character of the general who would be their opponent.

In most cases where Apaches faced field generals of armies, their identities did not matter; there was no need to know their character and their thinking. They were all alike in applying cumbersome field maneuvers, inept and ineffective against the Apaches. This general was cut from different cloth.

He was rated, as an Indian fighter, the equal of General Luis Terrazas and Colonel Joaquin Terrazas. Twenty years before, he had been sent south to subdue an organized uprising of Zapotec Indians. He had done so, effectively and with ruthless dispatch.

Recently, he had been ordered to Sonora with authority over all military operations. Unlike most generals, he respected the fighting qualities of the Apache, recognizing an unorthodox application of genius to their guerrilla operations. He allowed no military books or rules to prejudice his thinking.

Once when asked if he were a religious man, he had answered, "Only when I am not in northern Mexico."

"Why is that, General?"

"To be a religious man," he replied, "one must attend mass. In order to attend mass, one must bow one's head. In northern Mexico, I am sure; the priest before whom I bow my head could be an Apache in disguise."

He understood much, not all, but much of the Apache. More important, he was willing to learn more. He had very little egotism, a great deal of intelligence, and was therefore a very dangerous man. His name was General Geronimo Trevino and, at this moment, he headed six hundred crack troops riding

177

in a direct line toward Geronimo's band, not ten miles distant. To negotiate the narrow mule trail from Ures to Nuri, the troops rode two abreast, strung out in a long line. In the middle, the line was split; a quarter mile of space separated the leading three hundred troopers from three hundred who followed, a cautionary tribute to the Apaches' willingness to ambush any size force.

General Trevino was pacing his column, cantering across open flats and slowing down to walk over sharp rises and through arroyos. He was in a hurry, knowing the Apaches would flee toward the Madre, but broken horses' legs would not help. There was no moon and the low clouds hid even the stars. As he topped a rock-broken rise he halted suddenly. By his side, a colonel shouted, "*Alto!* Halt!" and the order was repeated back through the night. Horses stamped impatiently, jingling harness and creaking their leathers. Staff officers behind him rode up beside the general.

Through binoculars they studied a great bonfire on the flats three hundred yards in front of them. The fire was almost on the trail and spread a brilliant circle of light. Within the circle, a single rider sat his horse. He obviously meant to be seen and was waiting for that purpose. He wore a great sombrero, an army coat with crossed *bandoleros*. While the general and his officers studied him, his horse snorted and pranced, but the rider held the horse within the circle of light.

"*Guerrillero . . . irregular*," the colonel suggested. General Trevino continued studying the scene. He swept his binoculars across the small plateau but could see little beyond the circle of light. Bringing his glasses back to the man, he watched him for a time. Turning to an officer, he spat rapid orders, and the officer immediately raced his horse to the rear. The general raised the glasses to his eyes again, watching the rider in the firelight. "*Acaso*," he said mildly. "Maybe." Something about the man had set off an alarm in his brain; perhaps when the horse had pranced. The man had moved too easily with the horse, as though he were a part of the animal, the way an Apache rode.

The general relaxed in his saddle. Pulling a long black cigar from his coat, he placed it meditatively between his teeth. The colonel leaned from his saddle and struck a match. While a low murmur of protest ran down the line of troops behind him, General Trevino sat and smoked; and said nothing. He was waiting for the messenger he had sent to the rear to deliver his instructions. Five minutes ticked by; ten. The general raised his hand. *"Vamos!"* He led his column down the incline and onto the plateau.

As he entered the light circle, General Trevino motioned the colonel forward to interrogate the man who was now watching the troops with placid attention. Behind Trevino, his column broke into squads, and in a practiced maneuver, formed a semicircle around the rider and the light. Trevino sat his horse within ten yards of the rider, but off to the side so that he might observe without giving his attention to speech.

The bonfire was beginning to wane, lessening the light flickering over the rider and his horse. He looked small in the center of the growing half circle of soldiers that swept around him; but now he urged his horse forward, close to the colonel and officers. He was Fun.

Smiling, he flashed white teeth and touched his sombrero with an awkward salute. *"Buenas noches,* general!" he sang out pleasantly.

"I am Colonel," the colonel answered sharply. He had a civilized officer's disgust for *guerrilleros.* "What do you want?"

"Sí, Colonel." Fun's eyes swept the knot of officers who sat their horses off to the side. His gaze fastened on General Trevino. The general noted the eyes; they

were reckless, with a hint of wildness in them—perhaps a glint of humor. About what? What was there to be humorous about? The general shifted uncomfortably in his saddle and tried to peer past the light, into the darkness.

"Well!" The colonel spoke harshly. "What is it?" Fun turned his attention to the colonel. Apparently he was not discomfited by the colonel's irritation. *"Mi capitán."* Fun half-turned in his saddle and, lifting his rifle, pointed west, where the darker gloom of the Madre loomed past the plateau. *"Mi capitán,"* he repeated with exasperating monotony, "has sent me here to intercept you. We have the Apache killers of Nuri, yonder." Fun jabbed his rifle again toward the mountains. "They are caught in a canyon, Colonel. We need help. We have trapped them . . . but they are many. We need help."

The colonel looked toward the mountain and quickly over his shoulder toward General Trevino. The general advanced his horse to face the man, with him a dozen officers.

"Who is your *capitán?"* Trevino shot the question before he had halted his horse. Fun did not answer too quickly. He smiled, again raised his hand to his sombrero, holding it awkwardly until General Trevino impatiently snapped a salute in return.

"Mi capitán es Capitán Martinez, General," Fun said cheerfully, and added with enthusiasm, *"Es un capitán bueno,* General . . . *sí, bueno!"* Trevino pulled on his cigar, narrowing his eyes in the smoke as he watched the features of the young man. The firelight was growing dim.

"Are you Indio?" he asked suddenly.

"Sí," Fun smiled broadly, *"indio."*

"What nation?"

Fun's eyes swept the troops lounging on their horses. He could not see them too well, but he spotted the Papago scout. Fun did not speak Papago.

"Yaqui," he said. General Trevino nodded to an

officer at his side. The officer turned his horse and trotted into the ranks. In a moment he returned. Riding by his side was a slender man dressed in a Mexican trooper's coat. His legs were bare and he wore moccasins. Black hair fell below his shoulders. He was a Yaqui scout. Fun also did not speak Yaqui.

He knew he was trapped, but sat impassively as the Yaqui sidled his horse close, touching the leg of Fun. He stared intently into Fun's eyes. Slowly his mouth widened in a wicked grin. "San-o-le-yeh." His speech was deliberately spaced and menacing.

Fun did not understand him, but he returned the look, his own smile twisting into a sneer. He answered the Yaqui in Spanish, low and hissing, "I am well, Yaqui traitor dog!" The Yaqui's hand shot forward, and he jerked the sombrero from Fun's head. Bush hair fell from beneath the sombrero. The hair was held in place by a war band.

"Apache!" the Yaqui shouted. It was his last word. A rifle cracked from the darkness of the plateau and knocked the Yaqui from his saddle. Fun shot the colonel in the chest. Whirling and rearing his horse, he charged it into the group of officers before him. Another rifle cracked, and another, again, and again. An officer screamed at Trevino's side, falling and grabbing at the general. Fun sped his horse toward the darkness at the western end of the plateau. As he passed from the light, the soldiers had recovered from their shock and were shooting. Fun's horse coughed and fell. He flung himself free, striking the ground and rolling away from the puffs of bullets kicking up sand. Lying on his stomach, he groped and found the rifle he had dropped and looked back toward the dying light of the fire. The soldiers were not charging. They had backed away from the light and disappeared.

Fun crawled deeper into the darkness and saw the horses. Geronimo, Nana, and Chokole were standing by them, waiting for him.

"Behind me," Geronimo called as they swung on the horses. Fun leaped, settling himself on Geronimo's horse, holding him around his waist. Raising the horses to a gallop, they headed them toward the western lip of the plateau and the mountains beyond. Suddenly, before them, hundreds of small flames spouted in their faces, accompanied by ear-shattering claps of explosions. Rifles! Geronimo's horse fell, throwing him and Fun tumbling. Nana's horse fell immediately afterward and Chokole's made a galloping stride past them before it screamed, twisting in a fall that trapped her leg beneath it. As instantaneously as the rifle fire had begun, it stopped. There was silence.

Chokole ran her hand along the trapped leg. The leg had no feeling, it was broken. She still held her rifle and with the barrel tapped softly on the ground. It was Geronimo who crawled to her and, motioning behind him, brought Nana and Fun forward. The two pushed, lifting up the horse as Geronimo pulled her free. Two hundred yards away, from where the rifle shots had come, a fire flared, then another and another. Geronimo lay down beside Chokole and turned, his back to her. He motioned for her to place her body close, and as she did, holding his shoulders, he rolled to his stomach in an easy motion that brought him to his hands and knees with Chokole on his back. They began crawling toward the center of the plateau. Fires were flaring magically around the plateau's edge. In the center was the only place of complete darkness. They were trapped in a ring of light.

The plateau was a small mesa that sat like a round tabletop supported by rocky slopes that inclined upward to its rim. It was bare and flat. General Trevino had held his troops back from charging after Fun. He knew he had the Apaches caught; the messenger he had sent back to the three hundred troops at his rear had delivered instructions to circle and surround the mesa from the west. Now, at his instructions, great brushfires were being set, close together, completely encircling the mesa in a spectacular ring of leaping flames. Where the light fell, the little mesa was bright as day. The bonfires were built higher, making the light lap inward, like water eroding at the small circle of darkness in the center. General Trevino could not determine how many Apaches he had trapped there; perhaps he had all, or at least a goodly number of the killers of Nuri. From his force of six hundred, the general's captains detailed two hundred troops to feed the fires, and though their greatest efforts did not erode the small circle of darkness at the center, they were sure that no Apache could escape before morning. The mesa had no vegetation, no rock cover— not even a pebble. Its surface was sand.

Geronimo dropped to his stomach and rolled over gently, laying Chokole on her back. He had reached the circle of darkness and now did not look at the flaring fires; instead, he concentrated his attention on Chokole, running his hands over her leg. He grunted when he found the lump where the bone had broken, jagged and disconnected inside the flesh. Motioning for Nana and Fun to hold Chokole's shoulders, he jerked on the leg. The bone snapped in place. Sweat streamed down Chokole's face, dripping from her set jaw and chin. She made no sound as Geronimo pulled the leather *bandoleros* from his chest. Slipping the bullets from their loops, he bound the heavy leather around the leg and sat back for the first time, looking around them at the great fires.

Fun crawled close to him. "Geronimo?"

"Yes?"

"I saw a Papago with them . . . I did not see the Yaqui . . . maybe if I said I was Pima . . ."

Geronimo looked at the young man and half-smiled in the darkness. "They would have had a Pima too. It is the general, Fun, not you, that has put us here. The general is very smart. I did not think. Chokole shot the Yaqui at the right time."

Chokole had raised herself on her elbows and was looking at the fires. "Any time," she chuckled, "is a good time to shoot a Yaqui who is working for Mexicans."

Old Nana sat cross-legged beside her. He was working the breech of his rifle, blowing at the sand clogging its mechanism. "Well," he remarked dryly, "we may not have the Mexicans following us north, but I will say this for our plan. It is working. We have the entire Mexican army camped with us for the night."

Fun looked to his own rifle, slipping a bullet into the chamber, locking it in place. "Maybe," he said, "if we charged one place, toward the fires . . . maybe . . . we could . . ."

"No," Geronimo answered, "there is too much light. They can see us if we move ten feet from this place."

"In the morning," Fun said, "they will see us here . . . easy."

"Yes," Geronimo said. His voice was musing. "Yes, they will see us here in the morning . . . if we are here."

"You may have yours, in your pocket," Nana grunted, "but I forgot to bring my wings."

The fires were making great whooshing noises as soldiers threw brush on them, floating sparks high in the air over the mesa. Dimly from a distance, softly, a new sound was beginning. It lifted, growing stronger, and became a great chorus, rising above the crackling fire sounds. The soldiers were singing! They were singing together, six hundred voices that echoed on the still air. Now drum tappings and the brass sound of trumpets lifted with the song, savagely beautiful; the sound carried an ominous feeling of impending doom. Beneath the beauty, the song conveyed a feeling of ferocity that tingled the nerves and brought a knowledge that one was experiencing an expression of man's basest lust, loosed and unrestranied.

"It is the Dequela—the no-quarter song, the Death Song," Nana said, listening. "I have heard it before."

"I did not know," Fun remarked conversationally, "that the Mexicans had a Death Song."

Old Nana laughed. "Not their death. Ours. That is what they are singing. They are saying in their song they will give us no mercy. We cannot surrender. They are going to kill us without mercy. They will lance us and kill as slowly as they can . . . but they will kill."

Geronimo spat. "We already knew that. They are stupid to waste their song on Apaches."

Chokole rolled, picking up her rifle. It must be cleaned. She patted the stock. "For some of them," she said, "it is their Death Song, when they come in the morning."

"Yes," Fun echoed her, "for some of them." He still worried at his choice of being a Yaqui. However, he comforted himself, he did not speak Pima either.

Geronimo had crawled away from the four to the perimeter's edge of darkness. He sat cross-legged, his back to the group, looking above the fires. He was looking into the sky.

General Trevino recorded it in his notes for the record. His encircling maneuver had trapped the Apaches. Brush teams were working, feeding the fires. His soldiers were singing, passing the night. Their song was the Dequela, reminding their enemies of death in the morning. The air was heavy. There was no wind, not even a breeze. At some point, as the soldiers sang, a new sound began, far away, hollow, thin, wailing above the soldiers' deep chorus. For a time the soldiers did not notice. General Trevino noted that for a time he thought the sound might be in his own mind . . . not of the physical ear. As the sound persisted, rising, the soldiers' voices faded, dying, until only the fires crackling and whooshing upward—and the thin wail—came to their ears.

The air, General Trevino noted, became oppressive,

threatening, sullen. The general's choice of descriptive words is revealing; "threatening, sullen, oppressive" are descriptions of moods, of emotions. Only perceptive life, not dead matter, can be credited with these qualities.

Man has become enamored of the physical sciences, useful to the white man's material progress, but alien to the progress of the spiritual Great Force. Like a child playing with blocks, stacking them higher and higher, man cries in frustration when his materialism falls. He has learned to dissect, weigh, and measure the physical. He knows that the air around the earth weighs six million billion tons, that it is composed of 78 percent nitrogen and 21 percent oxygen, with smaller components of other gases. He knows heated air expands and rises, that cooler air moves downward, that air collects water vapor, condenses it, and carries rain around the earth, that nothing on earth could live without air or its activity. Carrying pollen and spores, air impregnates plants with Life, plunges into the earth to carry oxygen to the root mouths of all plants and into the waters to bring Life to the inhabitants of its body. Man knows with scientific certainty that air acts as an oxidizing agent, releasing heat and energy, Life, without which nothing could live. But man cannot control this, and so, with the arrogance of his mind mastery over the material, dismisses it as a natural happening whose purpose is mindless. When he cannot master or chooses not to understand the world, he interprets its material qualities only. He dismisses all else.

Not so with the Apache. For centuries the Apache had depended upon Will, Spirit, for survival. Considering themselves a part of, not a master of, all things around them and feeling no arrogance toward these things, they attributed the same Will and Spirit to them. They had observed that all things have Life, and therefore Purpose. Raising their hands, they had caught the pollen in the wind and observed its journey to the plants hungering for their Life's propagation. They had seen the wind bring rain, scattering it across the Life parts for their needs. If not a creator of Life, then Wind was a conductor of Life . . . as was man. Therefore, Wind had Purpose, and so, Spirit. To the Apache the moods of Wind were real, not poetic; sullen, tempestuous, tender, soothing, violent, fresh, stale, loving—expressions of their own Spirit temper.

That night General Trevino recorded the wind's effect. Nana, Chokole, and Fun told how it came. The thin, hollow wailing that reached the ears of Trevino and the soldiers was Geronimo. First, he faced the south, sitting cross-legged, arms resting before him. He began a tone chant. Turning, he faced the west, continuing the tone, then the north and the east. The tone rose higher, and as the decibels of sound reached the upper threshold of the human ear's ability to record them, they broke, in staccato notes; passing beyond the threshold, where the human ear could not hear, they became vibrations on the air, pounding at first, then pulsating in a rhythm, a harmony. This was the Life Chant of Geronimo, a petitioning for Life, in the way of the burro brush, the piñon, the cactus.

Chokole, Nana, and Fun, lying within the circle of darkness, felt the vibrations growing stronger. Fun later said that as he lay and listened, then felt, the hair of his head stiffened. Chokole and old Nana told of their skin tingling, of a great anticipation coming over them, an expectation.

Then, where the fires lighted the mesa, they saw the first tiny dust whirl. It lifted, dancing before a fire. Moving erratically in a pattern across the mesa, it joined another, larger whirl. These whirling miniature dust storms came together and gathered strength, one from the other. Now around the circle of light other tiny whirls were lifting from the mesa floor, merging,

187

gathering strength, until dozens of them, dancing, merging, became fewer and larger.

The dozens of dust whirls, forming no higher than a man's knee, raced toward the larger whirls, merging and growing taller than a man; still taller. They were no longer composed of dust. With their growing strength they were picking up sand from the mesa. Billions of sand grains, grating together, whipping in the force of wind, began a sound. Low and ominous in its monotony, the sound rose higher to an alto, and as the whirls merged together, lifting their open mouths to the sky, the alto became a soprano scream. The sand whirls were so great now, their force so powerful, that the scream rose higher, wild, hysterical. Imperceptibly the sound assumed a depth, a character, a mood; the emotion of the wind became a ferocity—a ferocity of madness.

Chokole, Nana, and Fun covered their faces. They could no longer see the fires, or Geronimo a few feet from them. They felt his hand as he touched each in turn; then, laying his body close to Chokole, he rolled her onto his back and began crawling through the storm. Nana touched the leg of Chokole as he crawled, and Fun behind him touched Nana's leg. Neither of them could see. Chokole knew when they reached the edge of the mesa, for the back of Geronimo tilted downward as he crawled. Off the mesa there were dim shapes; some she thought were soldiers, but she could not be sure. The shapes were low and rounded and could have been rocks, or soldiers hiding their faces from the wind and sand.

For a long time they moved downward; as they leveled off, ghostly outlines of bush and tree became apparent, whipping tortured in the wind. Chokole smelled the horses before they came to them, a long line, secured on a single rope. Geronimo rolled her to the ground and lifted her, swinging her astride the Spanish saddle of a big roan. Geronimo, Nana, and Fun selected their own horses carefully, mounted, and headed into the Madre with Chokole riding in the middle of their bunched horses.

The wind was at their backs, pushing them and rolling tumbleweeds and uprooted brush past them as they walked the horses. Upward, the ground tilting slowly, then becoming steeper. The horses scrambled to hold their footing until they reached the plateaus, then walked easily to the next ridge of mountain. Behind and below them they could hear the wind storm, howling and screaming through arroyos and whipping across flats. Here the air was quiet, tranquil.

When the first rays of dawn touched the sky, vast and bluing across Sonora's plains below them, they were three thousand feet high in the Madre, atop the prominence of a narrow mountain. Geronimo stopped their horses, and looking below with his binoculars, he grunted in satisfaction. Grinning, he passed the glasses to the others. Below them they could see squads of mounted soldiers chasing horses who had bolted in the storm. The air was still, clear, and wonderfully fresh. The sun sparkled on the tiny mesa here they had been trapped the night before; around it tiny wisps of smoke marked where the fires had burned and died in the storm.

For three days they rode over and through the back of the Madre, always to the southeast. Almost leisurely they allowed their horses to set the pace, up the sides of magnificent mountains, along the ridges of their spines, into swales of mountain cradles holding rushing waters and rich growths of trees and wild flowers. On the morning of their fourth day, from high on the peak of a rocky butte, they built a fire, and pulling a blanket from one of the horses, they smothered the fire briefly to allow one great ball of smoke to roll in the sky. Through binoculars they watched the south. Within the hour they were rewarded. From a high, narrow peak, far south, another smoke ball lifted lazily. Resuming their ride, they were met in the afternoon by a welcoming party of Nednis. Juh, jubilant to see them, was leading the riders. He had brought water bags filled not with water but with tiswin. Passing the bags around to Geronimo's band and consuming ample draughts himself, he would not have Chokole ride any farther. While she drank from a bag, his men fashioned splints for her leg and a free-swinging sling between horses. In this happy state they proceeded to the Nednis' rancheria, a small mesa backed by mountains with a sparkling spring.

The celebration continued through the night and next day. In the evening of the second day Geronimo was called upon to recite the exploits of his small party of riders. He was not among the crowd of celebrants. Juh found him at the edge of the mesa. He was lying flat on a high rock, studying the progress of a mule train, winding slowly, headed north across Chihuahua's plain.

The horror and outrage of Nuri had inflamed Sonora with a madness for revenge. Troops were being organized into striking forces. Some of these troops were being withdrawn, even from Chihuahua. And so Geronimo watched, and calculated, and planned.

15

Events far to the north would alter Geronimo's plans for a Chihuahua campaign. Chief Josecito of the Mescalero Apaches, with a party of prominent leaders of his people, had journeyed all the way to Santa Fe in the cause of peace. There he reported to United States government authorities that his people were tending crops and keeping peace. He and his leaders even requested that the United States build a fort in the midst of his country to protect his people from unscrupulous whites.

Chief Josecito was unaware of the murderous intent of the United States government. It was stated succinctly by Washington's own Indian Bureau agent, E. A. Graves, who wrote:

> That this race are destined to a speedy and final extinction, seems to admit of no doubt . . . all that can be expected from an enlightened and Christian government, such as ours, is to graduate and smooth the passway of their final exit from the state of human existence.

Josecito's entreaties were rewarded by the United States Army's surrounding his people and driving them from the White Mountains onto the reservation at Bosque Redondo. Here, on an arid region of flats, there were no trees, not even brush to build a wickiup. The Mescaleros dug holes in the ground, living like prairie dogs in heat that hovered above a hundred and ten degrees. No crops would grow. Rations from the Indian Bureau, dictated by Washington, were cut to starvation level. Swarms of biting sand flies and mosquitoes settled over the Mescaleros. They began to die. When Josecito protested this treatment, he was murdered.

Several years earlier General Carleton, commanding the Department of New Mexico, had made clear the United States Army's intent in an order to his subordinates: "Kill all Indian men wherever you find them. If they should attempt to ask for peace, tell them we have been sent to punish them for their treachery and their crimes; that we have no power to make peace." This order had been broadened by a "gentlemen's agreement" to unofficially authorize the killing of Indian women and children.

Given this background of officialdom's approval and intent of extermination, one might understand Lieutenant George Bascom's arrogance. Except for an infrequent raid on ranches or mining camps by outlaw Apache bands, there had generally been peace, with the Apaches submitting almost passively to the inevitable. Those who submitted died quickly and wretchedly almost without protest. Generally the United States Army had seen no indications of fighting qualities in these Indians and regarded the Apaches as no more than ragtag thieves.

By his actions, Lieutenant Bascom was to alter that impression. The United States government would discover the fighting qualities of the Apache in a war far more costly in lives, money, and materials than all the Indian wars in its history.

When Bascom sent word to Cochise to meet him for a conference at Apache Pass, Cochise saw no reason for alarm. He had kept his word. There was peace, despite the growing number of forts and the flood of white men into the Apache lands. He often visited the stage station at Apache Pass; he knew the white people there, and many of his own people supplied wood and forage for mules and horses to the station. He took a brother, two nephews, a woman, and a child to the conference. He carried no weapons, other than the knife he always wore.

Cochise noted the numerous soldiers around Bascom's tent, and when he entered and seated himself, Bascom appeared angry.

In the beginning Cochise had thought the lieutenant was joking when he accused Cochise of having kidnapped a half-breed boy* from a nearby ranch. Cochise laughed. But seeing Bascom grow furious, Cochise stated he knew nothing of the boy, but would investigate, that possibly Coyotero Apaches had the boy, and if so, he, Cochise, would arrange to have him returned. At this, Bascom had shouted a refusal of Cochise's offer, announced that he would hold the chief as hostage until the boy was returned, and ordered soldiers to arrest him. At this, Cochise leaped to his feet. Whipping out his knife, he slashed the tent and escaped in a hail of rifle fire. Although wounded twice, Cochise acted quickly. Racing into the mountains, he returned with a party of warriors and captured three whites from the stage station. More warriors joined him, and in the late afternoon he assembled them on the prairie in clear view of Bascom and the soldiers.

In the middle of the prairie Cochise raised a white flag of truce above himself, two warriors, and one of the hostages, a white man named Warren. Bascom, seeing the flag, advanced with two officers but no hostage. As they met beneath the flag Cochise again protested his innocence concerning the boy and repeated his offer to send his own warriors to search

---

*The boy, half Irish, half Mexican, had actually run away from a beating by his drunken stepfather. A band of Apaches had taken him in. He was later to be known as Mickey Free; he became a scout and interpreter for the United States Army and was universally hated by the Apaches.

him out and arrange his return. But Bascom had to release his hostages, whereupon Cochise would release his, meeting in the center of the field for the exchange. Bascom refused, insisting that the boy be returned first, and repeated his accusation that Cochise had kidnapped the boy. Angered, Cochise told Bascom to release his hostages or he, Cochise, would kill his own hostages. Bascom refused.

According to the officers present, the white prisoner of Cochise, Warren, spoke up. "Listen, Lieutenant, I know Cochise. He keeps his word. He does not have the boy. He will kill us. Go ahead and trade with him. He'll get the boy for you."

Bascom replied, "No. I will have the boy before I will release my hostages."

"For God's sake, man! He'll kill us! Are you crazy? Please . . . in Heaven's name . . . for the sake of Jesus . . . we will all help find the boy."

"No."

Angrily, Cochise retreated with his hostage, back to his warriors. While Lieutenant Bascom and his troops watched, Cochise staked the three white men on the flats, spread-eagled in plain view. Lining his warriors on horseback at a distance from the prisoners, Cochise raised his lance, gesturing a last time for Bascom to save the hostages. While the three men staked to the ground screamed and pleaded with Bascom, the lieutenant shook his head in refusal. Kicking their horses into motion, Cochise and his men galloped through the screaming prisoners. As they passed, they left behind silent bodies imbedded with cruel Spanish lances rocking gently in the wind. Bascom immediately ordered his men to seize three of his hostages, and in sight of Cochise, he hanged the chief's brother and two nephews from a crossbeam of the mule corral.

Later the woman, Dos-teh-seh, and the boy would be released from Fort Buchanan in a delayed and futile admission by the army of the facts of the case.

But the damage had been done. What the whites were to call the Cochise Wars had begun. Dos-teh-seh was the wife of Cochise. Of equal importance, she was the daughter of Mangas Coloradas. The boy was Naiche.

Lone riders on fast horses left the band of Cochise that night. They rode north and east and, most significantly, south—into the Sierra Madre. The riders carried a single message that would galvanize instant action: The bluecoats had broken their word. Geronimo and Juh came north, and with them a hundred warriors of the Nedni band.

Thirty days after Cochise's riders had delivered their messages, S. D. Jones made Fort Bowie and Apache Pass slightly past high noon—not an accomplishment to be taken lightly, considering his wagon train had broken dawn camp just west of the San Simon River, which split the San Simon Valley between Doubtful Canyon in the Steins Peak range and Apache Pass in the Chiricahua Mountains. But then, S. D. Jones was no tenderfoot freighter. A big hulking man with a perpetual cud of leaf Burley in his cheek, he was a master freighter and subcontractor in the freight-hauling business. All the way from San Antonio, he had rolled his wagons—monstrous vehicles that held eight thousand pounds in each of their twenty bellies, pulled by six spans of mules.

S. D. was called Cussin' Jones, a momentous tribute to his profane and imaginative vocabulary in the trade of mule skinning, where profanity was raised to a high art. His contract was with Beam & Company of Tucson, hauling for them at a rate of a cent a pound per one hundred miles. What Beam & Company got from the United States Army forts they supplied was their own goddamn business. Business was good. Forts were springing up magically in New Mexico and Arizona territories, the greatest concentration of military establishments in United States history. Some of the newest, not counting those already established in New Mexico, were: Fort

Bayard at Silver City, Fort Cummings near Deming, Fort McRae north of Hatch on the Rio Grande, Camp Ojo Caliente west of Fort Craig; Fort Seldon north of Doña Aña, Fort Stanton on Rio Bonito in Lincoln County, Fort Sumner on the Pecos, Fort Webster at Santa Rita, and Fort West on the Gila River. In Arizona, the new forts included: Fort Apache on the East Fork of White River, Fort Bowie at Apache Pass, Camp Grant on the San Pedro, Fort Crittenden near Fort Buchanan, Fort Goodwin near Fort Thomas, Fort Huachuca near the Huachuca Mountains and the San Pedro, Fort Lowell at Tucson, Fort McDowell at the junction of the Verde and Salt rivers, Fort Verde east of Prescott on the Verde River, and Fort Whipple at Prescott.

Forts crowded close on forts, some almost in sight of each other. Army patrols crisscrossed on short rides, overlapping each other in a veritable blue-blanketing of the territory. Soldiers at these forts had to be fed, clothed, armed, liquored, and whored. Tucson was a carousing settlement of four thousand drifters, profiteers, merchants, whisky dealers, gamblers, whores, pimps, and more army contractors per square inch than any spot on the globe. The "Apache War" was on.

If a tinhorn was holding six at five-card stud and was shot without witnesses present, the newspapers blazed headlines of another Apache massacre. It was good for business. Back east, citizens shuddered in vicarious horror at the bloody subhuman Apaches and solemnly agreed with Washington's thundering politicians that bigger appropriations, more forts, and more soldiers were needed to make life livable for Christian people in the "settling" of the West. A fair amount of the appropriations, flooding into the hands of the Tucson ring of contractors, found its way back, through bribes, into the pockets of the politicians, adding thunder to their speeches and hardening the policy of extermination for the Apaches.

Wealth flowed in such abundance that it brought life even to the miserable hovels of Tombstone, south of Tucson. Being far removed from the California Road, Tombstone felt obliged to attract its share of the golden flow with such enticements as soldiers will spend half their leaves in travel to reach—whisky and whores. Thus, Tombstone became a whore capital, so to speak, attracting the "fighting pimps" Wyatt Earp and his brothers, and other notables of the West later glorified in story, song, and motion pictures.

S. D. "Cussin'" Jones didn't give a shit. He was making his'n; dog eat dog, weak'uns suck the hind tit. He had never seen but one Apache in his life, a miserable, filthy thief that hung around the back doors of El Paso saloons doing odd jobs and stealing what he could to buy whisky. S. D. couldn't fathom what in suckin' hell the fuss was about. Whipping up on the Apache he had seen didn't exactly sound like much of a war; more like somebody was stirring donkey turds in mule piss to get up a stink. S. D. was all for it, as long as they didn't kill the miserable bastards off too fast. It would be bad for business.

S. D. slapped his skinning whip on the plank bar and attracted no attention from the half dozen soldiers drinking at a table. Freighters were a loud, common, and necessary nuisance. The bartender answered the summons "Seven dollars a bottle," and at S. D.'s nod, set the bottle before him, accompanied by an incredibly filthy glass. S. D. thumbed out his money, poured half a glass, and raising it, announced philosophically, "Piss on all of you," downing the drink. While his scalp tightened, drawing his lips backward from the blow, he meditatively turned and through the door watched his 'skinners across the road as they directed mule hostlers in unhitching and caring for two hundred and forty mules. The 'skinners were rushing the job, anxious to hit the bar.

Two of them were Anglos, seventeen were Mex. S. D. handled the lead wagon himself. It saved money.

This was a layover, with an army patrol scheduled to accompany him out of Apache Pass in the morning. All the way from El Paso he had had escorts. From Fort Bliss patrols had escorted him as far as Mesilla, where a patrol from Fort Thorn took over as far as the Mimbres River; there a patrol from Fort McLane had taken him across the flats below Big Burro mountains, through Doubtful Canyon and the San Simon Valley to Apache Pass. S. D.'s destination was Tucson, and while eighteen of his wagons were loaded with flour, bacon, whisky, dry goods, and sugar, two of them were stacked with breech-loading Spencer rifles with a thousand rounds for each. The army was careful of its guns.

Still watching the activity across the road, he poured another half glass of whisky, conversationally informing the bartender, "Tell the low-down, blood-suckin' pimp that bottled this bull piss to find a buffalo waller a little older. This here," he said, raising the glass preparatory to downing its contents, "ain't been off the bull's balls and in the barrel more'n forty-eight hour." Sucking in, he swallowed twice, emptying the glass.

The bartender, accustomed to such compliments, shrugged his shoulders. "Forty-rod," he recited in practiced defense, "straight from San Antone."

Something had caught S. D.'s attention across the road. He strode to the door. A Mexican youth wearing sackcloth, sandals, and a large sombrero was wandering down the line of wagons, peering casually under the canvases.

"Hey!" S. D. yelled. "Hey, you—Mex! Git yore greaser ass-wiping hands off'n them wagons!"

The youth sauntered on and apparently did not hear, or else did not understand English, for he continued down the line, looking into the back of each wagon. S. D. watched him for a moment with proprietary outrage before being summoned by the urge for another drink. He made a whisky-fuzzed mental note to place a guard on the wagons for the night.

Later, standing before the saloon with one of his 'skinners, he saw the youth again. The sun had set, and in the twilight he was plodding a decrepit mule westward out of Apache Pass. It reminded S. D. to place a guard. "Goddamn thieving greasers," he remarked to the Mexican 'skinner standing by him, who took no offense, not being a thief and therefore, logically, not a greaser.

"Sí," he agreed.

"He ain't only deef," S. D. remarked indignantly, "he's crazy, riding out by hisself at night."

"Sí, es loco!"

S. D. was wrong on three counts. The rider was not "deef," he was not crazy, and he was not Mexican. He was Naiche. This made S. D. "Cussin'" Jones dead wrong.

In the cool crispness before dawn, thirty troopers commanded by Lieutenant J. W. Davis swung, stiff and reluctant, into their saddles and headed west out of Apache Pass. Behind them S. D. swigged a generous anesthetizing swallow from his bottle, numbing his pain from the night before. Shifting the reins to his left hand, he uncoiled his whip, popping it sharply and cracking it across the heads of the mules spanned before him. Behind him more whips cracked, and the huge wheels of twenty wagons began grinding slowly away from Apache Pass, following the soldiers.

Dropping out of the pass, the road declined sharply and S. D. threw his right foot in the leather loop that hung from the brake pole. Pushing down with his foot and adding to this effort with his right hand hauling on the pole, he brought the back brakeshoes into contact with rear wheels. Twenty wagons shrieked like banshees rolling down the grade. S. D. hauled back on his reins, bringing the weight of his mules' rumps against the "butt brakes" that enabled the mules to hold backward on the harness and help to brake the wagon. It was hard work. By mid-morning S. D. and his 'skinners were glad to see the prairie ahead of them. The prairie was monotonous, but the work was light. The troopers, in unmilitary fashion, lounged on slow-walking horses a half mile ahead.

They were ten miles out in Sulphur Springs Valley before first night camp. The next night they camped at Sulphur Springs with the Dragoons looming to the west. Reaching the Dragoons in the shank of the afternoon, S. D. was for pushing on through, but Lieutenant Davis would have none of it.

"We'll dry camp here and get through the Dragoons tomorrow."

"Aunt Minnie's ass," S. D. said, reasonably enough, "there's four more hours of daylight. What are we gonna do, set here and pick our noses?"

"You can set and pick anything you like," Davis snapped. "You're my responsibility and this is smack in the middle of Cochise territory. We'll move in the morning."

The lieutenant allowed no fires and set guards moving along the train of wagons, rotating in response to shouted signals throughout the night.

At dawn they moved, creaking slowly through the narrow pass that threaded twisting between high peaks and canyoned walls. Now the troopers rode beside the wagons, rifles out of scabbards, resting across their saddles. They watched above them. Some of the troopers had fought Apaches. They knew that if an attack came, there would be no warning.

At high noon they sighted the desert through the last of the canyons and within the hour were clear of the mountains. Lieutenant Davis halted the train. Bringing his horse close to S. D.'s wagon, he raised binoculars, sweeping the horizon. Between here and Tucson lay seventy-five miles of desert prairie, no mountains, not even a hill for an Apache to hide behind, and not much vegetation beyond sage and cactus.

The desert bounced oven heat into the air, and the sun's light was white, blinding. S. D. was hot and irritated at the lieutenant's prolonged scrutiny.

"Welllll," he said crossly, wiping dripping sweat from his face, "do ye see any horse cars, er circuses, er nekkid women?"

Davis brought his glasses down. "I don't see any Apaches. I don't see the patrol from Fort Lowell either."

Davis was not a man to appreciate S. D.'s sour humor. He frowned, pondering his problem. His problem was orders. His orders were to escort the train past the Dragoons, to be met by a patrol from Fort Lowell. He had not been instructed what to do, army procedure, in the event the Fort Lowell patrol did not meet him. Lieutenant Davis was all army, and so pondered the problem in an accepted army fashion. He solved the problem.

"Look," he said brusquely, "my patrol will camp here at the mountains. I'll station lookouts there"— he pointed to a high, rolling ridge above them—"and we'll watch you until the Fort Lowell patrol meets you. We can keep you in sight all afternoon. Should the patrol not meet you, then we'll catch up to you for night camp."

"Suits me." S. D. patted the Spencer rifle standing by his leg. "They's nineteen more of these with nineteen 'skinners behind me, and twenty 'skinners with twenty Spencers ain't pushovers fer Apaches ner no other gents with screwin' on their minds."

S. D. "Cussin'" Jones cracked his whip, moving the wagons past the soldiers, into the desert and his destiny.

Lieutenant Davis ordered his troopers back into the sparse shade and smothering heat of a mountain butte. For over an hour in the dancing heat rays he and his lounging troopers could see the wagons with the naked eye as they rolled slowly across the prairie floor. Davis then sent two observers to the ridge above him with instructions for one man to keep his glasses constantly on the train. This was done, and after two hours of steady watch they observed the Fort Lowell patrol meeting the wagons. Being a dutiful officer, Lieutenant Davis himself mounted the ridge and observed the patrol, whereupon he hastened his men back through the Dragoons at a gallop. He had other pressing duties. His mission here was completed.

Later Lieutenant Davis was to call as his witnesses the two soldiers who had observed the patrol with him. He and the army were confused. Lieutenant Davis did not see what he saw. It was obvious. He and his two witnesses saw an illusion. The possibility was raised that Apaches, dressed as troopers, had taken over the train, but Davis and Army inquiry officers agreed that upon close scrutiny S. D. Jones and at least some of his 'skinners would have recognized them, whereupon there would have been action. There was no disturbance, as Davis and his two witnesses had carefully observed the patrol's routine meeting of the wagons.

Momentarily, the incident received notice as the case of the "disappearing wagons," but was soon forgotten in the furious waging of the war. The case was consigned to gather dust, unsolved in United States Army files.

For the Apaches there was no mystery.

When Naiche left Apache Pass on the decrepit mule, he did not ride it far. Within the hour he had turned off the trail into a rugged arroyo where a warrior waited with two fast horses. Riding hard, they sped across Sulphur Springs Valley into the Dragoons. In the hidden recesses of a particular wild area of "Cochise Canyon," three hundred Apache warriors sat well back in the darkness of live oak and piñon. In the center a small fire flickered, and around it were the men to whom Naiche reported. All together, they had led easily a thousand daring guerrilla strikes. Half a century and more of guerrilla war against the Mexicans was in the head of old Mangas Coloradas; fully forty years in each of the lives of Cochise and the brilliant Juh; and there was Geronimo, the War Shaman. Years of this roving warfare, undertaken out of love and concern for all Apaches, had made him a master of all terrains; this, with detailed knowledge of the habits of the enemy, made him a formidable strategist and field general.

Naiche's information had established the destination of the wagon train as Tucson. Geronimo's knowledge of army patrols, their routine maximum distance from forts, made it an easy matter to deduce the approximate point at which Lieutenant Davis's patrol would turn back. It was as simple to ascertain that the patrol meeting the train would be from Fort Lowell at Tucson.

By the time Lieutenant Davis and S. D.'s wagon train emerged from the Dragoons, and while Davis studied the prairie with his binoculars, the four Apache generals had already swung into action.

Mangas Coloradas and Juh had set out with over two hundred warriors the day before, traveling west toward Tucson. They were poorly armed with bows and arrows and an occasional smoothbore muzzle-loading musket. Forty miles east of Tucson on the California Road, they struck the dawn camp of fifty soldiers, the patrol from Fort Lowell.

Mangas and Juh used fewer than fifty warriors in the strike. The balance of their force waited to the north, in the foothills of the Santa Catalina Mountains. They made no attempt at a sustained engagement as they swept out of the early morning grayness through the camp, fired at the soldiers and retreated north. When the commanding officer of the patrol hesitated to follow them, they regrouped and struck again. The army patrol, armed with breechloading rifles, set out in pursuit with an ensuing running firefight from horseback that covered twenty-five miles, to the fringe of the Santa Catalinas. Here the patrol was surprised and cut off from retreat. Several of the troopers were killed as they fought their way back toward Fort Lowell.

During this time Cochise headed westward on the California Road to wait and meet the wagon train. With him rode thirty warriors carrying the preponderance of muzzle-loaders possessed by the Apaches. They wore bits and pieces of captured army uniforms, blue coats, and hats. This was the "patrol" Lieutenant Davis saw. Twelve hours before Cochise began his ride, Geronimo had left in the same direction. He had twenty warriors. They did not ride horses, but ran on foot, and carried no weapons beyond the long knives at their waists. Geronimo was the creator of the illusion.

S. D. Jones had no worries as he left Lieutenant Davis behind. He had passed the word to his 'skinners to keep a sharp watch on the vast horizons around them. They were all veteran freight haulers, tough and well acquainted with the Spencer rifle. To the rear of him, S. D. knew Lieutenant Davis was keeping watch, and in front, the patrol was coming from Fort Lowell. Around him, the wide, smooth desert floor made a surprise attack virtually impossible.

S. D. could turn his thinking to pleasanter things— like a coming week wallering around the saloons of Tucson, the bleached-out whore he was acquainted with, at thirty bucks a night. S. D. smacked his lips, took another swig from the bottle, whipped the mules a step faster.

An hour passed; two. The sun had dropped and was shining in S. D.'s face. He pulled his flop hat a shade lower over his eyes. It was hot, hotter'n a faced-up whore's belly after a hard night's work. But there was no wind. S. D. had seen the time he'd trade hot for the whipping, stinging sand when the wind rose on the desert. There had been a sandstorm recently, however, for as he rode along S. D. noticed mounds of sand that had been whipped into piles around sagebrush. The sage had broken the wind and drifted the sand. He even noticed, not long before his ride was over, that there had been a hell of a sandstorm. Close by the trail on each side, there were heavy mounds spaced here and yonder around the sage.

Even if S. D. had examined the mounds by the trail more closely and the bushes of sage that invariably topped the larger mounds, like tombstones, he would not have seen the heads, resting in the sage.

Even if he had known an old Apache adage— "Foolish men look far in search of joy . . . and expected death, both are close by them"—S. D. still would not have seen the heads. Who in hell looks for heads in sagebrush, heads with no bodies? And so S. D. Jones plodded his wagons by the mounds. As the last wagon passed the first of the mounds that S. D. had seen, a short figure rose miraculously from the sand, glided two steps and into the back of the wagon. It was Geronimo.

From the opposite side of the trail, a second figure rose and followed the first into the wagon. With a long knife held flat between his teeth, Geronimo crawled over the freight until he was crouching directly behind the 'skinner seated at the front. Swift, silent, the knife flashed beneath the 'skinner's chin. Without a sound, he was pulled backward into the wagon with his neck severed halfway through. Naiche, the second figure, seized the reins, climbed into the 'skinner's seat, and the mules continued steadily on.

Geronimo dropped down between the spans of mules, and threading his way through the harness along the trace-chained double trees, he made his way through the entire length of the mule team. Dropping to the ground, he trotted ahead of the lead mules and entered the second wagon. As he crawled beneath the canvas, another warrior rose from a mound beside the trail and jumped in behind him. The second 'skinner was dispatched in the same silent and efficient manner. Through the train of wagons Geronimo moved in silent, deadly concentration. Nineteen wagons! Over a distance of two miles, nineteen men had died; each time a warrior rose to take over the reins of the dead 'skinner.

By the time Geronimo entered the back of S. D.'s wagon, he presented a horrifying figure. Hot blood from the slashed neck arteries of nineteen men splattered and ran in rivulets from his forehead, down across the yellow stripes below his eyes. His face, bare chest, and arms were thick with blood, mixed with sweat that brightened its color and exuded a sweet smell of death.

Maybe it was the smell that first caused S. D. to turn, or perhaps he was only reaching for his bottle. In any event, from a corner of his eye, he caught a moving shadow beneath the canvas behind him. He turned full about to see the horror crawling silently, swiftly toward him, knife held flat between teeth that shined white from between bloody drawn-back lips. The black eyes were animal-hungry, ferocious for a kill. S. D. was paralyzed for a split second. But only for a split second. He tried to rise from his seat and would have screamed, but no sound would come from his throat. As he rose, strangling on his own straining neck muscles, he tumbled from his perch, over the wagon, and the monstrous wheel caught him across his thigh, grinding his leg mushily through his trousers. It was the last he remembered.

Search patrols from Fort Lowell found S. D. the following day, alive. His thrashing had coated and recoated the smashed leg, clogging his blood and preventing him from bleeding to death. He was the only living witness to the missing wagon train. Troopers had followed the tracks turning from the trail, south, but the tracks vanished after a few miles. Wind, and possibly brush dragged by Apaches on horseback, soon obliterated all trace of the wagon wheels.

S. D. talked incoherently of the "'Pache with the yeller stripes" and could add nothing more to the mystery. As far as can be determined, he never freighted again but hung around Tucson for a time, telling and retelling his moment of terror in the wagon train mystery. As the world turned, it apparently profited to no measurable degree by S. D.'s extended existence. He melted into Tucson's flotsam, disappearing forever from the history of the Southwest. But those identifying the "'Pache with the yeller stripes" were becoming more numerous.

For the Chiricahua Apaches the wagon train capture was a bonanza—not only for the food, which was sorely needed, but also for the arms. Modern Spencers and ammunition added firepower to many hard-riding warriors. The wagons' supplies were taken into the southernmost area of the Dragoon Range and distributed to patrols who carried them into the Guadalupes, the Chiricahua Range, and north toward the Big Burros. Following their guerrilla experience of centuries, the Apaches were breaking into smaller bands, scattering over the bosom of a populous enemy country. To remain concentrated in one large group, small in comparison to the growing enemy, was to court a concentration of the enemy forces upon them, and instant disaster.

These small bands were used with high efficiency in the war along the California Road. When the army concentrated troop patrols along the road so thickly that they were within shouting distance of each other, the Apache bands struck feeder trails carrying supplies to the forts. While Red Cloud, the great Chief of the Oglala Sioux, is deservedly given military credit for his campaign against and closing of Fort Kearny, the Apache generals were given no such credit. Yet their efficient use of small bands and deadly strikes forced the United States Army to close Fort Thorn, near Hatch, Fort McLane near Santa Rita, Camp Mason on the Santa Cruz River, Fort Tularosa near

Reserve, New Mexico, Fort Barrett near Sacaton in Arizona, Camp Grant in Arizona near the San Pedro River, Camp Calabasas near Nogales, Fort Conrad south of Socorro, and Fort Fillmore near Mesilla. The United States Army "officially" closed the forts as "no longer effective," which tells the truth, but not the reason why.

The heroic struggle of the Apaches, a people with no political power, no financial influence and no friends in the press, is missing from the pages of history. Yet this struggle of a small group of people resisting the attempts of two powerful governments to enslave and exterminate them is unmatched in history.

16

When United States troops were pulled from the California Road in an attempt to suppress raids on the countryside, the Apache bands virtually closed the road to all immigrant trains heading for California, supply trains, and the Butterfield Stage Line.

Tom Jeffords was superintendent of that line. In less than a year he had seen fourteen of his stage drivers and uncounted passengers killed and most of his stagecoaches burned between the Mimbres River and Tucson. He, himself, had been twice wounded. He was almost out of business and his pleas meant nothing to a helpless army. Jeffords was a determined man, mindful of his responsibilities and singular in his efforts to do his duty. He could speak the Apache language fairly fluently, having come into close contact with many Apaches during the years of peace.

One morning he abruptly came to a decision. Seeing a "friendly" Apache he knew lounging at the corrals at Apache Pass, he walked up to him and, extending a fistful of money, said, "I want you to lead me to Cochise." The Apache looked at him for a long moment.

Jeffords was crazy. For several years no white man had seen the face of Cochise and lived to tell it. The Apache shrugged; all white men were crazy. He took the money and led Tom Jeffords out of Apache Pass toward the Dragoons. Veering southwest once out of the pass, they angled across the Sulphur Springs Valley, making two night camps. Squatting around their campfire, they were a strange sight—an Apache and a red-bearded Anglo accompanied only by two horses and a pack mule, in the middle of a war where neither Apache nor white man camped in the open ... especially not together.

On their third day out they entered the rugged Dragoons far south of the California Road. Immediately they were in rocky terrain, steep slopes that taxed the horses, so they had to dismount and lead them. As they progressed, the mountains rose higher in a tangle of buttes, canyons, and sharp declivities that fell away unexpectedly a thousand feet. By late afternoon they were riding along the narrow floor of a deep canyon when a rifle cracked high above them. The Apache made no attempt to conceal himself. He was silhouetted, standing, his rifle pointed skyward. The shot had been a signal. In a moment another rifle report sounded far off. The signal was being relayed. The guide had stopped his horse.

"This is far as I go," he announced.

"Where's Cochise?" Jeffords asked.

The guide shrugged his shoulders. "This is his place. I do not know exactly where he is, but"—he jerked his head toward the lookout—"they will see that you do not have trouble finding him."

With that, the guide trotted his horse back down the canyon, turning to shout "*Adios*" to Jeffords with an ominous finality.

Tom Jeffords paused, in consideration of his imminent death, to light a long cigar; then shrugging his own wide shoulders, he proceeded. The canyon twisted, narrowing to admit a single horse between the high rock walls. Sheltered from the sun, Jeffords rode in a twilight, though the sky, high above, was light and blue. Suddenly he emerged into a wider box canyon with piñon trees. Somewhere he heard water running. This was a large ranchería. Tipis were scattered in great abundance among the trees. He rode slowly through them. Apache warriors were gathered ahead of him in a clearing. Women and children came from under the trees toward the crowd. The warriors' faces were painted, and they carried rifles.

Before he reached them, Jeffords swung down from his horse. He handed his reins to a surprised woman standing nearby and, unbuckling his pistol belt, handed this to her also. He walked straight toward the warriors. They parted as he came, opening a path that led to a large tipi. A tall Apache, arms folded, stood in front of it.

Jeffords stopped, facing him, and addressed him in Apache. "Are you Cochise?"

The tall Apache studied him for a while without answering. His eyes were calm and intelligent, but inside Cochise was shocked at the appearance of the white man. He answered, "I am Cochise."

Later, Tom Jeffords was to tell it in his slow drawl: "Well, I explained to Cochise who I was. I told him that my job was to keep the stage line running and I was about to lose my job. I said I didn't have no hatred for the Apaches, nor any war with the Apaches. I said I didn't want to steal their land nor cause trouble. I told him I would shore appreciate him letting my stage coaches pass through Apache territory without being attacked."

Cochise respected the courage and honesty of Tom Jeffords. There they found a friendship that was to last until Cochise's death. At this first meeting they formed a pact by which Cochise gave his word that no Butterfield stagecoach would be harmed. The word was kept by every Apache, forever. Tom Jeffords took no gifts to Cochise and the Apaches. He offered no rewards. No material benefits accrued, in any way, to the Apaches. This agreement led to many incongruous spectacles: Butterfield stagecoaches traveling the California Road unharmed, sometimes in plain sight of Apache warriors skirmishing with soldiers or attacking supply trains. No arrow or bullet fired by an Apache was ever again to injure a driver or passenger of the Butterfield Line. Cochise was approached by a white man without guile or ulterior motive. The record shows clearly that on every occasion when the Apaches were so treated, they returned unquestioned honor and fairness.

Sadly, the record of the United States Army falls short of the Apaches'. The famous mountain man Joseph Reddeford Walker was once leading a party of goldseekers west. As he camped his party at the old abandoned buildings of Fort McLane, a Mexican drover asked to join him through Apache territory. The drover was frightened. A few miles away a large band of Apaches was camped on the Mimbres River. He had recognized the huge figure around the band's campfire. He was Mangas Coloradas, the famous chief.

Walker and his men formed a plan. Ahead of them they faced nearly two hundred miles of hostile Apaches. If they could seize Mangas Coloradas and hold him as hostage during their sojourn through the land, they knew no Apache would attack them. Once through, they intended to release Mangas. Setting their plan in motion, they dispatched three men to Mangas's camp under a flag of truce. (Without fail, white men and army officers trusted the honor of "treacherous" Apaches.) The three men returned and reported the old chief said he would think upon their offer to meet and make peace. He would talk with them in the morning. The three also reported an "evil-appearing warrior present, seated beside Mangas." The warrior's cheeks were slashed with yellow stripes.

After the three men had left, Geronimo argued violently with Mangas, telling him the whites were treacherous and could not be trusted. Two chiefs present also joined Geronimo in pleading with Mangas not to go. They were Victorio and Loco, new chiefs of the Warm Springs band since the death of Delgadito. Mangas would not be persuaded.

As early as 1846, Mangas had sought peace with the Anglos. In that year he had approached United States military authorities and explained to them that his people, for generations, had fought off enslavement by the Spanish. He offered to ally the Apaches with the United States in their war with Mexico. The military authorities refused.

Texas cattle drovers pushing cattle west across Apacheria, many years before, left accounts in their diaries of meeting the towering chief named Mangas Coloradas. As the cattle drovers headed their cattle west toward California, they were invariably met by Mangas, sometimes with a hundred warriors. Each time, he had politely offered their services in showing the drovers water holes and assisting them across the land of the Apache. The drovers always accepted, and their diaries reflect high praise for the hard work and resourceful helpfulness of Mangas and his warriors. At the end of their drives, the drovers reported not a head of cattle stolen as the chief and his riders waited politely while the drovers cut out a few head in payment for their work, for which the drovers received a courteous *"Gracias!"*

Now Mangas was approaching eighty years of age. He was still a great warrior and could ride and shoot with the best of his men. He wanted an honorable peace with the Anglos; perhaps he knew the hopeless odds facing his people, squeezed on two fronts between the governments of the United States and Mexico.

Early the next morning he mounted his horse, unarmed. He carried a truce flag and proceeded toward the abandoned fort. What he did not know was that the night before Brigadier General Joseph Rodman West had arrived with two hundred troopers. West had served under Carleton and was an avid promoter of extermination for all Indians. The men of Walker's party reported what happened.

As Mangas rode into their camp, West ordered him

seized and bound. The chief attempted to talk to West, but was thrown into a room of an abandoned building, where he was kept all day. That night Walker's men heard West talking to his troopers. He had Mangas dragged from the building over to a campfire. His last orders to his men before he retired: "You understand. In the morning I want him dead."

Walker's party, from the shadows, watched the soldiers around the campfire with the old chief lying among them. The soldiers began heating their bayonets. As a bayonet glowed red, the soldier would rise from the campfire and walk to the place where Mangas lay and goad him with the hot glowing point. Some of the soldiers burned the old man's feet, others his stomach, groin, and back as Mangas twisted and turned on the ground. All night they tortured the figure on the ground. Mangas did not cry out, but attempted to dissuade them, speaking in Spanish. (He did not speak English.) Near dawn two soldiers approached Mangas, shouldered their rifles, and shot down repeatedly into his body. Mangas Coloradas was dead.

When West appeared, he ordered Mangas's head severed. An army surgeon scooped out the brain and peeled away the flesh, boiling the head in a pot of water. He measured the cranium and pronounced it as big or bigger, than Daniel Webster's. The head was sent to Washington, where it was exhibited widely to crowds of "civilized" Easterners before being placed in the Smithsonian Institution.

General West's official report of the incident reads: "Engaged Apaches in skirmish near old Fort McLane, killing several of enemy before they routed. Captured their chief, Mangas Coloradas, who was killed attempting escape. No losses."

That day, General West had no losses, but this would soon be altered. He had murdered the most revered of all Apache chiefs; worse, he had murdered the man who had been the idol of Geronimo since boyhood.

When Mangas did not return on the following day from his supposed meeting, Geronimo and several warriors slipped close to the old fort. Hidden, they watched the soldiers dispose of Mangas's headless body by throwing it into a ditch. All day they watched, helpless, while crows and buzzards pecked and tore at the bloating body. That night they recovered the remains. The Bedonkohe and Mimbre warriors were furious. Victorio proposed an immediate attack on the soldiers. But Geronimo, always cool and calculating, dissuaded him. Instead, he sent scouts to watch the soldiers' movements through the night. Geronimo planned.

Captain Weldon hid his irritation beneath a strict military countenance. He had no liking for General West. In fact, he hated the man. Not for West's attitude toward Indians—in this Weldon agreed; but West's officious, nitpicking manner filled Weldon with a deep revulsion for his superior officer, particularly his habit of issuing orders in the form of interminable lectures designed to reveal West's infinite wisdom and superior military thinking.

Now in the first gray of dawn over Fort McLane's old buildings, he stood at attention while West paced back and forth before him, hands clasped behind his back in a Napoleonic manner. He was pondering what might appear to be a great coming battle. Behind Weldon thirty mounted troopers sat half awake, restraining horses that stamped and snorted puffs of condensing air in the crispness of the morning cold. Weldon, sighing, almost snorted himself. General West paused and lifted a suspicious eyebrow toward Weldon. He was constantly alert to ferret out any show of irritation or impatience in his junior officers, which he labeled as "insubordination." Having paused, the general appeared to have come to a tactical decision based upon profound considerations, unfathomable to his junior officer. He had, in fact, smelled the breakfast fire and was compelled by this to dispense with Weldon.

"Now," West said, not looking at Weldon, but gazing afar as he always did. It gave him a look of Destiny, of a Man Deciding Future History. "Now," he repeated, "the immigrant train requesting escort left Doña Aña yesterday."

"Yes, sir," Captain Weldon answered, though it was not a question.

"Ummmm. Yes. They should have crossed the Grande the same day. By the time you reach them . . . coming this way, they will have made twenty-five miles. I am heading west. You should meet us within the week at Apache Pass."

"Coyote shit." Captain Weldon did not say it. He thought it. It would take at least two weeks. But instead he said, "Yes, sir."

"Now," West said, folding his arms and facing Weldon. He was not as tall as the captain but refused to look up and so he addressed the top button on Weldon's tunic. "Remember, Captain, I am responsible for you. You are responsible for my men. Keep your troops clear of the mountains, clear of any natural surroundings that might give the cowardly Apaches the opportunity to surprise and bushwhack you."

"Yes, sir."

"Apaches"—West gazed again into the distance and his tone became philosophically musing—"will not attack a well-armed . . . ah . . . force, no matter how small, if they are alert and avoid terrain that offers cover to the cowards."

"Yes, sir."

General West turned and strode toward the fire. Captain Weldon, however, was not tricked. He remained at attention. Halfway to the fire, West whirled. The trick had not worked. He frowned at the captain. Lifting and bending his arm majestically, he held a West Point parade salute. Captain Weldon responded, not to be outdone in majesty.

"Dismissed," West said sternly and retired to his breakfast. The captain was a cunning, insolent pup whom West was unalterably determined to expose. But as he ate his breakfast his mind was already on Apache Pass and beyond. Not much at the pass, but his ultimate destination was Tucson, where the citizenry and the newspaper appreciated and would welcome his arrival as he paraded his troops.

Captain Weldon headed his men southeast. He was an experienced and competent officer and in a short while had put his outrage at West behind him and turned his thoughts to the problem at hand—Apaches.

As he crossed the Mimbres River he dispatched two scouts north to check on the camp of the Apaches from which the old chief had ridden to be "captured." As he turned due east, two hours later, the scouts reported—the Apaches had broken camp and their tracks headed north into the mountains. Weldon grunted with satisfaction: good that the tracks did not lead southeast, but with Apaches the fact that they led north meant nothing. They could be anywhere. He exercised caution. Slightly changing his course, he dropped his troops farther south, away from the rock buttes where the Black Mountains tailed off into the prairie. He kept the mountains a good five miles distant to his left, but still breathed easier when the range disappeared behind him, leaving open prairie with sparse sage and cactus on every side.

Two hours past high noon, Captain Weldon was looking ahead through binoculars, a little prematurely, in anticipation of spotting the immigrant train. Despite the dry air he and his troops were wet with perspiration. A coat of alkali dust raised by their horses' hoofs had coated their uniforms and hats.

It was during one of his periodical binocular sweeps that he spotted them—not the immigrant train, but a body of horses angling from the northwest, whose course would eventually intersect his own. He pointed, and the sergeant riding to his left and slightly behind, raised his own glasses. After a time the sergeant eased up beside him.

"Horse herd," he said casually. "Three Mex drovers headin' 'em. They're wantin' to scrounge a little free escort off'n us."

Weldon studied the herd again. They were closer now, trotting; perhaps fifty or more of them. He could see the wide-sombreroed riders, one on each flank and one behind. They occasionally waved languidly at the horses, urging them on. Probably taking them to Fort Bliss where they would haggle with the army buyers.

For the next half hour the herd stayed to Weldon's left, leisurely moving closer. By this time they were a part of the landscape, an accepted part, identified, categorized in the military mind, and set aside in a proper pigeonhole.

Weldon casually checked them now as he swept the horizon to clear it of Apaches and in hope of sighting the train. On his last check he grew irritated. The Mexicans had pushed their herd into a gallop, raising dust, and worse, were set on a course that would cause Weldon to either slow his troopers or order them into a run to prevent them from colliding with the herd. In the intense heat he decided to slow his pace (a predictable and fatal decision) and hauled slightly back on his horse. As he did this the Mexican herd veered slightly inward toward him.

"Goddammit!" Weldon spoke to the sergeant. "Goddamn crazy Mexicans . . ."

The sergeant was not without humor. "They wear them big hats," he said, "so's they can make a shadder . . . light shines through their heads. Their brains is all in their asses."

When Weldon looked again from the sergeant to the horse herd, he felt a sudden alarm. Now the horses were coming at a run, drumming the ground in a wild charge! He and the troopers behind him waved their hats, shouting to head off the horses. Weldon sunk spurs into his own mount. The herd hit the troopers' line with stunning force, knocking horses to the ground, unseating riders, scattering soldiers in a wild melee. There were sharp reports coming from somewhere within the dust cloud. Rifle shots! Captain Weldon felt a heavy blow hit his back. His face showed surprise, unbelieving. He had been shot! Hat tumbling, he fell from his saddle, dead. Captain Wilton Weldon, first in his class at West Point, brilliant student of Marlborough, Napoleon, Wellington, had just had his entire command destroyed in fifteen minutes by Geronimo.

The Apaches had learned riding from old enemies, those superb horsemen of the plains, the Comanches, who each autumn had swept through Apache country on their way to Mexico. They no longer came, but the Apaches had not frogotten. Around the neck of each horse, a small loop dangled. Another encircled the horse's back and belly. Lengthwise, on one side of the horse, an Apache rode, his elbow resting in the neck loop, one heel in the belly loop. From the offside the horse appeared riderless, but with a flip of an agile body, the Apache could come astride his mount in an eyeblink, or if he chose, remain in his outstretched position, shooting from over or under the horse's neck. Geronimo did not invent this riding tactic, though he was skilled in it. But the unexpected appearance of the Mexican drovers, their long ride alongside the troopers, insinuating themselves into the soldiers' minds as a known quantity, a commonplace: This illusion was Geronimo's.

A corporal and two privates excaped, riding their horses to death toward Mesilla on the Rio Grande. There they told their story, of the lightning attack from nowhere, and in their telling, once again, the "warrior with the streaks of yellow across his face," was related to the U.S. Army. A large patrol from Fort Bliss found Weldon's dead command scattered along the trail for two miles. They were naked and swelling in the hot sun, stripped of uniforms and arms. Every body was headless.

Riding with Geronimo that day were Victorio, Loco, Juh, the warrior Fun, and a total of fifty horsemen. Naiche was not there. Two weeks before Geronimo had asked the youth to observe and gather information at a particular place. Naiche was two hundred miles northwest of Geronimo's action that day. He was alone.

17

Camp Goodwin did not look like a formidable out-post. It was designed originally as a base for army patrols in their efforts to clear the Gila Mountains and the surrounding area of Apaches. There was no wall around the camp. The blank, sturdy sides of adobe buildings served the purpose of a wall, in a squared U shape that left a spacious parade ground in the middle and opened in front toward the Gila River, a half mile to the west. Behind the camp, a good five miles, the high Gila Mountains rose.

West of the river which Camp Goodwin faced there was nothing except the desert. Like an ocean, endless, rolling slightly, with sagebrush, cactus, sparse ocotillo that cast thin silhouettes of shadow at the sun's sinking each day, seemingly into the western desert floor.

The vastness appeared empty, but was not. There was the wind. Where cactus needles stroked the wind, it was high, whining, and beneath, the sage leaves rustled a low alto, castaneted by grains of sand. Occasionally a jackrabbit streaked from one sparse hiding place to another, first checking the terrain for the sidewinder. Sometimes he was careless, and died, as is the way with the desert. A lone hawk covered a wide area; life, and therefore food, was lean and scattered. In the twilight cactus wrens snuffled in the security of their spiny homes, victorious in life for another day. But to the unpracticed eye the desert was empty, without the grace of a contoured symmetry of hill or rock; therefore it could hold no man in secret and was deserving of small scrutiny and no search whatsoever. And so it was here that Naiche lay and watched Camp Goodwin.

His position was approximately a mile west of the Gila, directly in front of Camp Goodwin's U opening. This was necessary, for he had to note the strength and the times of arrival and departure of the patrols from the fort. Before him he had small sticks. Each patrol he observed represented one of these sticks. He noted the sun's slant on that patrol's arrival or departure and so knew their routine. He placed the sticks in sequence, each representing a patrol.

When he reported these activities, he would look at each stick, and with a fantastic memory for detail, developed by a people without a written language, he would recite precisely the size of each patrol, the time of departure and arrival, the direction and length of time away from the camp.

He had been here nearly two weeks. In the center of a flat patch of prickly pear where no horseman would approach, he lay beneath a small scrounging of sage brush. He had sipped sparsely from his water bag. The water was almost gone. He had eaten the last of the jerked venison two days ago. Now as the sun dropped, flashing red on the buttes of the Gila Mountains, Naiche rubbed dust on his binoculars— always a necessary precaution, even though he was looking away from the sun—and lying flat, propped on elbows, he focused them on a particular butte in the mountains. He had done this every evening at the same time. At the spot he studied grew a piñon tree, standing alone. The piñon was tall, unbranched twenty feet from the ground. Its foliage was sparse, reflecting the scarcity of water and food at its roots. Near the top of the tree there was a small bunching of branches. Here it was that Naiche focused his attention. This time he was rewarded. In the branches was the large stick nest of a hawk. It had not been there yesterday at this time. No hawk is so foolish to build a nest that quickly. It was the tree and the sign of which Geronimo had told him.

A bugle sounding taps floated from Camp Goodwin. Naiche watched as the notes sounded solitary and haunting across the river. The bluecoats were lowering their cloth. *Superstitious white eyes*—Naiche smiled. He had watched them put up the cloth every morning and take it down in the evening. They did not trust the cloth in the night. It required several of them to retrieve the cloth, and Naiche enjoyed watching this ritual as they folded the cloth and marched, stiff and formal, across the parade ground. Now lights began to flare in the buildings. He waited, focusing his naked eye on a cactus standing fifty feet from him. When the cactus became indistinct, fading in the dying light, he rose, checking the desert around him, and trotted toward Camp Goodwin. A few yards from the river he lay flat while he accustomed his ears to the new sounds of water, sluggish in its bed, then crawled to the river bank and into the water. On the opposite side he crawled to the bank, listening again, before rising and trotting with an easy stride past Camp Goodwin and into the mountains beyond.

By the time darkness had deepened to reveal the tiniest stars, spectacular, dimpling lights in the vast, bending sky, Naiche was seated on the butte, his back resting against the piñon. He watched the lights blinking from Camp Goodwin far below to the west. The desert was giving up her heat, and a cooling breeze swept across the flat prominence where Naiche sat. He listened keenly, but did not hear the step, only felt the touch of Geronimo's hand on his shoulder. With him Geronimo had fifteen warriors.

After the destruction of Captain Weldon's command, Victorio, Loco, and their warriors had raced north to remove their people from an exposed rancheria. They knew quick and vengeful action would follow from the army. Juh with a small group had run to warn Cochise, embattled to the west. The warrior Fun, however, was still with Geronimo.

As they gathered, squatting in a tight circle, Naiche picked up his sticks and, without pause, recited a history of Camp Goodwin's patrols.

Geronimo had asked for particular details of the afternoon and evening arrivals and departures at the camp. Naiche was sure he knew why. When circumstances made it possible, Geronimo preferred to stage his illusions for the enemy in the twilight of evening.

When he had come to Cochise's rancheria asking for warriors, he had given a lesson to Naiche. In the twilight he had made a mark on the ground, asking Naiche to stand there. Pointing to a rock a hundred yards away, he said, "I have placed something on the rock. Look closely at it, Naiche, and tell me what you see."

Naiche narrowed his eyes, focusing his keen sight on the rock's face. He watched the object for a long time, attempting to discern its detail.

"I see," Naiche said uncertainly, "a piece of rope. It bends a little. Not much. This could be a dead snake, or perhaps it is only a shadow. Maybe you have not placed anything on the rock at all."

Geronimo smiled and said nothing.

Early the next morning, in the gray of dawn, he awakened Naiche and took him to the same mark and said, "Tell me what you see, Naiche."

Naiche looked. "I see a stick. It is as long as my arm with a width of my finger. There is a knot on the stick."

"Yes." Geronimo laughed. "You are right. It is the same stick that was on the rock in the twilight. The stick that was the rope . . . the snake . . . the shadow."

Naiche looked doubtfully at Geronimo. "Are you sure?"

"Yes. I am sure. I put it there. You have the same

amount of light this morning that you had yesterday in the twilight. It is not the same *kind* of light. Light is life. When it is born in the morning, it is like youth coming into the shadow world to deal with the physical shadows. It must see physical things distinctly. When the light is old, it is like the old person getting ready to leave the shadow world. The physical things are not important then. And so the light, and vision, blurs and is not distinct. It means nothing now for the old. If they have strengthened their spirit minds, they turn their sight inward and the spirit things grow sharp and distinct, for this is the world where they are going. If they have not strengthened their spirit minds"—Geronimo shrugged—"then they are lost there, too . . . in a twilight they cannot see before the darkness."

And so while Naiche recited his information of the patrols he expected that Geronimo would question him more fully about the afternoon and evening. Geronimo did.

Camp Goodwin furnished two major patrols of troopers on three-day alternating sweeps of their area. One, traveling north, kept the Gila Mountains to the right for twenty miles, then swept west in a half circle toward the new subagency at San Carlos and back down the Gila River to their home base at Camp Goodwin. The other patrol headed south, keeping the Gila Mountains on their left. Where the Gila and Blue rivers joined to form the San Simon, they forded, following the San Simon southward, then turning in a half circle toward the west and Fort Grant, they came back northward across the prairie to Camp Goodwin. These were large patrols of fifty troopers each. Thus while one was making its three-day sweep, the other was in quarters for the safety of the camp.

Naiche knew by the direction in which each patrol headed, and the direction from which it returned, almost precisely where it had been. He, like all Apaches of that area, knew the territory intimately and from the measured gaits of the horses easily figured the distance. As Naiche talked, Geronimo drew a map in the dirt. The map showed Camp Goodwin and the northern area. The northern patrol was due back at Camp Goodwin the next evening.

Captain Bartlett commanded the northern patrol. It was monotonous duty, riding an empty land of dust, wind, heat, and insects. The last Apaches he and his patrol had seen, a month ago, were a motley bunch of beggars grubbing in the ground on the slopes of the mountains. He and his patrol had chased them, but they ran, mostly women and children, into the deep canyons. He had turned back after a perfunctory search. Now, on the third day of this sweep, he was heading into Camp Goodwin; in fact, he could see a faint rise of smoke to the southeast that would be the camp. The troopers riding behind him were covered with dust and sweat. The last of the sun slipped toward the earth rim. Instant cooling and contracting of the air brought night wind.

Lieutenant Fairly rode beside Captain Bartlett, slumped in his saddle, a three-day beard stubble beneath the flowing longhorn mustache he affected. Bartlett had spoken to the lieutenant, on one occasion in a slightly deprecating tone, about the mustache. It was undignified, a style too well identified with miners, cowboys, and saloon trash. Bartlett himself wore an almost exact replica of Custer's modified Van Dyke—dashing, Bartlett thought, but having a dignity of command. Lieutenant Fairly had ignored his suggestive remarks, either from insolence or stupidity; probably stupidity, Bartlett surmised.

Bartlett had been in Apache territory five years. He had been a captain for twelve, and his hair was gray beneath his cavalry hat. He was hoping for a promotion to major before his retirement, and had requested this duty in Apacheria for that purpose. The loud clamor of the newspapers and political interest in the war had convinced him that here was the place to make promotions. If one could find action, he could overnight become a hero to the newspapers. Captain Bartlett, like most army officers, was an avid killer of Apaches, when he could find any. A killing could be termed a "skirmish," and if the Apache resisted or fired back, it could be reported as a "battle." The chain of command, all the way to the top, leaned over backward in collusion with all officers in magnifying reports. As in honor among thieves, all benefited from the loot: promotions, higher budgets from Congress, more enlistments and hence more power, successful lobbying to increase pay, benefits and pensions, glory in the eyes of the public—in army terms, "increasing the stature of the soldiers." It was a game everybody played. Everybody benefited. The newspapers loved it.

And so flagging from monotonous routine and somewhat discouraged by lack of the opportunity to kill Apaches, Captain Bartlett nevertheless had not given up hope. He was eager to sight an Indian . . . any Indian, preferably a group of Indians.

Consequently it was he and Lieutenant Fairly who heard the shots. Lieutenant Fairly shared Bartlett's ambitions and lifted his hand at the same instant as Bartlett. Halting their horses, they were almost run over by the tired, listless mounts of the troopers behind them, who served without hope or ambition.

"Goddammit!" Bartlett shouted at the sergeant whose horse had bumped his own. "Halt!"

"Halt!" was shouted back down the line.

"I heard shots!" Lieutenant Fairly shouted for all to hear. He was ever alert. There was a remote possibility of Indians, in which case the "report" had begun. His name must be duly recorded: "Fairly, First Lieutenant. Alertly reported hearing shots."

Captain Bartlett was not to be outmaneuvered. "I *heard* the goddamn shots, that's why I signaled the halt!"

"I signaled too, sir, I believe at the same time."

Fairly was cannily willing to share the halt signal with Bartlett. This stole half of Bartlett's credit for the signal, while Fairly was sole owner of the shouted warning of shots. He therefore was not in the least disconcerted at Bartlett's unmilitary "shut up!" and reclined rather smugly in his saddle. The sergeant, a big, red-faced drunkard, was studying the sky. He had heard nothing and moreover was fully confident there had been no shots. He was accustomed to wild-ass "signs" seen and heard by officers, and so kept his thoughts firmly on the bottle he had stashed in the barracks. It was a matter of mental discipline.

The sun still spewed a faint light at the horizon. A thin shadow had moved across the landscape, however, and would thicken—the beginning of twilight. Quickly changing temperature brought a steadily growing wind. The wind blew from the west, from across the desolate prairie. This time the entire patrol heard the shots. They were spaced, measured—one . . . two . . . three—the universal distress signal of the wilderness. The shots, from far away, were no more than faint crackings on the wind. Bartlett raised his binoculars. Three perhaps four miles, where the prairie rolled away against the sun's dying light, he saw the trooper. He sat on a nervous, scuffling horse. He had raised his own binoculars, and as Bartlett looked on he waved frantically.

"Trooper in distress!" Bartlett shouted first this time, while Fairly was still studying the landscape, and with some satisfaction noted the instant pout come to Fairly's face.

Captain Bartlett swung into action. Jerking his saber from the scabbard with some difficulty, he swiped the air, narrowly missing the ducking sergeant's head, shouted, "Follow me! Gallop!" and spurred his horse, coattails flapping, through the sage and cactus toward the figure on the skyline. Instantaneously Lieutenant Fairly whipped out his own saber and, sinking his spurs in his mount with a desperate jab, was riding beside Bartlett in a flash. As he spurred harder, passing the captain, Bartlett cursed, kicking his own mount to a greater effort. Hats flattened against the wind, they were soon charging at a dead run toward the lone figure several miles away.

The sergeant and troopers galloped behind. The sergeant knew horses. Within a mile Bartlett's and Fairly's horses had bottomed out, puffing and wheezing. They had begun to stumble and Fairly first, then Bartlett—somewhat triumphantly, for he pulled his mount down only when its head was past Fairly's—dropped the horses into a bone-jarring trot. The sergeant and troopers caught up. At the end of a trotting mile Bartlett again lifted his horse into a gallop, with Fairly still beside him. The twilight had deepened, making the bushes of sage appear unexpectedly and forcing the horses to dodge quickly to keep their feet. Twice Bartlett was almost unseated, but refused to sheathe his saber in favor of holding the saddle. Fairly would not sheathe his. Cactus, standing higher and silhouetted, was more easily avoided.

The distressed trooper had disappeared over the roll of prairie. Captain Bartlett was the first to see them, near the spot where the mounted trooper had been. A line of troopers on foot! The troopers appeared to be running away from Bartlett and his men, toward the roll of prairie. Close by his ear, Lieutenant Fairly shouted, "Infantry line directly ahead!" Before Fairly had finished his warning, Captain Bartlett had repeated it. His bellow was much louder and carried better on the wind than the lieutenant's somewhat treble voice. He felt satisfied he had destroyed any contention from Fairly that he had shouted first. Furthermore, he followed with an order, "Deploy right and left! Hooooo!" The column behind him split, still galloping as the troopers swung into a long line on either side of Bartlett. Now a faint puzzle entered the mind of the captain. In the dim light the infantrymen appeared to be running ahead of him, but they were not moving! His own mounted troopers were bearing down quickly on them. Alarmed, he had little time to shout "Passing through infantry line!" before he and his horsemen shot through the line of foot soldiers.

For fifty yards Bartlett galloped his riders. Ahead of him was nothing: dim shapes of sagebrush, cluttered mounds of boulders, cactus. He slid his horse to a halt, bellowing, "Halt!" Turning, his back now to a wind that was strong and steady, he could still see the line of foot soldiers. Now they appeared to be running toward him as he faced them, but they were making no progress! He could see them, their figures definitely in motion, toward him, but while they moved, they seemed to come no closer. Bartlett looked down his trooper line, to left and right. They were sitting as he was, staring ahead at the infantry line. The sergeant spoke near him, "What the hell?" —making his usual contribution of absolutely nothing.

Captain Bartlett advanced his horse slowly toward the figures and his troopers on either side reluctantly kept pace. As he came closer Bartlett felt the hair on his scalp definitely rise, and goose pimples broke out over his body. The wind was lifting at his back and the infantry ahead of him seemed to be running faster, but still did not move toward him. Except for the wind, a low moan, and the soft thud of the troopers' horses walking, there was silence. Now, moving closer, Bartlett and his men could hear another sound, small and distant, coming from the line of infantry—it was a light pattering, as of many feet running! Bartlett glowered at them. *Were the stupid bastards running in place?* An absurdly crazy suggestion entered his mind. *Are they performing exercises out here in the dark on the prairie, by God?* He shouted, "Infantry command! Who commands?" There was no answer, but the pattering grew louder.

Coming closer, the horses began snorting, shying

at the sound and sight of figures in the distorted light. The pattering was louder now. Bartlett's thoughts were half-hysterical. *What are the sonsofbitches doing,* dancing? Perhaps they had actually gone insane . . . with the heat . . . in which case, they could be dangerous. Getting closer, Bartlett recognized the pattering sound—not feet running, but coats flapping in the wind. The silly sonsofbitches had their coats unbuttoned, and now Bartlett could see the coattails whipping and popping in the wind.

It was Lieutenant Fairly who divined the puzzle's solution. Half in astonishment, half triumphantly, he shouted, "Why those are cactus and brush, with coats and hats on them!" He announced this again, shouting down the line. Bartlett was too relieved to resent Fairly's priority of discovery. He had been close to bolting either through or away from the infantry line.

Now the horsemen advanced closer. Before them, in a long line, cactus figures faced them, hats lifting and dropping in the wind on top of cactus trunks. Coats were neatly draped over the cactus, sleeves covering cactus limbs. The wind beating against the hats and coats had given the figures the appearance of running. Still, it was an eerie, ghostly sight, unexplained—so much so that Bartlett's troopers saw no humor in it, sitting their horses silently, facing the line of flapping coats and jiggling hats. The supernatural effect was heightened by the wind's low moaning in the brush, scattering small bursts of sand that rattled like dry bones over the sage.

An ear-shattering clap of rifle fire almost made Bartlett leap into the air. The fire came from behind him. A trooper fell woodenly from his horse, and another horse reared in the air, dropping a limp rider from his back. Bartlett felt a hot sting zip along his left arm. He was wounded! There was a brief pause, and again, a concerted fire of rifles. The firing came from behind them—from the boulders in the distance. Bartlett recovered his senses. This was action! He charged his horse straight through the uniformed cactus line, away from the firing, for fifty yards before sliding his mount to a halt.

He bellowed down the line, "Sergeant, order dismount . . . prone firing positions! Detach five men to the rear to hold horses!"

The sergeant, barely lifting his head from his prone position, shouted down the line. In a flash the troopers had followed the sergeant's example, lying flat, rifles extended. Only Bartlett was left standing, with Fairly hovering beside him. Bartlett had lost his hat in his first startled jump in the saddle. His hair waved in the wind. He lifted his saber now, pointing in the direction from which the rifle fire had come.

"Men!" he yelled into the wind. "I intend to hold this line against all charges! There will be no retreat! Not one damn inch!" He felt better now. He was no coward, and his feet were on solid ground. He had just made a brave, even a heroic statement. Let Fairly deny that in the record!

The Apaches, of course, had no intention of charging. In fact they were totally silent and did nothing. Bartlett felt confused. He had his men ready; why didn't the murderous scoundrels charge?

Fairly stepped close to him. "Sir, I notice you are wounded . . . ah . . . perhaps incapacitated. I am at your service to assume command." His tone was solicitous, sympathetic.

For a brief flash Bartlett felt a flood of unnatural kindness toward Fairly—a faithful retainer, willing to step into the breach to serve his master. But Bartlett was built of sterner stuff, topped by a steel-trap mind. True, he was wounded, perhaps desperately so. He faced an army of savages, but his keen mind recovered and he perceived the insidious motive behind Fairly's seeming faithfulness. He glowered at the lieutenant. Though his face was not six inches from his junior officer's his pronouncement was loud and forceful:

"Lieutenant, as long as I am able to stand, I will fight! As long as I can breathe and lift saber, I will command!" Bartlett was pleasantly shocked at his own utterance. It had just come out . . . he was sure he had not read it anywhere. Perhaps when a commanding figure stood at death's door, it was his soul speaking! Considering this, he breathed hard, leaning toward the lieutenant. His left arm hung limp, and placing his saber point in the ground, he sagged perceptibly, using the saber for support. The lieutenant felt compelled to step forward to hold him. Blood soaked the sleeve of Bartlett's upper arm. Where the bullet had torn the sleeve, Fairly ripped away the cloth. He made a gloating announcement.

"Sir! The skin is only grazed. It is a small furrow across your arm."

Bartlett shook him off bitterly. "Get away!" He had to do something, and quickly. Stepping before the line of prone troopers, he yelled with startling suddenness, "*Fire!*"

Taken unawares, the troopers required a full minute to begin firing, their rifles cracking and thumping down the line. Now from the boulders, two hundred yards distant, Apache rifles answered them. Captain Bartlett felt a surge of pride. This, by God, was not a mere skirmish, this was a *battle!* No commanding officer engaged in an action of this magnitude could be ignored. His intention now was to enlarge the engagement, increasing its size and therefore its importance. Looking around him, he noted that the non-West Point Indians had predictably performed a maneuver with a fatal weakness—they had not surrounded him! His rear was open. Summoning Lieutenant Fairly, he brusquely ordered him to send a rider to Camp Goodwin. A fast horse could cover the ground in thirty minutes and return with every soldier in the camp within the hour. The Apaches had foolishly attacked him near the camp and reinforcements! The messenger drummed away and the

Apaches made no effort to intercept him, another indication of their subhuman intelligence. Instead they continued a sporadic, desultory fire that kept Bartlett's men pinned down on their roll of prairie.

Within the hour the full complement of troops at Camp Goodwin was engaged. With mounting satisfaction and enthusiasm Captain Bartlett noted that the enemy had begun to fall back, farther and farther to the west. He pressed them, capturing and holding ground. Captain Jeremiah H. Bartlett was winning!

Camp Goodwin was silent now. Lanterns still lit in the mess hall spotted the parade ground with squares of yellow light. The soldiers had hastily mounted at the summons, thundering out of the camp behind Captain Simpson, toward the conflict not ten miles to the west. Left behind was a corporal and a squad of six men. They stood on a rooftop at one prong of the U and watched across the prairie, occasionally rewarded by a dim flash of firing.

Behind them, at the rear of the camp, four figures dropped silently from a roof to the ground. They wore trooper coats and cavalry hats. Their legs were bare. They wore breechclouts. Geronimo, Naiche, Fun, and Kaywahla moved shadowlike through the buildings. They found the one. A thick, small, windowless adobe. When they entered, Geronimo grunted with pleasure. Stacked in gleaming rows of well-ordered racks were rifles. Below the rifles ammunition boxes stood end to end. While Fun and Kaywahla began pulling the rifles from the walls, Geronimo and Naiche crossed the parade ground to the remuda. Here, with Geronimo whistling softly between his teeth to calm the horses, they selected and bridled four rangy cavalry horses. They put no saddles on them. In the adjoining mule corral they fashioned halters around the heads of eight big army mules and, pulling pack rigs from the corral's top rail, saddled the mules. Then they boldly led the horses and mules back across the open grounds to the ammunition storehouse.

Fun and Kaywahla were placing the rifles in sacks. Fun gloated happily, "Enough rifles and bullets here to kill *everybody.*"

"Yes," Geronimo remarked dryly, "and we will get to use them while you stand around being happy about it."

Fun laughed. "I am in the army now. If a bluecoat comes, I will touch my hat with the magic signal and he will touch his hat and we will be friends."

For half an hour they stacked the rifles, carrying them through the door and lashing them across the backs of the pack mules. Then, the ammunition boxes, cumbersome and bulky, were tied on the pack saddles. They could not get all the rifles. Geronimo called a halt when the last mule was loaded.

They mounted and rode, leading the mules, across the parade ground and through the opening of the U. The corporal, seeing them passing, ran to the end of the building roof.

"Hey!" he shouted. "Where the hell you fellows goin'?"

The riders leading the mules did not look up as they passed below and away from him, except for a slight, easy-riding private. The private looked up, flashing a broad white-toothed smile. Lifting his hand to his hat he snapped a parade-ground salute smartly at the corporal. While the corporal watched, the private saluted him again . . . and again . . . and fading toward darkness again.

"Smartass!" the corporal shouted.

Fun was disappointed; the bluecoat would not return the magic signal.

18

Major General George Crook was back in Apacheria.
He had been here before and endured a frustrating
four years of the Apaches' style of warfare. Crook
had neither the political ambitions of Custer and
Sherman nor Sheridan's pernicious penchant for
glory. He was a candid man, usually "telling it like it
is."

The day Lee surrendered at Appomattox, a Confederate cavalry general named Thomas Lafayette
Rosser struck the center of Crook's command. Crook
tersely reported his own disaster: ". . . forced to retire by overwhelming numbers." No excuses. Custer,
brought up to meet Rosser and routed, made a volu-
minous report excusing himself. Military records
emerging after the war failed to indict Crook's verac-
ity on any occasion. Sheridan, in contrast, got poor
marks. Thoroughly whipped and routed by Hampton
at Trevillian's, Sheridan fled across two rivers and
reported to Grant, "Found Hampton with all rebel
cavalry at Trevillian's and whipped him; but Brecken-
ridge's division of infantry came to his rescue, and as
I was about out of ammunition, I deemed it best to
come back."

Rosser gave a fair ranking to Crook, but said of
Sheridan, ". . . a dull man. His mind works too
slowly for the quick maneuvers of cavalry. All this
vaporing about Yankee victories *after* the South
yielded to starvation and poverty of arms, is the bray-
ing of the proverbial ass over the prostrate form of

the sick and dying lion." Rosser should have known. He mastered Sheridan, and "Little Phil" never forgot. As the vaporing thinned in the light of records released after the war, Sheridan turned his attention to the Indians. Indians didn't keep records.

Crook was as careful as any professional soldier of his record, but he was not a liar and had one irritating habit, as far as Sheridan was concerned. If he discovered an admirable quality in an opponent, he expressed it. His basic fairness led him often to these admissions. Of a Confederate operation in 1865 he said, "I consider it to be the most brilliant exploit of the War." He had inside knowledge. He was the victim.

On a cold night, February 21, 1865, General Crook was asleep in a hotel at Cumberland, Maryland, surrounded by ten thousand Union troops under his command. At midnight he was awakened by a polite Southern accent informing him that he was under arrest. Thirty Confederate Rangers had slipped through his army to capture him and General Benjamin Kelly, headquartered in the same hotel. In adjoining rooms, General Rutherford B. Hayes and Major William McKinley were also sleeping, but the Rangers regarded them as too unimportant to take along. As the Confederates rode their charges south, back through Yankee lines, Crook remarked, "I may as well enjoy it." He and his captors got along famously all the way to Richmond, with Crook joining in the banter over his embarrassment. General Kelly saw no humor in the situation.

Immediately after the War Crook further demonstrated his inability to nurse ill will. When he married a Miss Mary Dailey, her brother James Dailey was best man at the wedding. James Dailey was one of the Confederate Rangers who had kidnaped Crook.

For six years prior to his return to Arizona and the Apaches, General Crook held a command in the Department of the Platte. Exactly a week before

Custer's political dreams died with him at Little Big Horn, Crook had clashed with Crazy Horse on the Rosebud. He had retreated after the Sioux war chief had inflicted heavy casualties on him. His report of record gave Crazy Horse his due.

After Custer's debacle the nation and the United States Army called for vengeance. When Crook's cavalry swept over American Horse's peaceful camp of reservation Indians he was "sickened" by the sight of slaughtered women and children. The cavalry had not been particular in picking their targets. When the last of the Cheyennes, led by Dull Knife and Little Wolf, began their forlorn flight toward a homeland they would never see, George Crook was the general assigned to follow and capture them. Cheyenne blood made the trailing easy, and the miles were measured by frozen bodies of the old and the young, like wooden markers in the snow. The experience had a profound effect on Crook. After that he endeavored to help the homeless Ponca Indians and gave open support to Chief Standing Bear in his court petition to be named a legal "person." For this, Crook received the added disfavor of Sherman and Sheridan.

Now back at Whipple Barracks in Arizona, he had a broader view of humanity beneath his rough military exterior. The Apaches found him to be tough, a tenacious and relentless fighter (they called him Nantan Lupan, Chief Gray Wolf), but they learned they could trust his word. His sense of fairness led him to denounce the Tucson ring of contractors. This did nothing to enhance his popularity with the politicians and their friend, Sheridan. Disregarding Washington's ominous smoke signals relayed through an increasingly hostile press, General Crook set about his plans to secure peace in the Southwest. He opened persuasive negotiations with Mexican military authorities to forget old Yankee animosities and coordinate with him a clean sweep of the Apache sanctuaries in the Sierra Madre. Discarding cumbersome wagons, he employed mule packs in the rugged terrain, devising tactical methods that would be used as late as World War II in Asia and earn him the belated recognition of military historians as the top Indian fighter produced by the United States Army, outstripping Custer's and Sheridan's cosmetic glory. He shocked the military establishment by hiring the enemy—Apache scouts. Crook found the Apache scouts to be "ingenious trackers . . . tough, without equal in the mountains." Once hired, he reported, they maintained an "unfailing, even touching loyalty" to him. Also, he brought with him some of the West's most renowned frontiersmen, including Al Sieber.

It was Sieber who introduced Crook to young Tom Horn, and while most staff officers resented the unmilitary, flippant young man, their disaffection was tempered somewhat by Horn's display of courage on several occasions. Crook, however didn't hire Horn for his courage, commendable as it was. He spent long sessions with the young man discussing Apaches. From Horn, Crook began to understand the Apache from the inside—the thinking, customs, culture, and religion. Crook wanted to know what made the enigma operate, what it was that could sustain—indeed drive—a small band of people through the centuries of war with the Spanish. On his first tour of duty in Apacheria, Crook had dismissed the Apaches as simply "wild." He had paid for it with the usual frustrating defeats. This time he probed the complexities of a complex people with the surety of a surgeon. Tom Horn was a fountain of information. Politely, Crook never questioned Horn about his personal life, nor the persistent rumors that Horn "rode" with Geronimo on Mexican raids. The general was content to indulge all of the young man's conversational ramblings on the years he had lived with the Apaches, and only occasionally asked strategically placed questions.

Through this system of developing insight into his opponent, obtaining the increased cooperation of the Mexican military, and devising creative military tactics, Crook was steadily reducing the Apache threat. Toward the hostile Apaches, Crook applied only the professional soldier's code, to do his duty. He bore them no particular hatred, except one: Geronimo. For the War Shaman, he nursed an intense enmity. In this he had the total support of other army officers.

With the death of Mangas Coloradas, the Bedonkohe band had joined Cochise, becoming one band, known as the Chiricahuas. With them had come Geronimo. He had married again, this time a girl called Chee-hash-kish, described by the Apaches as "very handsome." She had borne him two children, a boy called Chappo and a daughter called Tozey.

Cochise, growing old and weary, was hard pressed to provide sanctuary not only for the Bedonkohes, but also for remnants of the Gila and Tonto bands, whose ranks had been depleted by Crook's army. Cochise had traveled as far as Santa Fe in the cause of peace and for a year he had neither headed nor ordered an attack north of the international boundary. Without a treaty of "word," however, no one could restrain the indefatigable Geronimo. During this time he was known as a *capitán* of Cochise and, with his usual energy, recruited warriors from all the Apache bands. He struck the bluecoats like a shark attacking a whale, slashing and disappearing. Efforts to hunt down Geronimo were described by one officer as "as futile as hunting deer with a brass band." The Chiricahuas got the blame. The *Arizona Citizen* wrote:

The kind of war needed for the Chiricahua Apaches is steady, unrelenting, hopeless and undiscriminating war, slaying men, women and children, until every valley, crest and crag and fastness shall send to high heaven the grateful incense of festering and rotting Chiricahua Apaches.

General Crook was infuriated by Geronimo's continuing attacks and taunting messages. Once a regular army patrol with a detachment of Apache scouts sighted him as they passed through Doubtful Canyon. He stood in plain sight, high on a rock ledge, and waved to them, shouting, "You cannot catch me shooting." Crook added an additional one hundred Apache scouts to the payroll, called in his officers and men, five thousand in all, and made ready to mount a major campaign against one man. He was halted by orders from Washington.

The Indian Bureau had more devious plans, designed to increase the bureau's power at the expense of the United States Army.

San Carlos was under the administration of the bureau and in the bureau's own words was to be made into a "place to concentrate all Apaches." A concentration camp. The bureau knew the most skilled of government liars couldn't invent the platitudes necessary to induce Apaches to come to this bleak and unlikely place. Therein lay the plan.

Bureau peace negotiators approached individual Apache bands and offered to set up reservations where each band could live "forever" in an area to their liking. Once the bands were settled, each farming its own reservation, and had turned in their weapons, then, and only then, would the United States Army move in, "capture" them, and remove them to San Carlos. Thus, the Warm Springs Apaches and the Coyoteros were settled. The Mescaleros, existing miserably at Bosque Redondo, were offered no such deal. They posed no threat. The major problem was the Chiricahuas.

The bureau selected a man as negotiator to approach Cochise, who was as naïve as the Apaches in the ways of bureaucratic treachery. General Oliver

Otis Howard was told only the "reservation forever" part of the plan. San Carlos wasn't mentioned. Howard had been a standout soldier at Gettysburg and had lost an arm at Fair Oaks. He was a Vermonter and a devoutly religious man. Universally disliked by his fellow officers, including Crook, who regarded his piety as ostentatious, he had a warm empathy with Indians, who discussed spiritual matters as routinely as the whites discussed their material dealings.

General Howard enlisted the aid of Victorio in contacting Cochise, and he induced Tom Jeffords and a nephew of Cochise's named Chee to accompany him. The three rode into the Dragoons among the towering peaks sheltering Cochise's stronghold. Howard had intended his visit to be brief, but he had no idea of the independent democratic process of the Apaches. Cochise informed him that he must have time to gather his *capitanes* so all might come in and share in the negotiations; otherwise, they would not be bound by it. Howard agreed to stay. His visit lasted nearly two weeks.

He later wrote that he was "pleasantly and delightfully surprised." He found the Apaches to be a friendly and hospitable people who accepted him warmly. He enthusiastically joined with them in prayer, confident in his pious old heart that the prayers "were the same . . . to the same God." He ate with their families seated cross-legged on the ground and laughed uproariously at humorous tales; he found Indian humor to be "refreshing." Forgetting his West Point dignity, the general played with the children and became a favorite of the ranchería. He taught the youth Naiche to write his name.

General Howard won the heart of the toughest war *capitán* present. In his old age, Geronimo would speak of him, remembering, ". . . he always kept his word with us and treated us as brothers. We could have lived forever at peace with him. If there is any pure, honest white man in the United States Army that man is General Howard."

Howard approached Cochise with ideas of his own on where the Chiricahuas should live, but he was not arrogant in his views. He listened to Cochise, finding him to be "an intelligent man with calm deliberation and reasonable manner." For the first and last time, an Indian chief changed the mind of a United States Army general through rational discussion. A treaty was made that incorporated the ideas of Cochise. The reservation would include the Dragoon and Chiricahua mountains and Sulphur Springs Valley. This was the homeland of the Cochise band and the treaty was warmly endorsed by them. As for his own and his *capitanes'* part of the treaty, Cochise pledged to guard the roads, including the California Road, and all settlements of the area against outlaw hostiles.

Geronimo was pleased with the agreement and had full confidence in General Howard, but he remained suspicious of the powers behind the general.

For two years the treaty was kept by both sides. During this time Geronimo made no raids north of the international boundary. However, he did continue to raid his old Mexican enemies. The government of Mexico called on United States authorities for enforcement of the Apache-containment treaty. "Forever" ran out.

Cochise was dying when they came to tell him his people were to be removed to San Carlos. He offered no resistance. Cochise had given up more than freedom; he had abandoned any hope of life for the Apaches. His emaciated body was depleted of its former magnificent strength. Calling his two sons, Taza and Naiche, to him, he made them promise that they would keep the peace. Then he asked for his old friend Tom Jeffords. Jeffords was alarmed when he saw Cochise's condition, and as he was about to leave to summon medical help from Fort Bowie Cochise asked, "Do you think you will see me alive again?"

Jeffords wouldn't lie to his old friend. "No. I don't think I will. What do you think?"

"I will be dead by ten o'clock tomorrow morning," Cochise answered. "It is not clear to my mind, but I think we will meet, somewhere up there."

By the time Jeffords had returned with a surgeon from the fort, Cochise was dead. Between Jeffords' leaving him and his death, Cochise asked to be carried upward from the valley floor, toward the sun. A long procession bore him up among the Dragoons' peaks, to rest him on a plateau, facing west. First his family members, then his *capitanes* knelt by his side to bid him farewell. Geronimo was the last. As he rose and walked away the thin Death Chant of Cochise began over the assembled Apaches. Cochise had put his earthly duties and farewells behind him. He was beginning his Journey.

Geronimo never spoke of that final exchange with Cochise, but the Apaches present were sure Cochise made no effort to extract a peace promise from Geronimo. As Geronimo rose from the side of Cochise and walked away the setting sun struck his hard cheekbones. They were slashed with yellow. The bluecoats had broken their word.

That night, while the Apaches mourned the passing of a great chief, Geronimo slipped away from the Chiricahua band and the approaching soldiers. Accompanying him were his family, his cousin Juh, and a handful of Nedni warriors. Crossing the California Road in the night, they struck an encamped wagon train. Only the women and children escaped in a wagon drawn by fast horses. Hastily the war party loaded the train's supplies on the backs of mules and disappeared north into the Dos Cabezos mountains above Apache Pass. While United States troopers made the usual futile search for him, Geronimo led his party across the San Simon Valley, through the Gilas and into the White Mountains. He was welcomed by his friend Victorio, but most of the Warm

Springs band were uneasy. Reprisals were following Geronimo. He had given his answer to the bureau's treachery, but now his followers were few. The bleakness of Geronimo's future did not attract many willing to share it.

19

John Phillip Clum had definite plans for Geronimo. Clum was the bureau's agent in charge of San Carlos, and as Indian agents operated, he was an oddity. He was honest. Demanding and getting good beef and quality supplies from contractors, he had set up a system of fair ration distribution at San Carlos unique among Indian reserves. Youthful and energetic, he was an accomplished organizer who had demonstrated a capable management of Indians and forced the United States military to stand aside—at a short distance. Using Apaches as policemen, he set up Indian courts with Apache headmen as judges, allowing the Apaches to punish their own for infractions of his rules. Clum found his fairness to the Apaches was rewarded by staunch loyalty for the most part. By now he had assembled on San Carlos the Coyoteros, whose "forever" treaty had ended, remnants of the Gilas, the Tontos, the Bedonkohes, the Chiricahuas, and a number of the Nedni band rounded up with the Chiricahuas. His next move was the Warm Springs Apaches and Victorio.

Clum had not kept aloof from his charges. He spoke Apache fluently and he spent endless hours interrogating the Apaches at San Carlos to ferret out the "troublemakers" of Apacheria. There was only one. The tales were fantastic but they rang true. The "warrior with the yellow stripes" was identified with monotonous regularity as the inspiration and guiding hand of the Apache war against the United States.

John Clum became obsessed with the solution to all Apache depredations: hang Geronimo. A fairly strong argument might be documented to prove him correct.

Through his Apache police, Clum had established a highly efficient spy service. In a short time he knew Geronimo was encamped with the Warm Springs band, and Clum had in his hand orders from Washington to bring the Warm Springs Apaches to San Carlos. Their treaty "forever" was ended. That they harbored Geronimo was a likely enough excuse, but first Clum somehow would have to get hold of the elusive War Shaman. Clum sent a delegation of Apaches to see him. Their message was friendly. Clum simply wanted to talk, a council. Geronimo consented, but he was cautious.

Always haunted by his Power's predictions, Geronimo was fearful for his family. He persuaded Juh and his warriors to take his family to the Nedni stronghold in the Sierra Madre, and the following morning he rode into the agreed meeting place at the Ojo Caliente Agency under a truce flag, with only seven warriors. He and his men were immediately surrounded by a hundred armed Apache policemen. Back-up United States cavalry, summoned by Clum, was on the way. Geronimo had been "captured," but only by treachery. It would be the last time.

Geronimo and his followers were put in chains, a blacksmith welded iron bands around their ankles, and they were thrown into a cell at the agency. Now Clum released the stories of Geronimo to the newspapers. The United States military already knew them, but had thought discretion the better part of embarrassment. Now the public heard. It was sensational. Headlines blossomed across the United States: "GERONIMO THE HUMAN TIGER," "GERONIMO RENEGADE MURDERER," "GERONIMO CRAZED KILLER."

Geronimo had arrived. Congressmen, hearing the public outrage, competed in marathon denunciations.

Without doubt, Geronimo salvaged the sagging fortunes of many a political hack. A man couldn't be *all* bad who was capable of expressing such outrage as ". . . not a drop of humanity's milk of pity should be shed to this blood-drinking scavenger from hell's corrupted depths. . . ." Newspapers gnawed the sensation to the marrow. "Black-handed assassin" alternated with "red-handed assassin." "Cold-hearted dog," for some curious reason, seemed to be a favorite. One enterprising newsman introduced a fresh note of horror to quicken the tempo of a nation already leaping like a lynch mob. He reported on sound authority that "Geronimo is known to have often *eaten* parts of his victims." Why only parts, or which parts, the reporter declined to explain. Even in his cell, Geronimo was credited with more current deaths as a scattering of righteous citizens burst blood vessels with indignation.

Governments of towns and territories, the United States Justice Department, and the United States Army squared off for the right to hang Geronimo. The "bloody renegade" was going down in history books, and the politicians or generals who sprung the hangman's trap would rate a line of immortality. The infighting was vicious.

One by one, the seven companions of Geronimo were released to San Carlos, free of their chains. Geronimo was placed in solitary confinement, where, in the semidarkness, he returned an inscrutable stare to the tormentors who scrambled to peek at him through a single high window. Several times a week he was informed that "his time was up." He said nothing. Geronimo had consulted his Power. Now he waited.

General George Crook was doing some consulting of his own. The storm over who would have the honor of hanging Geronimo was raging openly in the press. But hidden from Crook was the effect on several thousand volatile Apaches in the several thousand square miles for which he was responsible. It made him nervous. He didn't show it. Here in his office he appeared relaxed. His tunic was unbuttoned, chair tilted back; with booted feet crossed over his desk, he was chewing Burley and periodically hitting a spittoon ten feet away with ringing accuracy. Hands clasped behind his head, he studied the ceiling with a sleepy stare. Major Morrow sat stiffly erect in a corner chair.

God! Morrow thought. *A major general! He continuously encourages that impudent ass to act more disrespectful!* The impudent ass was slouched in a chair opposite Crook; in fact, he had a boot heel cocked on the corner of Crook's desk. It was Tom Horn, and he was cutting from a string of jerky beef with a bowie knife, plopping the cuttings in his mouth with noisy regularity. The two suggested an appearance more of disreputable saloon loungers than a major general consulting a subordinate.

Crook was talking. ". . . and so you say, Horn, that Geronimo's hanging is . . . uh . . . would have an inconclusive effect on the Apaches?"

Horn chewed speculatively before answering. "Well, naw, General, I didn't say that. I said they're kinda for it and against it, at the same time. Kinda scared for him to be hanged . . . maybe would breathe easier when he was. You know, General"— Horn pointed the bowie at Crook for emphasis— "kinda like maybe when they got Jesus . . . the people there, was wanting it . . . Jesus being kind of a troublemaker and all . . . but they was kinda scared at the same time."

Horn's comparison of Jesus' crucifixion to Geronimo's hanging brought an incredulous stare from Major Morrow. Crook, however, appeared to accept this comparison quite easily. With scarcely a turn of his head, he rang the spittoon before answering.

"You're saying Geronimo has a religious conscience? What kind of religion?"

" 'Pache religion, naturally, General."

"Naturally," Crook said dryly. "What is that?"

Horn chuckled. "You got a week to listen?"

"Skin it down to an hour." Crook eased his own knife from his belt, cutting a careful chew of Burley and slipping it into his cheek. He settled lower in his chair.

Horn sighed. "Well, the 'Pache believes if you keep the *high* laws, then you strengthen your spirit body. Each time you git on the Wheel . . . that is, git born again into a material body on earth, you exercise these high laws against the *low* laws that the material world goes by. Now as you strengthen your spirit body, then each time you die—or pass from this material world—your spirit body is stronger . . . if you done it right . . . kept the faith and all . . . and you move to higher and higher plateaus. The highest plateau, naturally, is the one where you're so strong, you don't have to come back. Gittin' 'saved' . . . so to speak. Which"—Horn inserted a beef cutting into his mouth—"which is more or less like Jesus put it . . . you got to be born again . . . just literal born again . . . and the Way is hard . . . which He said too. It's damn shore a hard set of rules by which to git saved."

Crook had not put up his knife; he was meticulousy cleaning his fingernails. "Not much different from the white man's religion, excepting maybe the reincarnation."

"Naw," Horn agreed, "not much . . . 'cepting the 'Pache don't look at it like reincarnation. I've heard you holler, General, that the Indian ain't got no regard for the value of time . . ."

Crook nodded. "Correct, absolutely none."

Horn ignored Crook's interruption. ". . . but that ain't right. You see, to the 'Pache, Time is eternal, going on and on with his spirit body . . . what he ain't got no regard for is the *material measurement* of Time . . . the damn clocks and calendars and such . . . nor not a hell of a lot for all the material building we're measuring ourselves with . . . shit, like he figures, everything material is going to die and rot, sooner or later."

"Correct." Crook nodded.

"Now, another difference," Horn said, "white man naturally has got to set him up a bureau to run things . . . and try to make it easy . . . including his religion, so's he can get it interpreted for his convenience. Thataway, he can run in the bureau church every Sunday, holler 'Jesus!' git his ass dunked in water, and he's 'saved.' This makes it a helluva lot easier than the 'Pache way . . . and the white man can git back to his material fixin's and puttin' up governments and other supervising bullshit. So . . ."— Horn spread his hands conclusively—"you see there *is* a difference."

"Yeah," Crook said, "I can see there is, but with no Bible, the Apache . . ."

"Oh, he's got a Bible," Horn interrupted, "yep . . . a long one of about a hundred stories, so to speak."

Crook pocketed the knife. "Let's hear one . . . one of the stories."

Horn frowned. "Well, you have to understand a lot of the stories has to do with fighting government slavery . . . since the 'Paches been fighting it about three hundred years. There's the one about the snake . . . him being a evil sonofabitch. He practices all the low laws, the lowest of which is he has a goddamn lust for power over everything. Now the snake goes to the eagle. He says to the eagle, 'Looka here, you're flying around ever' day to get food, but there ain't no *guarantee* you're going to git it. It's liable to run out, but you put your faith in me, instead of yourself and Usen . . . that's God . . . and I'll guarantee you got food, if I run things.'

"You see," Horn explained, "the snake here is practicing a low law, inspiring fear and killing the eagle's faith in hisself and his spirit. Then the snake

251

says, 'Looka there at the coyote, he can run a hundred times faster than you, and that ain't right. You let me have the power over things, and I'll fix it so he can't hop no faster than you.' You see . . . here the snake is using a low law of envy . . . and so on . . . until the eagle gives the snake the power over him. The snake talks to the coyote the same way, 'cept he creates envy of the eagle's flying and promises to keep him on the ground, like the coyote. Winds up, the coyote and eagle got their feet and wings bound up. They're scratching ground and planting corn for the snake and got *all* their attention on material security and things and have forgot their faith and honor, and courage . . . all the high laws.

"'Pache comes by and explains things to 'em . . . to make a long story short . . . turns 'em loose. They run free again, and depend on their spirit and their faith. That," Horn said with satisfaction, "is why you'll see a snake hide under a rock ever' time he sees a eagle or a coyote . . . or a 'Pache . . . which more or less proves it out."

Crook took his feet from his desk and turned to face Horn. "Who's the snake represent?"

"Well, like ah said . . . government . . . or the goddamn politicians which put it together."

"Then"—Crook smiled—"I guess to the Apache, I'm the snake."

"Naw . . ." Horn said thoughtfully, "not to most; but we're talking about the pure religion. Geronimo is a purist, and to him, you represent the snake. Y'see, General, to Geronimo it don't matter how fair you are. He says you ain't got no right to feed him, no matter how good the food is. You ain't got no right to house him . . . ner clothe him. He says you're stealing his faith when you do this . . . you're weakening and stealing his spirit body. That's what the government don't understand . . . why they call Geronimo a 'renegade' because he won't crawl up, like a good dog, to a handful of food. Geronimo believes that this reserve camp is a lower power idea that being brought about will come back . . . you can't destroy the idea now . . . it'll come back to haunt people . . . and have more and more people in it."

"What do you think Geronimo is thinking right now?" Crook asked.

"Ol' Geronimo," Horn said emphatically, "is settin' in that cell, calm as a butter biscuit. He knows he's done his duty to his Faith. He's waiting to see if the low laws git tangled up and spring him out. If they don't"—Horn shrugged—"he's got it made anyhow. He ain't scared of takin' the Journey."

"What about the women and children he's killed?" Crook asked casually.

"Well now, General," Horn said, "that's been kind of overtalked, but the ones he has . . . it's been for his own people's survival . . . he's been fightin' on his own ground for his people's right to live free. He ain't been in Chicargo trying to put hisself over somebody else . . . and," Horn said, "I wonder what excuse the U.S. Army has got for killing Indian women and children."

Crook rose abruptly. He did not look at Tom Horn, but walked to the window and stood staring out at the parade grounds. The big clock ticked loudly in the corner. Without turning, Crook said softly, "You may go, Horn."

"Yes, sir, General. Major." Horn walked from the room, closing the door quietly behind him.

Major Morrow rose, looking at the back of Crook. He cleared his throat, but the general gave no indication that he heard him. Morrow had come to respect General George Crook as a decent man, and so, although it was not like him, he blurted out his rage: "He's an impudent ass, sir, is Horn. Should be clapped in irons. If you'll allow me, sir . . ."

Crook turned and smiled wryly. "No, no, Major. He's a bright young man. I encourage him, I know. Take the bitter with the sweet . . ." Walking to his desk, he opened a drawer and pulled a bottle of whisky and two glasses from it.

Morrow stepped forward. "Allow me, General." He was careful to ration the whisky. Crook was not known as a drinking man.

"Here." Crook took the bottle from him and sloshed the glasses half full. He left the bottle uncorked and, taking his glass, walked back to the window and looked out. Morrow waited until Crook had downed his whisky before drinking his own. He set the glass on the desk. "General, I would like to reprimand Horn. I can . . ."

"No." Crook didn't turn. "I wasn't thinking of Horn, Major. I was thinking of that goddamn Washington bureau . . . of San Carlos . . . of snakes. I hope"— he sighed, still looking out the window—"that this is the last one."

The silence was heavy. Major Morrow couldn't determine if the general was referring to the "last one" of the bureaus . . . or San Carlos . . . or snakes. He felt embarrassed, feeling he was intruding on private thoughts.

"I have duties, General, if you are . . ."

"You may go, Major," Crook said. He didn't turn as Morrow left. It was irritating, even to a devoted subordinate like Major Morrow—this propensity of General Crook's to look at all sides.

20

Even as Crook and Horn talked, good news reached the United States Army. Juh was dead. After leaving Geronimo's family at his headquarters in the Madre, Juh had moved back north with his warriors. At Galeana he had attacked and destroyed two companies of Mexican cavalry. Returning from a "peace conference" at Casa Grande, Juh and his two eldest sons were riding well behind the rest of his warriors when Juh dropped from his horse into a shallow river, probably from a heart attack. His two sons could not pull his huge body from the river. He was still breathing, and while one held his head above the waters the other raced ahead and brought back the warriors. It was a fruitless rescue. Juh had died and been buried on the banks of the river.

Unknown to the warriors, a large force of Mexicans was trailing them, and the delay caused by Juh's death allowed the Mexicans to encircle and practically destroy the Nedni warrior band. There were a few survivors. Juh's sons, Delzhinne and Daklegon, were captured by the Mexicans and executed.

The last of the great triumvirate that included Mangas Coloradas and Cochise was gone. His departure touched off celebrations in Chihuahua and Sonora and brought optimism to a weary United States military. The United States government could count its war with the Apaches in decades; the Mexicans, in centuries. Now with most of the Apaches confined at San Carlos, with the destruction of the Nedni warriors, with Juh dead and Geronimo chained and waiting for the hangman, both governments could see the sun setting on the Apaches. But was it?

John Clum had nipped at the snake juice. Like salt water, it didn't quench, but created a thirst. He was now referring to "my Apaches." Clum wanted more. He fired off a telegram to Washington: "If your Department will increase my salary sufficiently and equip two more companies of Indian police for me, I will volunteer to take care of *all* Apaches in Arizona and the troops can be removed." The telegram set off an explosion. The United States Army high command was indignant. This was an invasion of *their* power. The threat of troop withdrawals alarmed the Tucson Ring—no more troops, no more money. Merchants in the territory held emergency meetings and contacted political cronies in Washington. Magically, overnight, John Clum was transformed from a hero into a villain by the press.

Pilloried unmercifully by the newspapers, he quit in a huff. He had a final reminder for the public: "You had better hang Geronimo . . . and quick!" The public was trying. It appeared a lynch mob would have to do it. The Southwest was a dust-kicking brawl. Greed, jealousy, fights for power and glory, and a half dozen more "low" laws were thrown in to make it no-holds-barred.

Henry Lyman Hart came on the scene to settle the dust. He was the appointed successor to John Clum at San Carlos. Henry applied the bureaucratic grease. When a hundred head of cattle were purchased for San Carlos, fifty were delivered, and the profits were spread among the fraternity. Short supplies of low quality were bought at full measure and premium price. The results were hypnotic. The dust began to settle, except for the fight over Geronimo. On this issue Mr. Hart demonstrated his wisdom in the ways of quieting troubled waters. Currying favor with the rumbling discontent of the Apaches under his starvation regime, he took the chains off Geronimo and assured the public that the "renegade" would be under close surveillance at San Carlos while awaiting hanging.

Curiously, there was no cry of outrage (except from John Clum and he no longer counted). Through four months of throat-throttling fights over Geronimo, the governments of towns, territories, the bureau, and the military had developed an enthusiastic hatred for one another that rivaled their hatred for the "renegade." Now each was jealously proud that the others had not gotten the prize, and each was confident his own political clout would reward him the honors. It was a bureaucratic masterstroke.

Geronimo entered a concentration camp changed since Clum's administration. Rations were short and consisted mainly of flour and meal working with weevils, rank and rotten beef, and even pork, which the Apaches abhorred and threw away. Smallpox was sweeping through the inmates and the United States government offered no vaccinations. Geronimo was a panther tossed among thinly domesticated and discontented wildcats. Moving from campfire to campfire, he preached the Faith with all his Shaman intensity. San Carlos blew up like a bomb.

Victorio bolted north with eighty warriors. Turning east and south, he recruited two hundred Mescalero warriors. Killing and burning, he struck for the international boundary. Old Nana, always ready to fight, rode with him. Small bands broke in all directions, like missiles flung from a spinning wheel. The bands were led by Mangas, son of Mangas Coloradas, Chihuahua, a raider leader of note, and Benito.

Several hours before these bands bolted San Carlos, Geronimo had been sitting and eating by a campfire before several witnesses who would later describe the scene. They all knew his family was three hundred miles away in the Sierra Madre. No messenger had arrived to bring him news, but suddenly he had dropped his food and stood up, announcing, "My family is threatened. My family needs me. I must hurry." Picking up a bow and arrows, he had run away into the darkness. He had "seen." As he left he cut the telegraph wires where they passed through the fork of a tree and bound the ends close together with rawhide so the wire would not fall. The break was hard to find, and the news of the escape was slow in reaching the nearby mining town of Globe and the United States military. When it did, the United States Army was furious. The bureau had managed to explode the Apache War, instantaneously, over a weary Southwest. The spark was Geronimo. Newspapers screamed, "GERONIMO ESCAPES," "HUMAN TIGER AT LARGE." The Southwest battened down. Historians estimate territorial militia, vigilance committees, and United States Army patrols numbered ten thousand armed and mounted men, crisscrossing the prairie and mountains of the Southwest, searching for him. As usual, Geronimo had vanished.

He crossed the San Simon Valley without being seen and entered the Chiricahua Mountains. But he would not stay in the mountain shelter; he needed speed, and emerged from the Chiricahuas to find a faster way south. In the Sulphur Springs Valley he stole a horse at the Stephens Ranch, killing a sheepherder in the process, and rode the horse to death between there and the San Bernardino River bordering the Sierra Madre. As the horse fell for the last time Geronimo hit the ground running across the international boundary into Mexico. His vision before the campfire had been ominous. He entered a Mexico that had changed.

The mountains were the same; the vast, rolling prairie, the ceaseless wind, all the Eternals of the Apaches' Time had remained as they always would. But the shadow time of men's shadow governments was changing. The shadow here in Mexico, as in the north, was deeper, darker, and lengthening.

The year 1877 had triggered the change. By that time Mexico had been a republic slightly more than fifty years. In that fifty years, the office of *presidente* had changed hands *seventy* times. The governorship of the State of Chihuahua had been occupied by *eighty-two* separate administrations. Each administration's change was balloted by the gun: revolutions, assassinations, firing squads. The Mexicans' cry of hopelessness, "Ay, Chihuahua!" is not derived from that state's desolate prairie. The year 1877 was "the year of yellow corn," a drought that yielded not a drop of rain. Corn scraggled an inch, no higher. Cattle ran themselves to death across the plains, crazed for water. At the bottom of the human pyramid, thousands of peons died.

The year 1877 brought Porfirio Diaz to power in Mexico City, and his iron fist of order began to reach Chihuahua. In the beginning it looked hopeless. Gangs of *bandidos* occupied and "taxed" whole towns, often taking over and operating rich silver mines for extended periods of time—routine practice in the state of Chihuahua. Ranchos had their own private armies for protection (and to join revolutions). Don Porfirio changed a faint hope into a reality. By 1880 it was done. Order had arrived. His methods were direct and simple; he organized the *bandidos* into the rural police, the dreaded Rurales. Putting them in flashy, silver-trimmed uniforms with rewarding pay, he armed them with the *ley fuga*, "law of flight." Anyone arrested by the Rurales could be shot "while fleeing." Everybody so arrested, apparently, did, and most certainly was. *Pistola* justice had arrived, and there was no need for courts, juries, or judges. Manipulations for power by the *guachupines*, the "wearers of the spurs," ground to a halt.

An ally of Diaz, General Luis Terrazas came to power as Governor of Chihuahua. The general was not a politician, hence, no demagogue. The don politicians had never fooled him. They had railed against the hated Yanqui in the north to cover their ineffectiveness in dealing with the *bandidos* and the Apaches on their doorstep. Leave the Yanqui alone. The *bandido* problem was solved. One obstacle stood between Chihuahua and a peace that would open vast lands to ranching and farming. Free from terror, that peace would bring wealth. The obstacle was the Apache.

This was the single-minded objective of General Terrazas, and for its consummation he appointed his cousin, Colonel Joaquin Terrazas. Already known as an effective Apache fighter, Joaquin was destined to be recognized as Mexico's greatest in the art of killing Apaches.

Even as Geronimo stood before the campfire at San Carlos, Joaquin's Tarahumara Indian scouts had searched out the headquarters of the last of the Nedni band. The War Shaman's reckless race through ten thousand white eyes would be too late.

21

Chokole watched the sunrise. The light, coming slowly, indirectly, shot high into the heavens beyond the mountains of the Sierra Madre that shielded the Nednis from Chihuahua's plains. As the sun's rim edged over the highest peak the light sped downward and brought a magic stirring of activity below Chokole, in Yaqui Canyon. She was lying on a broad ledge near the top of the canyon, five hundred feet above the Nedni rancheria. Breakfast fires were being set. Faintly, a child's shout mixed with laughter lifted to her from the canyon bottom. By looking over the ledge, she could see tiny figures playing in the icy waters of the Yaqui River that threaded thin and clear down the canyon's cradle. She allowed herself only a glance into the canyon, however; she had guarded the eastern access to the Nedni headquarters.

The high canyon walls were inaccessible to the Enemy. From the rim of the canyon, for three hundred feet downward, the walls were sheer smooth rock. No Enemy could descend this smoothness and live. The final two hundred feet sloped to the canyon floor and was thickly forested with fir, blue spruce, and live oak that furnished a cozy shelter from eyes on the canyon's rims. Besides, the Enemy had never penetrated this far into the Madre; there were too many rugged, impassable peaks and gorges.

Even with these assurances, the Nedni rancheria was apprehensive. Juh, bringing Geronimo's family, had reported the War Shaman's imprisonment in the north. He had left, taking every able-bodied warrior, with the intent of striking both south and north of the border and entering San Carlos with war prizes to arm a revolt and free Geronimo. Juh had been gone for a long time and no messenger brought news. Ishton commanded a Nedni band of twenty old men, one hundred fifty women, and nearly three hundred children.

Chokole had selected this ledge as an ideal vantage point, less than fifty feet below the canyon's rim. Carrying her rifle and Spanish binoculars, she had labored half a day climbing to this precarious height. She had already spent the night here and would remain still another day and night before being relieved.

From this point she could see the land above and beyond the opposite rim of the canyon, broken and cragged with rocks and dotted sparsely with cactus. A few piñon trees stunted from the rocks, leaning and twisted by strong winds. The sun swept onto the wall of the canyon. Its early light sharpened pitted surfaces and wind carvings into sculptured temples and ancient faces. The light worked over brilliant black layers of rock, softening them to deep lavender. Dark reds blushed bright before fading, pink and pale. A sandstone layer of yellow mixed with a startling blue below it and in the light washed sea green.

Reluctantly Chokole took her glasses from the wall. She studied the canyon to the east where it ran straight for a mile before twisting out of sight. The canyon's floor was feathered thickly with trees. The Yaqui River was almost hidden, sparkling through openings in the treetops. A cautious Enemy could move beneath the trees without Chokole's seeing them. She knew this, and watched the birds.

Half a mile away a cliff hawk sailed peacefully over the canyon to perch on the wall's rock face. His flight caused a martin to flash purple across the green of a spruce top. From somewhere far up the canyon a morning dove cooed sad and long, echoing. Chokole, flat on her belly, moved the glasses farther up the canyon, searching for the dove, then across a glade, open and grassy, in the trees. She brought the glasses back. A doe was in the glade drinking and lifting her head from the stream. Light spots dappled the underside of her tan coat, shining in the light. Timidly she set her mouth to the water; barely a sip, before jerking her head erect. The great ears moved and she turned her head toward the east. Poised. Magically she shot away into the trees out of Chokole's sight. Probably a mountain cat looking for an early morning kill. But Chokole did not like the way the doe acted. She had not lifted her nose to the wind, but had used her ears. Cats do not make a sound on a hunt. Chokole kept her glasses on the glade. A thrush shot up from the grass, into the trees. A woodpecker, dotting red through the foliage, fled down the canyon. She felt a rising apprehension as the glade was emptied of life. She watched.

The men came trotting from the trees and did not pause in the glade, but came on. They wore gray uniforms and their shoulders flashed with silver trimming. At first Chokole thought they were few, but these were only the first squad. No sooner had they disappeared into the trees than the glade was filled with soldiers again. This time the stream of men continued. Carrying rifles, they were running without caution. This meant that scouts, closer to Chokole, had already assured them there was no ambush. Her first impulse was to stand up and fire off her rifle to warn the camp, but she thought better of this. The troops were still a mile away. The scouts would be closer to her, and when she fired her rifle the scouts would hit the camp. Unless she could kill . . . could make them timid.

She dropped the glasses and raised her rifle, trusting her eyes to the trees. She did not move her eyes, searching, but focused them on a point in the center of the canyon, and waited. The canyon became a still picture on canvas; motion would disturb the picture. She was startled. Flashes of quick brown forms were everywhere in the trees—silent, darting and fleet, so that the eye could not be sure it had witnessed any movement. Chokole picked a brown flash that disappeared from the right behind the trunk of a live oak, two hundred yards ahead. She did not sight her gun on the oak. The movement had come from the right, and so, leaving the tree, would move to the left. Inches from the left of the tree, she sighted. The brown flashed and she fired. The movement halted, stunned in mid-air, and became a man, a naked man. He threw up both arms and fell. The canyon was alive with Tarahumara Indian scouts!

Chokole threw her cartridge belt in front of her, reloading and sighting at the flashes. Her first shot had boomed in the canyon, bouncing between the walls. Dimly, she heard yells and screams, but she did not take time to look over the ledge. She led another flash, firing, and saw the Indian plunge. Another. The flashes of their movement were close together now, and she crawled near the lip of the ledge, training her rifle fire down on them. The Tarahumaras were deer-quick, but Chokole was a long-practiced expert in the liquid movement and instant trigger squeeze of motion firing. The advance of the Tarahumaras was slowing down. She changed position, getting up on her knees so that she could shoot downward at a sharper angle. Now she was silhouetted on the ledge. Fifty yards ahead of her an Indian jumped from heavy spruces toward an oak, ten feet away. Her quick shot knocked him kicking on the ground. Now other rifles were cracking and booming in the canyon. Far behind her, to the west, she heard a crackling of rifle fire. Both ends of the canyon had been invaded!

She did not hear the shot. The blow knocked her

backward from her kneeling position. Lights popped before her eyes, and she could hear screaming below, but she could not see. The darkness pulled at her eyes. She tried to fight it, to push it back, to get up. She lost. The blackness put an end to her struggle.

When she awoke it was morning. She was lying on her back on the ledge. Her head was propped on a rock, and she could see the canyon stretching away below. The sun was in her face. The same cliff hawk was sailing across the canyon, perching on the same prominence of rock. There was no sound. Birds made flashes of color in the trees. Chokole's memory returned. She started to get up, but when her mind commanded her body to move, nothing happened. She looked around her. Her arms were outstretched, flung outward, but they were like separate objects. She could not feel them. She could turn her head only slightly from side to side, but she could not lift it from the rock. Her eyes traveled across the ledge.

When she had first arrived on her perch, she had inspected the bullhorn plant growing from the rocks. She remembered a favorite sport she played with the bullhorn as a child. Ants lived in the huge hollow thorns of the plant, and one need only to touch a leaf or stem and the ants would rush to defend the plant. She and her playmates had spent endless hours touching at bullhorns, watching little armies rushing to attack. When she had arrived for her guard duty, the bullhorn's three stems were standing almost naked; they had not yet bloomed. Now the stems were coated, thick yellow candles of color! How long had she been in the darkness? Two days? Maybe three. Her mind struggled to remember the time it took a bullhorn to bloom. As she watched the plant, she could see the ants. They had been disturbed by her presence. Her eyes followed a thin trail, traveling. She turned her head. The trail led across the ledge and into her hand. Her instinct on seeing the ants caused her to try to jerk the hand away, and she was shocked again when the hand didn't respond. The hand was a great ball, twisting and turning with moving ants. Chokole narrowed her eyes, watching the hand. Almost imperceptibly the hand was moving! The ants were pushing, pulling, carrying the hand, inching along the ground. When they found they could move it no farther, Chokole knew they would investigate. They would move up the arm.

She took her eyes away from the ants. Looking down over her body, at first she thought a rock had been placed on her breast. She studied it. It was moist, almost black; a great gobbet of blood that had fountained and, coagulating, built a soft, compact mound. Below the mound she saw two logs protruding down and outward from her breechclout. Her first sight identified them as logs, but Chokole had been on many battlefields and she knew. The logs were her legs. No blood had fed them. Inside the meat was rotting. Where it festered, putrid and swelling, the meat burst the skin, now black, and the white spewing from the cracks gave the appearance of bark bursting with sap and clinging to a tree trunk. Chokole knew then. She was dying.

At noon the fly came. His wings sang a heavy alto in the quiet air. He circled once and landed atop the blood gobbet on Chokole's breast. Six inches from her eyes he stared at her, great pimpled balls rotating on his head. His body was green, slick, and metallic. Washing his feet in the blood, he lifted fat balls to his mouth as he faced Chokole's stare. She pursed her lips, blowing hard at him, but he contracted his wings close to his body and would not move. Crouching lower on the blood mound, his hairy feet held tight. Finally gorged, he lifted off sluggishly into the air and flew down from the ledge. *He is the scout*, Chokole thought. *He will tell them I am here.*

She tried to move her head backward, to use it as

a grapple to pull her over the ledge. If she could reach the edge, she would crash five hundred feet. But her head would not move off the rock. She heard them coming, wings strumming a low chord below the ledge. They circled in her sight, a long endless string of flies. Settling green and hairy on the blood mound, they pushed and fought one another. The string continued from below and covered her legs, eating and laying their eggs for the maggots that were to come. Chokole blew at them over and over again until she was exhausted. They did not move from their feeding. Her sight blurred and faded then revived. Everything appeared brighter; clear.

A man was on the ledge. He was seated on a rock. Chokole was quite sure he was the Enemy, until he spoke. His voice was soft and musical, and he spoke Apache very well.

"I have been admiring your strong spirit, Chokole." He smiled, bending to pick up a handful of sand. He tossed the sand at the flies.

"It is not easy," Chokole whispered. Her throat would make no sound.

"Nooooo," the man said thoughtfully, "it is never easy to make the spirit body strong. The Way is hard. Most people choose the easy way, so their spirit bodies are flabby and weak. Everyone has a choice, you know."

"I guess they do," Chokole said. She blew at a huge fly advancing toward her chin. The man threw some sand at the fly, and it buzzed away.

"Thank you," Chokole whispered politely.

"It is nothing," the man said cheerfully, "but I should not stay long. I would like to show you something, if you will go with me."

"I would like to go," Chokole said, "most anywhere, but as you see, I cannot move."

"Yes, you can move." The man smiled and stood up. "Come with me."

Chokole rose without any effort at all. She looked

around. Her body was still lying on the ledge, covered with the flies. She followed the man, walking up the canyon wall. It was an easy walk.

From the canyon rim they walked south. Apache-like, Chokole kept note of her surroundings as they moved, it would make for a more successful escape later. They walked on the treetops, and where mountains blocked their path, they stepped over them. Everywhere around them now were mountains. They were jumbled and bare of trees. The terrain moved upward, harsh, where there was no life. Ahead of her, Chokole saw four mountain peaks. They rose from a base higher than the surrounding mountains, and looked like legs of a table supporting the sky, for they disappeared in the clouds. There was snow on the peaks. The man led her to the side of one of the peaks. They sat down.

"Are you tired?" the man asked kindly.

"No," Chokole answered.

"You have a strong spirit," the man said admiringly. "Look." He pointed his finger downward, between the four peaks. Chokole gasped. Ten thousand feet below them was a great sunken bowl completely enclosed by the high connecting bases of the peaks. The bottom of the bowl was green, shining like a deep emerald.

"Come," the man said. They stepped far down into the bowl. Here it was warm and Chokole stood in lush grass reaching above her knees. From one side of the bowl a great stream of water rushed, winding through the bowl until it reached the far side. There it disappeared into the tall mountain base. The water was clear and sparkling. Chokole could count the sand grains on the bottom. A great herd of deer, drinking at the stream, paid no attention to Chokole and the man. She followed him, walking beside the stream. She tried to count the deer, but there were too many of them. Groves of trees were set back from the grassy meadows, rounding the bowl with wide canopies of leaves. Chokole and the man sat down beneath the trees. Overhead in the branches there were flashes of color as birds chattered and played. Somewhere in the meadows a field lark sang, high and musical, and was joined by others. The man whistled an imitation of the field lark and was answered by half a dozen calls. He laughed and pointed far down the stream. "See the herd of white animals there." Chokole nodded. "They are mountain goats. Possibly"—he looked speculatively upward at the high sheer walls of the bowl—"they could climb out . . . but"—he shrugged—"there is no reason. Here they have plenty. All they would find when they reached the mountain tops would be rocks. Or"—he pointed farther down the expanse of grassland where brown flocks of quail rose in the grass to flutter and resettle again, feeding—"or . . . they might fly out, but when they reached the high winds overhead, they would come back."

"Did you make this place?" Chokole asked suspiciously.

The man chuckled. "No. Long ago, as earth measures time . . . even before I visited earth in a shadow body . . . heat from inside the earth pushed up. After it had pushed a few thousand feet, heavy rocks under the bowl resisted the heat, but around the bowl, the earth was weaker and continued rising. Then"—the man pointed to the snowy peaks, disappearing in the clouds—"the mountains themselves had four weak places, and they pushed even higher. Nooo," he said musingly, "I did not make it; but I help with the Laws that made it."

"An Apache," Chokole observed, "would never leave this place."

"No, I don't think an Apache would," the man said.

"But," Chokole said, looking up at the high walls, "I don't believe even an Apache could get in here."

The man followed her look upward around the

bowl. "Now, there just might be a way," he said hopefully. "Follow me."

At the base of the wall he walked between two huge boulders, and when Chokole followed him she saw a trail, leading upward along the side of the wall. The trail was wide enough for two, and Chokole walked beside him. The trail wound around rocky prominences in the wall and, sometimes steep, sometimes almost level, it gradually reached the top. But at the top a towering ridge of rocks and earth had blocked the trail.

"See"—the man pointed up at the great mass— "this is how the animals were trapped in the bowl. Part of the mountain slid down and blocked the trail."

He stepped to the top of the thousand-foot-high jumble. Chokole followed. The wind was cold at the top, and a scattering of snowflakes swirled around them.

"What do you think?" the man asked.

"Apaches could make it," Chokole said, a little pridefully, "if they knew where this place was, this exact spot."

"Yes," the man agreed, "I believe they could." He took Chokole's hand in his own. "We will have to go." She looked down longingly at the bowl. But she allowed him to lead her.

They went back to the Yaqui. The man sat down on a rock overlooking the canyon. Chokole sat down beside him. Below her she could see the ledge, and on it her body. But it was hard to make out the body's outlines; only the head, resting on the rock was clear. The rest of the body seemed to be twisting, heaving up and down in an undulating motion. The illusion of the body's motion was caused by the movements of the great mass of flies feeding on it, and beneath them, the white crawlings of maggots. Chokole shuddered and looked away.

"Messy," the man observed. He picked up a pebble, flipping it, arcing over the canyon, where it fell away, out of sight.

"As I remarked before," he said conversationally, "you have a strong spirit body. You have resisted the power-hungry god governments who would have you worship them because they feed and care for your material body. You've kept the high laws of Faith in your spirit . . . but . . ."—he frowned— "I have wondered if your fighting has been *all* for this purpose . . . or perhaps a little, because of vengeance."

Chokole blushed and looked at her feet. "Some . . ." she said hesitantly, "but not any at all for the low law of glory . . . or . . . well, the killing of my husband . . ."

"I understand," the man said, "but vengeance is a low law and weakens the soul muscle."

"But how are they to be punished?" Chokole asked.

"Nothing to it," the man said. "The low laws they practice put their spirits on lower plateaus and they must be born again into shadow bodies on the earth. They are their own descendants and so reap what they have sown. As they say, earth history repeats itself, over and over. Some resist in their following lives . . . some don't. That is the Choice, of course."

"I wish," Chokole said humbly, "that I had resisted the temptation of vengeance."

"Yes," the man said, "usually everybody wishes that, once they have departed the shadow body and see how weak their spirit body is. Once—I did not have to—but once I came back, deliberately, in a shadow body to demonstrate that the war between the low and high laws goes on always inside every person. I even let one of their god government bureaus put my shadow body to death—quite painfully —to demonstrate the spirit body can triumph if one resists all the temptations of the low laws. But . . . mostly it was misinterpreted by the religious bureaus. They like to have power too, you know . . . administering rituals with magic easy ways they claim will get you to the High Plateau. But always there is only the Choice."

"If I were offered the Choice again," Chokole said, "I would take it."

"Well . . ." the man said musingly, "I wouldn't be so quick to say that, not knowing what it is. You see, I have been worried about the children, down there in the canyon . . . some of them survived, you know."

"They did?" Chokole was surprised.

"Yes," the man said. "I have always had a weakness for children—the spirits who have come back, just beginning their shadow lives. They could be taken to the high valley we saw."

"Yes," Chokole said eagerly, "they would be free . . . and . . ."—she frowned—"but who can take them?"

"Well . . ." the man said, "Juh is gone from his shadow body and cannot come. However," he added thoughtfully, "Geronimo has escaped and is on his way here."

Chokole stood up in her excitement and almost fell into the canyon. "Then Geronimo will be here soon. Geronimo loves children. He will do it!"

"Yes," the man agreed, "Geronimo *could* do it—if he knew where the high valley was . . ."

"Who will tell him?" Chokole asked.

"That is your Choice," the man said, pointing down to the ledge.

Chokole averted her eyes from her body on the ledge. She felt sick. Then, hopefully, she said, "But even if I stay and tell Geronimo, he will want to take revenge on the Enemy. He might do that instead of taking the children to the High Valley."

"That," the man said, "is Geronimo's Choice, not yours, or mine."

Chokole closed her eyes. "I want to save the children . . . if this is the only way . . ."

She tried to open her eyes. The lids were heavy. They were weighted with ants. She blinked hard, pushing at the ants, forcing them to fall. Tears welling up kept the ants' probing mouths away from her eyeballs. The subtle, persistent sound was all around her. Thousands of tiny bodies, eating and crawling, made a mucking, stirring monotone over which hummed the metallic buzzing of fly wings.

With all her Apache will she fought the poison swelling her neck, reaching for her mind. A rush of air swept the ledge, and Chokole watched buzzards land. They tumbled, clumsy on the ground. Straightening, they stretched their necks, turning bald heads to inspect her. Wrinkled skin hung thick and scaly below their huge beaks. There were four of them and they opened and closed their wings as they looked at her and advanced in an awkward hopping stalk. Chokole was about to close her eyes when a swift shadow shot over the ledge. The shadow alarmed the buzzards. They stumbled away, jumping and hopping, flapping into the air. Chokole looked up from the shadow. It was a great eagle. He was tilting, turning against the wind and coming back. This time, he stretched taloned feet and braked against the air, landing close to Chokole. She saw him turn his head, looking at her. He kicked at the sand on the ledge. Chokole blinked her eyes. It was Geronimo.

He was kneeling, tossing sand over her body. Sweat glistened on his bare chest and arms. Some of the sand hit her in the face. She tried to call to him, but more sand struck her, almost smothering her. He was burying her! She blinked her eyes rapidly, but his head was bent as he scooped up more sand and threw it over her. A huge cloud of flies rose in the air. Desperately she pursed her lips, pushing air weakly between them. She whistled! It was thin, faint, but she saw his head snap up; the glittering black eyes met hers.

He was beside her, kneeling and washing her face

with cold water from a water bag. He tried to force water between her lips, she spat it out, afraid she would choke. His face was close to hers and now she begged him with her eyes, moving her lips. He bent closer. She whispered, "Can you hear me, Geronimo?"

"Yes," he spoke softly in her ear, "I hear you."

"All the Apaches do not have to die . . . like Cochise thought. God has not forgotten the Apache, Geronimo. Can you hear?"

"I hear, Chokole."

Her mind fumbled with the thoughts. She struggled, forming the words. "The children, Geronimo. There are children still living. Take them to the place, Geronimo."

"The place?"

"Yes . . . there is a place . . . listen, Geronimo." And in Apache fashion, Chokole began from the ledge, describing the journey south—each mountain and arroyo, the climb upward, the peaks that disappeared into the sky. She described the high barrier that led into the valley. Then she told of the high valley, all she could: the water stream, the deer, the trees . . . but her whisper was almost gone. She stopped, wanting assurance. The whisper was almost gone. Now it was only a breath. Chokole strained to make her swollen tongue and lips form the words.

"Geronimo?"

"Yes."

"Tell me you . . . will take them . . . the children."

He raised his head, looking at her, at her swelling face, her eyes closing into slits. Between the slits of flesh, her eyes were bright, intense. He said nothing.

She breathed deeply with a great effort. A croaking whisper came at last, surprisingly strong. "Your Word, Geronimo . . . give me your word."

His own eyes softened. "I give my Word, Chokole. I will take the children."

The great purpling mass of flesh that was Chokole's

face split imperceptibly. She tried to smile. She looked away from Geronimo, high up, where the last red of sun painted a cloud, drifting. Her whisper was thin: *"O Ha Le! O Ha Le!"* And the great spirit of Chokole faded quickly from her eyes. She was gone on the Journey, leaving behind the shadow body where she had strengthened her soul.

22

Geronimo buried the body in sand. As dusk crept upward from the canyon's deeper darkness he worked his way laboriously down the wall. The buzzards had led him to the ledge. He had been in the middle of the Nedni rancheria, searching for life, when he saw them. He had found no life.

For a mile along the banks of the Yaqui there were bodies of women and children, a few old men, scattered where they had fallen in flight. All of them had been scalped. Many were hacked, dismembered trunks of flesh. He had found Ishton. She still held a rifle beneath her. Close beside were two of her young daughters. But he had not found Che-hash-kish, nor Chappo or Tozey. He was sure they were here, but too many were unrecognizable. The canyon was black with whirring flies. Crazed by the stench of the bodies, they had attacked him and he flailed at them with a tree branch. Great flocks of buzzards, bold, or too gorged to fly, grudgingly hopped from his path. He had grown sick, and flinging himself at the Yaqui's bank, he splashed water on his face. He saw a child bloated in the water, caught on a rock. He believed it was Chappo, but he could not be sure. There was a certainty in him that his Power's prophecy had been again fulfilled.

Now as he came down from the wall, he moved away from the rancheria, up the canyon toward the east. Here the air was clear and fresh. Out of the numbness of his shock he felt rage rising in him as he stood by the river. He checked his weapons. He had gathered a rifle and cartridge belt. He still had his bow and arrows. Even in the dim light of the stars, he began searching for the trail of the Enemies. Then he remembered. His Word. He stopped, thinking on this. He did not doubt that Chokole had received a revelation from the spirit world. This was not an extraordinary occurrence with the strong-willed Apaches, but he doubted there were any survivors. He would test it. He had given his Word.

Breaking a cartridge, he spilled powder on the ground. Kneeling, he spread twigs over the powder and, striking two rocks together, set a spark into the pile. Flames shot up and he fed them with larger tree branches, finally adding dry trunks of trees until a huge fire flamed, lighting up the canyon. Selecting four arrows, he tied dried grass around their points, and dipping an arrow into the flames, he shot it straight upward. Rushing against the air, the arrow flared, making a bright red glow in the sky. As the arrow paused at the apex of its flight, the flames shot outward, spectacular in the night, before falling back into the canyon. He waited, measuring a star advancing over the canyon rim. Half an hour later he shot another flaring arrow. In this way he shot the four arrows. Now he stood near the fire, replenishing the flames, building them higher.

Hours passed. He was standing with his back to the fire when he saw light—many small lights, reflecting from beneath the trees. The lights were eyes. He shouted, "Geronimo! Geronimo!" And they came. A woman and several children were rushing toward him. She grabbed him in her arms, crying, "All are dead! All are dead!" Geronimo pushed her away from him and ran to the children, kneeling, looking for Chappo and Tozey. Across the stream two women appeared. One was carrying a baby, and several children clustered around them. They came into the water and Geronimo ran to them, splashing the water high in his excitement. He brought them back to the fire. More children were coming from the trees and he ran among them, searching.

An old man hobbled into the circle of light and Geronimo grabbed his shoulders. "Did you see Chee-hash-kish? Did you see my children . . . my children, Chappo and Tozey?"

The old man looked at Geronimo, dazed. He had blood on his face and one arm was limp. He shook his head. "I do not know," he mumbled, "I do not know."

He limped away to sit by the fire among the women and children, silent with shock. Some rocked their bodies back and forth, moaning. Geronimo moved among them, but they stared back at him blankly, not hearing his questions. He moved away from them. His heart was certain now. His family was dead. He was looking vacantly up the canyon when the movement caught his eye. As it came closer, it became a small figure, struggling resolutely with one ripped moccasin that dragged behind him. It was Chappo. His buckskin shirt was in tatters but he came steadily on, half-dragging a stubby figure behind him—Tozey.

Geronimo's heart leaped. His throat was choked and he wanted to run, to take them in his arms, but he did not. Instead he stood, waiting by the fire.

Seeing him, Chappo changed his course and came on, stopping three feet from Geronimo and announcing, "I did not cry, Father. Tozey cried. I looked after her. I told her not to cry, but she did."

Tozey stuck a thumb in her mouth. Her face was smeared with the mud of dirt and tears. Even now she was working hard to display her courage. Smothered sobs clogged her throat, and her chest heaved convulsively with the effort. She looked up, a little shamefaced, at her father, standing in the light over her. Her round black eyes were filled, but in a tiny voice between the snuffling intakes of air, she said defensively, "I did not cry much, Father. Chappo nearly cried."

Geronimo could not speak. He knelt and held them in his arms. He asked Chappo if he had seen Chee-hash-kish.

"I was playing with Tozey, in the water, when the Enemy came," Chappo said. "I did not see mother."

The Enemies' attack had been sudden, crashing into the rancheria from both ends of the canyon. Chappo, with a presence of mind beyond his years, told of hiding himself and Tozey under the bank of the river. As the fighting died, the Enemy ran up and down the river bank, searching out more victims. Chappo had pushed Tozey's head beneath the water and ducked down himself just as scouts of the Enemy stood almost over them. He and Tozey had stayed in the river through the night and most of the next day, until he heard crows and buzzards in the canyon. Then he had led Tozey out of the river into the trees where they had crouched, hoping to see others. It was here, Chappo announced, that Tozey cried, although he had assured her he would take care of her and kill any Enemies who attacked them.

Chappo talked incessantly, trailing on the heels of Geronimo as he dragged wood to the fire. Tozey tagged along beside him, refusing to relinquish his hand, although twice Chappo assured her, with some authority, that she must do so. Thumb in mouth, she had lapsed into a stoic acceptance of Chappo's indicting references to her crying. She was content to accept insults in exchange for companionship.

The warmth of the fire and the presence of the War Shaman brought a feeling of security, and sleep, to the women and children. For nearly a week they had hidden in terror. Now, near the fire, children slept, bunched close together in small huddles around the women they had chosen—comfort for a mother lost. Geronimo pulled more wood to the fire and sat down back from the flames. Chappo and Tozey stood over him.

Chappo was talking. ". . . And so, Father, I told Tozey that you would come. I told her that mother had escaped . . . and I know she has. . . . I said . . ."

Geronimo pulled Tozey down beside him, extricating Chappo's hand from her firm grip. He laid her head on his lap and she fell asleep instantly, holding one of his thumbs.

Chappo was saying, ". . . I believe mother escaped north . . . she has found another band, I am sure. If I had not had to look after Tozey, Father, I would have fought the Enemy, like you . . . but I did not cry . . ."

Geronimo reached up and pulled the boy down beside him, laying his head in his lap. He smoothed the torn buckskin of the boy's shirt where briers and thorns had gashed his back and arms.

"Sometimes, Chappo," Geronimo said softly, "I have cried."

Chappo was silent, burying his face in Geronimo's lap. And as he watched the fire, blazing high and crackling, Geronimo felt the tremor of convulsions in the small body beneath his hand. The sobs were smothered in his lap. Softly, Geronimo sang,

> O Ha Le . . . our shadow bodies come and go . . .
> But we are together . . . we have kept the Faith . . .
> O Ha Le . . . O Ha Le. . . .

And though the song was soft, it was musical and filled the canyon with reassurance, like the first sweet touch of warm wind after a harsh winter. The faces of the sleepers, reflecting the firelight, relaxed, giving up their tensions. Geronimo felt the body beneath his hand grow quiet. Chappo slept, snuggling his face deeper in Geronimo's lap. Even Tozey relaxed her iron grip on his thumb. Geronimo alone was awake in the canyon, singing. He watched the flames lowering. He had made the Choice. He would take them all to the High Valley.

He built the fire high against the chill of a gray dawn. Fog had dropped thick and glistening on the canyon's rock walls, dripping from the trees. Geronimo counted the sleepers: fifty-three children, a dozen women, one old man. He woke them, shouting *"Haaaa-eeeeee!"* and moved among them, organizing them for the journey to the High Valley. The old man he sent east, up the canyon, with the oldest children in search of strayed mules and horses. He led the women himself, down into the Nedni rancheria among the dead, to salvage supplies. They were timid, shy of the dead, but he urged them on. They moved swiftly, unhampered by the flies, sluggish in the morning cold. Gathering sacks of corn, dried beef stored in hides, cooking utensils, flour . . . Geronimo sent them in relays carrying the supplies back to the campfire. Before mid-morning he called a halt, and at the campfire he directed the loading and lashing of the supplies and equipment onto the backs of two horses and a half dozen mules rounded up by the children and the old man. By noontime they were on their way, asking no questions of the great War Shaman. Geronimo had allowed no pause, either for questions or for mourning.

And so he led them out of the canyon, the way Chokole had whispered, south, along high ridges, angling higher. By the evening of the fourth day they were near the tree line, and on the morning of the fifth they had passed it, moving upward sharply into high winds and bursts of snow. On the evening of the fifth day they camped, cold, wrapped in blankets with no fires, but Geronimo had seen the four peaks plunging up into clouds, striking red fire from the sunset with their snow sides. He woke the camp at midnight, anxious to reach the peaks. In near day-light of a full moon they crunched upward over frozen ground, their breath labored in the thin air.

Light was pinking in the east when he brought them to the base of the high rock barrier, just as Chokole had described it. The wind had not risen and the still air held steam clouds of breath suspended above them. Even the mules and horses were exhausted, heads down. There was no objection when Geronimo instructed them to remain where they were as he climbed the barrier, up the great slabs of granite to the top.

The first brilliant rays of the sun shot into the valley. Two miles below him the water reflected sparkling crystal lights and the green valley, wet with dew, blinked and rippled shiny in the sun. Geronimo raised his binoculars and studied a great gathering of deer grazing in the meadows, and farther away, the goat herd drinking at the stream. Snow from the high elevations of clouds had recently fallen and, striking the warmth of the valley, had turned to rain. The result was a burst of colors from wild flowers along the stream and dotting the meadows. Geronimo turned his face to the clear blue sky above him. He thanked Chokole for this gift, and Usen, who had led her here.

A small voice spoke beside him, "FFFather, I will teach Tozey to swim in the water. All the tttrees will take a long tttime to climb . . . but I will ccclimb them." Chappo's lips were blue in the cold wind, but he pointed, discovering the deer herd, and called Geronimo's attention to the thick quail coveys fluttering in the meadows. Looking back down the barrier, Geronimo called to the band to bring supplies over the rocks. Tozey, laboring upward, was already half-way to the top.

Some of the women stood without speaking when they saw the valley. Some cried. Carrying their loads, they clambered down the barrier, and the children ran ahead, yelling and shouting their excitement, making echoes which grew smaller as they disappeared into the valley's green warmth. Last over the rocks was the old man; Geronimo helped him with his burden.

Lingering on the trail, the old man said, "It is a great gift. Now we have life."

"Yes," Geronimo answered, "the treasure was Usen's. Chokole bought it, and paid for it, and gave it to us."

"We will not forget," the old man said. "We will remember." He turned, and despite his load, half-trotted down the trail.

Tozey was carrying a small sack thrown over her shoulder. Geronimo knelt and adjusted the load for easier carrying. Chappo was staggering slightly beneath an ambitious burden wrapped in cowhides. The cumbersome bulk of his load forced him, head bent, to peer out from beneath it.

"Are you ready, Father?" he asked a little impatiently.

"I am not going," Geronimo said.

"Why?" Chappo's voice was alarmed.

"Well"—Geronimo looked away, down into the valley—"it is not my purpose. I cannot go. If I stayed, the Enemy would search for me and destroy the valley."

"We would kill the Enemy, Father," Chappo argued. "I know we could . . . see, I am strong." He almost fell backward standing upright to demonstrate his strength.

"No," Geronimo said, "I cannot stay, but I will come many times and watch you from up here. I will signal you sometimes. You can see me when you look up."

Tozey snuffled, scrunching her eyes almost shut. Her chest heaved and she stuck a thumb in her mouth. Carefully balancing his burden, Chappo took her hand.

"Now, you must go," Geronimo said, standing.

"Yes," Chappo said, "we must go." He led Tozey a little way down the trail before he turned. "We will be looking up at the mountain, Father," he shouted. "We will watch for you."

"I will come," Geronimo answered.

Once, just before they disappeared around the trail's bend, Tozey looked back, timidly, quickly, and then they were gone.

For a long time, Geronimo watched the trail where they had disappeared. Then resolutely he climbed the high barrier, and on the other side, mounted the best of the horses. Leading the other and the mules, he descended downward through the cold winds and, at the tree line, turned loose all the animals except his mount. Then, dropping steadily in elevation, he headed north. Across his chest were cartridge *bandoleros*, and across his saddle he carried a rifle.

23

Geronimo had kept his word to Chokole, but in making the Choice, he had merely postponed his determination to find and punish the killers of Chee-hash-kish. Far to the north, in a canyon of the Dragoons, he had hidden rifles and ammunition. Now he needed warriors, and he began a search that was to range over two thousand square miles of Apacheria.

The Southwest was bustling. Where there had been villages, now there were towns—Globe, Safford, Silver City, Lordsburg. Tucson was growing in importance from the new railroad, and many of the old mining camps were blossoming into business communities. Wagon trains had disappeared from the old California Road. Frieght moved by rail, and people rode passenger trains of the Southern Pacific out of El Paso, across the prairie flats through Lordsburg and Bowie Station. At Willcox, close by the Chiricahua mountains, they disembarked to eat in restaurants, to be regaled with horror stories of the Apache, and to be reassured—the Apache was gone. With the last of the Apaches, the American Indian had disappeared. Sitting Bull was making his last appearance on vaudeville stages in New York City. The United States Supreme Court had declared that American Indians were aliens. In the East there were electric lights and telephones. In Tucson there was a drugstore, civic meetings, a ladies temperance society, even tourists.

For Geronimo the material march of the shadow

time made no difference. Nothing had changed. The mountains were where they would always be, the canyons, the springs and cactus, and the rocks. The Eternals were present in their proper places. And so, he was a man from another Time, as if Nature had warped his dimension, leaving him here in a war of the Spirit Time against the advance of man's material gods.

An army patrol camped at McIntosh Springs reported seeing him as he skirted their dawn camp. They pursued and were rewarded with two wounded troopers, a downed horse, and in the end, an empty prairie. Railroad repair crews telegraphed Tucson: "Geronimo sighted. Crossing tracks south of Santa Catalinas. Armed. Mounted. Headed north." No one doubted it was Geronimo. He was the only armed and mounted Indian in the United States of America. The Last Warrior.

He is known to have visited Bosque Redondo, slipping among the campfires in the night, searching for warriors. And here, at Bosque Redondo, the news was whispered to him, by the widows: Victorio had recruited two hundred of their men for his "war to the death." In Mexico, at Tres Castillos, he had been trapped by Colonel Joaquin Terrazas. He, his warriors, and many women and children were slain. Joaquin and his victorious army had paraded down the Avenida Juarez in Chihuahua City, displaying the scalps for which they received bounties of over fifty thousand dollars. Benito had surrendered to the bluecoats. Chihuahua. All had surrendered. There were no warriors.

In the night this band of Mescaleros disappeared. Army records report their disappearance "without a trace."*

---

*Modern-day historians of the Mescaleros write of this band's "vanishing from the face of the earth," never to be seen again. Geronimo is said to have escorted several groups and even

Geronimo "sightings" became common. Citizens of Santa Rita positively identified him near that town at the same time that Clifton, nearly a hundred miles away, was alarmed by a similar identification. Perhaps they saw him. He was drifting ghostlike through all the old mountain haunts, along the rims of Cochise's Dragoons, threading empty canyons where he had ridden with Mangas Coloradas. As he rode Geronimo conceived a plan. He was imbued with none of Cochise's hopelessness nor Mangas Coloradas's ominous feelings of defeat. His objective was the War Shaman's: to wage War in defense of the Eternals and in this there could be no defeat. He would recruit warriors by a method so audacious, so dangerous, that no white eye could conceive of his motives. He would recruit them from the inmates of San Carlos. In order to do this he must risk the hangman's noose again. He must become a prisoner himself! He had consulted his Power and was confident he could recruit the warriors. Once free of San Carlos, he would arm them with the rifles hidden in the canyon and raid the horse remudas of Gosoda. From there, he would strike and destroy Joaquin Terrazas, who, he was now convinced, had led the massacre on Yaqui Canyon. After that? He would lead them back north against the bluecoats, freeing the Apaches—all of them—from the camp. Turning his horse west, he moved closer to the borders of San Carlos.

Lahte had been given permission to report late to San Carlos. His old wife had been sick and dying when the bluecoats escorted his little band to the camp. He was old himself, too old and bent and shriveled to make war; and so they had given him permission to stay here in this canyon and wait with her for the Journey. The wait was over. She was gone.

---

individuals to the High Valley. See *The Vengeance Trail of Josey Wales,* page 196.

This day he had buried her, and now he lingered in the night by his campfire to sing after her, that she might wait. It would be a short time, and he would join her.

Darkness had come quickly to the canyon. As it deepened he felt closer to his wife. She was near. And so he had lit the small fire to show her the way and sat cross-legged, head bowed, while he chanted in his old cracked voice. Between his legs he held an *esadadne* and thumped it with his hands. The low hollow rhythm echoed in the canyon and brought life to the darkness. Now he could feel the Life. A Presence. Slowly he raised his head. Just above the flickering flames, black eyes glittering across the fire were watching him. Above the eyes, a war band; below them, slashes of yellow. The eyes hypnotically held his own. The ghost of the War Shaman had answered his chant! Lahte continued thumping the hoop drum. He was afraid to stop. The War Shaman's spirit might be displeased. The thumping of the drum and the crackling of the fire were the only sounds. Lahte broke beneath the tension.

"I have never harmed you, Geronimo." His voice cracked, thin above the *esadadne*. "I have never helped the Mexicans or the bluecoats against our people. I have been a warrior, now I am too old to fight." His eyes watered, not blinking, held by Geronimo's stare.

Suddenly the War Shaman spoke. "You are going to San Carlos?"

"Yes. In the morning—but only because there is nowhere else to go. There are no Apaches left . . . in the mountains." He watched the War Shaman's eyes, anxious in the silence. He had told the truth, and was surprised by the next question.

"Do you know Tom Horn?"

"Yes. I know him."

"Tell Horn this: I will meet Nantan Lupan here,

in this canyon, on the morning four days from now. I will meet him in peace."

"I will tell," Lahte said.

The War Shaman melted away into the darkness. After a short time Lahte heard a horse, walking over rocks. He rose from his campfire, walking north. He would not wait for morning. Geronimo was alive. Spirits have no need of horses.

And so General Crook, anxious to secure the most explosive and persistent threat to peace in United States history, came to Skeleton Canyon. He was too anxious.

"I want no more talk of hanging," Geronimo said. "I want all to be wiped clean of the past."

"I cannot stop the talk," Crook answered. "But you will be a prisoner of the army. A prisoner of war. You will not be hanged. You may see your people."

"Then," Geronimo said, "I surrender. Once I moved free as the wind. Now I surrender. Do with me what you will. That is all."

If Crook had understood the literal logic of the Indian, he would have asked Geronimo for his Word that he would maintain the peace, forever. He did not understand and so did not ask. Unlike the white man, the Indian allows no implications, interpretations, or suggestive double-meanings to a joke—or a treaty. Say only what you mean, mean only what you say. Nothing more. Indian-like, Geronimo carefully noted the exact, literal statements made and agreed to. Usually the Indian was the victim of such treaties. This time it was General Crook. When Geronimo said, "I surrender. That is all," he meant literally "That is *all* I do, nothing else." This misunderstanding on General Crook's part would lead him to bitterly denounce Geronimo as "treacherous . . . untrustworthy."

First, to ride out the storm of demands for a public hanging, Geronimo was placed in irons in solitary confinement. As the storm subsided he was escorted to San Carlos on that day when Naiche watched, worried by indecision, behind the brittle bush.

Moving among the campfires of San Carlos, Geronimo had been bitterly disappointed. The keeping of the High Laws was being eroded from the mind of the Apache. The people's attention, guided by the government administrators, was on food, clothing, housing, medical attention; how large or small these doles were determined whether an administrator was "good" or "bad." The High Laws, needed to sustain a free people's spirit, were being destroyed by the material largesse of the master. Deeply religious, Geronimo could see a slave mentality succeeding in the murder of a people's spirit where three centuries of Spanish lances had failed.

He was shaken, doubtful even of those who accompanied him through the sandstorm past Fort Thomas and through the Dragoons into the Madre. Being unsure, he had refused to reveal his plans for war. He was afraid they would not come, and so talked to them only of the freedom of the Madre, of the things and ways of the old life they loved.

Behind him, he left another front page sensation: "GERONIMO ESCAPES!" He also left General George Crook in deep trouble, and Sheridan gleeful at this opportunity to remove him.

Now as the sun tilted toward the high Madre peaks, Geronimo awakened beneath the mesquite where he had slept through the morning. He had felt rather than heard the vibrations. Listening now, he heard nothing. Behind him, where Naiche and the warriors slept, the mountain slope was in shadow. Somewhere to the north a crow cawed three times in alarm. He did not move, but watched the trees bordering the trail to the north. Flashes of color moved among them. The flashes were blue.

24

Gray light touched the sky above the mountains. Two of his scouts had called from high on the ledge, and Tom Horn helped them to lower the body of Marteen. Horn carried him past breakfast fires flickering against the darkness and laid the skinny corpse before Major Morrow.

"Geronimo," he said quietly.

Morrow tossed the last of his coffee at the campfire. "Damn!"

"Major"—Horn's voice was final—"the scouts have had it. After forty years of it, by God, everybody ought to. Ain't no mortal human being going to capture Geronimo. He's in the mountains and he's scattered his warriors. Marteen here"—Horn looked down at the dead scout—"he's Geronimo's message —don't call for me, I'll call you."

"I know that." Morrow stood, adding bitterly, "I know *all* of that." He tossed his tin cup on the ground. "I want some *thinking*, not cute observations." He looked at the fire. "General Crook is being hanged right now."

Horn sighed, "Well, I kinda hate to see it happen to ol' Crook and that's a fact. I been doing some thinking. From the single trails the scouts reported, 'pears like Geronimo has got hisself about a dozen warriors, which means he left all them women and children somewhere on the back trail, holed up."

"Where?" Morrow asked.

"I don't know," Horn said, "but my scouts can find

'em. Supposing we pull out of here, Major. You take the troops and camp out on the prairie in plain sight. Let me send the 'Pache scouts in to find them. Most of my scouts are related to the warriors and their families. Let them do the talking. Them women is scared of one thing. They don't want to risk their children being killed in a fight."

Morrow kicked thoughtfully at the fire. "And when we have the women and children?"

"Well," Horn said, "a 'Pache warrior has got one weakness as a fightin' man. He can't stand to be separated from his family. That's why he always takes his family with him on a reservation breakout."

"What about Geronimo?" Morrow persisted.

"Onliest power," Horn said emphatically, "stronger than Geronimo's over them warriors is their families'. If they surrender to be with their families, it'll leave Geronimo settin' alone. Maybe I can talk to him."

Major Morrow studied the fire for a long minute. Turning, he called to Captain Dawson in the distance, "Saddle 'em up!"

"We going to try it, Major?" Horn asked.

Morrow was strapping on his pistol and saber. "What else is there to do, Mr. Horn?"

"We could go home and fergit the whole goddamn thing. I git to looking at it, like ol' Crook, you might say, from a wider viewpoint. Here we are on God's little green apple, chasing Indians down here in Mexican mountains and when we git 'em, we take 'em back and we all set around up there looking at each other. Damned if I know what we're proving."

Morrow swung onto his horse. He didn't comment. Sometimes Horn made sense, sometimes . . . He raised his hand, waving the troopers forward, and set a hard pace.

As he led them out of the mountains, onto the flats, Tom Horn and his Apache scouts split off, following the back trail through the trees. Morrow was dismounting his men, ordering pack and horse inspection, when a sergeant yelled, "*Signals!*"

From a hundred miles away, on a peak of the Guadalupes, one of Crook's heliograph stations was flickering brightly, reflecting the sun. Morrow's own signal crew was setting up their tripod and in a moment gave an answering flash. Morrow stood behind the sergeant, printing out the message on a pad:

MAJOR MORROW YOU MAY RETIRE IF RESULTS APPEAR NEGATIVE REPORT FORT BOWIE MEXICAN GOVERNMENT AGREED TO COMMIT TROOPS SEARCH AND SWEEP MADRE FROM SOUTH CONJUNCTION WITH U.S. SWEEP FROM NORTH FOR GERONIMO REINFORCEMENTS TO ARRIVE FORT BOWIE UNDER GENERAL MILES AM RELIEVED OF COMMAND THIS DEPARTMENT ADVISE GENERAL CROOK

Morrow felt sick. He fumbled with the pad and pencil the sergeant handed him. Something *had* to be sent besides defeat. The signal crew was waiting. He scribbled:

MUST DELAY REPORT FORT BOWIE PROSPECTS ARE POSITIVE

He stopped, frowning. He ought to say something . . . something that would go in the record for Crook. He added:

CONGRATULATIONS CONSUMMATION YOUR WORK WITH MEXICAN GOVERNMENT GOOD LUCK NEW COMMAND MAJOR MORROW

* * *

Handing the message to the sergeant, he limped away. It was the best he could do—anyway, Crook, not Miles, should have credit for the Mexican agreement. He knew Miles as an ambitious brigadier pushing for major general, a glory boy who sent most of his flowery communiqués to the newspapers.

As the morning passed he fretted, consulting his watch frequently, walking at a distance from the troops who were now lounging on the ground, holding their horses. The rising heat was not helping their tempers. Morrow was beginning to feel like a fool. This scheme of Horn's could be another harebrained idea. The irresponsible fool was probably sleeping somewhere under the trees. Rations were distributed at high noon, but Morrow stayed apart from the camp, pacing. The sun passed its zenith, dropping toward mid-afternoon. Morrow stopped, facing the mountain. He had reached a hard decision and was about to turn and order his troopers to mount when the two figures came from the trees, walking toward him across the prairie. It was Tom Horn. With him was Loco. Horn was talking in Apache and the old chief was answering, nodding his head in agreement. Horn smiled as they stopped before Morrow.

"Well . . . Loco here is willing." He placed his arm buddy-fashion around Loco's shoulders.

"What does he say?" Morrow asked stiffly, feeling relieved and miffed at the same time.

"He says he didn't mean no harm. None at all." Loco grinned sheepishly and looked at his feet. "He says he wanted to be free for a little while. To be in the mountains. Just for a little while. He says he wasn't going to make war. Loco will go back—he says."

"Where are the rest of them?" Morrow interrupted.

Horn nodded toward the trees. "Back there. They're afraid of the soldiers. We didn't get 'em all. Some of the women and children slipped away in the mountains, but we got all the warriors' families—their wives, sisters, mothers. We got their children. They're in kinda bad shape."

Morrow checked the sun, slanting shadows over the mountain. "What do you suggest?"

"Well . . . the women say Geronimo ain't far. He promised to come back quick. I figured to send 'em down the trail with the scouts. The scouts have agreed to go with 'em and not carry guns. They'll rouse the warriors."

"All right," Morrow said, "but Loco stays here."

Horn spoke to Loco, who answered and promptly sat down. "He'll stay"—Horn indicated the old chief —"but he'll set here, not near the soldiers. We'll be back, d'rectly." Horn walked away across the prairie and into the trees.

Geronimo slipped silently from beneath the mesquite. Bending low, holding his rifle, he raced up the mountain. Halfway up the slope he sent the hard skeeing whistle of a hunting hawk through the brush and, halting in the cover of trees, whistled again. Immediately he was surrounded by the warriors.

Below them the scouts were emerging from the cover by the trail. Women and children were with them. The women were shouting and waving their arms. It was Fun who first recognized his wife. He shouted, waving, and the women waved back. They advanced toward the mountain.

"Kill the scouts!" Geronimo ordered harshly. The warriors looked around them. Some half-raised their rifles, but they were looking at Naiche, not Geronimo.

"No," Naiche said quietly. When Geronimo repeated his command, Naiche shook his head. "No, Geronimo. I will see what they want. Our families are among them."

He walked slowly down the mountain. Fun trailed behind him, then Ahkochne and the rest. Geronimo stood alone. The women and children were crowded around the warriors, talking excitedly, gesturing. It was Naiche who came back up the mountain. He stood uncomfortably, tall and lean beside the short stature of the War Shaman.

"We must go back, Geronimo. The scouts say the little bluecoat chief has promised better rations . . . better conditions. Maybe we have served our purpose. They have our families. We must go back. Will you come?"

Geronimo's eyes glittered, meeting Naiche's. "I will not come."

Naiche dropped his eyes to the ground. "I must go." He walked away, then stopped, remembering. "Tom Horn sends a message. He will be alone on the prairie at night. He gives his Word. He wants to talk." Naiche waited, but Geronimo did not answer and so he walked away, down the mountain.

Geronimo watched them through his glasses as they walked down the back trail. When they had disappeared, he followed, and saw them trailing north in the dusk, toward San Carlos. The soldiers were with them.

Night came. A campfire flickered, small on the prairie. Geronimo slipped cautiously into the brush, advancing toward the fire until he identified Tom Horn. Horn's horse was standing saddled behind him, reins trailing, and he was seated cross-legged by the fire, smoking a cigarillo. Geronimo walked forward openly and sat down. Neither spoke a greeting. Horn added a brush top and the fire crackled higher. He was poking more brush at the fire when he spoke.

"They are bringing in many thousand more troops to look for you, Geronimo."

"Let them come." Geronimo looked across the flames at Horn. "It will do them no good."

"You have no warriors."

"I will get more warriors."

"I have never lied to you." Tom Horn looked hard at Geronimo across the fire. "I will not lie to you now. I know they cannot capture you. I am not asking you to surrender. I want to tell you the truth. The bluecoats have a new treaty with the Mexicans. The bluecoats will begin at the north of the Madre and search every canyon, every rock, for you. The Mexicans will begin at the south. They will search all the Madre, they say, until they find you and come together in the middle."

Geronimo smiled. "They can never find me . . . they . . ." He frowned, thinking.

Horn watched his face. "If there is any . . . thing you do not wish them to find, Geronimo . . . they will find it."

Geronimo looked into the fire. For a long time he studied the flames, crackling lower. Shadows spread across his face, mottling the yellow stripes. When he spoke, his voice sounded far away and his speech was halting. "Tell Nantan Lupan I will surrender at sunset on the day following the full moon. Tell him I will wait at the river north of the Madre. Tell him this is my Word . . . and so, do not send the troops—or the Mexicans." He stood, easily and quickly.

Horn rose to face him. "Nantan Lupan is gone. The bluecoat chief will be Big-Wind-Double-Mouth. He calls hisself Miles."

"Then tell Big-Wind-Double-Mouth," Geronimo said.

"I will," Horn answered, "but . . . when you surrender, Geronimo, it will mean a big feather for Miles. You can git conditions. You better, or he'll have you hanged. Do you understand?"

"I understand," Geronimo said. "I will see you. At the river."

"No," Horn said quietly, "I will not be there. I will not come. I will not see you again. Forever."

They stood facing each other across the dying fire. A coyote yelped, lonesome on the prairie, and was not answered. Geronimo extended his hand and Horn gripped it.

"I understand," Geronimo said. "Thank you, Tom

Horn." He released his grip. "Good-bye." And turning quickly, he was gone.

"Good-bye," Horn said softly into the darkness.

But Tom Horn did not leave immediately. Instead he sat down by the embering fire, gazing into it. After a while, he touched a glowing brand to a cigarillo and smoked. An hour passed. The embers died, but Horn moved neither to replenish them nor to leave. Suddenly, from the mountaintop, a brilliant light shot skyward. High in the heavens the light paused, flaring, and fell plummeting, a red streak downward to the mountain . . . like a meteor . . . a falling star . . . or an arrow. As though this were the signal for which he was waiting, Tom Horn mounted his horse. He rode north.

25

Major Morrow ordered his mounted troopers to surround the women and children with their warrior hus-
bands. Gesturing and waving his arms, he explained
in broken Apache phrases to the scouts. He wanted
the prisoners strung out—a long line. Bunched together, they might bolt if alarmed, like cattle. With
his troopers alongside them and riding close behind,
Morrow led them at a slow pace, north in the evening
dusk. The mountains were too near, looming and
tempting. He must keep them walking north until
they were away from the mountains. He marveled
that, behind him, they made no sound walking through
the night. The men were carrying babies in their arms
and the women were leading the small children.

At midnight he ordered a rest but kept his troops
near and sent the Apache scouts walking among
them, talking. They made no protest when the march
was resumed. At dawn he ordered a halt and had
rations passed among them as they sat silent on the
ground. His troopers were dozing in their saddles,
worn out, and he wondered at the stamina of these
wild people, these women and children who had fled
across prairie and mountain without rest or sleep.
Walking among them in the growing light, he was
struck by their pitable condition. Their clothes hung
in rags. He extended their rest, and when the sun
rose, ordered his signal crew to send a message:

* * *

HAVE PRISONERS UNABLE TO TRAVEL
SEND FIVE WAGONS

By mid-morning, as they walked north, the dust clouds of the wagons were visible coming toward them.

And so Major Morrow brought them back to San Carlos, back to the heat and the aimless existence, the flies and bitter water from which they had so foolishly fled, following Geronimo. On his headquarters desk at Fort Thomas, he found a sealed letter and, opening it, read:

Major Morrow:
My appreciation for your dedicated service in a task assigned us both that at best has been distasteful. I hope we may meet again, sharing better times and happier circumstance.
General George Crook

He read the letter again. Crook had said it right—at best, distasteful. Possibly, at worst, a tragedy, but he didn't know what to do about it. Captain Dawson stuck his head in the door.

"Major, Tom Horn is here."

"Good!" Morrow rose. "Send him in."

"I . . . uh . . ."—Dawson hesitated—"I don't think he's coming in."

Morrow hastened to the door. Tom Horn was lashing a slicker behind his saddle. He was singing. Drunkenly.

"Horn!" Morrow said sternly.

Tom Horn turned. Pushing the big hat back from his forehead, he grinned owlishly at Morrow. "How y'doin, Major? Got yer goddamn medals shined and yer ass cleaned up fer Big-Mouth-Double-Wind?"

"You're drunk!" Morrow said accusingly.

"Naw." Horn wagged his head. "I ain't drunk, but I'm goin' to git drunker 'n a 'Pache on skull-pop juice . . . I'm goin' to git *Tucson* drunk . . . I'm . . ."

"What about Geronimo?"

"Geronimo?"

"Yes, *Geronimo!*" Morrow shouted.

Horn grinned. "Worried about him, Major?" He wagged his finger at Morrow. "Yessir, the military is worried about that old man. *All* the military brass from Washington to 'Frisco, struttin' around with their swords banging thisaway and thataway with their West Point asses all cocked out'n behind. The ol' warrior has whipped . . . I say *whipped* their paradin' butts for forty years, Major . . . y'hear? . . . *forty* years . . ."

Horn fumbled at his saddlebags. Extracting a bottle, he tilted it, gulping. He wiped his mouth and with drunken care, replaced the bottle.

"I done quit the army, Major, so you can't report me drunk. I *quit*, by God!" He considered this development for a while, staring at Morrow, then: "Geronimo will surrender sundown, day follering the full moon, by the river."

"How do you know he will surrender?"

Horn was making an unsuccessful stab at a stirrup with his boot. He stopped and whirled on Morrow. "Because he give his *Word*, you goddamn ninny. His *Word*. Suthin' the goddamn army guvment can't understand as they ain't got one."

He wheeled back for another try at mounting. This time he made it, swinging into the saddle.

Morrow stepped forward, holding the horse's head. "Aren't you staying for the surrender? It'll be big news all over the nation."

Horn's eyes steadied. He didn't look at Morrow; instead he gazed up at the sky, hot and blue. "One time, Major," he said slowly, "it mighta been fun, catching eagles . . . when there was a lot of eagles, and us being damn fools. There ain't no more, Major, they're all gone. You'll find the last one, when I said, down there by the river. It ain't no fun no more. I ain't staying. *Adios!*"

He jerked the horse's head from Morrow's grasp, whirling him tight and hard, and spurred him fast through the gates. He didn't look back.

Morrow frowned, watching him diminishing in the heat haze. He felt empty. The news would touch off celebrations. He'd had a part in it. There should be some feeling of triumph, by God. He shook his head, limping back to his office; maybe he had associated with General Crook too long. Passing Captain Dawson, he asked for a message orderly to be sent to him, and at his desk, he wrote his report in the form of a telegram, setting the time and date of Geronimo's promised surrender. In the fashion of Crook, he made no boasts, no judgments. Tom Horn was given full credit. He had finished when the orderly appeared.

"I want this sent to General Miles at Fort Bowie." He handed the telegram to the orderly, then: "Just a moment." He took the report back.

For a long time, while the orderly stood forgotten, at attention, he looked through his window at the parade grounds of Fort Thomas, where the pole stood, topped with Delshay's skull grinning white in the sun. Turning back to his desk, he picked up the pen and printed slowly:

RELINQUISHING MY COMMAND TO CAP-
TAIN DAWSON I SUBMIT MY RESIGNA-
TION EFFECTIVE IMMEDIATELY

and signed his name. If he hurried, he could make the evening train out of Tucson, heading east.

26

Tom Horn had seen the first of the flaming arrows. Dimpling the night, flaring and dying with persistent regularity, they continued. Below them, a great fire glowed on the mountain. Two hours passed before they came. Zalah led them, emerging from the darkness; she was holding Sanza's hand. They stopped at the edge of the light and it was Zalah who walked to the fire, looking into it. She could not see Geronimo standing back in the darkness, but she knew he was there. Her hair was torn from its binding, flowing loosely about her face and shoulders, and her face was bleeding, ripped by the undergrowth. Sanza's spindly legs were trembling and he collapsed on the ground near the fire.

"I knew you would not go with the soldiers." Zalah spoke to the fire.

"No. I would not go." Geronimo came from the darkness to place more wood on the flames. The flaring light revealed the women and children. Their clothes were ragged, torn by trees and brush. Many of them were barefooted, with pieces of moccasins hanging above swollen feet. Some of the women carried babies in breast slings.

He didn't count them. They were too many, and the flickering shadows partially hid them. He knew they were all here—the widows with their children who had persisted in accompanying him from San Carlos. There were no warriors.

He spoke loud, so they all might clear. "I had

meant to make war, with the warriors. The warriors are gone. I have made a choice. To do this thing I have chosen, I do not have much time, but I will lead you to a place where you and the children may live free. If you will follow me, the way will be hard, but when we reach this place, you will find that it is good."

No one spoke. After a long time Geronimo walked slowly around the fire. He knelt, lifted Sanza from the ground, and held him in his arms. He looked around the circle of women and children, and walked away into the darkness. No one hesitated. They followed.

And so Geronimo led them to the High Valley, across the mountains and upward toward the tree line.

He killed and fed them venison along the way and ministered to the children. But alone in the nights he was plagued with dreams of horror and screaming terrors. Although he had maintained an outward calmness during his solitary confinement, shackled in chains, the experience had been terrifying.

On the last-night encampment in the trees at the edge of the barren climb upward, he walked away from the camp. He prayed to Usen and asked that his Power speak to him. He could see—visions of the prisons where he would go, far from these mountains. He prayed to strengthen his spirit. A vision of Chappo and Tozey came to him. They were there, with him, in the prison. He saw them dying and he stood over their graves. He had never doubted his visions, and now his spirit, climbing this insurmountable anguish, almost found the Choice too hard to make.

He sat alone at the edge of the tree line, looking up on the sweep of rocky elevations leading away to the distant four peaks. His Power spoke to him, calling four times: *"Geronimo! Geronimo! Geronimo! Geronimo!"*

"I am here," he said. "I do not ask more for myself.

I will endure the prisons so the High Valley may live. I will learn not to love Chappo and Tozey if you will not take them. Let their shadow bodies live."

And his Power spoke: "You may not trade between the Choices, Geronimo. You must make the Choice. You must pay the price as Chokole paid. You may live free in the shadow world and keep the loves of your selfish possessions and so the High Valley will die. Or you may love unselfishly, as Chokole. That is the Choice. The way is hard. Ask nothing more."

Before dawn, he was leading them through icy wind and snow flurries across the rocks, climbing to the peaks. When they reached the barrier in the afternoon, he helped the women carry their babies and children over the rocky height. As the last of them hurried anxiously down the trail to reach the sunny valley below, he stood atop the barrier and placed Sanza in Zalah's arms.

The boy smiled weakly up at Geronimo as she cradled him close against the cold. "He will grow strong here, Geronimo." She spoke into the wind. "His spirit will not die here."

"No," Geronimo said, "his spirit will not die."

Her hair flared across her face in a burst of wind and she brushed it back. A scattering of snow swept over them.

"I have seeds," she said, looking hungrily at the valley, "many seeds that will grow there." She was lingering, sensing that Geronimo was not going to the valley.

"They will need seeds," he said.

"Are you coming?"

"No, I cannot come with you." He looked away.

"We will think of you," Zalah said simply. Shyly, she touched his arm, then picked her way down the barrier. At the bottom, she walked, looking back to the figure of Geronimo, dim in the bursts of snow. When she could see him no longer, she began trotting, carrying Sanza, hurrying to catch the others.

Through glasses, he studied the valley. Children were splashing in the stream. He thought he saw Chappo and Tozey, but he could not be sure. Wickiups stood beneath the trees, and far down the meadows, he saw a tilled field. He grunted with satisfaction. The field would bring corn, maybe squash and beans, and pumpkins. The way it had been, one time, long ago.

Leaving the barrier, he back-trailed down the barren slopes and camped below the tree line in a warm grove of spruce. He built his fire, sitting cross-legged before it, and chanted the old songs, taking him back in memory to his childhood.

The visions returned. He saw Chappo and Tozey standing by the fire. Chappo was holding Tozey's hand and she was looking at Geronimo, solemnly, with her round eyes. Chappo was talking.

"We built a council fire in the woods of the valley, Father; Tozey and me. We prayed to Usen as you told us to do. My Power spoke to me and said we must come and go with you. You are alone. And so we came. Tozey said her Power spoke to her and said the same thing, Father; but I think she is too young to have a Power . . . I think . . ."

Tozey interrupted, "My Power spoke too."

"You must go back," Geronimo said. "You cannot go."

"No, Father," Chappo insisted. "We cannot go back. You are our family, and so we must be with you."

"We cannot go back," Tozey added.

"I do not like you anymore," Geronimo said. "I hate you, both of you . . . I . . ."

Tozey stuck a thumb in her mouth. Her eyes wrinkled over her pug nose. Her chest heaved. The figures watered and blurred before Geronimo. He rushed around the fire and held them in his arms. They were not visions.

There was Time. The moon was not full. They wandered leisurely through the mountains, heading north.

Once, he had told Alope of the water spring where he drank, tasting, and there was no Time. And so now, they left the shadow time.

Early in the morning they followed bees flying a straight line from water, through trees on the heights turning red and yellowed leaves to the sunlight, into cradled hollows holding bursts of wild flowers in the late summer. They found the hollow log holding the hive. Chappo and Tozey squatted together, watching the bees working in the hollow log, but they did not disturb them.

They found a steep slope matted with piñon needles, and spent a golden afternoon sliding down the slope and crawling back to the top to slide again. Chappo the daring, Tozey on her fat little bottom, squealing as she tumbled and rolled, and Geronimo sliding and laughing and shouting with them. They were coming close to the north. At night Geronimo watched the moon.

The last morning, early, they dangled their feet in a clear stream and froze like statues to watch a doe come to drink, close to them. She raised her head, studying them with her liquid eyes. Tozey sneezed and the doe leaped in the air to send them laughing and tumbling along the bank. Chappo fell in the water.

In the slanting sun of late afternoon they began their descent from the mountain. They could see the river below them on the prairie. Geronimo paused to slide his rifle and cartridge belt beneath a rock. Chappo laid his knife beside it.

"I would not want them to think," Chappo said, "that I do not keep my Word, also."

Tozey left the stick she was carrying. Geronimo took her in his arms. He led Chappo by the hand. They came to the river bank as the sun hazed red over the water and the prairie beyond.

"We are not warriors anymore, are we, Father?" Chappo tried to keep the worry from his voice.

"Yes," Geronimo said, "we are warriors. You, and Tozey, and me. There are different kinds of warriors."

To the north a dust cloud was coming fast. They could see the bluecoats. Tozey stuck her thumb in her mouth.

The shadow time was September 4, 1886.

EPILOGUE

Chappo and Tozey died in bondage. Chappo is buried in the National Cemetery in Mobile, Alabama. Tozey is buried at Fort Sill, Oklahoma.

Tom Horn had been right. General Nelson Miles did not come immediately to the river. He sent soldiers. For days he communicated with them while they camped with Geronimo. Miles was fearful of Geronimo's reputation, that he would slip away, and so hurt Miles's career. In one of his messages to his officers, Miles hinted that they might simplify matters by murdering Geronimo. The officers refused. Finally, Big-Wind-Double-Mouth came, eager to make conditional surrender terms and promises. He reported, however, that he had "captured" Geronimo after a "long and hazardous" campaign, and so became an instant newspaper hero. General Miles's command never killed or captured a single hostile Apache.

Believing the story of the "capture," President Grover Cleveland ordered Geronimo hanged, but honorable officers present at the surrender revealed the terms. Cleveland was furious, but rescinded the hanging order.

They took all the San Carlos Apaches away with Geronimo and his children. The train carrying them across the desert was sealed, windows nailed shut, in temperatures of 110 degrees. Their dogs, running after the train, died on the prairie.

The Apaches were taken to prisons at Fort Marion and Fort Pickens, Florida, and Mount Vernon Barracks, Alabama. A third of them died there in the humid swamplands. The bureau in Washington came among them and took away their children to "educate" them at Carlisle, Pennsylvania. Many pathetic scenes were enacted as Apache mothers tried, unsuccessfully, to hide their babies and children from the bureaucrats. Nearly half the children died.

The Cherokees of North Carolina, hearing of their plight, offered to share their meager holdings with the Apaches. Their old enemies, the Comanches and Kiowas, moved by their inhuman existence, offered to take them in and share their own land. This was finally done, and the Apaches were taken to Fort Sill, Oklahoma.

Much of the improvement of their conditions may be attributed to General George Crook, who devoted most of the remainder of his life to helping the Apaches. He was assisted in these efforts by John Clum and other dedicated white men and women. Crook added extensively to his array of enemies in the Washington bureau. He died of a heart attack on March 21, 1890. He did not live to see the move of the Apaches to Oklahoma. At the time of his death he was leading a fight in Congress to stop the bureau from taking Apache children away from their parents, and other abuses. Of Carlisle, Pennsylvania, he said, "a place which, from whatever cause it may be, proves so fatal to them . . . Apaches are fond of their children and kinsfolk, and they live in terror lest their children be taken from them and sent to a distant school."

The Apaches were assigned farms on their reserve in Oklahoma. Here, they surprised United States military administrators by their industry and dedication to hard work. Their farms flourished and their cattle herds were judged to be the best in Oklahoma.

With their love of family, most of them established stable homes. Always, however, they longed to return to their beloved Southwest. It was not until April 4, 1913, that most of them were allowed to go, to the Mescalero Reservation, Mescalero, New Mexico. A few remained in Oklahoma.

Through it all, the energetic and alert Geronimo remained stubbornly unreconstructed. Army officers hated him. He taunted them often: "You could never catch me shooting." Most of his succeeding wives and children died in bondage. He was able to save one wife by divorcing her in prison; she and her two children went back to New Mexico. From these two children, Robert and Lenna, have come the only descendants of Geronimo, living today at Mescalero, New Mexico.

Geronimo was quick to learn the white man's economic system. He was a hard worker, thrifty with his money, and drove a shrewd bargain. But he was not greedy. When dictating letters to Apaches, he always ended with, "Tell me if you are in need. I have money and will send you some." And he did. He loved his people unselfishly. He was put on exhibit at world fairs and Wild West shows, sometimes wearing shackles, always with guards. Hundreds of thousands came to see "The Human Tiger."

Geronimo is the only known prisoner to participate in the inauguration ceremonies of a head of state. At the order of President Theodore Roosevelt, he rode, mounted on a horse with accompanying guards, in Roosevelt's Inaugural Parade. He caused a sensation. When taken to the White House to see the President, he expressed no awe. He demanded of Teddy Roosevelt that the Apaches be sent back to their homeland in the Southwest. When the President explained that he could not do this, Geronimo turned on his heel and walked away.

Tom Horn rode west that day from Fort Thomas.

He showed up at a rodeo in Globe, Arizona, in 1888, where he won several prizes. He later won the world's championship for steer roping and tying. For a short time he worked for the Pinkerton Agency. On one occasion he captured a notorious outlaw named Pegleg Watson. Watson was holed up in a cabin, and Horn, after shouting that he was coming in after him, walked across an open yard—with "cold courage," the report says—kicked open the door, and captured the outlaw. Later Horn showed up at a Pinkerton office and turned in his badge. "You got a good outfit," he said, "but I don't have the stomach for it." Horn was decorated for valor in the Spanish-American War. He drifted north, hired his guns to cattlemen in Wyoming and cleaned out the Hole-in-the-Wall rustlers. While drunk in Cheyenne, he boasted of his bushwhack killing of a sheepherder, and law officers arrested him. Sentenced to be hanged, he was offered life if he would reveal the identities of his employers. Horn refused. On November 20, 1903, he was hanged at Cheyenne. As he walked up the steps of the gallows, he sang:

> *Life is like a mountain railroad.*
> *If the engineer is brave,*
> *he can make the run successful*
> *from the cradle to the grave.*
> *Watch the curves, the hills and tunnels.*
> *Never falter, never fail.*
> *Keep your hand upon the throttle*
> *and your eye upon the rail.*

Tom Horn had kept his hand on the throttle.

Loco died at Fort Sill in 1905. His last words were: "I feel I have no country."

Nana died in 1896, having accepted nothing the white man offered. Totally unreconstructed. His last words: "I can see the mountains!"

Naiche lived on to be an old man; he and his wife Ha-o-zinne established a stable home. Three of their children died, but three survived. The youngest is still living at Mescalero, New Mexico.

Fun, the ebullient, carefree spirit, went into a deep depression in the Florida prison. His two children were taken by the government to Carlisle. The children died there, and on hearing of this, Fun killed his wife and himself—probably a pact between them, but there was no evidence except that they were found lying, entwined, on their bed.

Geronimo died at Fort Sill, February 17, 1909. With him when he died was Asa Daklugie, son of Ishton and Juh, whose birthing he had saved by trading with his Power on the mountain top. Before he died, he asked that his favorite horse be saddled and tied to a certain tree. He said he would come for the horse three days after he passed from his shadow body. But they didn't do it. The horse was not there. Geronimo was buried at Fort Sill. Many Apaches say he moved. Some say he went to the High Valley.

Asa Daklugie married a daughter of Chihuahua, named Ramona. He inherited the strong characters of Juh and Ishton, his father and mother, and he and his wife established an exemplary home. He became a leader among the Apaches when returned to New Mexico and has descendants.

In 1913, Pancho Villa told General Hugh Scott that he knew of "wild" Apaches in the Sierra Madre.

The last reported raid on a Mexican village by Apaches was in 1934. They came out of the Sierra Madre.

San Carlos languished, still there, but no longer a concentration camp. The "low" law seed that gave birth to San Carlos did not die. It lay dormant for many years in Washington. A generation passed; another, and another. Bureaus began pulsating from the seed. The descendants are arriving.

* * *

While the Apache death song recognizes death and its inevitability, it is significant that Geronimo's did not. His last words—singing on his death bed,

> *O Ha Le*
>> *O Ha Le*
>>> I am waiting for the *change!"*

Some Apaches say he never surrendered. Not even to death.

AMERICAN CAESAR

★ ★ ★ ★ ★

Douglas MacArthur 1880-1964

#1 NATIONAL BESTSELLER!
BY WILLIAM MANCHESTER

The author of *The Glory and the Dream* and *The Death of a President* brilliantly portrays the most controversial, most complex, and most hated or loved American general since Robert E. Lee: Douglas MacArthur! "William Manchester has written a masterful biography. Anybody who has ever wondered whether General MacArthur was a military genius or a political demagogue will find here evidence of both."—John Bartlow Martin. "Fascinating. Dramatic."—*Time.* "A thrilling and profoundly ponderable piece of work."—*Newsweek.* "Electric. Splendid reading. Like MacArthur himself—larger than life."—*The New York Times.*

A Dell Book $3.50

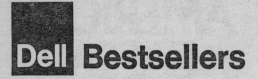
Dell Bestsellers

- [ ] TO LOVE AGAIN by Danielle Steel $2.50 (18631-5)
- [ ] SECOND GENERATION by Howard Fast $2.75 (17892-4)
- [ ] EVERGREEN by Belva Plain $2.75 (13294-0)
- [ ] AMERICAN CAESAR by William Manchester ... $3.50 (10413-0)
- [ ] THERE SHOULD HAVE BEEN CASTLES
      by Herman Raucher $2.75 (18500-9)
- [ ] THE FAR ARENA by Richard Ben Sapir $2.75 (12671-1)
- [ ] THE SAVIOR by Marvin Werlin and Mark Werlin . $2.75 (17748-0)
- [ ] SUMMER'S END by Danielle Steel $2.50 (18418-5)
- [ ] SHARKY'S MACHINE by William Diehl $2.50 (18292-1)
- [ ] DOWNRIVER by Peter Collier $2.75 (11830-1)
- [ ] CRY FOR THE STRANGERS by John Saul $2.50 (11869-7)
- [ ] BITTER EDEN by Sharon Salvato $2.75 (10771-7)
- [ ] WILD TIMES by Brian Garfield $2.50 (19457-1)
- [ ] 1407 BROADWAY by Joel Gross $2.50 (12819-6)
- [ ] A SPARROW FALLS by Wilbur Smith $2.75 (17707-3)
- [ ] FOR LOVE AND HONOR by Antonia Van-Loon .. $2.50 (12574-X)
- [ ] COLD IS THE SEA by Edward L. Beach $2.50 (11045-9)
- [ ] TROCADERO by Leslie Waller $2.50 (18613-7)
- [ ] THE BURNING LAND by Emma Drummond $2.50 (10274-X)
- [ ] HOUSE OF GOD by Samuel Shem, M.D. $2.50 (13371-8)
- [ ] SMALL TOWN by Sloan Wilson $2.50 (17474-0)

At your local bookstore or use this handy coupon for ordering:

WILD TIMES

BRIAN GARFIELD

The true and authentic life of Col. Hugh Cardiff

A two-part television special from Metromedia Productions.

The American west lives again in all its glory as Hugh Cardiff tells his tale—the story of an exuberant young nation and a hero larger than life.

"American history in full color. Garfield sees with near-perfect clarity. His episodes flash vividly."—*New York Times Book Review.*

"A passion that is contagious. Terrific entertainment."—*Los Angeles Herald-Examiner.*

"Vivid. Entertaining and fast-moving."
—*Chicago Tribune.*

A Dell Book $2.50   (19457-1)

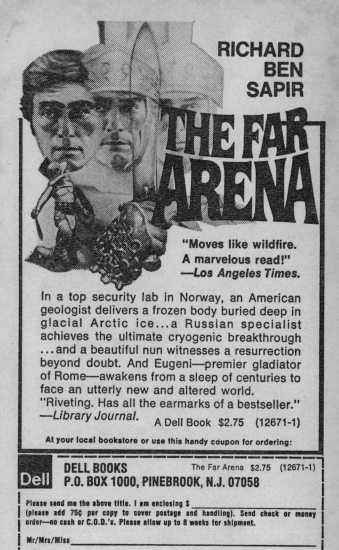

RICHARD BEN SAPIR

THE FAR ARENA

"Moves like wildfire.
A marvelous read!"
—*Los Angeles Times.*

In a top security lab in Norway, an American
geologist delivers a frozen body buried deep in
glacial Arctic ice...a Russian specialist
achieves the ultimate cryogenic breakthrough
...and a beautiful nun witnesses a resurrection
beyond doubt. And Eugeni—premier gladiator
of Rome—awakens from a sleep of centuries to
face an utterly new and altered world.
"Riveting. Has all the earmarks of a bestseller."
—*Library Journal.*   A Dell Book $2.75   (12671-1)